HAPPY DAYS

Graham Hurley

First published in Great Britain in 2012 by Orion Books,
an imprint of The Orion Publishing Group Ltd
Orion House, 5 Upper Saint Martin's Lane
London WC2H 9EA

An Hachette Livre UK Company

1 3 5 7 9 10 8 6 4 2

A CIP catalogue record for this book
is available from the British Library.

ISBN (Hardback) 978 1 4091 0125 3
ISBN (Export Trade Paperback) 978 1 4091 0126 0

Typeset by Deltatype Ltd, Birkenhead, Merseyside

Printed in Great Britain by Clays Ltd, St Ives plc

The Orion Publishing Group's policy is to use papers
that are natural, renewable and recyclable products and made from
wood grown in sustainable forests. The logging and manufacturing
processes are expected to conform to the environmental
regulations of the country of origin.

www.orionbooks.co.uk

For Lin,
again and always

Chapter one

D/S Jimmy Suttle had never had much time for Gill Reynolds. Not then. And certainly not now. The fact that she was a mate of Lizzie's made him answer the call but he tried to keep the conversation as short as possible.

She said she was worried about Faraday.

'Why?'

'He's not picking up.'

'Maybe he's busy.'

'No way.'

'How do you know?'

'How do you *think* I know?'

Suttle had pulled in beside a bus stop on the Eastern Road. Rush-hour traffic was flooding out of the city. His ex-boss's love life was no concern of his but he understood from Lizzie that Faraday's brief fling with Gill was well and truly over.

'You're together again?'

'Not exactly, but you don't stop caring, do you?'

The question was blunt, with a hint of accusation. Like Lizzie, Gill was a journalist on the *News*. And like Lizzie, she had a habit of trying to back the rest of the world into a corner. Suttle's wife managed it with a smile on her face. Gill didn't. No wonder Faraday had binned the relationship.

Suttle knew what was coming next. Gill was doubtless at

work. Gill was probably mega-stressed. And Suttle, in truth, was one of the few men Joe Faraday might count as a mate.

'You want me to go round? See how he's coping?' Suttle checked his watch. Nearly half six. Faraday's place was barely five minutes away. 'Gill? You still there?'

He waited a couple of seconds for an answer then realised she'd hung up. Faraday, mercifully, had seen the light. The woman, once you got beyond first impressions, was a total nightmare: needy, impatient, determined to shape life the way she wanted it. He glanced up at the rear-view mirror and eased back into the traffic. Maybe Faraday would have a Stella or two in the fridge. Maybe he'd be in the mood for a chat. Maybe Suttle could mark the old boy's card about manic divorcee *News* journos who refused to take no for an answer.

Faraday's place was called the Bargemaster's House. It lay at the end of a cul-de-sac that fringed Langstone Harbour, the stretch of water to the east of the city that helped give Pompey its island status. Suttle was vague about the origins of the property but assumed the house was connected to the nearby lock and the canal that had once ferried barges to Portsmouth Harbour. What he knew for certain was how much Faraday loved the place. He'd lived in it for years. He'd brought up his only child there, a deaf-mute called J-J or Joe Junior. And even now, maybe especially now, it meant the world to him.

The house was neat, square, brick built, with white-painted timber cladding on the first floor. Faraday's ancient Mondeo was on the hardstanding. Suttle parked and walked to the front door. His first ring produced no response. He rang again, then hammered at the peeling woodwork. Still no answer. He pushed the letter box open and stooped to peer inside. The house smelled damp, unloved, and there was a hint of a sweetness, a pungency, he couldn't quite place. As his eyes grew accustomed to the gloom of the hall, he saw the pile of uncollected post on the mat inside the door. He called Faraday's name, listening for an answer. Nothing. He tried the door. Locked.

Stepping away from the door and into the sunshine, he phoned Faraday's mobile number, returning to the letter box to push it open. Faintly, from the depths of the house, he could hear Faraday's distinctive ringtone, a soft peal of bells. The second he ended the call, it stopped.

He began to circle the house, sensing that something was wrong, knowing that he'd have to get inside. As Detective Inspector on the Major Crime Team, Faraday had been his immediate boss on countless investigations. Back in February he'd suffered a nervous breakdown and had been on sick leave ever since. His collapse had taken everyone by surprise. Colleagues who didn't know the man well, and that meant most of them, had blamed his condition on a road accident he'd suffered during a Christmas break in Egypt. Faraday, it was said, had gone through the windscreen and come back to work far too early.

A serious road traffic accident was plausible enough, but Suttle, who'd worked alongside Faraday on the inquiry that followed, had seen something else. His boss, in his opinion, had simply had enough. Twenty years of coppering had ganged up on him. His French partner, Gabrielle, had left in pursuit of a Palestinian child she wanted to adopt. These episodes had taken Faraday to a very bad place. Suttle had never seen someone so alone, so bewildered, so *lost*.

A gravel path led around the side of the house. Suttle paused beside a couple of dustbins. The space between was piled with Waitrose bags filled with wine bottles and empty beer cans. Suttle gazed at them a moment, then lifted the nearest dustbin lid. Two more bottles, malt whisky this time.

The rear of the house fronted onto the harbour. This, Suttle knew, was Faraday's pride and joy, the view that seemed to offer him endless solace. The last time Suttle had been here, a month or so ago, his ex-boss had handed him a pair of binos and talked him through the mid-summer birdlife on the harbour. Under Faraday's patient guidance, he'd settled on a gaggle of mallard, then a darting cloud of oyster catchers, ending with a single cormorant perched on a mooring post, the blackness of its wings spread wide in the last of the day's warmth. 'He's hanging himself out to dry,' Faraday had murmured, and the phrase had lodged in Suttle's memory. Was this the way his ex-boss imagined himself? Skewered by circumstance? Waiting for the dying sun to work some kind of miracle?

Suttle tried the windows and the French door on the ground floor. Everything was locked. Peering in, he could make out a glass beside the sofa in the big living room. The glass appeared to be empty but he couldn't be sure. He stepped back. For the first time, looking up, he realised that a sash window on the floor above was open. He stared at it a moment, wondering about a ladder.

He found one behind a shed at the far end of the garden. The garden itself, wildly overgrown after the recent rain, badly needed attention. He could see marrows and courgettes, unharvested, among the weeds. Some of the nearby tomatoes, hanging fatly in tresses, were beginning to split. Faraday had always been meticulous about his veggie patch. Now this.

Suttle carried the ladder to the house and propped it against the timber cladding. He'd never been upstairs in Faraday's place but guessed the half-open window belonged to a bedroom. He began to climb, aware of a quickening in his pulse. In his uniformed days he'd been obliged to force an entry on a number of occasions and rarely had what awaited him been good news. Faraday's gone off on a jolly for a couple of days, he told himself. Or maybe he's had one call too many from the ever-eager Gill and decided to emigrate.

The top of the ladder rested against the window sill. Suttle steadied himself and peered in. The smell here was stronger but it still took him a second or two to recognise the figure sprawled on the bed. Faraday was wearing jeans and a checked shirt. He lay face down on the duvet, one knee drawn up, one arm thrown across the pillow. The giveaway was his watch strap, a Russian swirl of embroidered flowers, a much-loved gift from his son J-J.

Suttle hesitated a second, then pushed the window open until he could squeeze in. Stepping towards the bed, he knew at once that Faraday had gone. His face had the mottled blues and greens of death. Vomit had filled his mouth and crusted in his beard and there was more of it across the pillow. Suttle flapped a hand, stirring the flies, shocked by what he'd found. He'd liked this man a great deal. He'd respected him, learned from him, and tried to return the favour by offering some small comfort when the going got tough. No one, he thought, deserved an end like this. Least of all Faraday.

Beside the bed, an upturned bottle had bled a dribble of red wine onto the whiteness of the rug. Suttle knelt beside the bottle, taking care not to touch it. According to the label, it was a Grand Cru Côtes-du-Rhône. He gazed at it a moment, wondering how special a bottle like this might be, then got to his feet again. On the desk beside the PC were two blister packs of codeine and a pint glass with half an inch of water in the bottom. The blister packs were empty. Suttle knew already that this sad little tableau probably told its own story but he knew as well that he was standing in the middle of a crime scene. In his shoes Faraday would already be reaching for his phone.

Suttle was downstairs by the time he got through to the office. Detective Superintendent Gail Parsons was a month into her new post, leading the S/E Hants Major Crime Team, and this was the last news she needed.

'Have you called anyone else?'

'No.'

'Stay there, then,' she said at once. 'We'll need to handle this.'

Suttle noticed the envelope moments later. It was lying on

the hall table. He recognised Faraday's careful script. Marked *Private and Personal*, the envelope had J-J's name on it. Among the clutter in the kitchen, tucked away in the cupboard beneath the sink, he found a new pair of Marigold gloves. He put them on and returned to the hall.

The envelope, when he turned it over, was unsealed. Inside was a single sheet of paper. The note – typed – was brief, the tone almost matter-of-fact. Faraday told his son he'd had enough of pretty much everything. The time had come to draw things to a close. He said he cherished the times they'd spent together and thought they'd made a great team. He wished him good luck for the coming years and told him that the Bargemaster's House, plus everything else in his modest estate, was J-J's for the keeping. If he wanted to sell the house, so be it. Otherwise, enjoy. The latter ended with a handwritten flourish. *Take care, my son*, Faraday had scrawled. *Your dad loves you*. Beneath, barely legible, was a brief postscript: *And remember the eagle.*

Suttle studied the letter in the gloom of the hall, trying to get inside Faraday's head, trying to imagine the pressures that must have led to a decision like this. The house was still a crime scene. There were still bends in the investigative road that demanded careful exploration. But this brief voice in the gathering silence surely pointed to Faraday taking his own life. Suttle slipped the letter back in the envelope and returned it to the hall table. He was still wearing the gloves when Parsons appeared.

He let her in and followed her down the hall. She saw the letter at once. Suttle explained what was inside. The mention of an eagle in the postscript drew an inquisitive frown. She wanted to know what it might mean.

'No idea, boss. Maybe we should ask his son.'

Parsons nodded, said nothing. Suttle sensed she was irritated by this sudden turn of events and found himself wondering to what degree Faraday had written himself out of her script. His illness had tidied him away. Faraday, alive, was no longer any concern of hers. Dead, on the other hand, he could be a real problem.

'I talked to Personnel just now,' she said. 'They think we're in the clear.'

'In the *what?*'

'In terms of procedure. We organised the counselling. We insisted he stayed the course. We were in touch with his GP. I just had to remind myself. That's all.'

Suttle digested this news while Parsons bustled up the stairs and took a look at the bedroom. She was a small, squat, big-chested woman who rarely let emotion trouble her unswerving progress towards ACPO rank. Among some of Suttle's older colleagues she'd become a byword for the kind of career pushiness that the bosses sometimes mistook for talent. Within seconds she was back at the top of the stairs.

'Horrible,' she said briefly. 'I think we're pretty safe with a Cat 2 death. Call the OCU.'

A Category 2 death is one stage down from an obvious homicide. Suttle needed a D/S from the Operational Command Unit to make an assessment of the facts. As he put the call through he was aware of Parsons leaving. She had a scheduled meet with the Police Authority at headquarters for half seven. With luck, she'd just make it in time for the pre-presentation drinks. Suttle heard the slam of the front door and then the growl of her new Audi TT before silence returned to the Bargemaster's House.

Still in the big downstairs living room, Suttle looked around. Like every detective, it was his job to tease a story from a scene like this, to coax out a sequence of events that would explain the body upstairs. For a couple of years now he'd been driving the Intelligence Cell on the Major Crime Team and his special talent lay in the careful compilation of other people's lives: what motivated them, what moved them out of their comfort zones, what made them angry, or hurt, or homicidal. To this end, before the Scenes of Crime blokes arrived, he knew he should be conducting a quick intel search, lifting all the usual stones beneath which most people hid their secrets: PCs, laptops, mobiles, landline messaging tapes.

That would mean another trip upstairs to Faraday's bedroom. His PC was on the desk beside the window. His mobile was probably up there too. Both might yield vital clues as to exactly why he'd necked a bottle of decent wine, swallowed a load of tablets and called it a day. That's where Suttle should go. That's what he should do. But the thought of the body on the bed was too much for him. It wasn't death that put him off. It was the fact that this needless collision with the buffers had happened to someone so close, and yet so distant. The real enigma, he sensed already, was the terrifying cul-de-sac Faraday had chosen for himself. Why had the guy been so desperate? And so alone?

The state of the body upstairs plus the post on the doormat suggested that Faraday had been dead for a couple of days. Suttle gazed down at the sofa, trying to picture how it must have been before he climbed the stairs that final time. The abandoned glass on the carpet had held alcohol – Suttle could smell it. He stepped across to the audio stack and hit the eject button on the CD player. He hadn't a clue about Mahler's Ninth Symphony so he reloaded the player, turned up the volume and waited for the opening bars.

The music was quiet at first, barely a whisper, but then came a passage on the violins full of sadness and regret and loss, and it was suddenly all too easy for Suttle to visualise Faraday stretched on the sofa, a glass of something consolatory in his hand, his eyes closed, his letter typed, his mind drifting off towards God knows where. The music gathered speed, bracing itself for the next hurdle, but the aching sense of desolation was still there, and Suttle shook his head, reaching for the stop button then turning away towards the big picture window with its semi-curtained views of the harbour beyond. If you listened to this kind of stuff too often, did topping yourself begin to make some kind of sense? Was Mahler a co-conspirator in Faraday's death? Had he orchestrated a lifetime's disappointments and somehow led him to his end?

Suttle didn't know. More importantly, he was honest enough to acknowledge that neither Hantspol, nor the Coroner's Office, nor any other branch of the judicial system had a reporting form with room enough for this kind of speculation. To understand Faraday when he was alive was challenge enough. To make sense of a death like this was, to be frank, beyond him.

Out on the grey shadowed spaces of the harbour a single swan was flying low, heading for the open sea. Suttle watched it for a moment or two then pulled the curtains back. He'd had enough of this gloomy half-light, of Mahler, of empty glasses and of the lifeless corpse in the bedroom above. He checked his watch and began to turn away from the window, but as he did so he caught sight of another letter. It was lying on the window sill. The masthead was all too familiar. Hantspol.

He picked up the single sheet of paper. It had come from a woman in the Personnel Department. She was pleased at the progress D/I Joe Faraday appeared to be making and noted that he had nearly a year to serve before he could retire on a full pension. Under the circumstances, she hoped he'd agree that a return to Major Crime would be inappropriate, but another vacancy had come up and she had great pleasure in making the formal offer. An interview would be unnecessary. The job was his for the asking.

Suttle checked the date. The letter had been written barely a week ago. Add the delay for second-class post and Faraday must have been living with this career-end curtain call for no more than a couple of days. He'd no idea what Theme Champions' Coordinator on the Safer Portsmouth Partnership actually entailed, and Faraday had probably been equally clueless, but it was all too easy to imagine the eternity of meetings that lay ahead. A body like this would speak the language of the new policing. The language of Service Performance Indicators and Victim Focus, of the Outcomes Matrix and the Neighbourhood Policing Offer. After years and years of life at the coal face, of multiple homicides and complex stranger rapes, of high-profile kidnaps and simpler acts of mindless brutality, what would any half-decent copper make of a letter like this?

From Hantspol's point of view, of course, it made perfect sense, the gentlest of landings after a bumpy ride. But for someone with blood in their veins, someone with an ounce of self-respect, someone who thought that coppering had some faint connection with justice rather than collective hand-holding, the thought of becoming a Theme Champions' Coordinator would have been the kiss of death.

The latter phrase drew a shake of the head from Suttle. He returned the letter to the window sill. A knock at the front door took him down the hall. There were two figures waiting to come in. He didn't recognise the D/S, but the duty D/I had decided to come too. Nick Hayder was probably the closest Faraday had to a friend in the job, a like-minded forty-something who rarely let sentiment get in the way of the facts. On this occasion, though, he looked shocked.

'What's going on?'

Suttle explained. Hayder nodded, made no comment, accompanied the D/S upstairs. Then came another knock on the door. Hayder, it seemed, had already contacted Scenes of Crime. There were two of them, a Crime Scene Investigator and the Imaging Specialist who'd tote his cameras up to the bedroom and put the lot on DVD. They both knew Faraday well. They took an appraising glance around the big living room and then followed Suttle up towards the bedroom.

Suttle had been through this routine on countless occasions. Normally, whether they were dead or alive, you were dealing with strangers. You stepped into the wreckage of their lives and did what you had to do. You were respectful and businesslike, but behind closed doors you often lightened proceedings with a muttered quip or two as the occasion suggested. Not this time. The CSI, a guy in his forties who'd had a great deal of time for Faraday, took one look at the body and left the image specialist to get on with it. There were windows to dust for prints, items to seize for analysis, the PC and Faraday's mobile to bag for the techies at Netley. Soon, the doctor would arrive.

On the landing Hayder was conferring with his D/S. Back downstairs in the living room, Suttle waited for them to finish. He'd found an old address book in a drawer and was leafing through it, amazed at how few friends or family Faraday appeared to have had. He was transcribing J-J's contact details when the CSI returned from the bedroom. He needed to know how far D/I Hayder wanted to take this thing. He'd boshed the bedroom and the bathroom and checked out the other windows upstairs. No signs of forced entry. Nothing remotely suspicious. Suttle shrugged. This was Hayder's decision, not his. As far as he was concerned, the story told itself. Faraday had slipped his moorings. Maybe death had been a kindness. Maybe the voice in the letter to J-J had it right. Maybe that's exactly the way he'd wanted it.

The CSI, drawn and pale, agreed. He said he'd check around downstairs just in case and then use the last of the daylight to have a nose outside. But, unless D/I Hayder had views to the contrary, he saw little point in turning this thing into a major production.

Suttle nodded. The two men looked at each other. In all probability Faraday had jacked it in. There was nothing left to say.

The doctor arrived within the hour. Suttle explained exactly how he'd found the body. Then he conferred briefly with Hayder and the D/S, and left them to it. Walking to his car, he suddenly realised how late it was. His wife, Lizzie, had long been used to the craziness of CID hours, but since the baby had arrived she'd been banged up at home on maternity leave, trying to coax some order into their domestic lives. Grace was

Chapter two

The news got to Paul Winter late that night. Suttle, he knew at once, was drunk.

'Son?' he said. 'What are you telling me?'

'He's dead. Gone. He topped himself. He did it.'

'But who, son. *Who?*'

'Faraday.'

There was a long silence. Winter didn't know what to say. The television was off. He was in his dressing gown. Intercepted on his way to bed, he could only stare out at the blackness of Portsmouth Harbour. Faraday? *Dead?*

'For fuck's sake ...' he murmured.

'Exactly.'

'How? When?'

Suttle did his best to explain. He was slurring. Badly.

'Where are you, son?'

'At home.'

'You want me to come round?'

'No.'

'You want to come here? Take a cab?'

'No.'

'Then what do you want?'

There was another silence before the line went dead. Then a shiver of wind blew in from the harbour, stirring the yachts moored beside the Gunwharf pontoon. Winter could hear the halyards rattling against the masts. He stepped closer to the window, the phone still in his hand, trying to understand what had just happened.

The last time he'd seen Joe Faraday was a couple of months ago. Jimmy and Lizzie had thrown a party to celebrate the arrival of their daughter, Grace. Winter, as godfather, had naturally been there, and he and Faraday had tucked themselves in a corner and sunk a couple of lagers. His ex-boss had seemed a bit vague, sure, and social chit-chat was something Faraday never found especially easy, but they'd talked about the new baby, about when Suttle might start thinking about the D/I promotion exams, and they'd shared one or two war stories from the old days on Major Crime. As far as the Job was concerned, Faraday seemed to have turned his back on all those years of nailing the bad guys, and when Winter had pressed him for some kind of explanation he'd simply shrugged and reached for another tinny. It felt like someone else's life, he'd murmured. It had come and it had gone, much like everything else he'd ever touched, and he'd never been one for nostalgia.

At the time Winter had put this down to the Stella. Shortly afterwards their conversation had been interrupted by a mate of Lizzie's, a looker with scarlet nails and a big leather belt. Winter couldn't remember her name, but she'd introduced herself with a cheesy little flourish before towing Faraday across to the brimming display of canapés, and somewhat later Winter had spotted them leaving together. Good on you, he'd thought at the time. Enjoy.

Now, though, he began to wonder. As a D/C on division, he'd spent a couple of years working under Faraday, and later they'd been thrown together on a couple of Major Crime inquiries. Winter had always recognised his D/I as a fellow loner, and when he'd left the Job and journeyed to the Dark Side, Faraday had been one of his few ex-colleagues to spare him the time of day. For that Winter had always been grateful. The man had more in his life than canteen gossip. He'd taken the trouble to try and figure out why someone as difficult and gifted as Winter would end up working for the city's top criminal face, and when circumstances had occasionally brought them together, he'd never rushed to judgement. On the contrary, he seemed to understand the path that Winter had chosen. That, of course, was why Faraday had been a decent cop. He was patient. He listened. He watched. He resisted the obvious conclusions. He let events play out, sharpened his pencil, reviewed the evidence, set a trap or two, and then joined the dots. Winter had always admired this MO because it so closely resembled his own. But then he, Paul Winter, was a survivor. Whereas Faraday, all too clearly, was anything but.

True? Winter eyed his reflection in the sliding glass door that led to the balcony. In his early fifties, he was Faraday's age, give or take. He was overweight by at least a couple of stone. He drank too much, ate too much and took full advantage of any passing opportunity. He was losing his hair, and physical challenge of pretty much any description was definitely becoming an issue. But he had resilience, and resilience mattered, and what he also had was self-belief. There were few decisions he'd taken in his life that he'd ever regretted, and if he'd finally arrived at a parting of the ways with Bazza then that, too, could be sorted. Because it had to be faced. Because it had to be done. Because otherwise, for all his matey confidence, he knew he'd end up like Faraday.

He thought about a drink, a private farewell toast to mark the man's passing, then shook his head. The light was still on in the bedroom, but Misty appeared to be asleep. Recently she'd taken to wearing a black silk camisole that cost a fortune and properly belonged on someone a bit thinner. She'd also installed her favourite stuffed animal, a pink leopard called Charlie with one eye missing and badly repaired damage around the hindquarters where Bazza had once attacked it with a broken bottle.

The beast stood knee-high and had occupied a corner of the

bedroom for a couple of weeks now, an affront to Winter's sense of independence. He'd loathed it from the moment it had invaded his space, and the more he saw of it the more he knew it had to go. It was chavvy. It was infantile. It clashed with his curtains and filled him with dread in case Misty turned up with the rest of the zoo he knew she kept at home. For years, at considerable risk, he'd been knobbing Bazza's mistress at every opportunity. Now, for reasons he still didn't fully understand, he and Mist appeared to have become an item.

Misty stirred. She wanted to know who'd been on the phone.

'Jimmy Suttle.'

'What did he want?' She was struggling to look at the bed-side clock.

'It was just a personal thing. Mutual friend.'

'Yeah?' She was up on one elbow now. 'And?'

'Dunno, really. The boy was pissed as a rat.'

Winter smothered a yawn, unsure why he was sparing her the details. Misty had met Faraday on a couple of occasions and thought him a cut above the usual Filth.

'So are you coming to bed, or what?'

'Yeah.' Winter didn't move. Earlier Misty had been worrying about her place over on Hayling Island. Bazza had acquired it years ago when his business empire was going from strength to strength. A whisker under half a million had bought a waterside property with views across Langstone Harbour, the perfect love nest for the aspiring entrepreneur. Misty had added a pool with underwater disco lights and found ample time for Winter when Mackenzie wasn't around. Bazza still paid her a visit from time to time, but Misty sensed his heart wasn't in it. Winter wanted to know more.

'I'm yesterday's shag,' she said. 'We do it for old times' sake.'

'So what's the problem?'

'I think he wants the house back.'

'Why?'

'To sell it.'

'*Sell* it?'

This was news to Winter. He knew exactly how tight things were in every corner of the business because that was his job, but he'd somehow overlooked the place on Hayling Island. That, in a curious way, was family. And Bazza had always been careful to keep family assets ring-fenced from the tax man and the recent credit crunch.

'Did he buy it outright?'

'I'm not sure. I don't think so.'

'What was the deal, then?'

'I think he raised a mortgage on three quarters of it. The rest he must own.'

Winter perched himself on the edge of the bed, doing the sums in his head. In today's market the house was probably worth around 650K. After expenses, that would still give Bazza at least 250K in equity. With the rest of his property empire in free fall, and the other businesses stretched to breaking point, there were a million pressing calls on a sum like this, but Winter's heart sank when he realised why Mackenzie might be serious about Hayling Island.

'Why all this? Why would he need the money?' he asked.

'Guess.'

'Kinder.'

'Of course. The guy's got Baz by the nuts. He can't get too much of all this politics shit. Honestly, my love, it's pitiful to watch.'

Winter could only agree. He'd seen it for himself. Leo Kinder had become a regular fixture at Mackenzie's Craneswater house. He was savvy, plausible and extremely well connected. Once, until they'd thrown him out, he'd been a full-time agent with the Tories, running parliamentary candidates up and down the country. Now, as a freelance political consultant, he was telling Mackenzie that – come the election – one of the two Portsmouth constituencies was his for the taking.

'Can't resist it, can he?'

'Never. You know what he told me last time we shagged?'

'Go on.'

'He told me Kinder was a genius. And he told me that when he gets in he's going to give the guy the freedom of the city.'

'He *said* that?'

'On my oath.'

'And he believes it?'

'Without a doubt.'

In certain moods, as Winter knew only too well, Bazza Mackenzie could be delusional. All he needed was a whiff of the big time, a glimpse of the summit, and he'd be off and running. All the usual obstacles would simply vanish. He'd charm and bully and buy his way to the top, exactly the same MO that had turned seventeen million quid's worth of toot into a sizeable business empire. For a while running this empire had been fun. He'd earned respect, won new friends, banked another fortune in legitimate profits, but then the recession had come along, and he suddenly needed something else to keep his attention.

With the wolves at the door, the world of balance sheets and employment contracts and meetings with lawyers was suddenly a pain in the arse. There had to be another challenge, something sexier, and in the shape of Leo Kinder he'd found it. First the possibility of standing for the post of elected mayor. Then, when the required legislation never happened, the chance of becoming an MP. This little conjuring trick was a tribute to the spell that a guy like Kinder could cast. Nowadays, from where Bazza was sitting, the city had seen enough of the same old faces. The people, the *voters,* had been shafted by the mainstream parties. Pompey, *his* Pompey, deserved better.

'So what's it costing?' Winter inquired. He had asked Bazza exactly the same question and got no answer.

'He says fifty grand.'

'Double it.'

'You're serious?'

'Yeah. And probably double it again. You know the man, Mist. He doesn't do losing. If Kinder puts a price on success, he'll take no chances.'

'Two hundred grand?' Misty was doing the arithmetic. 'That's what he'd pocket from my house.'

'Exactly.'

There was a long silence. Charlie the pink leopard had become a brooding presence in the room. Winter risked a glance, shut his eyes, shook his head. Then he felt the stir of bedsprings beneath him and a gentle tug on his arm as Misty tried to peel off his dressing gown. Moments later he was flat on his back while Misty busied herself with the knot on his pyjama bottoms. He knew exactly what was coming next. And he dreaded it.

Naked below the waist, he succumbed to her dancing fingers for a moment or two then levered himself half-upright. Supported on his elbows, he watched her bobbing head.

'So what will you do?' he managed at last.

Her head slowed. Her fingers closed around him and her face appeared. Winter recognised the smile she saved for special occasions.

'I'll move in here for real.' She nodded at the bedroom and gave him a little squeeze. 'You fancy that?'

Chapter three

Suttle was at Det Supt Parsons' office door at nine o'clock. For the first time in years a hangover had bent him over the toilet bowl. Lizzie, after a night of trying to cope with their daughter, had ignored him. Since he'd showered, dressed and risked a slice of cold toast, they hadn't exchanged a word.

Parsons wanted to know about the post-mortem. The thought of Faraday on the pathologist's table made Suttle's stomach heave.

'Half nine, boss. Up at the QA.' The Queen Alexandra Hospital was Portsmouth's newest and biggest, a sprawling complex on the fold of chalk overlooking the city.

'I want you there, Jimmy. I know it's tough but it has to be done.'

Suttle stared at her. For the first time he realised the role she'd assigned him over the coming days. Because Faraday's death wasn't being treated as suspicious, there'd be no need for a police presence at the post-mortem. But Parsons, as ever, wanted no surprises.

'Are you serious, boss?'

'Of course. We need to keep on top of this thing. You knew him. You worked with him. Intel's your speciality. We need a motive, some proof of *intent*. You get my drift?'

The inquiry was already tagged Operation *Castor*. Any kind of oversight role in the unexplained death of his ex-boss was the last thing Suttle needed. He briefly contemplated appealing to Parsons' better nature but knew it would be a waste of time. She wanted him to keep an eye on Faraday's immediate family too, offering them whatever support they needed.

'There isn't any, boss, as far as I can suss.'

'*None?*'

'Only his son, J-J.'

'Does he know yet?'

'I've no idea. He might.'

'Where is he?'

'London. Chiswick.'

'Then go up there and hold his hand, eh? After the PM.'

'Fine, boss.' Suttle glanced at his watch. 'I'd better make a move.'

Winter was summoned to breakfast at Sandown Road. Mackenzie's house was a big red-brick Edwardian villa with huge windows and an upstairs glimpse of the sea beyond the tennis courts at the end of the road. Bazza and his wife Marie had been living here for a while now, his most visible down payment on a new life among Southsea's moneyed professionals. Regular dinner parties and summer barbecues had fattened his address book, and – according to Marie – he'd recently treated himself to golf lessons at a pricey resort complex on the mainland.

Winter had phoned Mackenzie earlier, demanding an urgent meet, and when Bazza had enquired why, he'd just laughed. For nearly a year now there'd been only one subject to justify this kind of call: money. The Mackenzie empire, besieged on all sides by the recession, was leaking funds at an alarming rate. The company accountant, a talented refugee from the Inland Revenue with fingers in all kinds of city pies, had long been telling his boss that he had to start selling assets, but Bazza was temperamentally incapable of throwing the corporate gearstick into reverse. Making any kind of retreat simply wasn't his style. You got richer by taking risks. You survived by holding your nerve. One day, hopefully soon, the market would turn. In the meantime you manned the battlements, laid in stocks of boiling oil and repelled all boarders.

The big family kitchen was at the back of the house. Winter skirted the swimming pool and stepped in from the rain. Marie was laying the table. The smell of grilling bacon put a smile on Winter's face.

'Who else are we expecting?' There were four places at the long wooden table.

'Leo. He's been with Baz for a while now.' She nodded towards the door. 'He wants you to join them.'

Winter shed his dripping raincoat and made his way through the adjacent living room to Mackenzie's den. It was still early, barely nine o'clock. It wouldn't surprise him if Leo Kinder had moved in, sparing himself the near-daily commute from his trophy cottage out in the country. Misty was right. The world of politics had gone to Bazza's head. Only last week he'd described it as the new cocaine. Only better.

Kinder was a sleek thirty-something with a passion for designer jeans and crisp white collarless shirts. Most days he affected a hint of designer stubble and just now, to Winter's alarm, he occupied the leather recliner Mackenzie reserved for special guests. This, as Winter knew only too well, meant that Bazza's political guru, the company spaniel, had emerged from the long grass with something especially tasty.

'Listen to this, mush.' Mackenzie waved Winter into the other chair. 'Leo's come up with a media strategy for the big one. He's got the mainstream lot sorted already. Remember the stuff we had in the *Guardian*? The *Telegraph*? Lots more of that to come. But here's the kicker. We go into social media. Big time. We blitz it. We tie the whole fucking city up in knots. We get in their face. We go undercover. We go viral. It's votes, mush. It's all about votes. We set up these weirdo sockpuppet accounts and invite all those monkeys out there to join the party. Not any old party. But *my* party, *our* party—' He broke off suddenly and shot a look at Kinder. 'Sockpuppet accounts? Have I got that right?'

'You have, Baz.' Kinder granted him a nod of approval, then switched his attention to Winter. 'It's a group thing on Facebook. You make up a name and an email address, plant whatever seeds you like, and then step back and let it happen. You have to keep control, of course, but no one has a clue what you're up to or who you really are. In my game you need to boss the agenda. This is one way of doing it.'

'There are others?'

'Lots. Twitter. Getting stuck into the big aggregators. Digg. Reddit. Targeting specific forums. How much time have you got?'

Winter shrugged, aware of the blaze of light in Bazza's eyes. Switching him on had never been a problem, as Leo Kinder had quickly discovered.

Mackenzie was sitting at his desk. He swivelled towards his PC and reached for the keyboard.

'Take a look at this, mush.'

Winter found himself staring at a logo. The distinctive silhouette of the Spinnaker Tower reared out of an eye-popping wash of yellows and reds. Put it on a bottle of crap lager, Winter thought, and you might just risk a mouthful or two. Mackenzie bent to the keyboard again. Two words appeared beneath the same image: *Pompey First.*

'Brilliant or what?' Bazza shook his head in admiration.

Winter was still gazing at the screen. He'd heard this phrase before in muttered conversations between Kinder and his boss but had always ignored it.

'This is some kind of political party?'

'An aspiration, Paul.' It was Kinder. 'We'll need to badge the campaign, give it punch and presence. Starting a political party from scratch is a nightmare.'

'Yeah.' A vigorous nod from Bazza. 'All kinds of bollocks. Right, Leo?'

'Right. This way we get round all the nonsense from the Electoral Commission. Baz will be campaigning as an independent. That's exactly what it'll say on the polling slip. But as far as the rest of it's concerned, Baz is *Pompey First*. That's the way it works. That's the retail offer on all the stuff we're going to be putting out. That's what we're selling here.'

'*Pompey First?*'

'Exactly. And seventy thousand voters is a nice place to start.'

Winter nodded. His knowledge of the local political scene was rudimentary. The city was divided into two constituencies, Portsmouth North and Portsmouth South.

'So what are you going for, Baz? Where does all this stuff of yours end up?'

'Pompey North.' He gestured towards the window. 'I'm a Copnor boy, remember. It's home turf, my patch, and Leo thinks it's winnable. You know what MP stands for?'

'Tell me.'

'Mr Pompey.' He grinned. 'That's me, mush.'

Next year's general election dominated breakfast at Sandown Road. Winter, busying himself with scrambled eggs and four rashers of bacon, half-listened to the conversation, swapping looks with Marie when Kinder pushed her husband to the very edge of the known political universe. In this little game Bazza was a deeply willing accomplice, but Winter could only admire Kinder's skill in playing to his candidate's need to make the biggest possible splash in the claustrophobic little provincial backwater that was Portsmouth.

Watching him play Bazza, appealing to his vanity and his impatience and his raw appetite for mischief, Winter realised that Kinder had an almost feline talent for making the inconceivable – Mr Bazza Mackenzie, MP – seem a real possibility. How the city's favourite son could play Robin Hood to thousands of kids just old enough to vote. How he could turn his days with the 6.57 crew, a mobbed-up bunch of football hooligans, into evidence that he'd put his very life on the line for the city he loved. How Bazza's legendary business skills involved the kind of down-home aspiration that people on the hustings would readily understand. Bazza, Kinder kept saying, was real. He understood Pompey. He was passionate about the place. He was fluent in mush-speak. He smartened up failing businesses. He created jobs. He made the city a nicer place. Plus he wasn't afraid to voice an opinion or two. The voters of Portsmouth North, according to Kinder, were in for a treat.

On his second cup of coffee, Winter finally managed to bring the conversation back to earth. By now Mackenzie appeared to have signed up to a largish staff of talented young guys, mainly students, who would take the city by the throat and – in the name of *Pompey First* – set the place alight. Winter had lost track of what these people would actually be doing, but even in Bazza's world he knew that nothing came for free.

'So who's paying for all this?'

'Me, mush.'

'How?'

'I'll bung them a few quid. Make it worth their while. Students live on fuck all. Enough for a curry and a couple of pints? Easy.'

He seemed to think this settled the argument. Kinder disagreed.

'Why the fuck not, Leo?'

Kinder spelled out the big-ticket items: printing costs, premises, clerical salaries, a decent whack for someone with the right IT skills to get on top of the social media campaign, his own fee, plus another ten or twenty grand for something he called the 'stunt budget'.

'What's that?'

'It's a contingency, Baz. A lot of this stuff we can action

any time. That gives us a head start on pretty much everyone else. But when next year comes round and the thing gets going properly, you're in a different game.'

'I'm not with you, mush.'

'Anything can happen. Campaigns have to adapt. All the time. And to do that you have to make the weather.'

'Yeah?' Baz loved this. Winter could see it.

Kinder began to go into detail, calling on examples from previous campaigns: how to throttle another party's bright idea at birth, how to take a slip of the tongue and turn it into a major vote loser, how to find the skeleton in a rival's cupboard and give it a good rattle. In every case, he said, you needed to be quick on your feet, inventive and not afraid of spending a bob or two. To make that happen, you needed a war chest.

Bazza was grinning again. This was exactly the MO that had taken him from the backstreets of Copnor to up-market Craneswater.

'No problem,' he said. 'You want moolah, it'll be there for you.'

'How?' Winter again.

'Fuck knows.'

'I'm serious, Baz. The way things are going just now, we'll be lucky to make Christmas intact. Next year it's going to be even tougher. Unless you tell me where the money's coming from, this stuff's for the fairies.'

Mackenzie toyed with a corner of toast. For once he appeared to have been listening. Then his head came up.

'The guy who nicked my toot ...' he began '... that Skelley guy.'

'Yeah?'

'Get in touch. Tell him it's time he settled.'

Kinder caught the colder edge in Mackenzie's voice. He also saw the expression on Winter's face, the tiny turn of the head, the glance across the table towards Marie. Kinder wanted to know more about Skelley. Who was this guy?

'Forget it, Leo.' The grin was back on Bazza's face. 'Tell me more about that manga idea.'

Suttle had found a corner of the post-mortem room that was partly shielded by the pathologist and the mortuary technician who were bent over Faraday's corpse. The pathologist had just made a big Y-shaped incision, cutting twin lines from Faraday's shoulders to a point above his chest bone. From here, the scalpel sliced through the waxy yellowing flesh, stopping below the swell of belly that seemed to Suttle to have grown over the past couple of months. He heard the snap of bone as the front of the rib cage was removed and then turned away as the pathologist helped himself to the glistening jigsaw of organs that lay inside. In the grim parlance of autopsy procedure, this was termed the Pluck, a brimming double handful of windpipe, throat, lungs and heart carefully lifted and put to one side for later examination.

Suttle had been a witness at this procedure a number of times before. If you worked on Major Crime, it came with the turf. Yet never had he seen it happen to someone he liked to think he knew well. In one sense, it was difficult to associate the overweight body on the stainless-steel slab with Faraday. The essence of the man – his watchfulness, his humanity, the way he constantly worried about the real meanings of the word justice – had gone. Death robbed everyone of the person they'd been, and Faraday was no exception. What was hard, though, was trying to associate the pathologist's careful exploration with any real notion of what he might find.

Every post-mortem began with a complete external examination. In Faraday's case there'd been no visible signs of violence. No bruising, no abrasions, no ligature marks, nothing. Now, the pathologist was slowly emptying the rest of Faraday's body cavity. Each of the abdominal organs would be subject to careful inspection. There might be signs of damage from long-standing disease. Given Faraday's affection for a decent bottle of wine, his liver might come in for special attention. Tissue and other samples would doubtless confirm the chemical battering he'd probably given himself in the hours before he'd died. But that wasn't it.

Suttle's eyes returned again and again to Faraday's heart. It nestled beside his lungs in a big stainless-steel bowl, a knot of shiny muscle laced with arteries. Suttle doubted whether technology would ever be able to test for disappointment in a man's heart, but deep down he suspected that this, more than any other factor, had killed his ex-boss. Faraday was dead because, in the end, life hadn't measured up.

The Job, over two decades, had worn away his sense of belief in a society he'd once believed in. Not because he'd grown any less adept at proving guilt. On the contrary, some of his recent investigations had won quiet applause at every level. But because his belief in innocence had taken such a battering. In a moment of rare candour he'd recently confessed to Suttle that people, more and more, disgusted him. They seldom looked further than their own needs. They dug holes for themselves and others without the faintest regard for the likely consequences. And when the shit hit the fan, which it inevitably did, there was always someone else to blame.

This sense of disillusion, increasingly acute, had finally seeped into his private life. Suttle sensed that long-term relationships had never been easy for Faraday. A number of women had come and gone. But the abrupt departure of Gabrielle, his partner of three years, had been – for Faraday – the end of the line. He thought he'd known her. He knew he'd loved her. Yet, come the finish, neither had been enough.

Suttle watched the pathologist removing the last coil of intestine, aware of a choking sensation in his own chest. Barely twelve hours ago, back home after leaving the Bargemaster's House, it had been the same. He'd tried without success to explain it to Lizzie. Preoccupied with the baby, he sensed she'd barely listened. A bottle of red, followed by a couple of stiff vodkas, hadn't helped. Now, faced with the cold facts of Faraday's demise, he was completely lost. What did any of this have to do with the man he'd known? How could anyone's life be reduced to a set of clinical observations folded into a post-mortem report?

By lunchtime, mercifully, the pathologist had finished. Suttle left a message on Parsons' answering machine and set off for London. Twice he swapped stations on the radio, hunting for something, *anything,* that would take his mind off the body on the shininess of the post-mortem table, but nothing worked. Only an hour or so later, in a traffic jam on the M3, did he realise the full irony of the situation. Faraday, faced with something similar, would have probably felt exactly the same.

Chapter four

J-J lived in a terrace of houses three streets south of Chiswick High Road. The area, as far as Suttle could tell, had become a magnet for young professional couples with growing families. Mums pushing state-of-the-art buggies were everywhere, and it was hard to pass a parked 4 x 4 without noticing the baby seat anchored in the back.

Suttle found the address he'd copied from Faraday's book and slipped into a gap across the road from J-J's place. Yet another young mum was out in her modest patch of front garden, filling her recycling box with newspapers. From the car, Suttle could see her tiny daughter in the front bay window, jiggling away to unheard music, and he thought instantly of Grace, back at home in Southsea. His hangover was beginning to ease and he knew he owed Lizzie a call. He'd be crap at apologising for this morning's little episode but he dreaded the thought of returning to any kind of atmosphere. Parenthood wasn't quite as simple a proposition as he'd once imagined, as the woman with an armful of *Daily Mail*s doubtless understood.

He locked the Subaru and crossed the road. After the morning's rain, he enjoyed the sudden warmth of the sunshine on his upturned face. There was a single bell push on J-J's front door, and as he pressed it he wondered how on earth the man would hear him. Early on, Faraday had discovered that his infant son was deaf, a condition that seemed to have shaped the long years to come. In Suttle's book the fact that Faraday had coped so well told you everything you needed to know. J-J's mum had died with the kid barely six months old. How on earth would you set about being a single parent after a trauma like that?

The door opened, and Suttle recognised the tall skinny figure from a photo beside Faraday's bed. J-J was wearing a pair of patched jeans, no belt and a scarlet T-shirt several sizes too small. The message across the chest looked Russian – Cyrillic script, totally incomprehensible. He stared at Suttle blankly. He had a long bony face, utterly unlike Faraday's, and it was several days since he'd last had a shave.

Suttle, who'd sent a text earlier, wondered if it had got through. Evidently not. He produced his warrant card. When J-J looked even blanker, he pointed at the Hantspol logo, hoping he might make a connection or two. Nothing.

The two men looked at each other for a long moment, then Suttle nodded at the shadowed hall behind J-J and invited himself in. The back of the house faced south. A small conservatory was splashed with more sunshine, and Suttle could smell fresh coffee. He turned to find J-J standing uncertainly behind him.

In situations like these it was normal to alert the local police to deliver the death message. They usually sent around one of the uniforms on shift and offered the services of a Family Liaison Officer if circumstances justified it. Last night, before leaving the Bargemaster's House, Nick Hayder had asked the Met to do just this, but an email had been waiting for him this morning when he got back from the post-mortem, reporting that J-J didn't appear to be at home. Hayder had phoned Suttle barely an hour ago, knowing he was en route up to London to offer J-J help over the funeral arrangements. Would he mind doing a brief interview with the man as well?

Suttle had been happy to say yes. Now, looking at J-J, he was trying to work out exactly how to break the news. Sign language was beyond him. Lip-reading opened the door to countless ambiguities. The letter was his only option. Last night the Crime Scene Investigator had taken a copy on Faraday's printer before bagging the original as evidence. Suttle had tucked the copy in an envelope and brought it up. Now he gave it to J-J.

In conversation Faraday had always referred to him as a boy. In real life he was anything but. Doing the sums, Suttle calculated he must be in his early thirties, though his pallor and gauntness made him look older. He studied the letter, then read it again. When he looked up, he was visibly shocked, his eyes shiny with tears. He sniffed a couple of times and then wiped his nose on the back of his hand. Maybe Faraday was right, Suttle thought. A boy, after all.

Suttle shook his head in what he hoped was a gesture of sympathy. Then he tried to soften the news with a clumsy piece of mime, popping imaginary tablets in his mouth and then cushioning his head on his folded hands. Your dad took some codeine, he was trying to say, and then went to sleep. J-J followed him, gesture by gesture, not remotely fooled by this charade. He studied Suttle for a moment or two then drew a bony finger across his throat and raised an enquiring eyebrow.

Suttle nodded, extending a consolatory hand, patting him on the shoulder. He had no choice. There were a million ways of breaking this kind of news, but few were as brutal and bizarre as this.

The kitchen was next door to the conservatory. Suttle took charge, re-warming the pot of coffee and finding a couple of cups. J-J had disappeared and Suttle wondered whether there was anyone else in the house. Faraday had sometimes talked of a Russian actress his son was shacked up with, and Suttle hoped to God she was upstairs. In the event, to his immense relief, he was right.

She'd obviously been asleep. She stood in the kitchen, rubbing her eyes. She was slight, like J-J, but much shorter. The blue dressing gown she was wearing must have been his

34

because it came down to her ankles. Her eyes were enormous and lent her face the kind of startling beauty that would turn heads anywhere. Her feet were bare on the kitchen tiles and she'd painted a single toenail the colour of J-J's T-shirt.

'What's happened?' Her English was perfect, if heavily accented.

Suttle explained as best he could. J-J's father had been found dead. He appeared to have taken his own life. In all these cases the police had to make enquiries. He was sorry to have brought news like this.

She nodded and extended a hand. She said her name was Ulyana. She seemed neither shocked nor surprised by Faraday's death, and Suttle found himself wondering why.

'Did you know him?'

'Yes.'

'Well?'

'Only a little –' she shrugged '– but ...'

'But what?'

She glanced at J-J, obviously reluctant to go on, but her partner seemed to have ghosted away into a world of his own. He was gazing out through the conservatory windows. There were rags of cloud in the blueness of the sky over the nearby rooftops and his eyes were still wet with tears.

Ulyana angled her body towards Suttle, her face invisible to J-J.

'He wasn't well,' she said.

'How do you mean?'

'He was very nervous, always, and very sad.'

'This is recently?'

'Yes. And before as well. For years, maybe, since I first knew him, but it got worse.'

'And do you know why?'

'No.'

'Does J-J?'

'I don't think so. They were very close once. Now, not so much.'

Suttle nodded, realising that she was hiding her mouth because J-J could lip-read. He found a third cup and poured the coffee before returning to the conservatory. There were a couple of fold-up garden chairs and a battered old sofa, but it was impossible to get J-J to sit down.

'Is he the only next of kin?'

'I'm sorry?'

'Does he have any relatives? Family members?'

'I don't know. I don't think so.'

'Could you ask him, please?'

Ulyana got to her feet. J-J took a step back, but she reached out to him, folded herself into his chest, gave him a long hug. Then she began to talk to him, a flurry of sign. There was obviously far more to the conversation than the simple question Suttle had asked, but finally she returned with an answer.

'His mum's parents are still alive.'

'Where do they live?'

'America.'

'Anyone else?'

'He doesn't think so. There were never any aunts or uncles. Joe was ... how do you say?'

'An only child.'

'*Da.* Yes.'

Suttle nodded. Under these circumstances J-J would have to come down to Portsmouth asap. There was a long list of stuff to sort out, beginning with the arrangements for the funeral. It would be good, Suttle said, if he had a bit of support.

'Of course. I'll come with him.'

'It may take a while.'

'Sure. I have a couple of auditions but ...' She shrugged, leaving the sentence unfinished. She had her arms round J-J again, and for the first time Suttle caught the faintest hint of Faraday in his face, something vulnerable, something withheld.

36

'You have a key to the house down there? Or do you want me to sort one out?'

There was a brief exchange of sign.

'We have a key,' she said. 'Thank you.'

Suttle checked his watch and then found a visiting card. He gave it to Ulyana and told her to phone him any time if she needed help. He took her mobile number and asked when they might be heading south. She thought tomorrow, when J-J had had a chance to properly understand what had happened. Suttle looked at her, disturbed by what she had said.

'He's going to be OK?'

She smiled and then took Suttle's hand. 'Come.'

She led the way back through the kitchen. At the foot of the stairs she paused and then nodded up towards the first floor. For the first time Suttle became aware of a line of carefully framed photographs flanking the stairs. There were more of them on the top landing, all in black and white.

'Please,' she said. 'Go ahead.'

Suttle edged slowly up the staircase, pausing beside each photo. They were all studies of children, some young, some less so. In every case the child was looking into the lens, their young face side-lit, and what came through every shot was a trustfulness tempered with something else. As he moved from picture to picture, Suttle realised that these kids came from a special place. Something was missing. You could see it in their eyes. There was a vacancy, a lack of engagement, but there was also a sense that the person holding the camera, the person talking to them, the person winning their trust, had somehow secured himself visiting rights.

Suttle knew that J-J had won a bit of a reputation in art photography. In this respect, and many others, Faraday had always been immensely proud of him.

'J-J took these?'

'Yes. There was a special exhibition. It was a couple of years ago. Joe came up. His girlfriend too.'

37

'Gabrielle?'

'Yes.' Her eyes returned to a shot of a young girl. 'These kids are autistic. That's the whole point. If you understand that, you understand J-J. The kind of man he is, the kind of *person* he is.'

'You're telling me he's autistic, too?'

'Not at all. I mean he reaches out. He shows himself. He's never afraid. Like that you can get hurt, believe me.'

Suttle nodded. 'And these kids knew that?'

'Of course. Which is why these photos are so good. That's his gift. His talent. You understand what I'm trying to say?'

Suttle nodded. He understood exactly what she was trying to say. Like his father, J-J had the gift of empathy. He could get into other people's heads, other people's hearts. What Joe Senior had found there had begun to distress him, but it was this talent, all too rare, that had made him such a fine detective.

'There's a couple of other things ...' Suttle said. 'Do you think J-J has a contact number for Gabrielle?'

'Of course.' She looked surprised. 'Didn't Joe?'

'I can't seem to find one.' It was true. Suttle had searched both Faraday's address book and his email. All traces of Gabrielle seemed to have been erased.

'You want to get in touch with her?'

'Yes. She ought to know. She ought to be told.'

'OK.' She said she'd get the number from J-J's mobile before Suttle left. 'What else do you need?'

Suttle hesitated, unsure where investigation ended and intrusion began.

'Joe wrote J-J a letter ...' he said at last. 'I'm sure you'll read it.'

'I have. He showed me upstairs.'

'You remember the line at the end? The postscript?'

She frowned a moment, then nodded. 'You mean about the eagle?'

'Yes.'

'And you don't understand?'

'No.'

'You want to ask him?'

Without waiting for an answer, she took Suttle back to the conservatory. J-J, folded onto the sofa, was still watching the clouds. Ulyana signed to him. Suttle wondered which gesture meant 'eagle'. J-J took his time replying, but when the answer came it seemed to transform him. He stirred. His bony fingers were a blur of sign. His thin body was perched on the very edge of the sofa. When the punchline came, he turned towards Suttle and grinned.

'When he was a kid,' Ulyana explained, 'he and his dad played bird games. They'd go out all day, watching the birds. They had books, lots of books, and the books were all about birds. Sometimes there were programmes on the TV about birds. All the time, birds, birds, birds. That's the world they made for themselves. Birds everywhere.'

'And the eagle?'

'It's got to do with a poem.'

'Which poem?'

'He won't tell me.'

'Why not?'

She turned back to J-J and put the question. J-J shook his head, glanced up at Suttle and then put his finger to his lips.

'He still won't say?'

'No. I think it's private, personal.'

J-J was lip-reading. The nod was a nod of agreement. Then he stood up, extending his thin arms, and did a slow tight circuit of the conservatory, up on his toes, swaying and swoop-ing, a performance no less startling for being so sudden and so ungainly. Suttle watched him, wondering if he'd pushed the conversation too far. He needn't have worried.

'He's being an eagle.' Ulyana was smiling. 'He says it was his dad's favourite bird.'

*

Winter had been back in his apartment at Blake House for the best part of an hour before he noticed the message-waiting light blinking on the answering machine. He finished his coffee and hit the replay button. It was a woman's voice, faint, indistinct. The message lasted less than thirty seconds, but by the time it ended he knew exactly who it was. He reached for a pad and played the message again, scribbling down the numbers she'd left at the end. He'd no idea where the dialling code 00382 might take him, but that wasn't the point. Five years ago this woman had helped save his life. Fingers crossed, she might just do it again.

Feeling infinitely better, he stepped onto the balcony and gazed out. The busy clutter of Portsmouth Harbour had always been his favourite view. This, as he'd told so many visitors over the years, was where you could take the real pulse of the city. The Gosport ferries churning back and forth across the water, the hourly FastCat heading for the distant smudge of the Isle of Wight, the occasional warship ghosting towards the harbour narrows and the open sea, the big cross-Channel boats, outward bound for Le Havre and St Malo. This ongoing carnival – part pleasure, part commerce, part defence of the realm – never failed to gladden him. It was evidence that this city of his, so crowded, so claustrophobic, so *insular*, also had another face. From here, in Gunwharf, it looked outward. There were ways you could escape, he thought. Which, under the current circumstances, was just as well.

He shed his jacket and sank into the plastic recliner he kept on the balcony. The sun was warm on his face, and he shut his eyes, yet again reviewing his options. Martin Skelley was a Scouse businessman who'd trodden a career path very similar to Bazza Mackenzie's. Drug dealing in his early years in Liverpool had earned him a great deal of money, profits he'd sensibly invested in a delivery company called Freezee. Freezee had cashed in on the nation's passion for crap fast food, and it was Skelley's fleet of white Transits that now serviced cafés and burger bars nationwide. Skelley bought the burgers pre-frozen for zilch money and delivered them – strictly for cash – to anyone who'd pay. The margins he worked on weren't huge, but year after year the sheer volume of orders had grown to the point where he'd become a very rich man.

Like many ex-criminals, Skelley had retained a gut loyalty to a handful of mates he'd trust with his life, and one of them, it turned out, had found herself in possession of two and a half million quid's worth of cocaine, an insurance policy Bazza Mackenzie had put by for a rainy day. The circumstances of this episode were complicated. They involved four bodies in a burned-out farmhouse on the Isle of Wight and had pre-occupied Winter for much of the early spring. He'd won a kind of result in the shape of a £350K payout from Skelley's mate – a businesswoman called Lou Sadler who ran a stable of eastern European toms from premises in Cowes – but Bazza had always considered the settlement a rip-off, and Winter knew only too well that one day he'd be after the rest.

That day, thanks to his political ambitions, had now arrived. Quite why he'd look to Skelley for the money rather than sell Misty's house was anybody's guess, but that – thank Christ – wasn't the issue. In the shape of Martin Skelley, plus the forthcoming election, Winter had at last found a way of bringing his worst nightmare to an end.

His mobile was in his jacket pocket. Shading his eyes from the sun, still flat on his back, he accessed the directory and hit a number. Jimmy Suttle answered within seconds.

'Paul?'

'Me, son.'

'I'm on the motorway. What do you want?'

'A meet.'

'When?'

'As soon as.'

'You're kidding. I'm as busy as fuck. What's it about?'

'Skelley.'

'Martin Skelley?'

'The very same.'

There was a brief silence. Winter thought he could hear music in the background but he couldn't be sure. Then Suttle was back again.

'Where?'

'Here. My place.'

'Give me a couple of hours.' The phone went dead.

Chapter five

Winter was watching the early-evening news when Suttle thumbed the entry button at the main door downstairs. He got to his feet, made it to the hall, spared his video ID screen a passing glance and let Suttle in. The third can of Stella had definitely been a mistake.

Suttle knew at once that Winter had been drinking. They'd met a number of times since the early spring, in anticipation of exactly this moment, and Suttle was clearly impatient to get the thing sorted. Refusing Winter's offer of a lager, he settled on the sofa.

'So what have you got for me?' His eyes drifted towards the TV.

Winter did his best to look aggrieved. At the very least, an occasion like this deserved a little foreplay.

'Are you on the meter?' he inquired. 'Or can we behave like human beings?'

'Up to you, mate. I just want to know where you stand.'

'I stand where I always stood.'

'What the fuck does that mean?'

'It means that I work for the Man. It means that he's driving me barmy. Plus I've got a problem.'

'Like what?' Suttle was still watching the news.

'Like you blokes turning up with a European Arrest Warrant.'

He at last had Suttle's full attention. Winter reached for the remote and turned the set off.

'Why would we do that?'

'It doesn't matter.'

'To me it does. Don't play games, mate. It's a bit late for that.' He studied Winter for a moment or two. 'Has someone been on to you? One of our people?'

'No.'

'I don't believe you.'

'Suit yourself, son. The fact is I don't need a whisper. All you have to do is read the fucking paper.'

Winter had kept the cutting. It came from the *Daily Telegraph*. He fetched it from a drawer in the sideboard and gave it to Suttle. Under EU law, prosecutors Europe-wide could issue a warrant for the arrest of anyone suspected of being guilty of a criminal offence. The accused had no chance of challenging or even seeing the evidence before being shipped abroad for trial. According to the *Telegraph*, the Magistrates' Court at Horseferry Road was currently processing ten cases every day. Since the scheme started in 2004, extraditions had gone through the roof.

'I wouldn't have a prayer, son. I thought this was just about bent Polish plumbers and piss-head students in Magaluf, but I'm wrong, aren't I?'

Suttle was still reading the article. Finally he looked up.

'Depends,' he said.

'On what?'

'On what you've done.' He paused. 'Is it serious?'

'Yeah.'

'How serious?'

'Very.'

'So serious you need a deal?'

'Yeah.'

'And does it involve Mackenzie?'

'No.'

'You're sure about that?'

'Yeah.'

44

'OK.' Suttle checked his watch, then reached for his mobile. 'I'll have a Stella, if you're still offering.'

He made a call while Winter sorted a couple of cold ones from the fridge in the kitchen. Through the open door he could hear him trying to head off an earful from Lizzie. By the time Winter was back in the living room, Suttle was losing his temper.

'Later, eh?' He rang off without saying goodbye and tossed the mobile onto the sofa.

Winter gave him the tinny and a glass and made himself comfortable in the big recliner opposite. Way back on division, when Suttle was a young CID aide, Winter had taught him everything he'd known about the Job. He'd sensed from the start that Suttle had the makings of a quality detective, and within months they'd formed a partnership that had taken scalp after scalp. The boy was canny and brave and knew how to listen. He was also excellent company, and when Winter suddenly found himself fighting a brain tumour, it was Suttle who'd helped nurse him through it.

Winter had always liked to think that this was more than repayment for a blinding apprenticeship, and he was right. Suttle, in a way, had become the son he'd never had, and even Winter's decision to bin the Job and cross to the Dark Side had still left the relationship pretty much intact. Suttle had never hidden his feelings about the move Winter had made. Bazza Mackenzie disgusted him. The man had always been lowlife, and no amount of moolah and posh friends in Craneswater would ever change that. But Suttle had the balls, rare among Winter's ex-colleagues, to give any man a hearing, and his affection for Mackenzie's new lieutenant had somehow survived. Winter, he knew for a fact, was a class operator. He was also, deep down, a decent man. And so Suttle, despite everything, still regarded him as a mate.

'You look knackered, son.' Winter tipped his glass. 'Here's to crime.'

'Yeah?'

Suttle took a long pull at the Stella and then lay back, gazing at the wall opposite. The phone call to Lizzie seemed to have tripped a switch deep in his brain. The earlier impatience had gone. It had been his wife's suggestion to ask Winter whether he'd like to be a godfather to Grace, and just now he was deeply thankful he'd said yes.

'This is fucking horrible,' he said softly.

'What, son?'

'Everything. Lizzie. The baby. The lot.'

Winter, who'd never had kids of his own, could only nod. 'I bet.'

'I'm serious. Maybe we don't get enough sleep, maybe that's it, but you know what? Having a baby turns you into someone else.'

'Turns who?'

'Lizzie. Me too, probably. I just never sussed any of this would ever happen. You see kids in the park. You see kids on the beach. You see them in the fucking Mothercare catalogue. And it all seems so ... I dunno ... *simple*. And you know what? It isn't.'

Winter nodded, surprised by the admission. Suttle never moaned, never complained, never revealed a flicker of self-doubt. That was the way he coped. That was what had taken him to D/S and would doubtless push him further still. The guy was tough as well as honest.

'It'll pass,' Winter said. 'It'll get better, easier. Everything always does. Time, son. Give yourself time.'

'I wish.'

'I'm serious.'

'I'm sure you are. It's just that ...' Suttle shook his head, leaving the thought unvoiced. His glass was nearly empty. Winter was watching him carefully.

'You want another one?'

'No.' He shook his head. 'Thanks.'

46

The two men sat in silence for a while. To Winter at least it felt companionable and somehow necessary. Back at the start of the year, increasingly alarmed by his boss's behaviour, he'd made a private decision to find an escape hatch and bail out of the Mackenzie empire. Bazza had become too volatile, too cocky, too erratic. Like many rich men, he seemed to be living in a bubble of his own making. He thought that money and power and influence had put him beyond reach. In this, to Winter's certain knowledge, he was wrong. Reckless decisions would one day come back to haunt him, and when that happened Winter knew he had to be gone.

He'd shared this conclusion with Suttle, knowing that his young protégé would regard it as a key to all kinds of investigative mischief, and in this he hadn't been wrong. Within days Suttle had delivered an intelligence file on Martin Skelley to be used as Winter saw fit. In one sense this was an open invitation for Winter to rejoin the forces of law and order, albeit as an informant and provocateur, a pawn in the bigger game of entrapping his boss. In another, far more interesting as far as Winter was concerned, it marked the start of a path that would finally lead him to a safer place. Hantspol, he knew for a fact, would do anything to bring Mackenzie down.

'He's there for the taking, son.'

'Who?'

'Bazza.'

He explained about his latest caper, the bid to stitch up Pompey North and send the city's favourite son to Westminster.

Suttle looked shocked. 'As an MP?'

'Yeah.'

'You mean get himself *elected*?'

'Yeah. As far as Bazza's concerned, there's nothing that money and mouth can't achieve. These days, fuck knows, he's probably right. Either way, it's gone to his head. He's got himself an agent. He's putting a campaign team together. He's even worked out a policy or two. This, as I keep telling him, is going to cost a fortune, but the twat never listens. He just assumes the money's there. Happily, he's wrong.'

'Happily?'

'He's vulnerable, son. He's like a kid. The politics thing is a must-have. He wants it. He *needs* it. As far as Bazza's concerned, the money looks after itself.'

'How much are we talking? For this campaign?'

'A lot.'

'But he's a rich man.'

'That's what he says.'

'And you're telling me he's wrong?'

'Yeah. He's got assets coming out of his ears – property, businesses, whatever – but a lot of this stuff looks really dodgy. Take Dubai. We've got huge exposure, all on borrowed money, and you know what? The market's collapsed. Down 40 per cent in a year. Do the math, son. The guy's fucked.'

'No more toot?'

'Skelley had it all. As you know.'

'That wasn't my question.'

'Then no. The cupboard's bare. That's why the guy's there for the taking.'

Suttle nodded, brooding on the implications. One of the reasons he'd made a name for himself in Intelligence was his ability to see a pattern in events and turn it to his own advantage.

'I need to know about this Euro-warrant,' he said at last.

'No way.' Winter shook his head.

'Then why bring it up?'

'Because you need to be sure about motivation.'

'Whose?'

'Mine. Grassing up Bazza isn't something you'd do lightly. There has to be a reason.'

'Good point.' Suttle had the ghost of a smile on his face. His one-time mentor was as sharp as ever. 'So where do I go next?'

'Is that a serious question?'

'Of course it is.'

'OK.' Winter bent forward in the chair, abandoning his glass. 'For my money we play it long. Bazza wants me to sort Skelley. Skelley is a top face. I've read that file you gave me. Bazza hasn't a clue what he's getting into. Best, says me, to first try and find the funds elsewhere.'

'Like how?'

'Like Montenegro. We've got 10 per cent of a big fuck-off development in a place called Bicici. The rest is owned by a Russian guy. The way I hear it, he might be happy to buy us out. I start negotiations. I get him on the hook. I'm looking at decent money. The election's getting closer. Then Brown's away to the Palace or wherever he fucking goes, and the election's kicked off, and guess what? The Montenegro deal falls through. By now, in Bazza's little head, he's got one foot in Parliament. He's nearly there. All he needs is a whole whack of money to make it happen. So guess whose door I'm knocking on ...'

'Skelley's.'

'Exactly. By now Baz is dribbling big time. He wants Pompey North so bad he could practically *eat* it. That's when he starts being very silly indeed. And that's when we take him.'

'We?'

'We.'

Suttle smiled again. He could see the logic. It was neat. It was devious. And it might even work.

'So what do you think?'

'I think it's cool.' Suttle's smile turned into a frown. 'The election's months away. Next year probably. April or May.'

'Exactly. That's what I mean by playing it long.'

'But what about the arrest warrant? What happens if someone comes knocking on your door?'

'You sort it.'

'You mean some kind of indemnity?'

'Yeah. Protect me. Keep the fuckers off.'

'That's not easy.'

'No, but it's not impossible either.'

'And what would you want after that?'

'Money. And somewhere to live. And maybe a new ID. Standard deal. Yeah?'

Suttle conceded the point. Winter watched him toying with his drink, swirling the last of the Stella around the glass. Decision time, he thought.

'So ...?'

'Fuck knows. It's not me who'll be calling the shots. You've been there. You know the way it works. People like Parsons and Willard – they're the ones with the exposure.'

Winter nodded. Det Chief Supt Geoff Willard was Head of CID. He'd tried to nail Mackenzie on a number of earlier occasions, and each time he'd failed.

'He's still interested? Willard?'

'Of course he is. Mackenzie behind bars sends the message of his dreams.'

'So why wouldn't he buy in?'

'Because he doesn't trust you.'

'Ah ...' Winter nodded. 'And how about you? Do *you* trust me?'

'Of course not. But I understand you. And that makes a difference.'

'It does?'

'Yeah.'

'Why?'

'Because I know when you're lying.'

'You're sure about that?'

'Of course.' Suttle offered him a weary smile. 'Most of the time.'

Lizzie was in the bath with Grace by the time Suttle finally got home. He could hear the splash of water from upstairs and the muted gurgle that his daughter made when she was in a sunny mood. He crept up the stairs, armed with the placatory bottle he'd bought in the offie round the corner. A decent Rioja. Lizzie's tipple of choice. And, as it happened, Faraday's too.

Up on the narrow landing Suttle paused. He could feel one of the floorboards shifting under his weight. They'd only moved into the tiny terraced house a couple of months ago and he still had to find time to get a carpet down. The bathroom door was an inch or two open, and through the crack he could see his wife blowing bubbles for the baby. Lizzie was small-boned and neat and moved with a precision and quickness that had always stirred him. Regular jogs along the nearby seafront had quickly shed the extra stone or two she'd put on during pregnancy, and only last night she'd announced that she was back at the weight she'd been when they first met. Preoccupied with events at the Bargemaster's House, Suttle had let the news slip by him. Time to make up.

Easing the door open, he stepped quietly into the bathroom. Grace saw him at once, her tiny face creasing into the big rubber grin she saved for moments like these. Lizzie stiffened, aware of another presence in the room, and when her face came round Suttle realised he had even more ground to make up. Then the alarm in her eyes gave way to relief and she reached up for him.

'Kiss me,' she said. 'Bastard.'

Later, after Suttle had put the baby to bed, they opened the bottle. Lizzie appeared to have forgotten all about the earlier conversation on the phone. A couple of mates had been round for a bit of a catch-up. She hadn't seen either of them for months and they'd made a huge fuss of Grace before beating a tactful retreat at bath time.

Suttle was busy at the stove. He wanted to know more about the surprise callers.

'Megan and Andy. Megan's still at the *News*. Andy used to work there but chucked it in. At least that's what he says.'

'You think the man lies?'

'I think he's not the kind of guy that really fits. He's awesome in all kinds of ways – really bright, really cluey – but he hates all the corporate stuff and doesn't bother to hide it. Even the *News* must have noticed in the end.'

Suttle had never heard of these people. Even married, both he and Lizzie tended to hang on to their own sets of friends. Paul Winter, oddly enough, was one of the few people they shared.

Suttle scraped a dice of onion and garlic into the frying pan. It was all too easy to imagine the conversation with Megan. Newsroom gossip. Stories that hadn't worked. Who was screwing who. Lately, he'd begun to sense that Lizzie couldn't wait to get back.

'You miss it, don't you?'

'I do.'

'You miss it badly?'

'Badly enough to bore Megan shitless about how lucky she is.'

'Maybe she feels the same about you.'

'I doubt it. She and Andy aren't getting on. You could see it. The guy fascinates me. I've never met anyone ... I dunno ... so *shameless*. He's impatience on legs. Whatever he's thinking, it's all over his face. She obviously bores him stiff. Pity, really. She can be really sweet.'

'So what's he up to now?'

'No idea. I did ask but he's always full of bullshit. I think he views unemployment as a career opportunity. The big novel? Some new twist on social media? The trillion-dollar website? Either way, he's lucky Megan's still earning. Which is probably why he's hanging in there.'

'Nice.'

'Exactly. Are you getting the picture here, Mr Chef?'

She stepped across with the bottle and gave him a kiss. Suttle abandoned the stove and held her for a long moment. For reasons he couldn't explain, he'd always loved the snubness of her nose and the way she cropped her hair. In certain lights, like now, she looked about twelve.

'Friends?' he murmured.

'Always.'

Over supper he told her about J-J. He described breaking the news about his dad's death and showed her the mime he'd used to try and soften the blow. When he told her that J-J and Ulyana were due down tomorrow to try and pick up the pieces, she offered to do whatever she could to help. Suttle wasn't quite sure how this might work, but he loved the generosity of the gesture and the fact that she obviously cared. She'd only met Faraday on a couple of occasions, but both times she'd come to the same conclusion. Now, halfway through another bottle they'd found, she said it again.

'He needed mothering. He needed a bit of a hug.'

'Yeah? You think so?'

'Definitely. The guy was all over the place. He needed looking after.'

'You're right.' Suttle emptied his glass. 'Maybe it's a man thing.'

Lizzie said nothing. Then she pushed her plate away, got to her feet, extended a hand and nodded towards the stairs.

'My pleasure, Mr Chef.'

That same night Winter dreams about Brett West. He remembers the morning Bazza drove him across to Southampton Airport. He pictures the little charter jet waiting for them on the apron in front of the terminal building. Mackenzie has already dispatched Westie to Malaga with instructions to keep a low profile and has now laid hands on a professional hit man from south London called Tommy Peters to tidy the situation up. As Bazza's enforcer, Westie has shown a real talent for hurting people but he's also overstepped the mark once too often. Mackenzie has no patience for that kind of liability. Hence the presence of Tommy Peters.

A hired Mercedes van is waiting for them at Malaga Airport. Winter has yet to figure out exactly what's to come. They drive into the city and then take the coast road north. Beyond the town of Rincon de la Victoria the van hooks a left and climbs through the suburbs. High in the foothills overlooking the sea, Winter is dropped outside a half-finished bar in a housing development still under construction. It's late afternoon but still very hot. There's no one around. Bazza gives him a holdall. Inside, in high-denomination notes, is £25,000. The money belongs to Westie, Bazza says. Make sure he counts it.

Winter remembers the cloud of dust as the van takes Bazza and Tommy Peters and couple of other guys away. He walks into the bar. The place smells of cement dust. Nothing's finished. He takes a seat at a table and waits. After a while an old man appears and gives him a drink. Later still Westie turns up. He's brought his girlfriend. She's German, very pretty, nice to talk to. Her name is Renata. She's some kind of artist. Westie is still counting the notes when Tommy Peters reappears. He's carrying a gun. He shoots Westie twice, both times in the head.

In the dream Winter is inches away from Westie when Peters pulls the trigger. He can feel the warm spray of blood. It's all over his face, his hands, his shirt, everywhere. The girl is on her knees, trying to help Westie. She looks up. She sees the gun levelled at her own head. She's pleading for her life. Winter can taste his own shock, his own fear, the terrible realisation that he doesn't belong here, that he should never have been any part of this slaughter.

He turns to Peters, tells him to put the gun down, tells him to spare the girl. Peters gives him a look, eases him out of the line of fire, moistens his lips, half-closes one eye. Winter looks at the girl. He wants to say sorry. He wants to be forgiven. But he knows that will never be possible. Of Bazza, needless to say, there is no sign.

*

Winter woke with a tiny gasp. After a moment or two, totally lost, he realised he was trembling. Then he recognised the shape of his bedroom window in the throw of light from the promenade below and dimly made out the silhouette of the stuffed leopard at the foot of the bed. Bathed in sweat, still trembling, he reached out for the comfort of Misty. He wanted to wake her. He wanted to tell her about the dream. But there was no one there.

Chapter six

For the first time for months Suttle slept in. Normally, to keep the peace, he was first up for the baby. This morning, a Saturday, it was Lizzie who slipped out of bed at the first tiny cries from the baby's room next door. Making his way downstairs, hours later, he found Lizzie dribbling feed into the goldfish bowl while Grace, strapped in her rocker in front of the TV, tried to make sense of the morning cartoons.

'You're a star,' he mumbled, giving her a kiss.

'Your boss phoned.'

'Parsons?'

'Yeah. She wants you to give her a ring.' She looked at him a moment, then gave his hand a squeeze. 'Enjoy.'

Parsons was at home. She was about to descend on Sainsbury's but first she needed an update on Operation *Castor*. She was having lunch with the Head of CID and it seemed Det Chief Supt Willard wanted to be absolutely sure.

'About what?'

'Us. And Faraday.'

'I'm not with you, boss.' Suttle was still rubbing the sleep from his eyes. 'The guy committed suicide.'

'We're sure about that?'

'Positive. I talked to D/I Hayder last night.'

'No evidence of ...' she paused '... negligence?'

'By who?'

'Us.'

Suttle was looking at Lizzie. Good journalists listen to everything, and she was one of the best. He bent to the phone again.

'We gave him support, boss. I understand we offered him a job. What else could we do?'

'Nothing. You're right. I'll tell Mr Willard. Anything else I should know?'

'Yeah, boss. Winter.'

'What about him?'

'We had a long chat last night.' He glanced at his watch. 'What time are you seeing Mr Willard?'

It was never Suttle's intention to invite himself to lunch, but when the return call came fifteen minutes later it seemed that Willard had insisted. He and Parsons had been planning to meet at a gastropub out in the country, but under the circumstances Parsons had cancelled the booking and would be getting something together in the privacy of her own home. She anticipated a lengthy discussion, and the last thing she needed was an audience.

Willard was a big man, physically imposing. He'd won a force-wide reputation as a detective's detective and commanded respect as well as a degree of fear. Suttle had never seen him out of a suit.

'Winter?' he said.

They were sitting around a highly polished table in Parsons' dining room. There were only single-course settings, and Suttle was wondering why she bothered with a silver candelabrum at midday. At least she hadn't lit the candles.

Suttle explained about the meet he'd had last night. Winter had tired of life with Bazza Mackenzie. He was definitely looking for a way out, and if the price of the ticket was stitching up his boss then so be it.

'And you believe him?'

'Yes, sir.'

'Why?'

'Because Mackenzie's started to frighten him.'

Willard wanted to know how. Suttle explained the political campaign he was trying to mount. The man's ambition knew no limits. In Winter's view, Mackenzie had lost touch with reality. He was in denial about the gathering storm that threatened to swamp his various businesses, and in the shape of Leo Kinder he'd found the playmate of his dreams. As ever, the world was his for the taking. Next stop Westminster.

The news that Mackenzie might be facing ruin drew a smile of grim satisfaction from Willard. He'd always believed that one day Mackenzie would be the cause of his own undoing. Maybe that time had come.

'I'm still not clear about Winter,' he said. 'Why so sudden? Why now?'

Suttle had been anticipating exactly this question. He should of course tell Willard about the possibility of a European Arrest Warrant but knew that this would be the end for Winter. In Willard's book the ex-D/C was public enemy number two. Turning your back on the Job, betraying everything that it represented, was the cardinal sin. Nothing would please him more than to know that Winter might spend the rest of his life in some khazi of a foreign jail.

'I think it's been building, sir. I think it's a long-term thing. Mackenzie's an animal, and even Winter's realised nothing's going to change.'

'He knew that all along.'

'Maybe not in the way he knows it now.'

'So what's happened?'

'I don't know, sir.'

'Would he tell you?'

'He might.'

Willard nodded. One of the reasons he was a hot favourite for ACPO rank was his talent for seeing through every variety of bullshit. This skill had served him well as a sharp-end detective, and Suttle was uncomfortably aware that the conversation was about to become deeply personal.

Parsons appeared with a basket full of rolls, hot from the oven. Willard reached for one without taking his eyes off Suttle.

'Winter's a godfather to your daughter. Am I right?'

'Yes, sir.'

'Was that wise? Given the fact that you're a serving officer?'

'Probably not, sir.'

'*Probably not?* You're a policeman. Winter's taking money off a known criminal. He works for the man. He probably does a good job. He probably makes him feel safe. And you treat him as a *mate*? Some kind of *family friend*?'

Suttle said nothing. At this rate he'd start next week by looking for a new job.

'They go back a long way, Geoff. And if Jimmy wasn't still in touch I dare say we wouldn't be having this conversation.'

It was Parsons. She'd been listening from the adjoining kitchen. Now she stepped back into the room with a bowl of salad and a bottle of wine. She gave the wine to Willard and fetched some glasses from the sideboard.

Suttle wondered whether to volunteer his services with the corkscrew. He liked her use of Christian names and was grateful for Parsons' intervention. He'd known for months that hoisting Winter on board for Grace's christening hadn't been a great career move, but Lizzie had been keen, and in the end Suttle hoped no one would notice. Wrong.

'Do you feel compromised?' Willard had put the bottle to one side.

'No, sir.'

'Why on earth not?'

'Because I know where the line is.'

'What line?'

'Between the job and everything else in my life.'

'And you think that's the same for Winter?'

'Yes, sir. I do.'

'Why?'

'Because when the chips are down, like now, he treats me as a friend. And that, sir, might be an opportunity for us.'

Willard eyeballed Suttle a moment longer then granted him a tiny nod of approval. Nice answer. Clever. Neat. Almost plausible.

'Winter's a rat,' Willard said softly. 'We shouldn't be dealing with rats.'

'But Mackenzie's the same, sir. Only nastier.'

'And you think that justifies cosying up to Winter?'

'That's your word, sir. All we've done is have a conversation.'

'And you trust him?'

'Of course not.'

'But you think we should have him on board?'

'I think we should be putting Mackenzie away.'

'And you think Winter can do that?'

'I think he can make it possible, yes.'

Parsons was ferrying dishes in from the kitchen. With the pasta went a big dish of chilli con carne. While Suttle explained Winter's plan to bait the campaign-funding trap with the drug debt owed by Martin Skelley, Willard wrestled the cork from the bottle.

'That means we'll be talking months,' he said. 'Next spring, probably.'

'That's right, sir. But that's generally the way with u/c.'

Willard nodded. An effective undercover operation often took upwards of a year to prepare. In this case Winter would, if anything, be shortening the time frame, chiefly because he was already at the heart of Mackenzie's life. No need to insert someone new, give them a legend, let them groom the major parties, lulling them into a false sense of security before the trap was finally sprung. In Suttle's view Winter's offer was a major windfall, a great fat plum that had just dropped into their laps.

Parsons agreed. 'Jimmy's right, Geoff. There's no one else I can think of that Winter would trust. Maybe we owe him a vote of thanks.'

Willard ignored the invitation. He helped himself to a plate of food then looked up at Suttle.

'The man's a nightmare.'

'Who, sir?'

'Winter. Assuming we do something, assuming we think it might play to our advantage, we'll need to manage the bastard, tie him hand and foot, make him understand he's not a free agent any more. These things are tricky. We could get burned. Badly.'

'Of course, sir.'

'So who'd do it? Who'd take the responsibility? Who'd rein him in?'

There was a long silence, broken, in the end, by Parsons. She smiled across the table, loops of pasta hanging from her fork.

'That would have to be you, Jimmy, wouldn't it?'

Winter spent the day at Misty's place out at Hayling Island. He brought her two bottles of Chablis, a bunch of pink roses and news he assumed would put a big smile on her face.

'Bazza's not interested in selling up, Mist. Fuck knows why, but he seems to think you need this lot.'

They were sitting beside the pool. The sun was hot after a couple of early showers, and Misty was lying topless on her B&Q recliner. A couple of savage Bacardi and Cokes had settled her down after a late lunch, and droplets of sweat were beading in the coat of factor 20 that masked her face.

She reached out for his hand. Earlier she'd suggested he join her in the pool, but there was no way Winter could squeeze into Bazza's cast-off Hawaiian surf shorts. Now, nursing a Stella, he sat beside the patio table in the shadow of a big striped umbrella. He'd shed his jacket and from time to time he mopped his face with a corner of Misty's towel.

'I've been thinking ...' she said.

'About what?'

'Us.' She gave his hand a little squeeze, turning her head sideways to bring him into view. 'What if you came to live with me?'

'Here?'

'Yes, pet.'

'You mean ...' Winter frowned '... full time?'

'Yes. Does that sound so terrible? Someone to look after you? All those little needs of yours?'

She struggled onto one elbow and slipped her sunglasses to the end of her nose. For a woman in her late forties, she still had a wonderful body. Winter had given up pretending not to look at her breasts.

'I'd bore you shitless,' he said. 'Give it a month and you'd chuck me out.'

'Never. You're good for me. You make me laugh.'

'Yeah? And what else?'

Winter had known Misty Gallagher far too long to take anything at face value. However disarming the smile, she always had another agenda, and one of the reasons they'd been good together was the fact that she knew she could never bullshit him.

Misty admitted times were getting tough.

'How?'

'Money-wise.' She waved a manicured hand towards the house. 'Baz has always been good about paying the bills but lately he's started making excuses. It's getting tricky, pet. I'm not sure what a girl's supposed to do.'

'You think he wants you out? You think I'm wrong about that?'

'No. I think you're right. I think he's skint. If he could help me out I'm sure he would. To be honest, it's a bit of an embarrassment.'

She explained about a recent bathroom refurb. She'd got a

guy in to rip out the old bathroom suite and install a power shower and a new Jacuzzi. He'd done a brilliant job and she was really pleased, but she was looking at a bill for nearly 5K and hadn't got a clue how to pay it.

'Baz?'

'He says he can't. He knows the bloke well. Suggests I bung him a couple of freebies.'

'And?'

'You don't want to know.'

'Try me.'

'The guy's an animal. We did it once. Never again.'

'Charge him five grand.'

'That's exactly what I did.'

'And?'

'He just laughed.' She reached for her drink and pulled a face. 'He wants it regularly, preferably Wednesday evenings. That's the night his wife goes to Pilates. The problem with builders is they never know when to stop. Believe me, pet, there wouldn't be anything left by Thursday.'

Winter smiled. He didn't know whether to believe this little tale, but something told him it was probably true. Misty's appetite for sex had been the real come-on for Bazza. In the world of Pompey gossip nothing spoke louder than having Misty Gallagher as your regular shag.

'So I'd be the muscle, right? Keeping your creditors in line?'

'Absolutely. And you'd have squatter's rights.'

'But I've got those already, Mist.'

'Yeah, but more often.'

'You'd wear me out.'

'That's what I told the builder, but he never listened. An hour and a half? Do you think that's reasonable? No chatty little breaks? Nothing to drink? Not a word between us? It was weird, pet. God knows what he's like at home.'

'He's probably a puppy. Or maybe his missus has gone off it.'

63

'That's what I said. That was the other bit. He went totally mental. Told me I couldn't hold a candle to the way she did it. Just wasn't in the same league.'

'So why bother with you?'

'Thanks, pet.'

'That's not what I meant.'

'I know.' She shot him a smile. 'Next time I bollock you for not trying, just say "Builder." Five minutes? Tops? Then off to sleep? Bring it on, pet. Move in whenever you like.'

Winter laughed, knowing she was probably serious. Since Bazza had abandoned territorial rights Mist had definitely wanted something closer and more permanent, but Winter found this prospect a bit of a let-down after the scary excitement of nailing Bazza's mistress when his boss was busy elsewhere. He could rely on Misty for a lot of things, including the best sex he'd ever had, but he wasn't at all sure about cosy nights around the flame-effect gas fire.

'So why me? You could have any bloke you fancied.'

'Of course I could, but it's not the same, is it? You can't build a whole fucking life around some bloke who happens to take your eye.'

'Then stay single.'

'You're not supposed to say that, pet. You're supposed to find life impossible without me.'

'I do. Often.'

'Sure. That's when you want a shag. And that's when you lift the phone. So what else am I in your life, Paul?'

Winter stiffened. This was getting serious. She very rarely used his Christian name, and when she did it usually spelled trouble.

'Are we talking the L-word?' he enquired.

'Yeah. Lulu. That's me. A fucking lulu. Off my head. Putting up with all this.'

'All what?'

'This.' Her head jerked back towards the house. 'Trying to

64

keep it all together, trying to make things half-decent for us, trying to kid myself I'm not getting shagged witless by some half-arsed cheating bastard monkey I happen to owe money to.'

Shocked, Winter realised she was crying. Proud as ever, she'd tried to turn her current situation into some kind of joke, but it hadn't worked. Life was getting to her, big time. Especially now.

He abandoned his chair and squatted beside the recliner. Misty tried to push him off. She was angry as well as upset. She hated being seen like this. Crying was for a different kind of woman.

'Fuck off, Paul. You don't need me. Just go.'

'Who says?'

'You don't have to say. It's fucking obvious. I thought you were different once, but you're not, are you? You're just like the rest of them. You take what you want and come back when the mood suits you. At least Baz said he loved me.'

'When?' Winter was astonished.

'A couple of years ago.' She dabbed at her eyes with a Kleenex. 'He was pissed, if you want the truth, completely out of his head, but at least he said it.'

'And me?'

'What about you?'

'You think I don't love you?'

'I don't know. You never say.' She spared him a tiny enquiring glance. 'Well …?'

'Of course I do.'

'And is it such a tough fucking thing to say?'

'Yeah.' Winter nodded. 'It is.'

'Why?'

'Because …' Winter frowned, hunting for the explanation, wanting somehow to make things better for her.

She was looking at him. She'd taken her glasses off. She sniffed a couple of times.

'Is it me? Am I that evil?'

'No, Mist, you're not.'

'What is it then? Aren't we right together? Or am I so stupid I've missed the fucking obvious?'

'Like what?'

'Like this is some kind of game?'

'No, Mist, it's not a game.'

'Then what is it? Just tell me the truth for once. Go on, Paul. Do us both a favour. Be brave.'

Winter didn't know what to say. His knees were killing him. He shifted his weight, propping his back against the recliner. Across the harbour he could see the tiny dot that was the Bargemaster's House. He gazed at it for a long moment, thinking of Faraday. He too had messed up in relationship after relationship. Maybe it was a man thing. Or maybe it was something that came with the Job. The latter thought took him back to Jimmy Suttle. The coming months were going to be extremely challenging. One wrong move and he could end up like Westie. The last thing he needed was to fall out with Mist.

Winter closed his eyes. The sun was warm on his face. He let his head fall on Misty's shoulder, then reached for her hand.

'Well?' She was still waiting for an answer.

'You know it already, Mist.'

'Know what?'

'That I can't live without you.'

Chapter seven

D/I Hayder wrapped up Operation *Castor* in less than a week. Analysis of Faraday's recent correspondence, emails and phone calls yielded a handful of contacts which Hayder regarded as useful. Emails to a couple of birding magazines had cancelled both subscriptions. A letter to his solicitor had asked for a meeting which hadn't, in the end, taken place. A couple of days later, in a two-minute call to a local jobbing gardener, Faraday had apparently had second thoughts about a minor landscaping project. When Hayder traced the guy and paid him a visit, he said he hadn't been surprised. He'd helped Faraday out on a number of occasions but lately he seemed to have lost interest. He hadn't done any weeding for weeks. Neither had his plantings been watered. More telling still, evidence on Faraday's PC of repeated visits to his secure page on the HSBC website indicated a sudden interest in the state of his bank balance.

To Suttle, briefed by Hayder, this kind of activity formed a pattern. These were, he suggested to Parsons, the actions of a man tidying up his life prior to ending it. The tox results from the post-mortem were yet to come through, but the pathologist had already established respiratory failure as the proximate cause of death. Faraday, a couple of days before Suttle had found his body, had necked a great deal of red wine, swallowed two packs of codeine, drifted into unconsciousness and choked on his own vomit.

Parsons wanted to know about Gabrielle.

'Have you talked to her?'

'Yes, boss.'

'Where is she?'

'Gaza. She took the child back and seems to be living with the little girl's aunt. She was a bit reluctant to go into details, but I think she must be working with some NGO. Maybe Médicins Sans Frontières, I'm not sure.'

'And Faraday? You told her what happened?'

'Of course.'

'And?'

'She said she couldn't believe it. She was really upset. I couldn't get anything else out of her after that.'

'Do you think Faraday had been in touch? Recently?'

'She says not.'

'So when did they last talk?'

'Months ago. She said he used to phone a bit. In the end I think he just gave up.'

'Poor man.'

'Yeah ...' Suttle nodded. 'Too right.'

Parsons asked about the funeral. It was important, she said, that as many of Faraday's former colleagues as possible attend. She'd be sending round a reminder to that effect and knew that headquarters would dispatch a sizeable contingent. Given the sadness surrounding Faraday's departure, she said, the least we all owe him is a decent farewell.

Suttle nodded but in his heart he was already blaming himself and maybe a couple of others for not keeping in closer touch with his ex-boss. The more he put the intel picture together, the more obvious it became that Faraday had ended his days without any support whatsoever. This was probably his own choice because he'd never been one for socialising, but both Suttle and Lizzie agreed that company of the right kind might have made a difference. Depression, like a spring tide, could simply sweep you away. A shame, therefore, that no one had been around to drag him back to safety.

Parsons was obviously having similar thoughts.

'Was there *anyone* he was close to?'

'Not that I know of. As far as I can tell, he just turned his back and shut himself away.'

'Meaning none of us knew.'

'Meaning none of us bothered to find out.'

Parsons shook her head, disagreeing. You could only help people if they wanted to be helped. That was the way it worked. You lifted the phone or pinged off an email, and that way you could get people to your door. It was unreasonable, she said, to expect busy people to be psychic.

The word busy brought the flicker of a smile to Suttle's face. This was Parsons preparing herself an alibi. She'd probably sleep better at night if depressives like Joe Faraday had the good sense to behave like rational human beings.

Suttle gave her an update on arrangements for the funeral. Faraday's remains had been released by the Coroner. J-J had been down all week. He and Ulyana had spent their first night at the Bargemaster's House, but sleeping with the ghost of his dead father had spooked J-J badly and by the morning, according to Ulyana, he was a wreck. She'd phoned Suttle, asking about a cheap B & B, and it had been Lizzie who'd insisted they come and stay at their place. Suttle had been nervous about the arrangement at first, but J-J had bonded at once with Grace, who couldn't take her eyes off his hands, and by the end of the week they'd all become best mates. J-J had even asked Suttle to read a poem at his dad's funeral.

'Poem?'

'Don't ask me where it comes from, boss. I think it's something by Tennyson.'

'Does it have a name?'

'Yeah. Guess.'

Parsons gazed at him for a long moment, thinking back

to the night she'd taken Suttle's call and driven out to the Bargemaster's House.

'*The Eagle*?'

Suttle nodded. According to J-J, Faraday used to read the poem aloud to his infant son, doing all the moves, pretending he was the bird in the poem. Deaf and not yet able to lip-read or understand sign, J-J had been entranced by his dad's performance, especially the bit at the end.

'So what happens?'

'Can't say, boss. You'll have to wait and see.'

'But it's good? Fitting? You know ... *appropriate*?'

'Absolutely. I thought at first there was nothing of Joe in J-J, but I was wrong. Faraday could be off the planet sometimes. You had to look very hard to see it, but it was there. His boy's got that in spades. I've never met anyone like him. The guy's a total one-off.'

'And the girl? The Russian?'

'She's a bit of a fruitcake too. Nice, though. And she really cares about him.'

Parsons smiled, calling up her diary on her PC. 'So when's the funeral?'

'Thursday, boss. Half three at the crem, then Faraday's place afterwards.'

'J-J doesn't mind going back there?'

'Not in daylight. It's the dark that gets to him.'

Suttle said that Lizzie and Ulyana would be getting a few nibbles together and something to drink. Parsons was still looking at her computer screen.

'I've got a couple of meetings scheduled at Winchester that day. Both involve Mr Willard. I'm sure he'll cancel. What time did you say?'

'Half three, boss. We're talking the whole of the afternoon, really.'

'Of course.' She typed in the details, then looked up. 'I take it you'll sort out the guests? Get the invitations circulated?'

Suttle nodded. He'd already been in touch with Personnel and had a longish list of Faraday's ex-colleagues to contact. With luck, there might be more than a token scatter of mourners at the funeral.

Parsons wanted to know about Winter. Would he be coming, too?

'Of course. In a way they were close. Especially over the last year or so.'

'You mean mates?' Parsons couldn't believe it.

'Not really. But they'd been through some of the same old shit together, and I guess that matters after a while. Faraday knew Winter was a rogue, but he always got the job done. Occasionally they used to get a bit pissed and swap war stories. I was there a couple of times. It was nice to see.'

'And this happened often?'

'Not often enough, boss, if you want the truth. Especially towards the end.'

Parsons nodded, not wanting to take the conversation any further. Instead, she scribbled herself a note and asked whether the Bargemaster's House might be available after the guests had gone.

'What for?'

'A meet. Mr Willard, myself, you ...' she offered Suttle a thin smile '... and Winter.'

It rained on the morning of Faraday's funeral. Suttle had taken the day off, and while Ulyana helped Lizzie get the food ready for the Bargemaster's House, he drove J-J to some of the places he knew Faraday had loved. Favourite of all was the tip of Spice Island, a spit of shingle that curled around the bottom of Old Portsmouth. Here, beside a pub called the Still and West, was a waterside area that had recently been tarted up to help put Flagship Pompey on the map. Faraday hadn't much liked what the planners had done, but nothing could spoil the real magic of the place.

Faraday had come here often, especially when an investigation was threatening to hit the rocks. Most of the time he'd be alone, nursing a pint beside the railings, staring out at the incessant comings and goings in the harbour, but sometimes he'd take Suttle along, quizzing him about this or that aspect of a case, wanting to know how much weight the intel could bear, wondering whether they were heading in the right direction, abruptly breaking off to direct Suttle's attention to a lone cormorant, inches above the racing tide, heading out towards the Solent and the open sea.

It was that quiet, dogged, relentless professionalism, spiked by moments of childlike excitement, that hung in Suttle's memory. He wanted somehow to get just a little of this magic across to J-J, but in the absence of Ulyana, for all J-J's lip-reading skills, he knew it was beyond him. Instead, they stood in the drizzle, doing what Faraday used to do, just gazing out across the water until it occurred to Suttle that there was no need for explanations. J-J, wholly his father's child, understood instinctively. Moments later, as if to prove the point, he took Suttle's elbow and steered him into the pub. He had a wet ten-pound note in his hand and brooked no argument. Drinks were on him.

By early afternoon the rain had cleared. Rags of cloud scudded in from the west, and the sunshine glittered in the puddles of standing water during the long drive out of the city. At J-J's insistence, Lizzie and Suttle rode in the limousine behind the hearse. Lizzie had parked Grace with her mum, who lived at the top end of the city. The cortège took the motorway north across the harbour, and J-J sat bolt upright, his eyes never leaving his father's coffin. His face was a mask. Suttle had borrowed a suit for him from a mate. It was far too big across the shoulders and made him look like a refugee. In some respects, Suttle thought, the effect was fitting. Like his dad, J-J was one of life's windfalls.

The crematorium was at Portchester, on the mainland. The

previous funeral had just finished, and a thin straggle of mourn-ers was filing away towards the Garden of Remembrance to inspect the flowers. Faraday's cortège turned into the drive. Outside the Chapel of Rest there were faces Suttle recognised, chiefly the hardened smokers, lingering in the sunshine before going in. At the sight of the approaching hearse, they ducked into the entrance and disappeared. Suttle had toyed with trying to arrange some kind of modest guard of honour for Faraday's last journey, but Ulyana had told him that J-J was against the idea. He didn't want any fuss, she said. He just wanted to say goodbye.

The hearse came to a halt. Suttle and Lizzie joined J-J and Ulyana as the undertakers hoisted the coffin onto their shoulders and began the slow carry into the chapel. To Suttle's quiet satisfaction, there was a good turnout. The chapel wasn't big, and the pews on either side of the aisle were packed. He reached for Lizzie's hand, nodded at a face or two, suddenly overcome by what this moment really meant. Faraday was no longer among them. The man he'd trusted, admired, respected, liked, had gone.

Spaces had been saved for them at the front. Suttle stood aside, letting Lizzie squeeze into the pew, then took his place beside her. Mercifully, no one could see his face. He swallowed hard and reached for the Order of Service he'd had printed. On the front was a photo of Faraday and a much younger J-J, lifted from J-J's laptop.

Father and son were squatting together on the stony strip of foreshore in front of the Bargemaster's House, Faraday's arm around the child's skinny shoulders. J-J, barely seven, im-mensely proud of himself, was holding a tiny green crab by one leg, showing it to the camera, while his dad's attention appeared to have been caught by something else. For Suttle, it had been impossible not to wonder what that something was, but he now realised why J-J had treasured the shot.

Only last night, through Ulyana, he'd told Suttle that there were two things he'd always remember about his dad. One was his bigness and his smell, both of them an enormous source of comfort, and the other was his curiosity. Dad, he said, was always on the lookout, always interested, always nosy. And for that alone he'd loved him.

A Schubert impromptu came to an end and the moment of silence was broken by the vicar. The music for the funeral had been Ulyana's choice. She remembered Faraday telling her about solo piano pieces that had touched him at a concert he and Gabrielle had once attended, and she'd selected two impromptus plus an extract from a Beethoven sonata, telling J-J that his dad would have loved them. Reflective, beautifully paced, intensely moving, the music was perfect.

The vicar extended a welcome to the congregation. Suttle, half-listening, let his mind drift away. He'd noticed Winter at the back of the chapel and wondered whether he shared this sudden gust of overwhelming loss. Then, his opening remarks complete, the vicar invited Detective Chief Superintendent Willard to come forward and make his tribute.

Willard was in full-dress uniform. Dwarfing the vicar, he spoke without notes. Faraday's death, he said, had come as an immense shock. Not because he was so young. Not even because those that knew him might have sensed that all was not well. But because an event like this, so sudden, so final, was a terrible reminder of how easily the best qualities in a man could be lost.

Faraday, he said, was one of the finest detectives he'd ever had the privilege of serving alongside. He was utterly honest, immensely hard-working and never let anything stand between himself and the best possible outcome. He never hogged the limelight. He kept himself away from the usual swirl of canteen gossip. But best of all he could read other people like a book. In the service of justice, said Willard, this was a huge gift. But as a human being it made Faraday someone pretty rare. The man listened. The man understood. The man reached out. And

– in all three respects – he was a lesson for us all.

Suttle felt an audible ripple of agreement behind him. This was powerful stuff. He'd no idea Willard had it in him. But Willard hadn't finished. Turning to J-J, on behalf of his father's ex-colleagues, he offered their most profound sympathies. In his view, it was a mark of Faraday's uniqueness that J-J had lost more than a father. Because, when it had mattered most, Faraday had been his nipper's sole contact with the world. He'd brought him up single-handed. He'd built a bridge to the strange, mute happenings around him. He'd been there until the time had come for J-J to flee the nest. And only then had he let himself get on with a life of his own. That had demanded a degree of love, and commitment, and selflessness all too rare in today's world. And for that, Joe Faraday, we salute you.

He turned to the coffin, bowed his head and then returned to his seat. Suttle could hear someone sobbing a couple of rows back. Lizzie's hand was knotted in his. For the second time in ten minutes he was close to losing control himself. Beautiful, he thought. Spot on.

A couple of prayers followed. Then it was Suttle's turn to squeeze out of the pew and join J-J beside the coffin. Last night the pair of them had rehearsed for this moment. A bottle of Côtes-du-Rhône had helped. Now Suttle produced the carefully folded text from his jacket pocket, nodded to J-J, and began to read.

'*The Eagle* …' he announced uncertainly '… by Alfred Lord Tennyson.'

He made the mistake of glancing up. A sea of white faces, blurring again at the edges. He fought to regain control of himself, aware of J-J beside him, his bony hands outstretched, already miming the opening line. Suttle bent to the text again and began to read:

'*He clasps the crag with crooked hands*
Close to the sun in lonely lands

75

Ringed with the azure world, he stands.
The wrinkled sea beneath him crawls,
He watches from his mountain walls,
And like a thunderbolt he falls.'

Suttle looked up. J-J's performance had got wildly out of sync and he was already sprawled at Suttle's feet, the fallen thunderbolt, but it didn't seem to matter. The soft applause came from Ulyana. The vicar picked up the cue, joining in. Then everyone else did the same, uncertainly at first, then louder and louder before Suttle helped J-J to his feet and silence returned.

Back in his pew Suttle closed his eyes. Lizzie reached up and kissed him. There were more prayers, a reading or two, and then an address from the vicar about the welcome awaiting Faraday on the other side of the grave. Over the last week Suttle hadn't managed to find anyone who had a clue whether Faraday was a believer or not. It was yet another side of the man that would remain a mystery. Yet just here, in this small moment of time, Suttle sensed that there'd be some one, some thing, some presence that would take care of Faraday. Not because he'd been to Sunday school or collected for Oxfam or found some other way to stack his credits up. But because he'd been a good man. The vicar appeared to agree.

'Like all of us, Joe Faraday is a child of God. May the Lord be with him.'

The service came to an end minutes later. The curtains closed on the coffin and Suttle found himself listening to another Schubert impromptu, sunnier this time. J-J was standing at the end of the pew closest to the aisle. His task now was to lead the mourners out of the chapel but he couldn't take his eyes off the curtains. Suttle was trying to get inside his head, trying to imagine what this must feel like. Did he view this as some grotesque conjuring trick? Would he expect to meet his dad again in the Garden of Remembrance? Or had he managed to make some kind of peace with Faraday's going?

Suttle didn't know, and seconds later it didn't matter because Ulyana had taken him firmly by the elbow and was steering him down the aisle towards the door. Out in the sunshine people knotted together, seemingly lost for words. Several of the women gave each other hugs. Then a D/I, Cathy Lamb, appeared from nowhere and took Suttle to one side. As a D/S years ago, she'd been a favourite of Faraday's. Suttle had served under her himself as a rookie detective on division and understood why. She was solid and warm-hearted, and had turned out to be a brilliant skipper.

Looking at her now, Suttle realised she'd been crying. Her eyes were puffy and her mascara had streaked. He fumbled for a handkerchief and then mumbled something about not having brought one.

She waved his apology away. 'That poem was unbelievable,' she said. 'Joe would have been really proud of you.'

Chapter eight

Most of the mourners made it to the Bargemaster's House. J-J had insisted on picking up Grace from Lizzie's mum's place and he circulated among the guests with the child in his arms, jiggling her up and down and giving her a nuzzle from time to time. Watching him from across the room, Suttle realised how helpful this was. Grace was an icebreaker. People were a bit wary of J-J. You never knew quite what to say to someone who was profoundly deaf, and his performance in the chapel – Suttle now realised – hadn't been to everyone's taste. There had been something frankly odd about it, something way over the top, and people could be nervous around stuff like that.

Grace, though, made it easy for him. Whenever he stopped, especially with the women, everyone communicated through the baby. How sweet she was, how cute, how well behaved. Happy in J-J's arms, Grace played her role to perfection. Even Willard seemed smitten.

The turn-out for Faraday had been impressive. Many of these faces Suttle knew from his recent service on the Major Crime Team. Dawn Ellis and Bev Yates were there, two D/Cs who'd served alongside Faraday for years. Meg Stanley, a Crime Scene Coordinator who'd worked with Faraday on his last case, had rallied half a dozen officers from various corners of the Scenes of Crime empire, and there was an enormous floral bouquet with a message from Jerry Proctor, an older

CSC who was currently on attachment in Afghanistan. Proctor had always been a big fan of Faraday, as was Dave Michaels, a vastly experienced D/S who now helped run the force surveillance teams. Michaels had put up with a series of twat bosses in his time but had always regarded Faraday as something a bit special.

'Broke the mould, didn't he? All that birdwatching? I couldn't believe the man when I first met him. To be frank, mate, I thought he was away with the fairies, but I was wrong, wasn't I? The guy was tougher than he looked.'

'Really?'

'Yeah.' Michaels helped himself to half a Scotch egg. 'Until last week.'

Suttle moved on. One of Faraday's bosses from the early days, a uniformed Chief Superintendent called Neville Bevan, had driven up from his retirement cottage in west Dorset. He was a stocky Welshman with thinning hair and a huge belly. Suttle could imagine exactly the kind of guvnor he'd been – plain spoken, no nonsense – but his affection for Faraday seemed genuine. Much the same was true for others in the room, men and women who'd accompanied Faraday through investigation after investigation. Each of them seemed to have their own take on Faraday, a special story they wanted to share, and Suttle was beginning to flag when he was drawn aside by a softly spoken guy in his early fifties. Unlike most of the guests, he was drinking tea. He had a runner's build – slight, lean – and there was something in his eyes that spoke of laughter.

'Nigel Phillimore.' He gave Suttle's hand a tiny squeeze. 'I'm sorry about your friend.'

Something in the simplicity of the gesture caught Suttle's attention. The name Phillimore meant nothing. He thought he might have been a cop, another colleague from Faraday's early service, but Suttle was wrong.

'I'm a priest,' Phillimore said, 'for my sins.'

They talked for a couple of minutes. Nearly a decade had

gone by since Phillimore had met Faraday. He'd been working with the diocesan staff in the Anglican cathedral and had become involved in the death of a young girl who'd fallen from a tower block on the edges of Somerstown. Faraday had been in charge of the subsequent investigation and was, in Phillimore's opinion, a revelation.

Suttle had heard about this case. Faraday had mentioned it a couple of times.

'The girl from Old Portsmouth?'

'That's her. Helen Bassam.'

'And she had a crush on some older guy? Am I right?'

'You are.' He smiled. 'That was me.'

'Jesus.' Suttle blinked, then realised what he'd said and apologised.

Phillimore said it didn't matter. The important thing was Faraday. His experience of policemen was mercifully limited, but he'd been amazed by the man's sheer humanity.

'People in my line of work know a thing or two about awkward situations,' he said. 'In some respects this was a real challenge, but he handled it magnificently. In fact I like to think that we became friends as a result.'

Suttle said that all this was way before his time but agreed that Faraday had always had a talent for drawing the heat out of tricky situations.

'How do you mean?'

'He always looked beyond the immediate facts. That's rarer than you might think.'

'I see.' Phillimore nodded. 'That explains a lot.'

'In what sense?' It was Suttle's turn to be intrigued.

'In the sense that he probably put more of himself into his job than might have been wise.'

'You felt that? At the time?'

'Definitely. I imagine you must often be dealing with a great deal of grief. It's the same with us. It's not always obvious to people why things happen the way they do, why everything can sometimes feel so unfair. But that's the way it is. If you look for any kind of justice, any kind of *rightness* in life, you'll end up a disappointed man.'

'And Faraday?'

'He took that risk. Definitely. I felt it at the time, and nothing I've heard today tells me I'm wrong.' He paused. 'You worked with him a lot?'

'Yes.'

'I imagine this must be very painful for you.'

'It is. I didn't think it would be but it is.'

'Then I'm sorry.'

'Don't be. I hate to say it, but in our job it sometimes pays to have a very thick skin.'

'You mean you ought to be less sensitive?'

'Exactly.'

'But then you wouldn't be such a good detective. Am I wrong?'

Suttle looked away and smiled at the thought. Faraday's instincts had always been to get close and stay there. As far as the Job was concerned, it was definitely a high-risk strategy. Coupled with the disappointments of his private life, it had probably killed him. None of the women in Faraday's life had attended the funeral. Not even Gill.

The door across the room opened to admit the last of the guests. Heads turned. It was Winter. He stepped across to Lizzie, gave her a kiss and looked round. The buzz of conversation had stopped and there was a moment of near-silence before Winter became aware of the uniformed bulk of Willard, standing alone beside the window. The two men eyed each other, then Winter walked across and extended a hand.

'You did him proud, sir,' he said. 'Fantastic.'

Willard, for once, was caught off guard. He looked down at Winter, at the proffered handshake, then turned away.

*

An hour or so later the mourners had gone. J-J, Ulyana and Lizzie gathered up the remains of the eats and carried them out to Lizzie's battered Clio. Willard had yet to exchange a word with Winter. Parsons sat between them in Faraday's living room, flicking through a pile of birding magazines.

Suttle returned from seeing Lizzie off. If this was to be a serious attempt to get Winter onside, he thought, then they had some way to go.

Parsons had appointed herself chairman. Mr Willard, she announced, had to be back in Winchester by half past six. Best, therefore, to establish exactly what was on offer.

Offer was a word Winter didn't much like. He said he wasn't here to sell anything. He was simply pointing out that his days with Mackenzie were numbered and there might be some mutual advantage in the way he chose to end the relationship.

Willard wanted to know whether he was definitely getting out. Winter said yes.

'Why?'

'Because the man's off his head.'

'You must have known that for years.'

'I have. In a way. But it's getting worse.'

He reached inside his jacket and extracted a white envelope. Inside was a press cutting. He passed it across to Willard.

'That's from today's *News*. I don't make these things up.'

Willard studied the cutting without comment, then passed it to Suttle. Mackenzie had evidently held some kind of news conference. In the accompanying photograph he was sitting next to a younger man – sleek, tanned, linen jacket, designer jeans. This, it seemed, was Leo Kinder, his political consultant. Together they'd announced the launch of *Pompey First*, a bid, in Kinder's words, to return the constituency of Portsmouth North to the people who really mattered: the voters. Beside the story was the *Pompey First* logo. Suttle recognised the Spinnaker Tower. Mackenzie's choice of background colours

– bilious reds and yellows – reminded him of a particularly violent crime scene.

Parsons was looking nervous. Willard's silence didn't bode well.

'And that's why you want out?' she said. 'Because Mackenzie's standing for Parliament?'

'Yes.'

'But what difference does it make?'

'All the difference in the world. I joined him to run a business. To be honest, there's fuck all left.'

'And he knows that?' Willard this time.

'Of course he does. The guy's brilliant with figures, always has been, but he's crap at handling bad news. Show him a balance sheet, tell him how much money we're losing, and he doesn't want to know. He's got a new toy now.' Winter nodded at the press cutting. 'Everything else is history.'

'So where does it all end?' At last there was a flicker of interest in Willard's eyes.

'We're heading for a car crash, big time. He'll go bust. He'll lose the lot, the hotel, everything. It's all secured on debt.' Winter drew a finger across his throat. 'Endgame. Finito.'

Willard wanted to know more. It was his understanding that Mackenzie had built his business empire on the millions he'd stashed from wholesaleing cocaine.

'That's true. That's exactly the way it worked in the early days. He'd launder the money through buying café-bars or tanning salons or whatever he could get his hands on, but it never stopped there. Once he started investing abroad he needed money upfront, so the guy ends up with a trillion mortgages on the UK stuff plus a bunch of foreign investments that have gone down the khazi. Even the hotel belongs to the fucking bank.'

Suttle thought he detected the ghost of a smile on Willard's face. The Royal Trafalgar Hotel was Mackenzie's trophy buy. Situated on the seafront, it had recently won a fourth AA rosette.

'So you're telling me he's skint?'

'That's exactly what I'm telling you. I've been telling him too, but he never fucking listens.'

'So why doesn't he go back to what he knows best?'

'Toot, you mean?'

'Exactly.'

'Because he thinks he's put it all behind him. Because he likes to kid himself he's a cut above all that lowlife shit. Bazza never goes backwards. Not unless he has to.'

'But you're telling me that's exactly where he is. You're telling me he has no choice.'

'Yeah. But like I say, the man just tunes out.'

Willard seemed to accept the logic of Winter's case. What still wasn't clear was exactly why he wanted out.

'Because it's going to get ugly.'

'Ugly how?'

For the first time Winter faltered, and for a moment Suttle wondered whether he was going to mention the European Arrest Warrant. He still hadn't got to the bottom of why Winter was so worried but knew Willard would move heaven and earth to find out. But Winter, it turned out, had something else on his mind.

'You want the truth?' he said.

'The truth?' Willard was laughing now. 'Is that some kind of joke?'

'I'm serious.'

'Go on.'

'Mackenzie is a talented man. He's got a brain in his head. Plus he's done some decent things for this town.'

'Like the 6.57? Like flogging seventeen million quid's worth of Class A narcotics?'

'Like the Tide Turn Trust. Like getting alongside kids. Like giving Southsea a bit of a makeover.'

'And that makes it OK, does it? In your book?'

'It helps.'

'I bet it does.'

'But you're right. It's not enough.'

'Why not?'

'Because he goes over the top. Because he doesn't know where to stop. And because sometimes he hurts people.'

'Ah ...' Willard had folded his arms. 'And you're telling me that comes as some kind of surprise?'

'In some cases, yes.'

'Tell me more.'

'No.' Winter shook his head. 'You asked me a question and I've given you an answer. There are some days the man disgusts me. And there are others when I disgust myself. That has to stop. And if you want the truth, that's why I'm here.'

'Some kind of redemption then? Is that what we're talking about?'

Winter held his gaze. It wasn't clear from Willard's tone of voice whether he was taking the piss, but that's what it sounded like.

Parsons tried to move the conversation on. As far as she understood, there was a very easy way of encouraging Mackenzie back into narcotics.

Willard wanted to know more.

'There's a Level 3 called Martin Skelley, sir. I think I've mentioned him before.' Level 3 was CID-speak for a top criminal.

'You have. This is the guy that ended up with Mackenzie's little nest egg. Am I right?'

'Allegedly, sir, that's the case, yes.'

'And you think we can put them together?'

'I think Winter can, sir.'

Willard turned back to Winter.

'Is that true?'

'Yes.'

'Why should I believe you?'

'Because Mackenzie will have no choice.' He reached for the press cutting. 'He needs to fund this lot and Skelley is his only option. I can dress it up to begin with. I can go and poke around various places abroad. I can try and magic up the money he needs from other sources. But in the end it's not going to work. And that's when we try to nail Skelley.'

'We?'

'Me. And my dickhead boss.'

Willard was considering the proposal, weighing the pros and cons. You didn't need much imagination to realise the possibilities. A Level 3 like Skelley wouldn't put up with any shit, least of all from an upstart Pompey mush like Bazza Mackenzie. On the other hand, an operation like this carried considerable risks.

'You'd be happy to become our informant? You don't mind grassing Mackenzie up?'

'It's something I have to do.'

'But you understand we'd have to manage you? Draw up an agreement with the CPS? Treat you as a tasked witness? Put a handler in? Make sure you play by the rules? Make sure you don't do anything silly that fucks the whole thing up?'

The CPS was the Crown Prosecution Service, the government lawyers who would – fingers crossed – be getting a result in court.

'Yeah, I understand that.' Winter didn't seem the least bit surprised by Willard's finger-wagging. 'Two conditions, though. One, I want a deal for afterwards.'

'I'm sure you do. And the other?'

'The handler.' Winter was looking at Parsons. 'Last time we tried something like this, you lot nearly got me killed.'

It was true. Years back, Parsons and Willard had cooked up something similar, dismissing Winter from the force in the knowledge that Mackenzie would probably pick him up. On that occasion his handler had let him down badly, and in the end Winter had decided to stay with Mackenzie for real. Now, though, that decision wasn't looking so clever.

Willard said that the choice of handler would be his and his alone.

'Fine.' Winter got to his feet and reached for his jacket. Willard stared up at him.

'Where are you going?'

'Home.' He glanced at his watch, then nodded at Suttle. 'I'm happy to work with Jimmy. No offence, sir, but anyone else and I'm afraid I'm out.'

It was nearly seven by the time Suttle made it back home. Faced with Winter's ultimatum, Willard had been unyielding. Once Winter had gone, he told Suttle to stay in touch. In his view there were pressing reasons why Winter had made the approach in the first place. Sooner or later the devious little scrote would be back because he probably had no other option. When Suttle enquired who else he had in mind as a handler, Willard said it was irrelevant. In any negotiation you had to be sure who was bossing the thing. Letting Winter have his way from the start was a short cut to disaster. There had to be rules. There had to be a protocol. And Winter had to understand who was in charge.

Shortly afterwards, with Parsons in tow, Willard left. Suttle circled the house a couple of times, tidying up, wondering whether he'd ever set foot in the place again, then locked up and made his way out to his car. There was rain in the air again, and he paused at the kerbside, glancing back towards the Bargemaster's House. J-J was already making arrangements to put it on the market. In a month or two, thought Suttle, there'd be no trace left of Faraday.

Arriving home, Suttle recognised the red Mazda sports car parked behind Lizzie's Clio and his heart fell. Gill.

She was sitting on a stool in the kitchen, nursing a glass of what looked like vodka and Coke. She was dressed in black, a formal suit with a single red rose pinned to one lapel. Her face was puffy, and Suttle knew at once she'd been crying. J-J was at the stove, preparing something with garlic and tomatoes, and every now and then Gill sneaked a look at him, as if she couldn't quite believe what she was seeing.

'Lizzie's upstairs,' she said. 'With the baby.'

Suttle nodded. He'd heard Grace crying the moment he'd opened the front door. He knew he ought to play the host with Gill but couldn't think of anything to say. She watched him heading for the door, then called him back.

'I'm sorry I didn't make it,' she said.

'Make it where?'

'To the funeral.'

'That's OK.'

'No, but really …'

'Really what?'

'You know … I really wanted to be there … I really *should* have been there.'

'Why?'

'*Why?* Because I like to think we meant something to each other. Is that such a bad thing?'

'Not at all. If you felt like that then you're right. You should have come.'

Suttle had stepped back into the kitchen, manoeuvring himself so that J-J could lip-read the conversation.

'I got as far as the crem,' she said, 'but I just couldn't face it.'

'Shame.'

'You think that's cowardly?'

'I dunno.'

'No, be honest. Just tell me. Was I right not to come?'

'I've no idea, my love. I'm assuming he mattered to you or you wouldn't have made the effort.'

'Of course he mattered to me. Shit. How can you *say* that?'

Suttle shrugged. Spread his hands wide. No idea. Gill studied him a moment longer, then reached for the bottle beside the modest pile of recipe books. Suttle had been right. Stolly.

He watched her pour herself a generous slurp, wondering

where this conversation was heading. She left the top off the bottle and didn't bother with more Coke.

'I drove back down to Lee, if you must know. We used to walk there. By the sea. A lot. It felt right. Righter than the crem.'

Lee-on-the-Solent was a beachside township with views across the water to the Isle of Wight. Apartments on the seafront were much favoured by wealthy retired couples who spent their days watching the big ships outward bound from Southampton. The sunsets were said to be fantastic, but Faraday had always hated the place.

'You live that way?'

'Yeah. I have done for years. Joe used to stay over. We could have made it work. I know we could.'

'Really?'

'Yes.' She was frowning now. 'You know something? You're just like him. You don't trust people. You don't believe them. I can hear it in your voice. It must be something to do with the Job.'

'Joe was out of the Job.'

'I know. I know. And he hated it. Absolutely hated it. Didn't have the first clue what to do with himself ...' She sniffed, gazing at the glass. 'My poor lamb.'

'You miss him.' It was a statement, not a question.

'Of course I miss him. We were so good together, so fucking good. I knew it from the moment I met him. From that very first time. It was here. That party for Gracie. I expect you remember.'

'I do.'

'But he's shy, isn't he? Like a child? Maybe I should be gentler. Maybe I frighten him. Next time, eh?'

She raised her glass in a toast, swaying gently on the stool, and Suttle began to wonder how many she'd had. Her use of the present tense was baffling. Suttle had always believed that journalists made most of their stuff up, but this was seriously deranged.

She wanted to get more off her chest. How they'd been hatching plans to go away together. How she'd been badgering him to sell the Bargemaster's House and move across to Lee. The sleepless nights she'd passed since the news broke about his death. So many memories, she said. And the promise of a life together once they'd had a proper chance to sort everything out.

After a while Suttle made his excuses and went upstairs. Lizzie was in the room she called the nursery, reading Grace a story. Suttle stooped low, giving them both a kiss, and volunteered to take over.

'Is she still down there?'

'Yeah.'

'Pissed?'

'Yeah.'

'I'll phone for a taxi. Put you out of your misery.'

Lizzie clattered downstairs and Suttle settled himself beside the bed. He was a couple of pages from the end of the story when he heard the *parp-parp* of the waiting cab in the street, followed by an emotional farewell on the doorstep.

Back downstairs, minutes later, he found Ulyana giving J-J a hand at the stove. Of Lizzie there was no sign.

Ulyana had a question from J-J. How long had his dad been seeing the woman with the red lipstick?

Suttle held up five fingers.

'Weeks?' Ulyana translated J-J's next question.

'Days. Your dad couldn't stand her. Big mistake.'

'You're sure?'

'Totally.'

'Absolutely certain?'

'Believe me.'

J-J nodded, gave the frying pan a poke, then signed something to Ulyana.

Suttle wanted to know what he was saying.

'You want it for real? Word for word?'

'Please.'

'He said thank fuck for that.' She shot J-J a glance. 'I think he was getting worried.'

Chapter nine

A month later, while he was still shaving, Winter took a call. It was Carol Legge, a spirited social worker who worked on the city's Child Protection Team. Over the years Winter had leaned on her for a number of favours. and she'd always obliged him with a stern sense of motherly indulgence. More lately he'd asked for a very big favour indeed, and – after a couple of days' thought – she said she'd do her best. After a week she had come up with a name and an address. Winter got the form from the Post Office and used the photo booth in the corner to acquire four head shots. The girl behind the counter had warned him not to smile for the camera because the agency didn't accept smiles any more. Winter held her gaze for a moment then told her it wouldn't be a problem. Smiling was the last thing he felt like doing.

Now Winter asked Carol how she was getting on.

'It's ready, pet,' she said. 'And he'd like the money in notes.'

Karl Sparrow lived in a carefully converted council house on a neat estate at the top of the island. Winter had never met him, but Carol Legge had explained everything he needed to know. Karl's nickname, she'd said, was Birdy. Half a lifetime ago he'd taken a cheapo summer break at a holiday camp in north Devon. The second night, out of their heads on cider and various other substances, he and his mates had decided on a midnight swim. Birdy dived into the wrong end of the pool, hit the bottom and surfaced with a strange numbness below his neck. His mates managed to get him out, and Birdy was still putting the numbness down to Strongbow when the paramedics arrived. Only a day and a half later, in the neurological unit at the Royal Devon and Exeter Hospital, did a consultant confirm that he'd broken his neck. Barring miracles, Birdy would be paralysed for the rest of his life.

Winter rang the doorbell, wondering how you'd cope with an injury like that. After a while he heard footsteps, and the door opened to reveal a youngish black woman in a white smock. The nose stud was a fetching shade of lime green and she was peeling off a pair of surgical gloves.

'You the guy Carol sent round?' Pompey accent.

'Yeah.'

'He'll be with you as soon as I've finished, OK? Kitchen's at the back. Help yourself.'

Winter went through to the kitchen and made himself a mug of tea. A glass door offered access to a tiny paved area at the rear of the property. At this time of day it was in shadow but later, Winter thought, it would turn into a bit of a sun trap. He was eyeing the row of tomato plants beside the fence when the girl returned.

'He's ready now.' She nodded back towards the hall. 'First on the left.'

Winter could smell the disinfectant on her clothes. He stepped out of the kitchen and followed her directions. Karl Sparrow was lying in bed, propped up on a mountain of pillows. He was a big man, Winter's age, with a shaved head and tattoos on both arms. The room, tiled, was bare except for a big motorised wheelchair, a mobile hoist parked tidily at the entrance to the adjacent bathroom and an ancient TV perched on a chest of drawers at the foot of the bed. The disinfectant smell was stronger, laced with something more earthy.

Sparrow's hand lay on the whiteness of the sheet.

Winter gave it a pat. 'All right, Karl?'

Sparrow studied him a moment. 'No,' he said, 'since you're asking.'

'What's up then?'

'Pressure sore.' He nodded at the spotless duvet. 'Takes months to clear up. Mona's a fucking saint. In her shoes I'd put me down.'

Winter gazed at him, wondering how far to take the conversation. Mercifully he had very little experience of conditions like this. All he really knew about Birdy was Carol Legge's undying admiration for what she called his pluck. As the medics had warned all those years ago, the guy was paralysed from the neck down, no feeling, no control, nothing. He survived, she said, on a rota of call-in nurses who changed his nappies, sorted out his catheter and urine bottle, and fed him a diet of chicken soup, wholegrain bread and salad from the garden, plus liberal helpings of local gossip. This, it seemed, was all Birdy needed. The rest of his life happened in his head.

'You got the money?'

'Yeah. You want to count it?'

'Very funny. Do it on the bed, yeah?'

Winter had the notes in a Jiffy bag in his jacket pocket. He made a space for himself on the duvet and began to lay them out. Carol Legge had told him £3,000 in twenties, and Winter was surprised how long it took to count.

'OK?' he said at last.

'That far pile. Count it again.'

Winter did so. Five hundred quid. On the button.

'Where do you want it?'

'Top drawer. Under the telly.'

'It'll be safe in there?'

'Sure. I've got decent neighbours. Bloke next door'll do anything for me. Sorts me out money-wise. Keeps an eye on things.'

'And he knows about this?'

'You're joking.'

'So how do you explain three grand?'

'Fuck knows. Rich relative? Insurance settlement? Either way he won't care, won't say a word. All he has to do is give matey a ring and tell him it's on.'

'What's on?'

'The new plasma.' He nodded at the far wall. 'Sky Sports? Twenty-four-hour news? A million channels? Bring it on, eh?'

It dawned on Winter that he might just have opened an important door in Birdy's life. From now on, whenever he fancied it, he could watch the outside world tearing itself to pieces. This knowledge was oddly comforting. He gathered up the notes and stuffed them back in the Jiffy bag. Carol Legge, as ever, had been punctilious about the small print of this deal, but Winter had to be sure.

'No previous, am I right?'

'Nothing.' He couldn't take his eyes off the Jiffy bag. 'Luck of the fucking devil.'

'And you've never been abroad?'

'Never. Always fancied it. Never got round to it.'

'And from here on in?'

'No fucking chance. An hour in the back garden is a major production, believe me.'

'OK.' Winter circled the bed. 'Top drawer?'

'Yeah. The brown envelope's for you, mate. Check out some of those DVDs while you're at it. Magic, eh?'

Winter opened the drawer. The plain brown envelope was addressed to Karl Sparrow, and Winter could feel the outline of the passport inside.

'What do you think?'

'Thanks. I'm grateful.'

'I meant the DVDs.'

'Ah.'

Winter quickly sorted through the DVDs. There were dozens of them, all classics, mostly black and white. *Casablanca. The African Queen. The Cruel Sea.* He'd seen *Gone with the Wind* three times himself. Clark Gable had always done it for his late wife.

'Brilliant, eh?' Birdy was watching him. 'Matey next door's gonna set the whole lot up for me – plasma, recorder, player, the lot. I tells Mona it's gonna be like travelling without all that airport hassle. She thinks I'm bonkers, that girl.'

Birdy cackled with laughter, then began to cough. Within seconds Mona was at the door. Birdy beckoned her into the room with a tiny backwards jerk of his head and whispered something Winter didn't catch. She nodded and fetched the hoist before glancing across at Winter.

'You want to help me here.' It was a statement, not a question.

The nurse folded down the duvet, releasing a gust of foul air. Birdy's bum was swaddled in a big disposable nappy, crusting brown at the edges, his pale skinny legs poking down towards the bottom of the bed. A reinforced plastic sheet lay beneath the nappy. The nurse disconnected Birdy's catheter, gathered up the ends of the plastic sheet, which folded around the bulk of his torso, and linked them to the lifting strap that dangled from the hoist. The hoist was operated by a remote control. The strap tightened and Birdy began to rise from the bed.

'Wheelchair?'

Winter did her bidding. He jockeyed the chair into position beside the bed and then stepped back. Birdy was still in mid-air, revolving slowly beneath the hoist, his arms and legs slack, his chin on his chest, his eyes closed. Inch by inch, the nurse released the tension on the strap, lowering the flaccid bundle of flesh and blood onto the wheelchair. He must have been through this a million times, Winter thought. Poor bastard.

'Feet?'

Winter knelt on the cold linoleum, stationing each of Birdy's feet on the wheelchair's metal supports. His flesh was icy, the nails yellow and brittle. Then Winter stood aside as the nurse

96

wheeled Birdy into the bathroom. When Winter enquired whether she needed any other help she shook her head.

'We're fine.' She said.

Grateful for the chance to leave, Winter gave Birdy a parting nod and left. Out in the street, heading back to his car, he slipped a thumb under the gummed flap of the envelope and took a look at the passport. The photo didn't really do justice to the sternness of the expression he'd tried to muster in the Post Office booth, but the rest seemed completely authentic. Beside the Lexus he paused, glancing back towards the house, knowing that the image of Birdy dangling from his hoist would be with him for a very long time. The guy was completely kippered, totally parcelled up, utterly at the mercy of whatever might happen around life's next corner. That's me, Winter thought, as he slipped the passport into his jacket pocket.

That same morning, an hour or so later, Suttle received an abrupt summons to Gail Parsons' office. At first he assumed she wanted a debrief on the morning's top story. Yet another young mother had been stranger-raped after a break-in, this time in front of her two-year-old son. This latest incident was the fourth in a series of similar city-wide attacks and there was every reason to assume that they were linked. Suttle had been building the intel file for several weeks now, uncomfortably aware that his own wife was the perfect target for the mystery rapist, and anticipated a detailed grilling from Parsons. Wrong.

She waved him into a seat in front of her desk and made sure the door was shut.

'This is about Mackenzie,' she said. 'And Winter.'

Suttle blinked. He hadn't thought about Winter for weeks, not – to be honest – since Faraday's funeral.

'So what's happened, boss?'

'This ...' She had a file open on the desk. She passed across a two-page report. Suttle scanned it quickly. Yesterday's date. And the signature of a uniformed Inspector who rarely let the manic drumbeat of events get in his face. On this occasion, though, it had evidently been very different.

Suttle looked harder. 'Safer Neighbourhoods Initiative' rang a bell.

'This is the community policing thingo?'

'Hearts and minds, Jimmy. It might not be to your taste, nor mine, but that's not the point. At ACPO level, believe it or not, these things matter.' She nodded at the report. 'As you can probably gather.'

Suttle hadn't seen the pencilled comments at the foot of the last page. The Chief's handwriting was unmistakable: flamboyant, beautifully formed, 90 per cent indecipherable. Suttle looked at the front page again, confirming that the Chief and his secretariat were on the circulation list, and then returned to the hieroglyphic at the end.

'So what does he say?'

'He says this is unacceptable. He says it has to stop. What he means is that this man is not to get anywhere near the democratic process.'

'Mackenzie?'

'Of course.'

'So who stops him?'

'Good question. I was rather thinking that Winter had an idea or two.'

Suttle read the report again, properly this time. The Safer Neighbourhoods Initiative, or SNI in the parlance, had organised a series of public meetings. The most recent had taken place a couple of evenings ago at a comprehensive school in the north of the city. For once, to the Inspector's delight, the SNI had managed a decent turnout. He hadn't done a headcount but he estimated more than two hundred punters in the school assembly hall. Audiences like this – concerned, civic-minded, determined to add their voices to the swirl of public debate – deserved to have their worst fears about policing and public order put to rest. With that in mind, the Inspector had assembled an impressive PowerPoint presentation, using a blizzard of stats to prove that North End, Copnor and all the other bits of Pompey at the top end of the island were as safe – if not safer – than anywhere else in the kingdom.

Bazza Mackenzie, though, had other ideas. He'd arrived early, in company with a couple of other guys, and commandeered prime seats in the front row. Thanks to the *News*, plus his own efforts, there was a growing buzz across the city that Mackenzie might be heading up some kind of challenge in the coming general election, but it hadn't dawned on the Inspector that his carefully organised meeting was about to be hijacked.

Suttle read through to the end of the report. This was the work of a very angry man, but it was hard not to smile at some of the choicer quotes.

'Mackenzie actually said all this stuff?'

'As I understand it, yes.'

'Have you talked to anyone else at the meeting?'

'Of course not. The man's a police officer. He's got ears. He's got a brain in his head. We don't need corroboration.' She nodded at the report. 'The moment the likes of Mackenzie stand up and start telling us how to do our job, we've got a problem.'

Suttle could only agree. Halfway through the PowerPoint, seconds after the Inspector had been underlining how much police time went into hi-vis patrols, and how the community could therefore sleep easy at night, Mackenzie had got to his feet and told him he was wrong. The reality, according to Bazza, was exactly the opposite. Pissed kids. Rowdy students. Dickheads pulling stunts on cross-country bikes. Mad drivers burning rubber on some of the wider side roads. Drunks pissing in next door's hedge. Incident after incident, each carefully logged by Pompey's tyro politician.

At this point other voices had been raised, all in support of Mackenzie, and in the end the Inspector had abandoned the PowerPoint in a bid to regain some kind of order. By now something told him that most of this chorus of dissent had been planted, probably by Mackenzie himself, but it made little difference. The evening, he wrote, had been a public relations disaster, made infinitely worse by the fact that this full-on drivel had come from a man whose business success had been entirely based on the profits from a decade or so flogging Class A drugs. 'I get the impression this might be the first of a series of similar stunts,' the Inspector warned, 'which I find personally troubling and professionally offensive. Maybe we should be putting Mackenzie where he belongs instead of giving him a platform like last night's.'

This was a sentiment with which any Chief Constable would doubtless concur. Hence Parsons' summons to Suttle.

'He's serious,' she warned. 'And I don't blame him.'

'So what do we do?'

'We find Winter.'

'And then what?'

'We get him onside. Take him at his word. *Enlist* him, Jimmy.'

'You think it's that desperate?'

'I know it is.' Her hand touched the phone. 'I had Mr Willard on before you came. I think he's realised the damage Mackenzie could do if he really does stand for Parliament. We're not just talking the city, Jimmy. This thing could go national. This is just the kind of idiot stunt the media love, and I bet he's planning others.'

'He won't get the thing off the ground. It won't fly. The bloke's a dickhead. He can't string two words together. The other candidates will hammer him.'

'That's not the point. It's the campaign that's going to do the damage, not the result. You know what? Sometimes I start to wonder about democracy. Maybe it's more trouble than it's worth.'

Suttle laughed. He assumed she was joking, but one glance at Parsons' face told him otherwise.

'You don't think that?' she asked. 'You don't think there's something wrong with a system that lets the likes of Mackenzie stand for Parliament? You don't think that's an insult?'

'No.'

'What is it then?'

'A failure.'

'Whose failure?'

'Ours.' Suttle tapped the report. 'This guy's right. We should have scooped Mackenzie up years ago.'

'But that's exactly it, Jimmy.' Parsons was angry now, leaning forward over the desk. 'We have to stop him. And if it's Winter who can make that happen, then so be it.'

Suttle sat back, taking his time. To the best of his recollection, he said, it was Willard who'd brought the courtship of Winter to a grinding halt.

'How?'

'By insisting on total control. By binding Winter hand and foot.'

'You think there's a better way?'

'I know there is. Because I know Winter. We burned him once before, you know we did, and people like Winter have a long memory. Like it or not, we have to be ready to let him have some kind of guarantee.'

'Like what?'

'Like me, for starters.'

'As Winter's handler?'

'Of course.'

Parsons said nothing. Then her eyes strayed to the phone.

'I happen to agree with you.' Her voice was low. 'The problem is Mr Willard. He doesn't like Winter, not at all, and there's no way he'll let the man boss any kind of negotiation.'

'With respect, boss, that's daft. We're not talking negotiation. Winter, believe it or not, is a bright man. He's also a realist. He knows there's no way he's going to be in charge of anything except his own survival. And that's why he wants to do this thing through me.'

'You're telling me he doesn't trust anyone else?'

'I'm telling you he did once and it didn't work out. So I guess the answer is yes.'

'OK ...' Parsons was frowning now. 'And if Mr Willard won't have it?'

'Then we have to find someone else to put in alongside Mackenzie.'

'You think that's possible? In the time we have left before the election?'

'No, boss –' Suttle returned the inspector's report '– I don't.'

Bazza Mackenzie had left a message on Winter's mobile to be at the Royal Trafalgar by eleven o'clock. Minutes later a reminder in text form had arrived. This kind of attention to detail was a novelty in Mackenzie's world. Winter, reading the text for a second time, could only assume that Kinder had taken over completely. That, or something truly important was about to kick off.

'His name's Makins,' Mackenzie grunted, 'Andy Makins. He's downstairs in reception, and a little bird tells me he's exactly what we're after.'

The three of them – Bazza, Kinder, Winter – were sitting in the basement office Mackenzie had taken to calling the War Room. A huge street map of the Portsmouth North constituency dominated one wall. The map was divided into electoral wards, and someone – presumably Kinder – had taken the trouble to record ward-by-ward voting patterns in the most recent local election.

On the adjoining wall was a display of *Pompey First* posters, while the area to the left of the door had been converted into an impromptu darts arena. Mackenzie himself had raided the Internet for photos of the likely candidates standing for Pompey North in the coming general election, and each of them had been allotted his or her space on the *Pompey First* dartboard. As a guide to Mackenzie's gut take on how best to triumph at the hustings it was crude but unsurprising. You chose your favourite arrows. You took careful aim. And then, one by one, you did your best to nail the bastards.

This strategy, as far as Winter understood it, had won little traction with Kinder, who favoured putting the New into New Politics by completely blanking the opposition. That way, he contended, they could hug the inside lane in the coming elections, demonstrating time and again that *Pompey First* had a uniquely special rapport with the locals. Kinder's word for this was traction. Neither Bazza nor Winter had a clue what he meant, but they both sensed that his tolerance of the darts arena was at least a nod in the right direction. *Pompey First* was grounded. *Pompey First* spoke a language people understood. *Pompey First* would do exactly what it said on the tin.

A long conference table occupied most of the rest of the office, a declaration of collective intent over the coming months, and on his few visits to the War Room Winter had noticed that Kinder always sat at the head of the table. That gave him chairman rights at every meeting he summoned, and – much to Winter's surprise – Mackenzie didn't appear to object. Kinder, he'd once told Winter, was a real pro. Given the kind of money he was paying him, the man could sit wherever he fucking liked.

Kinder wanted to know more about Makins. He, like Winter, had never heard of the guy. Where had he come from? What was he offering?

'He's a journo,' Mackenzie said, 'or at least he used to be. That feature piece in the paper last month? Gill Whatever-her-name-was?'

'Reynolds,' Kinder said.

'Yeah. Nice lady. Did us proud.'

'Did *you* proud, Baz. I'm not sure she grasped what we're really trying to achieve. Nice try. *Nul points.*'

'Whatever.' Mackenzie shrugged. 'All I know is she phoned

me last night, told me about this bloke Andy. The way I read it, he's exactly what we're after. The guy's young, savvy, spends most of his time on the Internet. Plus he's really in tune with the kids, knows what makes them tick, what turns them on, which is more than us lot fucking do. Gillie says he's got some ideas we might use. She also says he's a fucking genius. So ...' Mackenzie spread his hands wide '... I thought it might be worth a sniff or two.'

'Gillie?' Winter raised an eyebrow.

'Yeah. Gillie. Great tits. Great conversation. First time we met she drank me under the table. Turns out she worked with Makins before he left the *News*. That's why she sent him our way. The guy's at a loose end. She says he's given up on all the corporate bollocks and wants to do something real with his life. If we can get him for fuck-all money, so much the better, eh?' He glanced at his watch and produced a mobile. The receptionist answered on the first ring. 'Trace? Baz. Send the guy down.'

Andy Makins appeared at the door within seconds. He was small, thin, pale, intense, with thick-lensed glasses and a scary side parting, a greasy lick of hair falling over one eye. He wore a Ramones T-shirt under an ill-fitting tweed jacket he must have picked up in a charity shop and had a Palestinian scarf wound round his scrawny neck. The black jeans had definitely seen better days, but the lime-green Nike High-Tops looked brand new. He stepped into the room, unpeeled the scarf and blinked at the faces around the table. Kinder, Winter sensed, couldn't believe his eyes. His brand of political consultancy had little room for a fashion statement this muddled. Baz, on the other hand, loved him at first sight. The way Makins went round them all, damp handshakes, major eye contact and a smile that blossomed like a firework. This was the kind of guy you don't come across too often. Definitely a trophy find.

'Welcome, son. Take a seat.'

Makins settled in. Bazza asked him whether he'd like a

coffee. He said he'd prefer Coke. Bazza made another call then asked him how much he knew about *Pompey First.*

As it happens, Makins was facing the wall of sample posters. 'Cool.' He nodded in approval. 'I like that one.'

'Which one?'

'The one on the left.'

Baz was beaming. It was his favourite too. *Pompey First – Because the Last Lot Screwed Up.*

'So why do you like it, son?'

'Because it's simple. And because it works. *First? Last?* They're the keys. The best commercial messages are like poetry. Same principle. Keep it simple. Compress. Bombard. *First. Last.*' His tiny fists flailed the air. 'Bam bam.'

Baz was hooked. Winter could tell. Even Kinder seemed to be taking an interest.

'But how much do you know about us?' he asked.

'Not much. I know you're local, obviously. I know you're a bit off the wall. I know you probably want to kick the shit out of the other lot. Beyond that, to be honest, it's a all a bit of a mystery.'

'How come?'

'Because I know zilch about politics.'

'Might that not be a handicap?'

'No way.'

'Why not?'

'Because it's a selling job. This is retail, not politics.'

'Really?'

'Of course. I've no idea what you guys really believe, but that's not the point, is it? The point is you want to make an impact, you want to get your names out there. So ...' he peered round '... maybe there's some way I can help.'

'How?' This from Bazza.

Makins gazed at him for a moment. Then he ducked his head and picked at his fingers and mumbled something about

Gill. She'd given him the impression that *Pompey First* might be up for something a bit radical. Like social media.

'We are, son. We are.'

'Then I'm the guy you need.'

'Why's that?'

'Because it's not just a question of Facebook and Twitter. Those are just the doors you have to kick in. It's what you do when you get through to the other side that matters.'

'Are we talking sockpuppet accounts here?' Baz was grinning now. He'd picked the term up from Kinder but Winter wasn't convinced he really understood what it meant. Kinder, meanwhile, was watching Makins with some interest. Social media was his baby and he didn't want her kidnapped.

'Well?' he said.

There was a note of warning in Kinder's voice but Makins ignored it. His eyes had never left Mackenzie.

'Sockpuppets are a must,' he said. 'But how do you use them? Who do you target? Where do you cause most trouble?'

'Tell me, son.'

'You get to the people who don't normally vote. You get to blokes, especially. You set up groups. You get in among the lads' mags crowd, the Pompey fans. There's a squaddies' website, full of gossip - that's a must. You lob in the odd hand grenade, stir it all up, get them onside, make these guys want to get out and vote. Most of them wouldn't know a vote from a hole in the road. Why? Because it isn't cool, because it's not on their radar. This city's full of guys who don't care a fuck about politics. By next year that has to change.'

'And this is how you do it?'

'This is one way, yeah. Even if they vote for a laugh, the vote still counts.'

'There are other ways?'

'Of course.' Makins was revved up now, full throttle, the fox in *Pompey First*'s hen coop. 'YouTube's an obvious tool. You'd be mad not to use it. You need a couple of guys with the right equipment to start making those punchy little movies that are going to tune people in. Once you've shot and edited the footage, this stuff's for free.'

'So who does the donkey work?'

'Students. These people are ten a penny. The uni's full of guys who think of nothing but making their name on screen. Put the word around, and you'll have queues at the door.'

'And what do they make? What are these movies about?'

'That's down to you. This place can be a nightmare on a Friday night. Why don't you start there? Why don't you start hoovering up all that stuff in Guildhall Walk when the clubs start chucking out? Why don't you get stuck in when it kicks off at the burger bars and the kebab vans afterwards? If you get the packaging right, a dozen pissed clubbers kicking the shit out of each other are worth a hundred votes.'

'For us?'

'Of course.' His eyes strayed to another of the posters. *'Pompey First – Because Enough is Enough*. That's a great message. All I'm talking is delivery. All the images are out there. All we have to do is put them in the right order.'

Bazza nodded in agreement. Winter had seen this reaction before. He was spellbound. 'And you're telling me you can make this happen?' he said.

'Of course I can. Plus lots of other stuff. I need more time to get my head round what you guys really want, but like I say we're talking retail, branding, all that bollocks. Conversation costs nothing. Believe me, anything's possible.'

'So what would you need? From me?'

The question brought Makins to a halt. Winter was watching Kinder. Me, not us. Bazza had taken over, and he knew it.

'Well, son?' Bazza wanted an answer.

'I'll need a space of my own and some money to make it happen.'

'A space here? At the hotel?'

'Yeah.'

'And the money? We're talking wages?'

'No, I'm talking some kind of development budget. If you buy into the student thing, I need to nail down the production costs. Plus I've got some other ideas that might be a little pricier.'

'Like what?'

'I don't want to say. Not yet. But this is stuff no one's ever tried before, which is why you'd be mad to say no.'

'How's that?'

'Because the real exposure's gonna come from the mainstream media. My job is to take them into the jungle, show them all kinds of exotic stuff, get them chattering, get them impressed, get the buzz going. That way you get two hits for every quid you spend. And I'm not just talking Pompey.'

Mackenzie pulled a pad towards him and scribbled himself a note. Then his head came up.

'How much then? For development?'

'A couple of grand to start with. That may be more than we need.'

'And you? Wages?'

'Four grand a month. The moment I don't deliver, we call it quits.'

'Two grand.'

'Three. In cash.'

'Deal. I'll sort you a room upstairs. Sea view or something round the back?'

'Sea view.'

'Good call, son. You know rule one in this fucking world? Never undersell yourself.' Mackenzie extended a hand across the table. Then, as an afterthought, he glanced at Kinder. 'You've been a bit quiet, Leo. All this stuff OK with you?'

Kinder said nothing. Mackenzie got to his feet. A waitress from upstairs had appeared at the door with a frosted glass of Coke, but Makins ignored her. He was looking at Winter.

'I'm sorry,' he said. 'I didn't catch your name.'

Chapter ten

Suttle did his best to raise Winter on his mobile but failed. Parsons had wrung a grudging go-ahead for renewed negotiations from Willard at headquarters and she was now demanding feedback by close of play. With a busy afternoon of intel meetings, mainly on the stranger rape, Suttle knew he had little alternative but to pay Winter a visit before lunch. With luck, he might be in his Blake House apartment.

Suttle left his Subaru in the big underground car park at Gunwharf and emerged into bright sunshine. Shedding his jacket, he strolled along the canalside promenade, trying to plot the shape of the coming conversation. Every undercover operation, he knew, was fraught with difficulties, but this one would be especially tricky. By recruiting Winter, as he'd already pointed out to Parsons, they'd spare themselves the time and effort of inserting someone new into Mackenzie's business empire, but the fact remained that Winter was a loose cannon.

Suttle knew him far better than anyone else in the force and liked to think that the kinship they'd established in their early years would survive whatever lay ahead. But it was Winter himself who had taught Suttle the darker arts of CID work, and the instincts he'd acquired from this apprenticeship told him to be extremely cautious. By turning informant, Winter was putting everything on the line. As, indeed, was Suttle. In both cases the gamble might well pay off. Winter would be a free agent again, armoured by the Witness Protection Programme, while a result with Mackenzie would do Suttle's promotion prospects no harm at all.

Suttle smiled to himself, thinking of Lizzie. Only this morning, wearied by the traffic and the shrieking covens of fat single mums, plus all the other hassles of living in Pompey, she'd floated the idea of moving somewhere a bit quieter. This was music to Suttle's ears. He'd grown up in a council house on the edge of a small village in the New Forest, and something deep inside him had always wanted to get back to the country, but it had never crossed his mind that Lizzie might feel the same way. As a working journalist, she'd always relied on the flood of stories that a city like Portsmouth could generate, but those days were over now, at least for a year or two, and it was obviously becoming harder and harder to keep the place at arm's length. Lizzie had always regarded her own space, her own turf, her own peace of mind, as sacrosanct, but the fact was that Pompey had a habit of getting in your face. Enough, she seemed to be saying.

Blake House lay on the other side of the canal. Suttle pressed Winter's button on the video entry panel and waited for an answer. When nothing happened, he tried again. Finally came a voice he dimly recognised. Not Winter at all.

'Jimmy Suttle.' She was laughing. 'You look so much older.'

'Trude?'

'Yeah. Come in.'

Suttle rode the lift to the top floor. Trudy Gallagher was Misty's daughter. Years ago, before he wised up to the inevitable consequences, she and Suttle had got it together. For a couple of giddy months Suttle had wondered whether he might even be in love, but shagging the daughter of Bazza Mackenzie's mistress was deeply reckless. No way was Mackenzie going to allow the Filth anywhere near his nearest and dearest, and the relevant message had been delivered one wet night outside a Gunwharf nightclub. As a result of his injuries, Suttle had spent a couple of nights in hospital, emerging on crutches to explain himself to his bosses, and since then his contact with Trude had been limited to a single exchange of Christmas cards. In hers Trude had suggested eloping to South America. It was a sweet suggestion, underscored with a line of fat kisses, but – with some regret – Suttle had declined.

Now she was waiting for him in the hallway outside Winter's flat. Her hair was tied back in a way he'd never seen before and her jeans were splashed with white paint. She had a deep tan and had lost a lot of weight.

'You look great ...' he said '... fabulous.'

'So why don't you kiss me?'

Suttle obliged her with a hug. She smelled of burned toast.

'Paul says you're married.'

'He's right.'

'With a kid.'

'Right again.'

'Happy?'

'Yeah.'

'Really?' She held him at arm's length.

'Yeah.'

Barefoot, she led him into the flat. Most of the carpet in Winter's big living room was covered with a dust sheet. A pair of wooden steps was propped against the far wall, and a roller tray at the foot of the steps was full of paint. Magnolia. Winter's favourite.

'So what's this?'

'What does it look like?'

'Since when have you become a painter and decorator?'

'Since Saturday. It's Mum's idea. Paul's selling the place, and she thinks a coat of paint might get the punters through the door.'

'Selling the place?' Suttle tried to keep the surprise out of his voice.

'Yeah. Paul's moving in with Mum, over in Hayling Island.

She says she can't wait, the old slapper. Can you imagine that? Mum and Paul going legit?'

Suttle couldn't but didn't say so. Instead he wanted to know about the tan. Trude led him through to the kitchen and put the kettle on. She'd been out in the Canaries, she said, working as a rep with a company in Fuerteventura. The hours were shit and the punters were worse, but she'd hooked up with a local guy who ran a windsurfing school. Hence the tan.

'You can windsurf now?'

'*Sí. Y hablo español.*'

'I'm impressed.'

'Don't be. I can order a beer and tell the guys I don't fancy to bugger off, but that's about it. When it comes to windsurfing, I spent most of the time in the fucking water.'

'And the boyfriend?'

'Nice man. Juan. Totally ripped.' She shot him a grin, and for a moment Suttle thought he was in for another hug, but she backed off when she caught the expression on his face.

'You look different,' she said.

'Yeah?'

'Yeah. Round here ...' she touched the skin around her eyes '... and here.' She patted her midriff.

'You're telling me I'm getting fat?'

'Not fat. I dunno ... more solid, more *sturdy*. Maybe it's the married look. Am I right?'

Suttle grinned, but Trude wasn't fooled for a moment.

'It's tough, right?'

'What?'

'Marriage. Babies. All that.'

'I dunno, Trude. It's certainly different.'

'To what?'

'To the way it was before.'

'Better?'

'Different.'

'Does she cry a lot? Does she need lots of attention?'

'Yeah.'

'And how about the baby?'

Suttle shook his head and turned away. Trude, like Misty, could read body language like a book. In another life she'd have made a great detective.

'You still want coffee? Or have I upset you?' She touched him on the arm.

'I'll skip the coffee, thanks. What I'm really after is Paul.'

'He's out.'

'I can see that, Trude. You know where he is?'

'At work, as far as I know. Give him a ring.'

'I've done that. He's on divert.'

'Maybe he's busy. I'm seeing him later. You want me to give him a message?'

'Yeah ...' Suttle glanced at his watch. 'Tell him something's come up with Grace. Tell him we need to talk.'

'Grace?'

'The baby.'

'She's OK?'

'She's fine.'

'So how come Paul needs to know so much about Grace?'

'Because he's her godfather.'

'Paul Winter? You're serious?'

Suttle nodded. Trude held his gaze for a long moment then reached behind her and switched off the kettle.

'You'd better let me get on with it then.' She nodded towards the lounge. 'I've got three more rooms after this.'

Winter was riding north through the city in the front of Bazza's new Bentley. It was a grey Continental GT, most of which Mackenzie owed to the insurance settlement after Winter had written off the old one. Winter, without much success, had been trying to pin Bazza down on various money issues. The way Winter figured it, the latest addition to the *Pompey First* campaign team was going to cost Mackenzie at least 26K, and if the guy came up with more stunts that took Bazza's fancy that figure could easily double.

'You're right, mush. So here's hoping, eh?'

They were en route to an outpost of Bazza's empire called Pompey Reptiles, a converted terrace house that now did a thriving trade in snakes, baby alligators and Peruvian lizards. Given the state of his boss's diary, the journey there and back was Winter's only opportunity for a decent chat.

'Tell me about the money, Baz. Just pretend I don't know we're broke.'

'We're not broke. We've got assets everywhere. Sell something.'

'Like what?'

'Fuck knows. Make a few calls. Have a nose around. I read in the *Telegraph* that Spain might be on the up again.' He swerved to avoid a cyclist and nearly clipped a traffic island. 'What about those apartments in Almería?'

'They're all mortgaged. And the *Telegraph*'s wrong, by the way. If we sold now we'd still be owing the bank. The market's on its arse, Baz.'

'France?'

'All mortgaged.'

'I don't fucking believe you.'

'You should, Baz. It was your decision.'

They glided to a halt at a set of traffic lights. Further up the road was one of the city's biggest comprehensives. Once the traffic was moving again, Mackenzie gave the empty playground a derisive wave as they sped by.

'Did Leo tell you about the other night?'

'Where?'

'There.' He gestured back towards the school. 'We did a spoiler on one of the Filth's little road shows. Safer neighbourhoods, my arse. By the time we'd done those muppets over, there wasn't a single punter in the hall who'd risk walking home by himself. Brilliant job, mush. Leo's idea but me in the driving seat. You know how many signatures we took on the door afterwards? Over a hundred. That's where it matters, mush. That's where you get them. Law and order. Never fails.'

Winter said nothing. Kinder's latest strategy called for a series of what he termed informed interventions, posh code for gatecrashing other people's meetings, scaring the public witless and converting volunteered names and addresses into complimentary membership cards. Over the last month alone, according to Kinder, *Pompey First* had harvested nearly six hundred new supporters. It was people like these, said Bazza, who would take him into Parliament.

'This Skelley—' He braked hard to avoid a young mum crossing the road. Two kids off the leash and another in the buggy.

'What about him?'

'He's the go-to guy for money. He owes us. And more to the point, he fucking knows it.'

'So what are you suggesting? A letter?'

'Don't take the piss, mush.'

'What then?'

'A visit. Tell him we'll settle for a million. As long as it's cash.'

'A million is way over the top. He's given us £350K already.'

'That was a deposit. We need the rest. I'm serious, mush.' He glanced across. 'We have to get this thing sorted.'

By now they were in Copnor. Mackenzie took a left without bothering to signal, dismissing the guy behind with a derisive wave of his hand. Pompey Reptiles was first right at the end of the road.

'You coming in? This guy's a laugh, the only Vietnamese I ever met who can speak half-decent English.'

Winter eased his bulk out of the car and followed Mackenzie into the shop. The smell hit you at once, an overpowering mix of sawdust and reptile shit, thickened by the big wall heaters. Winter looked round. All his life, snakes had terrified him.

The shop, he guessed, had once been the front room of the property. Now it was stacked high with cages. Through the smudged glass, on closer inspection, Winter could make out an occasional stirring among the sand and wood shavings, but anyone expecting thick coils of python or rearing wide-screen king cobras would be sorely disappointed. Maybe snakes kipped at lunchtime, he thought. Very sensible.

A tiny shrunken figure emerged from the back of the shop. He appeared to be wearing pyjamas. Looking hard at the seamed yellow face, Winter would have been pushed to guess an age.

'Sanouk? This is Paul, a mate of mine. I don't think you ever met.'

Sanouk bowed. He had a tube of expanding foam in his hand. A huge bubble of yellow foam had dribbled from the nozzle and hardened in seconds. Winter shook his outstretched hand, sticky with the foam. Sanouk, he knew, was a refugee from one of the city's many cannabis factories. Imported from his smallholding in the Mekong Delta, he'd been scooped up in a raid by one of the city's drug squads. Smart defence work by his brief had put him back on the market, and the sight of his face in the *News* had caught Mackenzie's fancy. Pneumonia had just carried off the last manager of Pompey Reptiles, and within a week Sanouk found himself in charge of the livestock.

'Listen, my friend.' Mackenzie had turned down the offer of tea. 'We might have a problem ...'

Kinder, it turned out, had identified Pompey Reptiles as an electoral own goal. Once the pressure was on, he'd explained, the name would doubtless be used against him, especially as the *Pompey First* candidate was so proud of his city roots. Bazza Mackenzie. The Pompey Reptile.

'We change name?' Sanouk was looking confused.

'Afraid so, son.'

'What we call us?'

'Jungle Jim's.'

'Yungle Yim's?' For some reason Sanouk couldn't manage Js.

'That's it, son. You need to sort someone out to do the business, get the paint out, change the name. And another thing. If anyone turns up asking about me, whether I own this place or not, just tell them no, OK?'

'Sure.' The frown had deepened. 'So who own this place?'

'I do.'

'Sure.'

'You understand?'

'Sure.'

'I can count on that?'

'Sure.' He bowed again, none the wiser, and then wiped his hand on his pyjama bottoms and showed them to the door.

Back in the Bentley, Winter inspected his hand, still sticky with the foam. Mackenzie wanted to talk about Skelley again, but Winter had a better idea.

'Montenegro, Baz.'

'What about it?'

'That development in Bicici. The one next door to Budva.'

'Kubla Khan, you mean? Nikki Kokh?'

'That's it.' Winter nodded.

'And?'

'We've got 10 per cent, right?'

'Right.'

'Nikki priced it at fifteen mil, yes?'

'Yeah. In euros.'

'Which makes one and a half million. As long as he's happy to buy us out.'

Mackenzie said nothing. Nikolai Kokh was a budding Russian entrepreneur, one of the younger sharks feeding on the remains of the old communist state. Bazza had first met him in a casino in Marbella. It turned out they had a great many shared passions. One was football, another was finding a decent return for laundered narco-cash. Since Montenegro offered near-perfect facilities for the latter, Bazza had agreed to take a 10 per cent stake in a beachside development Nikki was planning. Kubla Khan would, he told Bazza, offer five-star hotel facilities, including a conference centre, a casino and an adjacent block of top-end apartments for clients who wanted to turn their holiday experience into real life.

According to Nikki, any serious investor would win twice over – once by buying into a profitable money machine with the capital protected by the booming Montenegran property market, and second time around because the casino operation offered limitless opportunities for money laundering. No matter where your money came from, Kubla Khan would wash it white as snow.

At the time, back from Marbella, Bazza had no doubts about the venture. He and Winter did a number of Internet searches, which all confirmed that Kubla Khan was a kosher project. The virtual tours looked sumptuous. The boasts about eco-friendly heating systems and world-class cuisine seemed real enough. And when Winter checked the claim about backing from the regional planning authorities, that too stacked up.

A couple of months later Mackenzie met Nikki Kokh again, this time in London. He'd flown in that morning from Moscow for a Chelsea home game. Bazza signed a memorandum of agreement, handed over a 5 per cent deposit on a 10 per cent stake, and agreed to wire the balance as soon as his solicitor was happy with the due diligence checks. The checks were complete by August 2008, at which point Bazza paid for the rest of the stake. A month later Lehman Brothers collapsed. Since when Bazza had heard virtually nothing.

Now he was having a serious think. Winter was happy to ride back to the hotel in silence, knowing that he'd finally got his boss's attention. In ways Winter had never anticipated, *Pompey First* had become a crusade. Thanks to Leo Kinder, and now Makins, Pompey's one-time cocaine king genuinely believed he could make it all the way to Westminster. If he ever got there, he would doubtless end up as frustrated and over-worked as every other MP, but that wasn't the point. What mattered, just now, was the coming battle, and Bazza had absolutely no interest in anything but winning. That's what made him get up in the morning. That's what fuelled the endless late-night strategy sessions with Leo Kinder. The pair of them were determined to lay siege to the fucking Establishment wankers, and if the price of success was his stake in Nikki Kokh's Montenegran venture, then so be it.

Only when they were on the seafront, approaching the Royal Trafalgar, did Bazza voice his decision.

'Get out there, mush,' he said. 'See if Nikki wants to play.'

Chapter eleven

Suttle waited all afternoon for Winter to get in touch, checking his phone between meetings in case a message had been
left. Parsons, he knew, had to be on the road by five for a
conference at headquarters in Winchester. When there was still
no word from Winter, Suttle walked the length of the Major
Crime corridor and tapped on Parsons' door.

'Well?' She looked up from her PC.

'Nothing, I'm afraid, boss.'

'*Nothing?*'

'I can't find him. He's not responding. He'll get in touch in
the end but maybe not today.'

Visibly irritated, Parsons checked her watch and closed
down her PC.

'Bloody man,' she muttered.

Suttle hesitated a moment, caught between agreement and
something more personal.

'We don't own him, boss,' he pointed out. 'At least not yet.'

'We don't, Jimmy.' She was reaching for her coat. 'But we
will.'

Winter was back at his flat in Blake House by half five. Hoping
that Trude was still at work, he was disappointed to find her
gone. He'd always got on with her, and in the week or so since
she'd arrived back from the Canaries, she'd been one of the few

bright spots in what he sensed was the gathering darkness. She was funny. She made him laugh. And, if he'd ever let her close enough, she'd be amused by his current plight. That Winter should find himself wedged between the apprentice politician and a bunch of outraged Filth determined to head him off was all too predictable, but even Winter acknowledged that the fault was his own. He should have seen this coming. And he should have done something about it.

He circled the flat. For years and years he'd associated the smell of paint with spring. Back in the old days, before Joannie died, she'd always begin the climb out of winter with a brisk coat of emulsion and a trip to the laundrette with the lounge curtains. Once he'd even caught her marking up the calendar to remind her to break out the colour charts and inspect last year's brushes. Nearly a decade later he could even remember the date, 8 March.

He paused beside the big picture window, staring out across the harbour. By late September, at this time of night, the light was already dying in the west. The big council flats on the Gosport waterfront were etched black against the paleness of the sky, the first pricks of light visible on the upper floors. Next week it would be October. Soon the clocks would go back. After which his fears about the darkness would be all too real.

He checked his mobile again, wondering whether Suttle had left any more messages. All afternoon he'd fought the urge to get in touch, to ask him how the land lay, to share a joke or two, to hear a voice he trusted, but just now he knew it was important to keep him at arm's length until his own strategy – how he intended to handle the coming months – was clearer. From his office at the Royal Trafalgar, he'd done his best to get hold of Nikki Kokh, but for some reason the Russian wasn't returning his calls. Instead, in the end, he'd phoned the guy who served as Kokh's lieutenant.

Arkady was a big, broad, potato-faced Muscovite with huge hands and a ready sense of humour. Twenty years older than

Kokh, he'd once been a cop. Kokh had plucked him out of near-retirement, flown him to Montenegro and installed him as his eyes and ears at the Hotel Georgi, the first of many flags Kokh had planted on the Adriatic coast. From time to time the pair of them turned up at English Premiership games, and Winter still remembered the moment when Bazza had done the introductions.

They'd all met at a city restaurant for lunch before going to Fratton Park to watch a home fixture. In situations like these Bazza was never slow to point out that Winter was a trophy signing from Pompey CID, but Arkady needed no clues. He'd known at once that Winter was a fellow cop. That night, while Bazza wined and dined Kokh at the hotel, he and Arkady had gone on the piss, strolling from pub to pub, trading war stories, chuckling at the madness of trying to impose any kind of order on the reliable chaos of city life. What made the evening especially sweet was the realisation that they'd both traded a career as cops for something altogether more interesting, and by the time they made it back to the hotel they'd become brothers in arms.

Afterwards Winter had kept the relationship going – the odd phone call, a postcard when work sent him abroad, an occasional present at Christmas – and talking to Arkady late this afternoon he knew at once that the rapport was still there. Kokh, it seemed, was holed up in his motor yacht at a place called Kotor. Getting a meet with him would be no problem. Winter was to fly to Dubrovnik, take a cab across the border to Budva, and present himself at the Hotel Georgi. Arkady would take care of everything else.

Winter checked his watch, wondering about the time difference. The Balkans, he assumed, would be an hour or two ahead. He'd booked a BA flight that put him on the ground in Dubrovnik early tomorrow afternoon. Looking at the map, he estimated a two-hour taxi ride over the border to Budva. Arkady was setting Kokh up for an evening on the yacht at

Kotor. By Wednesday morning, fingers crossed, Winter would be free to pursue the real business he had in mind.

The country code for Croatia was 00385. Checking the slip of paper he kept in his wallet, he dialled a number. The number rang and rang, and he was beginning to think that she was at work, or in the shower, or otherwise engaged, when she finally answered.

'You're really coming?' Five years had done nothing to change her voice.

'Yeah.'

'When?'

'Wednesday. Where the fuck's ...' he peered at the scribbled name beneath her number '... Porec?'

'A long way from Montenegro.' She was laughing now. 'I hope you like coaches.'

Suttle was home early for once. Lizzie was in the kitchen, sing-ing along to Radiohead while the baby watched her stuffing the week's laundry into the washing machine. Suttle gave his wife a kiss, which got a big grin from Grace. Lizzie had acquired a lightweight portable rocker from a friend of Gill's. It sat neatly on the kitchen worktop, giving Grace a perfect view of pretty much everything. A system of straps kept her safe from falling out, and Suttle loved the way she kicked her legs and waved her chubby arms to get the thing moving.

'My girl,' he whispered, putting his face to hers. Nothing in his life had prepared him for the softness and sweet scent of his daughter's infant flesh. If there was anything closer to perfection, he'd yet to find it.

Lizzie wanted to tell him about Andy.

'Who?'

'Andy. Andy Makins. You remember Megan? My best mate?'

'Sorry.'

'Yeah. Well it seems Andy did a runner in the end, just the

way I knew he would. The guy's a total bastard. Megan's in bits.'

'And ...?'

'It turns out he's hooked up with Mackenzie.'

'Mackenzie?' Lizzie at last had Suttle's full attention. 'So how does that work?'

Lizzie explained about the feature Gill had done on *Pompey First*. To no one's surprise, Mackenzie had taken a fancy to this forty-something vision in thigh-length boots, and the encounter had survived beyond the interview.

'So what happened?'

'Gill bigged up Andy. Told Mackenzie he was a genius, just what he needed if *Pompey First* was ever going to make it.'

'And Mackenzie?'

'He bought it. Big time. Hauled Andy in for an interview and gave him a job.'

'As what?'

'God knows. Andy lives and breathes the Internet. He knows exactly what's possible. I'm assuming Mackenzie needs that kind of talent.'

'And Gill?'

'She's stoked.'

'Why?'

'Because Andy's copped himself a hotel bedroom. Sea views. Fridge. Hot and cold everything. She couldn't be happier.'

'Why's that? You're telling me Gill's into Mackenzie?'

'You're joking. The man's an animal. It's Andy, my love.' She stepped across and gave him a kiss. 'I thought you were the detective in the family?'

It was dark by the time Winter got to Misty Gallagher's place. He killed the headlights the moment he turned in through the gate and let the big Lexus ghost to a halt. Misty was in the kitchen, her back to the window. She had the phone wedged between her shoulder and her ear and was painting her nails.

Winter lay back against the warm leather, wondering who she was talking to. After tomorrow's trip, if things went the way he anticipated, there'd be no way out. He'd have made a decision that would probably shape the rest of his life. He'd be back by the end of the week, committed to a double life that he'd have to sustain for the best part of six months. Was he up to that kind of deception? Could he withstand that kind of pressure? And if so, who would be the losers? Mackenzie? Definitely. His immediate family? Without doubt. But Misty? Who loved him? Who wanted him? Who still made life extremely sweet for him? Where would she find herself in six months' time? If things panned out OK?

He shook his head, knowing that there was no room for guilt or regret in the script he was writing for himself. What he needed just now was the raw gut conviction to keep his nerve. In essence, he told himself, the thing was simple. His years with Bazza had taken him to a very bad place. What little was left of his conscience was beginning to trouble him, but infinitely worse was the prospect of arrest and deportation. A European Arrest Warrant, all too likely, would trigger an abrupt rewriting of his life plan. Did he really want to spend umpteen years banged up with a bunch of foreign scrotes in some Spanish jail? Was that any way to end his days?

Misty's phone conversation had come to an end. Winter leaned across for the holdall he'd packed at the flat. Misty was keen for him to make the move in one go, to rent a van and haul his entire life across to Hayling Island, but Winter knew he couldn't cope with that. Until he found a buyer, it had to be one token item at a time, a down payment – as he argued it – on a permanent relationship.

With this Misty was far from happy. She knew he cherished his independence. She was aware of how much he adored his little perch on the edge of Pompey harbour, but she had a view as well, and water at the bottom of her garden, and ample room for Winter to hide himself away and play the single man if that was what he really wanted. This argument had been going on for weeks and was still far from settled, but only last night Winter had pointed out that it was much easier to sell a flat that still felt lived in, and this, for the time being, seemed to have done the trick.

Fumbling with his key, Winter let himself in. Still drying her nails, Misty circled him with her arms and gave him a kiss. Winter could taste Bacardi. She fetched him a Stella from the fridge and perched herself on the bar stool in the big kitchen, watching him pour it. Winter could smell one of the curries Misty had mastered from a recipe book he'd given her at Christmas. There was more Stella in the fridge and afterwards they'd curl up next door with a DVD or two. By half ten they'd both be pleasantly pissed, and if Winter could muster the energy there might be some action before Misty doused the bedroom lights and folded herself around him. Not a bad life. Not considering.

Winter raised his glass in the usual toast.

'Us ... yeah?'

Misty didn't move. Her glass was empty.

'I had Trude on earlier,' she said. 'What was Jimmy Suttle doing in your flat?'

Chapter twelve

Winter was at Gatwick Airport in good time for the morning BA flight to Dubrovnik. He'd booked the ticket in the name of Karl Sparrow, and there were no problems when he presented his new passport on the way through the departure channel.

An hour's wait for the flight to be called gave him the opportunity to give Misty a ring. He'd left her before she'd really woken up, telling her he'd be back by the end of the week, and she'd grunted something that might have been affectionate before turning over and going back to sleep. He'd spent most of last night trying to explain why he'd accepted the role of godfather to young Jimmy's baby but he was still unsure whether she believed D/S Suttle had been paying a purely social visit to Blake House. In Misty's world the Filth were always the Filth – no exceptions, no room for negotiation – and what alarmed her most was the fact that she'd had to learn about this cosy little arrangement from her daughter.

'So why didn't you tell me, pet?'

'Because you'd never understand.'

'Understand what?'

'That you can stay mates with someone like that.'

'Filth, you mean?'

'Yeah.'

'You're right. I don't. It makes me very nervous, pet. And I'm someone who loves you.'

'Meaning?'

'Others might not be so trusting. Like Baz for starters. He gets funny about Filth, especially some knobber who once shagged Trude. You think that's unreasonable?'

'Not at all. But it's my life, Mist, not his. I taught that kid everything he knows.'

'Which makes him a great detective?'

'The best.'

'Then put yourself in Baz's place. What's he gonna think? Someone that sharp sniffing around? Baz didn't get rich by accident, pet. He's got a brain, believe it or not. Plus he knows a set-up when he sees it.'

'You think this is a set-up?'

'Either that, pet, or you're losing it.'

'Then maybe I'm losing it.'

'No, you're not. If that was the case, I'd be the first to tell you.'

At this point, with the curry in danger of overcooking, they'd called a truce. Only later, in bed, had Mist raised Suttle again. She'd tried to rouse Winter and failed completely. Up on one elbow, her face silhouetted against the bedside light, she'd hung over him.

'Maybe you should move in properly,' she'd murmured, 'then Baz need never know.'

'About what?'

'Jimmy.' She'd smiled. 'Deal?'

Now he waited for her to pick up. As far as he knew, she'd been planning a raid on the autumn sales in Southampton. He was right. On his third attempt to get through, she was on the motorway, heading west.

'You ...' she said.

'Me,' he agreed.

She laughed, then said she wanted to apologise for giving him a hard time last night. On reflection she'd decided he was right.

'Right? I'm not with you, Mist.'

'I think you *are* losing it, pet. But I still love you.'

'And?'

'I've booked a van for Saturday. Trude says she'll be around to help. Isn't that sweet of her?'

'A van for what, Mist?'

'All your clobber. It's a weekend deal. We can do several runs. That OK with you, pet?'

The line went dead, leaving Winter staring into the middle distance. According to the nearest bank of screens, the Dubrovnik flight was delayed for an hour. Great, he thought, pocketing the mobile.

Headwinds over southern Europe put another thirty minutes on the journey, and by the time Winter stepped onto the tarmac at Dubrovnik Airport it was nearly three o'clock. He scored a cursory nod from immigration, carried his single bag through customs and queued for several minutes beside the cab rank outside arrivals before agreeing a fare to Budva.

Winter climbed into the back of the Mercedes and put a precautionary call through to Arkady.

'I'm going to be late,' he said. 'The flight was delayed.'

Arkady told him to head for a seafront hotel called the Neptun where a room had been reserved. The Georgi, it seemed, was full.

'What name have you used?'

'Winter.'

'I'm travelling as Karl Sparrow. You want to tell them that?'

'No problem.' Arkady didn't seem the least surprised. 'Take care, my friend.'

The cab driver, mercifully, spoke no English, so Winter settled down to enjoy the trip. The border was half an hour down the road. Soon after they crossed into Montenegro, beyond a rash of new hotels, the road wound round a huge fjord that reached deep into the mountains. The scenery was spectacular, the water a flawless shade of green, fluffy white clouds crowning the surrounding peaks. At the head of the fjord Winter caught signs to Kotor, and minutes later the Mercedes slowed as the traffic began to thicken.

The town of Kotor sprawled along the waterfront. At the heart of it was an ancient walled settlement that obviously pulled thousands of tourists. A huge white cruise ship lay docked alongside the marina, and Winter wound down the window for a better view as the Mercedes crawled past. Beyond the cruise ship lay a line of fuck-off gin palace motorcruisers, neatly parked stern first to the waterfront promenade, and Winter twisted round in the seat, wondering which of these trophy toys belonged to Kokh.

Half an hour later, after a fast run down a valley back towards the coast, the road climbed again, and around the shoulder of the next mountain Winter found himself looking down at Budva. In the literature he'd consulted on the plane this was the go-go engine at the heart of Montenegro's economic revival, and looking down at the sprawl of hotels he could well believe it. The town filled the bowl of a broad valley, suburbs spilling up the foothills of the mountains behind, and wherever you looked the view was spiked by cranes. A grey-looking beach marked the long curve of the bay, and the promontory on the far side had morphed into a gigantic construction site.

According to Bazza, this stretch of coast had become a magnet for Russian money, most of it dodgy, and already Winter had lost count of the bulky new-looking 4 x 4s that permanently hogged the outside lane. Budva chic obviously called for wrap-round shades to go with the darkened windows, and it was rare to spot a driver who didn't look like he spent most of his life in the gym. Already Winter sensed these were serious people. They took no prisoners at traffic intersections. They liked to ride with sensational-looking women. They didn't smile much.

The Hotel Neptun was tucked into a compound behind the

beach. Winter paid the driver and made his way to reception. The girl took a cursory look at his passport and told him that payment for the room had been taken care of. When he asked whether anyone had left a message she reached under the counter and gave him an envelope. The scribbled note inside was from Arkady. He apologised for not being around in person, but just now his schedule was impossible. A car would be calling for Winter at half past seven, and Nikki was looking forward to meeting him in Kotor. In the meantime he might like to take a look at Budva's wonderful waterfront. The letter ended with a big fat exclamation mark: *Enjoy!*

Winter wondered whether Kokh's lieutenant, who had a well-developed sense of humour, was being ironic. He was. After dumping his bag in the room, Winter left the hotel and made his way towards the sea. The shadows were beginning to lengthen beneath the scrawny palm trees but there was still warmth in the air. Fat women lay sprawled on the beach among pockets of litter and driftwood, enjoying the last of the sunshine, while a lone drinker at an otherwise empty café sat staring out to sea.

Winter paused for a moment, trying to picture the scene at the height of the summer. Even then, swamped with tourists, it wouldn't have been pretty. Everything seemed abandoned or half finished. A beachside amusement park had succumbed to fly-tippers. Peasant women squatted in the shadows guarding piles of bulky knitware which might – or might not – have been for sale. Even the tribes of feral cats, foraging listlessly for scraps, seemed to have lost the plot.

Strolling on, Winter began to wonder whether this was what happened when you threw a lot of money at a pretty coastline and didn't bother too much about the consequences. He was closer to the development across the bay now, and from this perspective it was even bigger than it had seemed from the cab. Maybe this was the answer, he thought. Maybe the serious investors ring-fenced the best sites, turned their backs on all the other rubbish and created a little fantasy world of their own. That way you'd be selling exclusivity, privileged access, round-the-clock security, plus a bunch of like-minded punters who wouldn't get in your face.

He walked back to the main road and hailed a cab. Yet another Mercedes. The phrase Kubla Khan drew a nod from the driver. They rode out past the big development and into the next bay.

Winter leaned forward. 'This is Bicici?'

'*Da.*'

Bicici, on first impressions, was Budva without the charm. The speed of development was no less intense but there were still large tracts of land – overgrown, litter-strewn – advertised for sale. In the middle of the bay the cabby slowed and indicated a sizeable white complex with a nod of his head.

'Kubla Khan,' he muttered.

Winter got out and paid. A huge roadside hoarding advertised the benefits of making a down payment on one of the beachside apartments attached to the hotel. A sleek, bronzed twenty-something in a red bikini was mugging for the camera beside an enormous pool. Her mates, equally gorgeous, were tastefully arranged in the background. A waiter with a tray was lurking on the edge of the shot. This could have been a scene from any of a hundred resort destinations. On offer was limitless sunshine, world-class cossetting, and – if you were lucky enough to score – quality sex. In essence, thought Winter, these guys were selling everybody's wet dream. *Why Wait?* went the strapline.

Why wait, indeed. At the bottom of the hoarding was an email address and the name of the developers. Melorcorp was the vehicle Nikki Kokh used in Montenegro. Winter walked down towards the beach along the flank of the site. The skin and bones of the complex were in place, but glaziers were still fitting windows on the seaward side and an enormous lorry was offloading what looked like interior panels.

As far as Winter could judge, the bulk of the development consisted of an artfully cantilevered building which served as the hotel, while a matching block beside it housed the apartments. On closer inspection, some of the units on the upper floors seemed not only complete but occupied. Shading his eyes against the low slant of sunshine, Winter could see Venetian blinds at some of the windows, pot plants on balconies, even a beach towel draped over a smoked-glass retaining screen.

Winter stepped back, wondering how the sums stacked up. He had no way of telling whether this construction site would deliver all the promotional boasts he'd checked out on the Internet, but he liked what he saw and assumed it would play well with the clientele Nikki Kokh had in mind. Given full occupancy at the hotel plus speedy take-up on the apartments, Melorcorp might be looking at a nice little earner. Maybe he should be pitching for more than £1.5 million tonight. Maybe he could squeeze a little more from Bazza's favourite Russian.

Back at the hotel he treated himself to a bath and a kip. When he awoke, the room was in semi-darkness. He fumbled for his watch. Five past seven. He had a shave and stepped back into his suit. By the time he got to the lobby, his transport to Kotor was already parked outside, a big Audi 4 x 4, regulation black. Expecting Arkady, Winter bent to the front window. Only one of the two guys spoke English. Both had the look of bodyguards, presumably part of Kokh's entourage. They wore designer jeans and white T-shirts. Heavily muscled, they had the blank-faced fuck-off arrogance that goes with decent wages and a place in the fast lane. These guys owned the world. Neither had much interest in conversation.

They sped through the town, heading north towards Kotor. Bruce Springsteen played softly on the music system. From time to time Winter caught a murmur of conversation and once, with a glance in the rear-view mirror, a low chuckle. On the road north, along the valley, Winter glimpsed more construction sites, fenced-off enclosures stacked with sewer pipes and huge piles of aggregate. The whole of Montenegro, it seemed, was on the rise. Then came a tunnel Winter remembered from the earlier trip and suddenly they were back in Kotor. The dockside cruise ship was bathed in light. Flocks of elderly tourists were waiting for gaps in the traffic before they wandered into town.

The Audi slowed and then slipped into a side road that led to the marina. Kokh's motor yacht was one of the biggest, a sleek confection in gleaming white.

A boarding ramp offered access to the fantail from the dockside, and Winter made his way aboard, stopping briefly to gaze down at the name emblazoned on the stern. *Starburst.* Gibraltar.

Nikki Kokh was waiting for him, a small slight figure in jeans and a rumpled denim shirt. He wore his hair long, tied in a ponytail, and the wire-rimmed glasses gave him the look of a student. Bazza had already mentioned Kokh's taste in clothes, the way he liked to present himself, and only yesterday he'd warned Winter not to jump to conclusions. The guy dresses like a hippie, he said. But don't be fooled for a moment.

Kokh extended a hand, the lightest touch, barely a hand-shake at all.

'Welcome,' he said. 'You've come a long way.'

They moved into the saloon. If wealth has a smell, thought Winter, it was surely this: new leather, wax polish and the faintest hint of perfume in the air. The lighting was soft after the harshness of the marina neon outside. An extremely pretty girl stepped out of the shadows and asked what Winter would like to drink. Like Kokh, her English was flawless. Winter opted for a lager.

'Not champagne?' Kokh was smiling. 'We have Krug.'

Champagne, to Winter, suggested some kind of celebration. Under the circumstances it seemed churlish to say no.

Kokh led him to a huge crescent of sofa. Like everything else on board, the white leather looked showroom-new. The girl, who said her name was Olenka, popped the bottle of Krug and poured two glasses. Kokh, it turned out, was drinking fruit juice. He raised his glass.

'Kubla Khan,' he murmured.

'Happy days.'

'You went to Bicici this afternoon? Had a look round?'

'Of course.'

'And you like what you see?'

'Very much.'

'Good. Very good.' He glanced across at the girl and said something in Russian. She nodded, checked her watch and slipped out through a glass door at the far end of the saloon. Kokh turned back to Winter. It was best, he said, if they talked business first. Afterwards they could enjoy a meal together. Olenka was a fine cook. She'd given the resident chef the night off and insisted on preparing the meal herself. Kokh hoped Winter liked wild boar.

Winter, who'd never tasted wild boar in his life, said he loved it. But where was his friend Arkady?

'Arkady has a date in Podgorica. He's sorry not to be here.'

'Is he back tomorrow?'

'I think yes.'

'At the hotel?'

'At the Georgi, yes. You must get together. He talks about you often.'

Winter smiled and said nothing. Towards the end of their evening in Pompey Arkady had confided that Montenegran women were extremely hot. Maybe that's what had taken him away for the evening.

Kokh fetched the bottle from the ice bucket and topped up Winter's glass. Then he settled on the sofa again. He said they needed to be frank with one another. The project was coming along fine at last, and they were nearly back on schedule, but the last nine months had been a nightmare.

'How come?'

'For people like us life here can be complicated. You know what I mean?'

'No.'

'The Montenegrans, they love money. They'll sell you anything. Land. Water. Drugs. Women. Anything. And when there's nothing left to sell, they sell you yourself.'

'I don't understand.'

'They make things hard for you. They give you big problems. And then one day they come along to your office and they knock on the door and they're very polite and they tell you they can make all the problems go away. For money, of course.'

'You're telling me you pay protection?'

'Of course. They call it business. These are mountain people, my friend. Life is tough in the mountains. They don't like strangers. The only stranger they find room for is the stranger with money. And if he doesn't share his money they chase him away.'

'We're talking serious money?'

'Enough. More than enough.'

'And this came as some kind of surprise?'

'Of course not.'

'So why invest in the first place?'

'Because we can make the sums work. Because we're good at what we do. Because this is a beautiful place and we believe in the project. But everything in life is relative, my friend, and these are greedy people.'

'So what are you telling me?' Winter knew exactly what was coming.

'I'm telling you that the project has been in trouble. And I'm telling you that there may be more trouble to come.' Kokh put his glass to one side. He had delicate hands, perfectly buffed nails, and he used them to develop and shape the case he was trying to make. 'There are two kinds of Montenegrans. The ones in the government, the ones who run the country, the ones

136

with the rubber stamps, they make it very tough for you to do anything and they rob you blind in the process. The other sort don't bother with the paperwork. You either pay what they demand or your life becomes very difficult.'

'How?'

'They cause trouble at the construction site, they intimidate your workers, they take your chief engineer for a ride one night and scare the shit out of him. Next morning you wake up and he's gone. This is a cowboy town, my friend. On a bad day it reminds me of Chechnya. On a very bad day it can be worse.'

Earlier, back at the hotel, Winter had prepared a little speech about his own boss's problems. How much damage the credit crunch had done Bazza. How most of the business sector was suffering. How the time had come to turn one or two investments back into cash. Not because the original decisions had been wrong or the prospects going forward looked dodgy, but because they had no choice.

'You want to leave the project?' Kokh was watching him carefully.

'I'm afraid we have to.'

'You mean liquidate the entire holding?'

'Yes.'

'And do you have a buyer?'

'No. That's why I'm here.'

Kokh looked briefly pained, as if this news had come as some kind of shock.

'You want *us* to buy back your stake? The full 10 per cent?'

'Yes.'

'And do you have a price in mind?'

'Of course.'

'How much?'

Mackenzie had told him to start at two and a half million. Winter doubled it.

'Five million?' Kokh was laughing. 'Is this some kind of joke?'

137

'Not at all. We think the project's fabulous. We know you're selling apartments already. The design, the setting, the promotional stuff, it's all spot on. Five million is a compliment. Five mil means you guys have done brilliantly. I'm surprised the locals are such a pain in the arse, but I'm sure you can see them off.' Winter shrugged. 'This kind of bollocks you'll find everywhere. It's what happens when you do business in the Third World.'

'You think this is the Third World?'

'That's what it feels like.'

Kokh was chuckling now. Surprise had given way to amusement.

'You're asking me for five million? When you've just told me you have no choice?' He shook his head. 'You want some more Krug?'

Winter emptied the glass and held it out for a refill. He was beginning to enjoy himself.

Kokh got to his feet and fetched a bowl of nuts from a table near the door. When he returned to the sofa he had a proposition.

'Three hundred thousand,' he said. 'In euros. A third on signature. A third on project completion. The rest when we declare the first dividend.'

'Three hundred grand?' It was Winter's turn to laugh. 'When we paid you a million and a half?'

'Things haven't been easy. These people have cost us a lot of money.'

'But three hundred grand?'

'Then turn it down. Stay in the game. Stay at the table. You're welcome, my friend. We like you. We appreciate your support.'

'That's nice to hear –' Winter tipped his glass '– but we can't afford you any more. Like I say, times are hard.'

'Then take the three hundred ...' the softness of his hand closed over Winter's '... before I go lower still.'

'I can't.'

'Very wise. I wouldn't either.' He glanced at his watch. 'Shall we eat?'

The rest of the evening passed more quickly than Winter had anticipated. The plates of wild boar, despite Olenka's best efforts, looked like something out of a crime scene. The meat was blood-red and extremely tough. The arty scoops of mashed potato might have come from a tin, and the decorative crescents of red cabbage badly needed seasoning. The wine, on the other hand, was excellent. Winter had the best part of a bottle of Chambertin to himself, and by the time Olenka escorted him off the boat, he was beginning to regret it.

On the fantail he turned to give Kokh a goodbye wave, but the Russian seemed to have disappeared. Conversationally, over dinner, the stand-off on a price for Bazza's stake in Kubla Khan had given them nowhere to go. Winter's knowledge of football was rudimentary, and Kokh hadn't shown much interest in talking about anything else. In the end Winter had found himself discussing the Battle of Trafalgar with the girl. It turned out she had a degree in naval history from St Petersburg University and was deeply impressed by Nelson's boldness in breaking the French and Spanish line.

As he stepped onto the gangway he gave her a peck on the cheek.

'England expects.' He squeezed her arm. 'That's all you need to know.'

Olenka smiled and told him to take care. There was something in her voice that might, under different circumstances, have sounded a warning note, but Winter was far too pissed to notice.

The bodyguards were waiting in the black 4 x 4. They watched him plotting an uncertain course across the dock and one of them leaned back to release the rear door. The moment he got in they were on the move, pulling a tight U-turn and carving a path back into the traffic on the main road. An angry *parp-parp* from an oncoming truck brought Winter to his senses. He forced himself upright on the back seat, steadying himself as the guy behind the wheel weaved around a slowing bus and floored the accelerator.

'In a hurry?' he said vaguely.

There was no answer from the front. He was aware of the driver's eyes in the rear-view mirror, scanning the road behind, and the other guy half turned in his seat, peering back. Winter thought nothing of it, and once they'd cleared the traffic and found a clear road before them, he lay back against the plumpness of the leather seat and closed his eyes, trying to review the evening aboard the yacht.

He and Kokh had been through the pantomime of negotiation, as Winter had planned. The last thing he'd wanted was a decent-sized cheque to get *Pompey First* off the hook – that would have to wait for Skelley – and he'd therefore tabled a bid he knew Kokh would reject out of hand. At that point, in the way of these things, he'd assumed there might be some appetite or room for compromise, but the ruthlessness of Kokh's counter-offer had taken his breath away. Not for a moment had he believed all the bollocks about extortion rackets and protection money. Neither did he buy how difficult and costly it was to get state backing. On the contrary, according to Bazza the locals were falling over themselves to flog off vast areas of the coast. No, Kokh – like every other Russian businessman – could scent blood in the water. If Bazza's little empire was haemorrhaging money, then Kubla Khan's junior partner was there for the taking.

He opened his eyes. They were in the tunnel now, speeding away from Kotor. The traffic was thinner here, but the guy in the front passenger seat was still peering back, checking the road behind. Winter did the same. Maybe four hundred metres behind them he could see a pair of headlights. The vehicle looked like another 4 x 4, white this time.

The guy in the passenger seat murmured something to the driver. Already the 80 kph signs were flashing past, but Winter felt the punch of the big engine as the Audi surged forward. By the time they burst out of the tunnel back into the darkness, the digital speedo was showing 187 kph.

They slowed briefly for an upcoming bend, accelerated hard again, then the Audi began to shudder as the driver stamped hard on the brakes. Winter had time to register the blur of a T-junction before they were drifting sideways onto the major road. The manoeuvre was a punt. They were on the wrong side of the road, still travelling at speed, but luck and blind faith spared them oncoming traffic. A twitch of the wheel took them back to the right-hand side of the road. In the throw of the headlights Winter caught the glitter of broken glass in an approaching lay-by. Seconds later the driver hit the brakes again, hauled the Audi off the road and killed the headlights. Winter, still peering out of the rear window, hung on to a grab handle as the Audi bumped to a halt on the rough gravel.

Back down the carriageway the white 4 x 4 had stopped at the T-junction. After a second or two it turned left, away from the lay-by, towards Budva, and disappeared into the darkness. Winter did his best to compose himself. Maybe, after all, Kokh had been right. Maybe Montenegro was as lawless as he'd claimed. Maybe Winter had stepped into an ongoing turf war, which would explain a great deal about Kokh's treatment of his junior partner. He turned back, meaning to pursue the thought a little further, but his attention was caught by the guy in the passenger seat. He had a mobile in one hand and an automatic pistol in the other. Mercifully, as he began a muttered conversation, he returned the gun to the glove box beneath the dashboard.

Winter was back at the hotel by midnight. A circuitous route had taken them up through the mountains on one flank of the valley, via a succession of tight bends and dizzying drops, to a much bigger road that approached Budva from the east. Winter had tried to coax conversation from his minders but failed completely. Knowing his reliance on these guys was total, he sat in the darkness resigned to whatever might happen next. Tomorrow, he told himself, he would take an early cab back over the border. From there he could find a coach north along the coast. By lunchtime, with luck, he could be light years away from the madness of Montenegro. When he finally reported back to Mackenzie, he'd salt the disappointment of Kokh's offer with a full account of exactly how these guys did business. You're lucky I'm still in one piece, he'd tell Bazza. Nikki Kokh? Kubla Khan? Melorcorp? Best of fucking luck.

Some kind of celebration was in full swing at the Hotel Neptun. Winter collected his room key from reception, picked his way through a scrum of partying twenty-somethings spilling out of the hotel's function room and headed for the lift. His room was on the top floor of the three-storey building. He shut the window and pulled the curtains across to soften the noise from downstairs. In the tiny bathroom he cleaned his teeth, rinsed his face and spent a moment or two eyeing his image in the mirror. A couple of years ago an evening like this – especially with Bazza in tow – might have yielded a laugh or two. Now he knew he simply wanted out. He was too old, too battered and – to be honest – just a little nervous. Bazza had a talent for short cuts, but life had a habit of getting even, and Winter didn't want to be around when their collective luck ran out. No, he told himself. Now is the time to acknowledge the odds and draw the only sane conclusion. He and Bazza had come to the end of the road. What he needed now was deliverance. Back in the bedroom Winter set the alarm, stripped to his boxers and climbed into bed. The party downstairs was as noisy as ever, but thanks to the Chambertin he was asleep within minutes.

Hours later, he'd no idea when, he surfaced again, trying to remember where he was, trying to put together the grey shapes of the built-in wardrobe and dressing table beyond the foot of the bed. The party was over. Out in the grounds of the hotel he could hear the soft patter of rain. From miles away, through the gap in the curtains, he caught a brief flicker of lightning followed by a low growl of thunder.

He rolled over, wondering what time it was, peering in the half-darkness at the digital clock. 03.41. He lay back for a moment, listening for the next peal of thunder, then he became aware of another sound, much closer. There were footsteps in the corridor outside. They paused at his door. He heard a low voice, male, followed by a muttered reply. Then came the scraping of a key in the lock. His lock.

Winter was halfway out of bed, his bare feet on the carpet, when the door eased open. Against the lights of the corridor outside he could see the silhouettes of two men, then a third. They slipped into his room, turned on the light, closed and locked the door behind them. Two of them were big, thick-necked, heavily muscled across the chest and shoulders. The third was smaller, thinner. All three wore ski masks. The ski mask on the little guy carried a Lamborghini logo.

'What the fuck—'

Winter was trying to get to his feet. One of the bigger guys lifted him bodily by his upper arms, spun him round, then threw him to the floor. Winter, trying not to vomit, could taste Chambertin. Moments later he felt the bite of cable ties around his wrists. Someone had their foot in the small of his back. He tried to lift his head, tried to struggle, but it was hopeless. Whenever he moved, he took a kicking, first his ribs, then his head. His head was exploding. He knew, at all costs, he musn't succumb to the waves of blackness threatening to engulf him. That way he'd probably end up dead.

'What the fuck do you want?' he managed.

Through one half-closed eye he became aware of a face close to his. He wasn't sure but he thought it was Lamborghini. He tried to focus on the oblong of scarlet Lycra around the mouth.

The man's breath stank. He had thick lips, oddly distinctive, and evil little ferret teeth. Winter tried to turn his head away.

'We have lots of time. Time is not a problem.' Heavy accent. And a strange high-pitched laugh at the end that told Winter he was probably doomed. These guys were psychos, no doubt about it. Definitely party time.

'Just tell me what you want,' Winter mumbled.

Lamborghini had got to his feet again. Winter heard the click of the minibar opening and a rattle of glass. Then came the sigh of bedsprings and a soft *fizz* as someone settled on the bed and pulled the tab from a can of lager.

Lamborghini seemed to be in charge. Winter could see his runners, brand-new Nike High-Tops, just like Makins.

'Mr Kubla Khan,' he said. 'Welcome to Montenegro. Welcome to Budva. You like it here? You like our country? You like that you can make money from us? That makes you feel good? Taking our money?'

Winter tried to explain he'd no intention of taking their money. On the contrary, he'd come to give his stake *back*.

'To who?'

'Kokh. Nikki Kokh.'

'Kokh is a dog. Worse than a dog.'

'You're right.'

'Kokh would screw a donkey if there was money in it.' He translated the joke for the benefit of his mates. One of them laughed. Then he turned back to Winter. 'You like Kokh? You think Kokh is OK?'

'I think Kokh screws everyone. You, me, everyone.'

'So why do you do business with this man?'

'Because that's the way it is.'

'And now you regret it?'

'Now I wish you'd leave me fucking alone.'

Winter saw the High-Top coming. He tried to turn his head away, but the blow caught him high on his temple above his ear. More pain.

'You think we're joking, Mr Kubla Khan? Because that would be a mistake. Maybe you should have come as a tourist. We like tourists. We treat tourists like friends. But you're a businessman. And businessmen are dogs.'

Winter was wondering whether they had a white Audi 4 x 4 outside. And whether this encounter would go on until they were tired of kicking the shit out of him. One way or another, he knew he had to move the conversation on.

'You want money?'

'Of course.'

'Take it.'

'Thank you. What else have you got for us?'

'Nothing. Money's all I've got.'

'An apology maybe? You want to say sorry? About Kokh? About Kubla Khan?'

'Whatever.'

'Whatever?' Lamborghini didn't understand.

'Yeah. I'm sorry we put money in. I'm sorry I ever heard of Kubla Khan. Is that OK? Is that enough?'

The laugh again – soft, weirdly intimate, a small whisper of delight from someone who very definitely liked hurting people. Winter hadn't a clue what might happen next and knew there was no advantage in trying to guess. The last thirty years had put him in some dodgy situations, but he'd never been as kippered as this. Karl Sparrow, he thought. But worse.

Someone was at the minibar again. Another finger tugging at a can pull-tag. Winter caught a murmured exchange from the direction of the bed. Then came that same laugh, a gesture of approval.

'Gin or vodka?' Lamborghini enquired.

Winter shook his head. The last thing he wanted was a drink.

'Please ... choose ...'

'No.'

'I said choose.' The ribs this time.

Winter gasped with pain. 'Vodka,' he managed.

'You don't say please in your country?'

'Please.'

'Good. Very good. You know something about business-men? They learn very fast.'

Winter swallowed hard, fighting the rising gusts of nausea, wondering how on earth he was supposed to drink in a position like this. Then he caught the tiny scrape as someone twisted the top off the miniature and moments later he felt the trickle of liquid as the bottle was upturned over his bare back. After this came another bottle. Then a third. Winter was trying to visualise what it must look like, the spirits running over the whiteness of his flesh. Then came Lamborghini's question, freezing his blood.

'You mind if we smoke? My friends and I? You mind if we light up?'

As if to make the point, he crouched low beside Winter's head again. Winter could see the lighter. It was a Bic. Lamborghini flicked it twice, inches from Winter's eye.

'You know what happens next? All that booze? You know what we do at Christmas? Before we roast the meat? You know what we use instead of vodka or gin? We use slivowitz, plum brandy, and you know how that works? It burns. In the end it makes the meat crisp. Beautiful smell. Beautiful taste. Happy Christmas, Mr Businessman, eh?'

Winter turned his head away. He didn't want Lamborghini to see the tears in his eyes. This was worse than dying. This was humiliation, total abasement. In a minute or two these animals were going to set him on fire. And watch.

Nothing happened. No conversation. No more taunts. Winter still had his head turned towards the bed and the window. There came another fork of lightning, much closer this time, the thunder deafening. Winter could see one of the two big guys sitting on the edge of the bed, his huge hands folded over his knees, his eyes flicking back and forth behind the ski mask, a punter with the best seat in the house, waiting to see whether the main attraction measured up.

Winter stirred, wondering whether his burning flesh would trigger the fire alarms and who would eventually arrive to find his charring body. Over the years, like everyone else in the world, he'd seen news footage of protestors dousing themselves with petrol and then striking a match. There was a terrible fascination in watching a human being engulfed in flame, and he'd always marvelled at their commitment. To bear the pain without flinching – totally immobile, often cross-legged, the way it happened with Buddhist monks – was beyond his imagination. That kind of courage spoke of a belief he simply didn't have. When the time came, as it surely would, he knew he'd wriggle and howl and scream exactly the way these guys had planned it. They probably had their mobiles ready for the moment he caught fire, and once they legged it would doubtless circulate the pictures to anyone foolish enough to cross the Montenegran mafia. Our country. Our coastline. Your fucking profits.

There was another clap of thunder, virtually overhead. The entire hotel seemed to shake. Winter began to shiver, knowing he couldn't take much more of this, all too aware that the waiting – in exactly the way they'd planned it – was probably worse than the event itself. He'd had enough. He wanted it over.

'Do it,' he said.

'What you say?'

'Do it. Just fucking do it.'

Lamborghini muttered something he didn't catch. The guy on the bed nodded and stood up. He stepped out of view and moments later came the tug of a zip and Winter became aware of the guy looming above him. Then he felt the splash of something warm on his bare back. He tried to put a picture to what he was hearing, to what he was feeling, and then he realised the guy was pissing all over him, sluicing away the alcohol from the miniatures. A couple of cans of Heineken at least, Winter thought. Thank God for lager.

'Your lucky night, Mr Businessman.' It was Lamborghini again. The spotless High-Tops. 'Next time not so lucky ... eh?'

The big guy had finished. He zipped himself up, gave Winter a playful parting kick and then joined his mates by the door. To Winter's immense relief they appeared to be getting ready to leave. For a second or two he wondered whether this was simply his imagination playing tricks. Maybe his brain was scrambled. Maybe he'd already burned to death and by some trick of the mind had been spared the agony until later. Maybe this whole thing was some grotesque nightmare. But then Lamborghini was back in his face. He was holding what looked like a scrap of white paper between his forefinger and thumb.

'We leave you this, Mr Businessman. A little present. A little gift. From Montenegro.'

Winter felt a blade sawing through the cable tie around his wrists. Then, quite suddenly, his hands were free. The blood surged back into the stiffness of his fingers, a hot scalding pain as bad as anything he'd suffered, and he rolled onto his side in time to see his tormentors leaving. Lamborghini was the last through the door. He didn't look back.

Winter waited and waited, praying they didn't have second thoughts and come back to finish him off. The rain was much heavier now, and when he'd locked and bolted the door and finally made it across to the window, the patches of grass visible beneath the security lights were already beginning to flood. For a long moment he watched the darting blue fingers of lightning against the blackness of the surrounding mountains, dazed, trembling, his bare flesh icy cold, and then he pulled himself together, knowing he had to get organised, repair a little of the damage, make a plan.

Limping towards the bathroom, he noticed the scrap of paper on the carpet. He paused, eyeing it. Bending, even breathing, was incredibly painful. With immense difficulty, he

retrieved the paper. It was a bus ticket. For tomorrow. 09.35.
To somewhere called Herceg Novi. The message couldn't have
been plainer. Leave.

Chapter thirteen

On those nights when Bazza Mackenzie couldn't sleep – increasingly common – he'd taken to creeping out of the big double bedroom in the house on Sandown Road and making his way downstairs to the privacy of his den. Marie, who was a light sleeper herself, had been aware of this for weeks but had chosen to say nothing. Like everyone else in the family she'd recognised that something was happening to her husband, that something was changing him. Her daughter, Ezzie, had put it down to the excitements of the coming election, but Marie, who knew Baz best of all, wasn't so sure. A phrase of Winter's had stuck in her mind. Paul had said he was becoming unhinged. In some deep and maybe permanent way he'd lost it. What 'it' comprised was not clear, but Marie, like Winter himself, was fearful about the consequences. For one thing, her husband had started calling her Ma.

Marie lost track of how long she spent that night lying in the darkness waiting for Baz's return. Once, carried on the wind, she caught a distant church bell toll four o'clock. A while afterwards she heard the low rumble of the first of the day's FastCats powering up for the run across the Solent to Ryde Pier. Finally, when Baz still didn't appear, she slipped on a dressing gown and went downstairs.

Mackenzie was sitting at his desk in the den, staring at his PC. When the door opened behind him he didn't seem the least surprised to see Marie. He gestured at the screen and told her to pull up a chair.

'Fucking extraordinary, Ma,' he said. 'The boy's a genius.'

'You mean this Andy?'

'Of course.'

Marie sat down. She'd never met Makins but had no doubt about the impact he'd made on her husband. Guys who wanted to sell you their services, said Baz, were ten a penny. Even consultants like Kinder weren't that hard to lay hands on. But truly special individuals, genuine one-offs, were bloody rare, and in the shape of Andy Makins Baz had found a prime example.

'Here ... look.' Mackenzie scrolled back to the beginning of what looked like a very long email. Marie peered at the subject heading.

'Smoutland?'

'That's code for Pompey.'

'But why Smout?'

'They're a family, Ma, three generations, all dysfunctional as fuck, total muppets.'

The Smouts, Bazza explained, were Pompey born and bred. The oldest couple, Arthur and Marj, had an allotment at the end of Locksway Road. It was the love of their tiny lives and nothing would ever spoil it for them. Not the bastard little scrotes who broke in at night and necked vast quantities of White Lightning and trampled all over their veggies. Not the thieving pikeys who jemmied the lock off their little garden hut and stole their power tools. Not the man from the council who harassed them with letters about late payment for use of the communal stand pipe. Not even the black aphids that laid waste their crop of tomatoes. No, in the world of Arthur and Marj there was room for only one emotion.

'Which is?' Marie, in spite of herself, was interested.

'Gratitude. They're grateful, Ma, and you know why? Because life has never given them anything, not a penny, not a single decent break. And so bad news, all the shit and aggravation I've just mentioned, is all they expect.'

'That's ridiculous.'

'No, it's not, it's funny. And weird. But it gets better.'

He scrolled on through the email. The middle generation of Smouts was represented by Dave and Jackie. Dave occupied one half of a cell in Winchester Prison after being nicked on a drugs offence. Jackie, bless her heart, visited him every Thursday afternoon, half past three, on the dot.

'In real life, Ma, you get to meet in the visiting room, but Andy wants to go one better. He's after one of those glass partitions. What Jackie does, she arrives every Thursday with a week's supply of the *News* and holds the pages up against the glass, one by one. That way she doesn't have to say very much, which is fine by Dave, and he gets to stay in touch. Plus we obviously hand-pick the bits of the paper that get the message across.'

'Message?'

'Inbreds stoning the swans on the lake down at Great Salterns. Kids living rough in bus shelters. OAPs treble-locking their doors at night to keep the Kosovans out. Welcome-to-Pompey stuff.'

'This is some kind of film?'

'Video, Ma. Andy's going to upload it to YouTube. Kind of soapy thing. Lots of episodes, all shot specially.'

'But why someone like Dave?'

'Because he's just like his dad. Grateful. Humble. Doing his bird the way he should. No complaints. No one to blame but himself. Start watching this stuff and you'll piss yourself laughing.'

'I don't get it.'

'You will, Ma, you will. Because Dave and Jackie have a daughter – and you know what? She's just the same. Sweet as you like. Takes life on the chin. Grateful as fuck for sweet fuck all.'

Young Shelley, said Baz, lives in a council flat in Somerstown way up on the tenth floor. The men in her life drift by from time to time, but she's the one who has to sort out the kids.

'How many?'

'Three. Tyler, Jordan and Scottie. They're nippers, tearaways, totally out of control. In episode one Scottie dumps the family cat out of the window. This girl has fuck-all money, zero prospects, never goes out of an evening, never has a chance to enjoy herself, plus she really loved that cat, but you know what?'

'She's grateful.'

'Yeah. Big time. She loves the council. She loves the view. She even loves the old dosser in the flat next door who's always trying to get into her knickers. He's had a hard life. It's not his fault his dick's got a mind of its own. Plus, of course, she loves her kids to death. The cat thing was a mistake. Tyler never meant to set fire to the sofa. Jordan only ran away because she got into a bit of a muddle. Brilliant. Can't fail.'

'But what's the point –' Marie nodded at the screen '– to all this? What does it mean? What's it trying to *say*?'

'It's not trying to say anything, Ma, except that people like the Smouts are total retards. They trust everyone and get fuck all in return. People are going to die laughing when they watch this lot, especially the kids. The Smouts are weirdos. They're so not 2009. Compulsory viewing, Ma. *Cult* viewing. Do us no end of good.'

'Us?'

'*Pompey First*. Andy's doing it so every episode ends with our logo. That's all you need, just the association. Andy calls it viral. It's a marketing thing. We're spreading the word, but doing it in a way no one's ever done before.'

'But I still don't get it. What are you really saying about these people?'

'The Smouts? That they're old-style Pompey. That they haven't moved on. That they're too stupid and trusting to look out for themselves. That they leave themselves wide open and get turned over as a result. This is a pitch for the kids, Ma, like I say, and when Andy says it'll put us on the map I believe him. YouTube goes everywhere. We're talking an audience of millions.'

'Kids as in adolescents?'

'Kids as in students. Over eighteen. With a vote. And it doesn't stop there, Ma. These days you can be thirty-plus and still be a kid.'

With some reluctance Marie nodded. From what she could see, the Smout storyline was silly and cruel and – to be frank – offensive. But maybe Baz was right. Maybe that's what it took to sell a political message these days. One way or another, you had to make an impact.

'That's right, Ma. That's exactly what Andy says. You have to give the punters a smack in the face to get their attention. Either that, or you make them piss themselves laughing. After that you can probably sell them any fucking thing.'

'Through the Smouts?'

'Exactly. This is about a bunch of muppets banged up in their own little world. Of course they're bizarre. Of course it's bad taste. But we're talking relics, Ma, real dinosaurs. Life ain't like that any more, and everyone knows it, especially the kids. You grab what you can and you make sure no other bugger gets it off you.'

'Great.'

'You're complaining?' Mackenzie gestured round. 'Six bedrooms? Sea views? Couple of decent motors in the drive? Money to make sure the kids are OK. You think all that happened by accident?'

'Of course it didn't.'

'Well, then …' He put his hand on her arm. 'Chill out, Ma. Like I say, the guy's a genius.'

Marie knew the conversation was at an end. The last thing she wanted was any kind of row. What her husband needed now was a good night's sleep, and she knew he'd find his way back upstairs in his own good time.

'I'm going back to bed,' she said. 'Any word from Paul?'

Mackenzie shook his head, returning his attention to the screen. Winter, for the time being, was off the plot. The future, just now, belonged to the Smouts.

Chapter fourteen

A long hot shower did wonders for Winter's morale. He'd
checked the door again and wedged a chair under the handle,
but on balance he didn't think they'd be back. Lamborghini and
his mates had come to deliver a message, and whichever way
you looked at it there was fuck-all room for ambiguity. Foreign
investment, on the wrong terms, was deeply unwelcome. Kubla
Khan, for whatever reason, had pissed them off. Winter, with
his pathetic 10 per cent, was part of that operation, and they
wanted him out of town. No problem. He might not be on the
09.35 to Herceg Novi, but one way or another he was about
to head north.

He reached for a towel and with great care began to dry
himself. He could be back in Croatia by mid-morning. A coach
would take him the rest of the way. The prospect of what
lay at the end of this next stage in his journey was more than
welcome.

He wrapped the towel round his waist and inspected the
damage in the mirror over the sink. His face and torso were
already red and swollen from the beating. Breathing was painful, and a cough or even a laugh didn't bear thinking about. A
visit to a doctor or a hospital might be wise, but he suspected
broken ribs and knew there was little you could do but wait
until they healed.

He brushed his teeth, grateful that they at least were still intact, and then popped a handful of Ibuprofen before making his way slowly back to bed. To his intense pleasure, a single miniature had survived the raid on the minibar. It was cognac. He sank heavily onto the edge of the bed and tipped the bottle to his mouth. The spirit caught at the back of his throat, making him cough, and the pain from his ribs was every bit as savage as he'd feared, but the warmth that came afterwards justified the rest of the bottle.

Feeling immeasurably better, he climbed into bed. By now it was nearly five in the morning. It was still dark outside and rain was lashing at the window, but the storm was drifting inland and the occasional rumble of thunder sounded like shellfire deep in the mountains. He put his head on the pillow and closed his eyes, taking a tiny shallow breath from time to time, waiting for the tablets to kick in. He knew that the images pasted on the back of his retina – the High-Top Nikes, the circle of scarlet Lycra around the fleshiness of Lamborghini's mouth – would probably be with him for ever, but he hadn't been barbecued and for that he was deeply grateful. With the beginnings of a smile on his face, he drifted off to sleep.

When he woke up it was broad daylight. For a moment everything that had happened in the middle of the night felt unreal, a passing nightmare, but then he saw the damp stains on the carpet and caught the sharp sour smell of piss and knew once again that he'd been lucky. He eased himself out of bed and limped to the bathroom. Everything hurt, and when he checked himself in the mirror he scarcely recognised the face that stared back. One eye had nearly closed, and a huge bruise down the side of his face was beginning to purple. With infinite care he washed and shaved and then shuffled back to the bedroom. The rain had stopped now, and he opened the window to try and get rid of the smell. From somewhere below came the clatter of cutlery. Breakfast time, he thought, amazed that he felt the slightest bit hungry.

Under the circumstances he settled for room service, ordering a plate of ham and eggs. By the time it turned up, he'd managed to get dressed. A sullen young girl handed over the tray, stared at his face and hurried away. He sat on the bed, ate the eggs and most of the ham, and then glanced at his watch. Five to nine. He lifted the phone and waited for reception to answer. He checked that the room had already been paid for and ordered a cab. Putting the phone down, he suddenly remembered his wallet. His Blackberry, he knew, had left with his visitors, but last night, before going to bed, he'd tucked his wallet under the pillow. To his surprise it was still there. Reception phoned ten minutes later. Mr Sparrow's cab had arrived.

The driver for once spoke decent English. He didn't spare Winter's face a second glance.

'Hotel Georgi?'

'Sure.'

'And afterwards you can take me to Dubrovnik?'

'No problem.'

They settled on a price. The drive to the Hotel Georgi took them to the northern arm of the bay, up beyond the Old Town. Looking down from the corniche, Winter could make out the lines of the citadel, stone grey against the blueness of the sea. The weather had cleared after the storm, and the Adriatic was a shade of blue you'd barely believe on a poster. A guy from the café beside the citadel was putting out sun loungers on the beach and one was already occupied. To Winter, after last night, images like these were deeply comforting. They meant that Budva could, after all, deliver what it said on the tin.

The Hotel Georgi stood on the edge of a sheer drop to the ocean. According to the cabby, the place owed its name to a legendary centre forward in one of the Moscow Spartak teams. Given Kokh's passion for football, that seemed all too possible.

'Back in half an hour.' Winter eased himself out of the cab. 'Or maybe less.'

In reception he asked to speak to Arkady. He'd no idea whether or not the Russian had returned from Podgorica but thought it was worth a try. One way or another, once they'd done a little catching up, Kokh's lieutenant might have an idea or two about Lamborghini.

The young man behind reception held Winter's gaze then lifted the phone, confirmed Arkady was in his office and told Winter to take a seat. Minutes later Arkady stepped into the lobby. The broad smile on his face vanished the moment he set eyes on Winter. He stared down at him, then shook his head.

'Don't tell me ...' he said.

'Yeah.' Winter struggled to his feet. 'Welcome to Montenegro.'

Arkady's office was up on the first floor. The position of Security Chief had earned him a breathtaking view across the bay. Winter gazed at it, then accepted Arkady's offer of a chair.

'You want coffee? Something stronger?'

'No, thanks.'

'So tell me ...' Arkady gestured at his face.

Winter kept to the bare details. He'd been jumped in the middle of the night by three monkeys who didn't have much time for either Kokh or Kubla Khan. They'd known where to find him and – more to the point – they'd made themselves at home.

'Description?' Arkady had pulled out a notebook.

'Hopeless. Nothing to go on. They all wore ski masks. Two big guys. One not so big. Locals, as far as I could judge. That's all I can tell you.'

'But you want me to do something about this?'

'I want you to tell me who these guys might have been.'

'I've no idea.'

'Montenegrans, you think?'

'Might have been.'

'Local hoods?'

'It's possible.'

'But that's all? Just possible?'

Arkady was frowning. In Budva, he said, the line between

business and crime was very thin, but most of the serious players rarely pulled this kind of stunt. They were too disorganised, too lazy. These guys had more money than they knew what to do with. Nights were for shagging. Why make things complicated?

'So who, then?'

'I told you. I've no idea.'

He opened a drawer and settled a bottle on the desk. Next came two glasses. Winter was staring at the bottle. Slivowitz.

'You're staying a while?'

'No.'

'Pity. I thought maybe tonight ...' One huge hand reached for a framed photo on the desk and angled it towards Winter. The girl had draped herself around Arkady's suntanned shoulders and was blowing a kiss at the camera. Winter recognised the fantail on Kokh's yacht. Judging by the crowds on the beach in the distance it must have been high summer.

'Her name's Milena.' Arkady grinned his big conspiratorial cop grin. 'And she has lots of friends.'

'Afraid not. I have to go.'

'We can't tempt you?'

'No.'

'Shame, eh? You want to see more?' Without waiting for an answer he dived into the drawer again and produced a photo album. 'Start at the back. It's more interesting.'

While Arkady splashed slivowitz into the glasses, Winter leafed back through the album. This time Arkady was up in the mountains, same girl. A fresh fall of snow gave the shots the look of a fairy tale, two pairs of ski tracks snaking away into the distance.

'Nikki has a place up near Zabljak. Come back in the winter. After Christmas is best. Milena will find someone nice. You'll be our guest. Everything on the house, eh?'

Mention of Christmas, like the bottle of slivowitz, took Winter back to last night. He wondered about sharing some of the smaller print with Arkady but decided against it. While Arkady rhapsodised about the après-ski, Winter turned page after page. The shots were much the same, all featuring Milena, but then came something different, a bunch of skiers gathered on some kind of terrace. Behind them the snow-capped mountains were in deep shadow. Someone must have just made a joke, or maybe the day's skiing had been especially sensational, because all these guys were in stitches. It was a nice shot, companionable, celebratory. It was one of those unforgettable moments you'd stick in an album like this and keep for ever. Winter was about to move on but then a particular face caught his eye in the very middle of the group. He was shorter than the rest. Like everyone else he was laughing fit to bust, his mouth wide open, thick lips, a tiny row of teeth. Winter felt a sudden chill. The scarlet ski jacket was badged with the Lamborghini logo.

'Who's that?' Winter showed Arkady the shot.

'Which one?'

'That one. Him.'

'His name's Radun. We all call him Coco. You know the clown? Coco the Clown? He's a real madman, this guy, a real jester. He does favours for us sometimes. Nikki loves him.' He paused and looked up. 'Why do you ask?'

Winter was struggling to his feet. He swayed for a moment, his hand extended. Thanks to Arkady, everything was suddenly all too clear.

'It's been a pleasure, mate.' He managed to muster a smile. 'Give Nikki my best, eh?'

It took a while for Winter's anger to cool. He rode in the back of the cab, staring out at the endless construction sites, wondering why it had taken him so long to suss out exactly what had happened back in the hotel room. It wasn't the local mafia warning him off; it was Kokh himself. As they passed through Kotor again, on the way up to the Croatian border, he was tempted to get the cabby to stop so he could pay the yacht a second visit, but then he realised he had nothing to say. It was, yet again, the old story. Russians were gangsters. They robbed foreigners the way they robbed their own people. Get involved with the likes of Bazza Mackenzie and this is what happened. You fell into bad company. You risked first your dignity, then your liberty and finally – if you were very unlucky – your life. Was that what he really wanted? Was that any way to end his days? Winter shook his head. This thing had to end, he told himself. Not on Mackenzie's terms but his own.

By the time they got to the border, Winter had found a kind of peace. A conversation with the cabby had wised him up about coach options north along the coast, and it turned out that the guy even knew Porec.

'Nice place,' he said. 'You'll like it.'

Winter took him at his word. Dubrovnik coach station lay alongside the ferry terminal. Winter settled the cab fare and made his way to the booking office. By now it was gone midday. Porec was up on the Istrian Peninsula, at the very top of Croatia. To get there by coach you had to go to Rijeka first. The coach left in an hour's time and wouldn't be in Rijeka until way past midnight, too late for an onward connection to Porec until the next day.

Winter asked about alternatives. A flight might be possible, but he'd have to go via Zagreb and nothing was guaranteed. There were no trains and the last thing he fancied was renting a car.

'Fine. I'll take the coach.'

He bought a ticket for Rijeka and retired to a café around the corner. He'd promised to phone ahead about his travel plans, but without his Blackberry he was stuffed. He ordered a coffee and sat back, enjoying the warmth of the sunshine on his battered face. She'd given him the address of the apartment she was renting in Porec and had offered to meet him off the coach but he'd told her it wouldn't be necessary. Once he'd made it to the bus station, he could find his own way. Better, he told himself, to simply turn up. Life, after all, was full of surprises.

It was Misty's idea to make a start on Winter's packing. She drove over from Hayling Island immediately after lunch and stood outside the communal entrance to Blake House, waiting for her daughter to buzz her in. The redecorating was going more slowly than Trude had planned. She'd taken yesterday afternoon off to go shopping with a girlfriend and had only just started on the spare room.

'What are you doing?'

Trude was watching her mother emptying Winter's big double wardrobe.

'I'm moving Paul out. He's coming over to Hayling.'

'Does he know about this?'

'Of course he does. He can't wait.'

'But this ...' Trudy nodded at the twin lines of suits hanging from the picture rail, one for chucking out, one for keeping. 'Doesn't the poor man even get a say?'

'Paul trusts me. I've got taste, pet. He hasn't. A lot of this stuff is tat.'

Trude shrugged and returned to the spare room. She had Winter's radio on full blast and was soon singing along to Muse.

Misty had brought a couple of big cardboard boxes over from Hayling. Back in Winter's bedroom she began to fill them with underwear, socks, shoes, belts for his trousers – anything, in short, that he couldn't do without. The logic was simple. If everything Winter needed was over at Misty's place, then he had to be there too.

Trude had reappeared at the door. She'd sussed what Misty was up to.

'That's evil, Mum. I feel really sorry for the guy.'

'Men are lazy, pet. They hate making decisions. Baz was always the same. They get so far then all they need is a little push.'

'There's nothing little about that.' Trude nodded at the brimming boxes. 'Paul's going to be really pissed off. You can't just walk into someone's life like this and help yourself. That's kidnap.'

'Nonsense.'

Misty hadn't finished. At the bottom of Winter's wardrobe, once she'd emptied it of shoes, she'd found a black briefcase. She carried it through to the big lounge, where the light was better, and settled herself on the sofa. A lot of this stuff would be personal, she knew that, but only a couple of days ago Winter had assured her that he had nothing to hide, that everything he owned was hers to share, that there was no one more important in his life. This little declaration, at the end of a decent bottle of Chablis, had done wonders for Misty's confidence, and now she couldn't wait to cement the foundations of their new life together. Misty had never expected a great deal from any of the many relationships in her life. This time she promised herself it was going to be different.

The briefcase was unlocked. Inside, among a litter of assorted photos, she found a large Manila envelope stuffed with legal-looking documents. She took it out and opened it. Winter's birth certificate. A couple of insurance policies. His wedding certificate. A couple of old driving licences. Agreements relating to the sale of the Bedhampton bungalow he'd shared with his wife. And, last of all, a smaller white envelope stamped *Personal*.

Misty hesitated for less than a second. Inside the envelope were two documents. One was a death certificate. Joan Christine Winter had died on 23 September 2000. Cause of death was recorded as pancreatic carcinoma. Misty looked at it a moment, then turned to the second document. She recognised Winter's handwriting at once – impatient, difficult to read, much like the man himself. She bent over the script, deciphering it word for word, knowing at once from the layout that it was a letter. He'd written it to Joannie, and judging by the date on the top he'd done it the day after she'd died.

The letter was confessional, full of regret, a long list of things he said he'd never had the time, nor the decency, nor the bottle to tell her. He said that she'd been brave, braver than he could ever be, and that she'd gone far too early. He said that she'd had more patience than anyone he'd ever met in his life, which was just as well because he knew he'd let her down. He wrote that he'd always loved her, truly loved her, but that he'd never quite got the knack of putting it into words. At the end, for the first time in his life, he realised that they should have had kids. Kids would have left him a tiny bit of her. Instead of now. When he had nothing.

Misty looked up. Trudy, standing with a paintbrush in her hand, was a blur.

'Mum ...?' She said uncertainly.

Misty shook her head, fumbled for a tissue.

'That's so fucking sad.' She nodded at the letter and blew her nose. 'I never realised.'

Embarrassed in front of her daughter, Misty fled to the kitchen. She'd make some tea, rustle up some biscuits, whatever. Trudy appeared at the open door. She wanted to know more.

Misty didn't know what to say. Parts of Winter that had always been a mystery to her – his reticence, the way he ducked certain kinds of questions, his refusal to talk about large tracts of his past – were suddenly a whole lot clearer.

'He's a good man, Trude. A good, good man.'

'Paul?'

'Yeah, Paul. I've always loved him. I've always loved his cheekiness, the risks he takes, how he gets away with stuff. Baz is the same. But you know something? I've always missed the poetry in him, the *soul*. And you know why? Because deep down I didn't think he had any. I thought what you saw was what you got. Turns out I'm wrong, thank fuck.'

They shared a pot of tea, nibbled a biscuit or two and talked a whole lot more about Paul Winter. How easily he seemed to have handled the move to the Dark Side. How long it had taken Baz to accept that this guy was for real. And how hard he'd worked, especially recently, to keep the Mackenzie show on the road.

'Some nights, Trude, he's just so knackered he can barely talk. I never like to ask because I can be a coward sometimes, but lately I don't think things are going too well. We rely on Baz, me and you, probably more than we like to admit. But here's hoping, eh?'

'Hoping what, Mum?'

'That Paul sorts it.'

Trudy agreed. She liked Winter a lot, always had. He was a laugh. He made you feel good. Nothing seemed to bother him.

'Exactly, pet. Which is why I know something's going on. He's not the man he can be. Not at the moment, anyway.'

'Yeah? You think so?'

'I know it.'

Trude slipped off the kitchen stool and gave her mother a long hug. Then, with a tact that took her mother by surprise, she went next door and began to carry the suits back to Winter's bedroom. Misty did nothing, just sat on the other stool staring into nowhere. By the time she summoned the energy to find out what her daughter was up to, the suits were back in the wardrobe and the boxes on the bed were empty.

Misty gazed round at the neatness of the bedroom, then blew her nose again.

'You think that's for the best?'

'Yes, Mum. And I think you should check the answerphone.'

'You what?'

'The answerphone. Next door. The call came in when I was painting earlier. Maybe you ought to have a listen.'

Misty went back to the lounge. Trude was right. There was a message waiting on the phone console. Misty pressed the replay button and turned to the window. A woman's voice, difficult to place. Could have been young. But maybe not.

'What's going on? I've been waiting for you to call. Are you still coming? Have you changed your mind? Does it spook you staying at my place? Or are you still in the UK? Just give me a clue, eh, and tell me we're still on.'

Misty played the message a second time. She didn't know whether she wanted to cry or do something a whole lot angrier. Paul had gone abroad to sort out a partner of Bazza's. Now this. She checked the display window on the answerphone. An eleven-digit number.

'Mum?'

She spun round to find Trudy behind her. Misty wanted to know about the prefix 00385.

'You looked it up?' she asked.

'Of course I did.'

'And?'

'Croatia.'

Chapter fifteen

Winter hadn't seen Maddox for five years. He'd first met her back in the Job when he'd busted a high-class brothel in Old Portsmouth. The place was run by a gay ex-radio DJ called Steve Richardson who'd spotted a niche in the market and persuaded a wealthy Iranian to stake him. He'd bought a brand-new penthouse apartment overlooking the Camber Dock and installed a couple of part-time toms. They were tasty, intelligent and cultured. One was an ex-student, the other a Latvian blonde with a qualification in sports physiotherapy.

Richardson, who was a talented cook, offered candlelit soirées with the best wines and the best food. After you'd feasted on foie gras and lobster, swapping gossip, impressing the girls, you could step next door for the fuck of your dreams. An evening chez Richardson wasn't cheap but he had no problem attracting customers. City solicitors, executives from Zurich and IBM, even the occasional naval officer, phoned for a discreet booking. When it came to the girls, they always had a choice. And most of them phoned early to reserve Maddox.

She was the ex-student. She had a rich father who lived in Paris. After the frustrations of an unfinished year at RADA, she'd done three years at Bristol studying English literature, earning herself a decent degree along with an enduring passion for a French poet called Arthur Rimbaud. Winter's first sight of her was on a DVD he'd seized when they busted Richardson.

Maddox, naked apart from a string of beads, was straddling an overweight businessman seconds away from coming. She had a body that reminded Winter of the showgirls Joannie liked to watch on TV, and when her bedmate climaxed she did something startling with a polythene bag full of ice cubes. For weeks afterwards Winter had treated the icebox in his fridge with something approaching reverence. Applied by the right person in the right place at the right time, a bag of ice cubes plainly took you somewhere very special indeed.

Maddox was undoubtedly the right person. In ways that Winter recognised only too well, she hid behind veil after veil of clever deceits, but once he'd managed to strip most of them away it turned out they had a lot to offer each other. In the shape of a punter who'd begun to frighten her, Maddox wanted a little protection. This, Winter was only too happy to provide. In return, when he became inexplicably sick, she had the grace and the patience to look after him.

By now Joannie was dead. The medics arrested Winter's brain tumour just in time, but he knew then, as he knew now, that he really owed his survival to two people who were a great deal closer. One of them was Jimmy Suttle. The other was Maddox. The fact that she could fuck you witless in three languages was immaterial. She'd become a mate.

An hour out of Rijeka, the coach to Porec was winding through the mountains. Winter was sitting at the back to spare passengers joining the coach the sight of his face. He'd enjoyed a decent night's sleep in a modest hotel near the bus station and was feeling a great deal better. Not least because of the prospect of being with Maddox again.

Once they'd seen off the brain tumour, he and Maddox had parted. She'd sold her apartment on Southsea seafront and lent Winter most of the profits to enable him to buy his perch in Blake House. On Winter's insistence, they'd drawn up a legal agreement and she'd thus acquired a 50 per cent share in the property. In the early years in Gunwharf, buoyed by the money

Bazza was paying him, Winter had toyed with buying Maddox out, but she'd disappeared to South America and the occasional postcards she sent never included any contact details. He'd therefore let matters slip, assuming she'd get in touch if and when she needed the money.

This, as it turned out, was exactly what happened. Only last month Winter had taken a call. For a moment or two he hadn't recognised her voice, but then he was suddenly back in the world of body oils, scented candles and desperate couplings before he got news of the latest CT scan. Now Maddox was selling real estate in Croatia. It was a nice enough life she'd found for herself, but the market was flat on its face and she was running out of money. She didn't want to make things tough for Winter but might he be able to repay the loan?

Winter, of course, had said yes. Partly because he owed her a great deal more than a simple cheque could ever repay and partly because it gave him an excuse to sell the flat and move on. Quite where his new direction might take him was anyone's guess, but now, just thirty-four kilometres from Porec, he knew he had a day or two in hand. He'd told both Misty and Baz he'd be back by the end of the week. Plenty of time to see what might be possible.

The bus station at Porec was five minutes from the waterfront. He showed the address Maddox had given him to the girl in the ticket office and she drew him a map. If you ignored the many developments that sprawled along the coast, she said, Porec itself wasn't a big town. Take the main road to the harbour. Turn right. Follow the road to the square. Carry straight on. Then look for a road on the left. Trgbrodogradilista was a nice address. Her friend happened to live in the same street.

Winter set off, following her directions. Minutes later he was on the waterfront. To the left a newish-looking marina. To the right a long thin promontory that must once have been the heart of the old town. Winter could see a church steeple and a row of hotels. A sleek catamaran advertising day trips to

Venice lay beside a pontoon. A thin scatter of tourists, mostly elderly, walked arm in arm in the afternoon sunshine. The air was still. The temperature was just right. He could smell baking chestnuts from a stall in the tiny waterfront market. The water, astonishingly clear, lapped at the ancient harbour wall. Winter peered down, watching the fish darting among the pebbles on the seabed, wondering if the Romans had got here first, and then he went across to a bench and sat down, determined to savour this moment. He felt unthreatened. He felt he'd finally turned some kind of corner in his life. He felt wonderful.

It was late afternoon before he moved again. Out in the bay a returning fishing boat was towing a cloud of seagulls. He watched until it found a berth beyond the marina, then got to his feet. He knew nothing about the working day in Croatia but guessed that Maddox might be home by now.

Trgbrodogradilista was a quiet residential street running up from the waterfront on the other side of the promontory. Number 8 lay halfway up the hill, a flat-fronted two-storey house in pitted yellow stucco with a narrow alley beside it. Winter paused at the front door and rang the bell. When there was no response, he tried again. Then he stepped back into the street and gazed up. A window on the top floor was open. He called Maddox's name, listened for a moment or two, then turned to the gate that barred access to the alley. Unlocked, it swung inward at his touch. He followed the path along the side of the property, body-checking around a pile of empty beer crates. At the back was a square of grubby courtyard with a drooping basketball hoop lashed to a spindly tree. The back door to the house was ajar. From deep inside came a buzzing noise, intermittent, distinctive, penetrating. It sounded, thought Winter, like a trapped insect. He knocked on the door and then pushed it fully open. Inside was a kitchen, surprisingly roomy. A tap was dripping onto a pile of dirty plates in the sink and among the clutter on the battered pine table Winter recognised a carton of aloe vera. Maddox had been mad about aloe vera. Some weeks she'd drink nothing else.

After a brief pause the buzzing started again, much louder this time. Winter crossed the kitchen and found himself in a dimly lit hall. The first of the doors on the right was an inch or two ajar and a light was on inside. The buzzing stopped. Then came the softest giggle, a woman's giggle, girlish, intimate, before the buzzing resumed. Winter hadn't a clue what Maddox might be up to, but he knew he owed her a decent entrance. He paused for a moment at the door and then went in.

The room was bare except for a table and two chairs. There was a faint smell of disinfectant. A woman sat in one of the chairs, her naked back angled towards the door. A lamp on the table threw a pool of light onto an elaborate rose tattoo between her shoulder blades. The tattoo was half finished, and a big guy in a grey T-shirt was in the process of adding another thorn to the stalk that snaked down towards the top of her jeans. He was mid-thirties, sturdily built, with a shock of blond hair, and the irritation on his face as he turned towards the door spoke of a deep concentration. There was a protocol here, house rules, and Winter had just broken them all.

'Maddox?' he queried.

The woman looked round. She was a girl. She was still in her teens. Winter couldn't speak a word of Serbo-Croat but it was obvious she wanted to know what was going on.

Winter apologised and made his excuses. He was looking for someone called Maddox. He thought she lived here.

'She does', the guy said. 'We both do.'

'So do you know where she is?'

'Of course. Who are you?'

Winter introduced himself, said he was expected.

'You're from England? You're the cop?'

'Used to be.'

'Josip.' He put his tattoo machine to one side and extended a hand.

Winter did his best to mask his disappointment. Not once, for some reason, had he expected another man in Maddox's life. Not here. Not now.

'I should have phoned,' he said lamely.

'No problem.' Josip checked his watch. 'You need to go to the agency. She works late on Thursdays.'

The agency was a couple of streets away. Winter lingered outside for a moment, scanning the properties for sale in the window, wondering how anyone could justify asking 240,000 euros for a tatty-looking flat-roofed bungalow with a rusting child's swing in the garden. Inside the agency, as far as he could see, the reception area was empty. He pushed the door open and stepped inside.

The door must have triggered some kind of alarm because at once he heard movement overhead. Then came a clatter of footsteps down a flight of stairs and the door behind the counter flew open. Maddox.

In five years she'd aged more than Winter would ever have expected. She was thinner, gaunter, and the long fall of black hair was threaded with grey. But her poise, her presence, the way she held herself, the way the suddenness of her smile warmed the space between them, told Winter that she still had it. This was the woman who, five years earlier, had charmed the grouchiest turnkeys at the Custody Suite in Pompey Central. Nothing in that respect had changed.

She reached out, touching his battered face, and then put a finger to her lips when he started to explain. Upstairs she settled him in a chair by the window and gave him a gentle scolding for not getting in touch. She was, as ever, a working girl. She'd had to start late today in case he'd turned up at the apartment. And her boss was a lot less forgiving than Steve Richardson.

Winter was determined to get Montenegro off his chest. When he'd finished telling her about the guys in the hotel room she asked him what the police had said.

'I never told them.'

'Why not?'

'No point. The way I hear it, they're as bent as everyone else.'

'Then maybe you should have phoned home. Called for the cavalry.'

He gazed at her, remembering Josip's line about the English cop, and realised what he'd never told her.

'I left the Job,' he said. 'I binned it.'

'You're not a cop any more?'

'No.'

'So what do you do?'

'Good question. Later, eh?'

She made coffee. He wanted to know what she was doing here, flogging godforsaken bungalows on the edge of the Balkans, and most of all he wanted to know about Josip.

'You've met him?'

'I have. Tell him I'm sorry breaking in like that. Tell him old habits die hard.'

Winter's take on their brief introduction made Maddox laugh. The girl was Joe's star patient. She'd just signed a record contract in Zagreb and had millions of kuna to spend. Josip thought she was a bit in love with him but that was typical.

'Of what?'

'Joe. He makes life up. He does it all the time. The truth is he went to school with her eldest brother and gives her special rates for old time's sake.'

'He comes from round here? Josip?'

'Yep. Born and bred.'

She'd met Josip, she explained, in a bar on the Venezuelan coast. She'd been travelling with a friend, dropping down from Nicaragua en route to Brazil. He was skippering a charter yacht for a party of rich Americans who were relaxed about extra company.

'So what happened?'

'I never got to Brazil. Not by bus, anyway.'

They'd spent that summer afloat. Josip had a favourite cousin he'd virtually grown up with. The cousin was now a bridge officer with a shipping line headquartered in Split, and a decade at sea had made him a great deal of money. A loan had bought Josip an old schooner they'd found in a marina in Martinique. Joe, whose second passion in life was DIY, had fixed it up, and they'd spent the following couple of years island-hopping around the Caribbean.

'So what's Joe's first passion?'

'Apart from me, you mean?'

'Yeah.'

'Art stuff. Painting. Sketching. That's what got him into tattooing. He's an interesting man, Joe. It's not obvious at first, but he's really unusual.'

Tattooing, she said, had paid their way. Every time they dropped anchor, she and Joe would put fliers around. Guys on the yachting circuit paid ninety-five dollars an hour. Adapting his technique to black skin had taken Joe a while to perfect, but in the end it had worked just fine. Instead of money, the locals paid with fruit and fish. Unlike other visiting yachties, they never got robbed.

'So why did you come back?'

'Joe's mum got sick. And so did I.'

'What happened?'

'She's still in hospital. I don't think it's going to be long.'

'I meant you.'

'Don't ask.' Her fingers briefly touched her midriff. 'But I'm fine now.'

At Winter's insistence, once she'd packed up for the evening and locked the agency, they went to a nearby sports bar. There was football on the plasma screens, but Inter Milan v. Roma had failed to pull the crowds in. Winter found them a shadowed table at the back.

'So tell me ...' she said.

Winter explained about his journey to the Dark Side. How his bosses had screwed up on a u/c job to kipper Pompey's drug lord and how Winter had nearly died as a result. How he'd decided to bin the rest of his CID service and join Bazza Mackenzie for real. How well it had worked for the first couple of years – good money, good company, good everything – and how more recently it had begun to destroy him.

'That's a big word, my love.'

'I mean it.' He reached for her hand. 'It's killing me in ways you wouldn't believe. I thought I went into this thing with my eyes open. Turns out I was wrong. You do stuff, you let yourself get involved in stuff, and it comes back to haunt you.'

'What kind of stuff?'

He gave her a look. In the half-light she was the old Maddox, a woman who could rob you of your deepest secrets without you scarcely knowing it. She worked a particular magic, an allure all the more potent for being so understated, and he realised how much he'd missed her. She was, in a word, classy.

'I got caught up in a contract killing in Spain. It wasn't down to me, but I was the one closest to the action. That's not a distinction that's going to cut much ice with a Spanish jury.'

'They want to *arrest* you?'

'They will. In the end it's bound to happen. Fuck knows, they may have a warrant already.'

'So what are you doing here?'

'Here's fine. There's no extradition treaty between Spain and Croatia. Not yet, anyway. Not until this lot join the EU.'

'So you're safe?'

'Yeah. Pretty much.'

'So how long are you staying?'

'A day or so, max. We just need to get things ironed out.'

They talked about the apartment in Blake House. Winter said there'd be no problem getting a buyer. The market for property in the UK wasn't great, but places in Gunwharf were holding up OK and he'd be disappointed if he didn't get at least 500K.

'Fifty per cent is 250K. Will that be enough?'

'That'll be plenty. We're buying another boat. Once Joe's mum's gone, we're off again.'

Winter's heart sank. An hour locked in conversation with this wonderful woman and he'd forgotten all about Josip.

'Somewhere nice?' he inquired.

'Greece. The islands. Then wherever. What about you?'

This, Winter knew, was the question he couldn't dodge. Since yesterday he'd thought of nothing else. His days with Mackenzie were definitely numbered. Exactly how he dug the tunnel and hoodwinked the guards was yet to be negotiated, but afterwards he needed somewhere to hide, somewhere to rest up, somewhere safe beyond anyone's knowledge, and anyone's reach. Except, perhaps, Maddox.

'I was thinking maybe here.'

'*Porec?*'

'Yeah.'

'Why? How would that work?'

He gazed at her for a long moment. Rule one in a situation like this was to trust nobody. The fewer people you shared stuff with, the closer to your chest you played your cards, the smaller the chance of it all falling apart. Yet there had to be someone in your life you could rely on. Otherwise that life wasn't worth living.

'I was thinking you might be able to find me somewhere to get my head down, somewhere to live. You must know places.'

'Of course I do. I sell them.' She'd withdrawn her hand. 'You're planning on buying?'

'I dunno. I'm not sure. Maybe some kind of rental first, see how it goes, then get something more permanent if it works out.'

'You'd need a job?'

'Probably not.'

'But you think you could cope with it? Hack it? Life out here? The language? No friends? No contacts?'

'There's you.' Winter offered a weak smile. 'And Joe.'

'Sure. But we'll have gone.'

'Yeah.' Winter gazed down at his empty glass. 'Of course.'

The silence thickened between them. The Roma centre forward poked a lovely pass over the bar. A lone drinker in the corner shook his head and turned away.

'What about tonight? Have you got somewhere?'

'No.'

'I can sort something out. I've got the keys to a place down the road. It's a bit pokey but it'll do for a night or two.' She leaned against Winter and then cupped his face between her hands. She'd always read him like a book. 'You're hurting, aren't you?'

'No.' Winter shook his head. 'No way.'

'You are. I can see it.'

'Yeah?' He risked a look at her face. For some reason he felt close to tears. 'It's been a shit couple of days, love. I need to have a think about things.'

'You do, my love. We'll talk again tomorrow.'

'When?' He jumped in too quickly. He was definitely losing it.

'Maybe lunchtime. Maybe late afternoon. Fridays are always a bit difficult. Give me a ring, eh?'

'I can't. They nicked my phone.'

'I've got a spare. It's back at the office. We'll pick it up when I get the keys.'

Winter nodded. Something he'd been looking forward to, something he realised he'd taken for granted, was evaporating in front of his eyes. She had a life, this woman, and to no one's surprise Paul Winter wasn't part of it.

'When I do a runner I'll be in for the full makeover,' he said.

'Name. History. Inside-leg measurement. The lot. You think Joe might do me a couple of tatts?'

Maddox was still very close. He could smell the wine on her breath.

'I'm sure he would.' She kissed his ear. 'You know how he describes what he does?'

'Tell me.'

'He says he gets a sense of what a person is really like. And then he puts what's inside outside.'

'Horrible.' Winter sat back and closed his eyes. 'Who'd want to look at that?'

The room that Maddox sorted out was small and airless with a tiny window that looked out onto the street at knee level. The shower in the tiny bathroom dripped all night, and by the time the first grey light filtered in through the curtains Winter was wide awake. Lying in the half-darkness under the thin duvet, wondering what else he had to say to Maddox, he realised he'd never felt more lonely in his life. If this was the shape of the years to come, he thought, then maybe he'd be better off in some Spanish nick. Either way, he felt life pressing in around him. Tiny rooms. The rough company of strangers. And an eternity of empty bars.

He had breakfast at a café on the waterfront. A plate of scrambled eggs cheered him up a little, and he was amused by a brief conversation with an elderly couple on the next table. They'd come on a coach from Blackburn. They were staying in a nice hotel at the back of the main square. And they'd decided between them that Winter must have been in a road accident.

'Easily done, love.' The woman leaned across and patted him on the arm. 'No one wears the seat belts on these coaches, do they?'

Winter decided to use the morning to explore the curve of bay to the south, telling himself the least he owed Porec was a bit of a poke around. If he was going to be spending a bit of time here, he ought to get to know the place. He paid his bill, said goodbye to the couple from Blackburn and set off.

As soon as he got to the marina, it was obvious that the season had come to an end. Boats were chocked up for the winter on the dockside and a lone cyclist had stopped to feed a small army of cats. Beyond the marina the waterside path led to a concrete lido. There was space for hundreds of bathers, and in high summer Winter could picture the mayhem, but now a man of uncertain age lay staked out on his towel, the lido's sole occupant, enjoying the September sunshine.

Winter found himself a bench and did the same. After a while the sunbather struggled to his feet and slipped into the water. Winter watched him swimming way out into the bay, a steady breaststroke, nothing splashy, no drama. He made it to a line of buoys and back, and Winter wondered if in his place he'd have the self-discipline to adopt a routine like this. He could certainly lose a pound or two, and if the life he had to lead was to be this solitary then too bad. He could take up gardening. He could make a real effort to understand football. He might even read a book or two.

Beyond the shrouded signs for deckchairs and jet ski hire a waiter was giving his café tables a wipe. Winter had no idea whether this was simply optimistic, but he knew the guy had to make a living and – his mood lifting – he decided to show a bit of solidarity. He walked across, took the table with the best view, ordered a lager and asked for the menu. Miles away, across the water, he could see the white bones of a huge hotel complex. It looked like a cruise liner that had somehow ended up among the pinewoods on the mountainside, and by the time the waiter returned with his lager he was determined to find out more.

'You get lots of English here? In the summer?'

'English?' He shook his head. 'No. Germans, yes. Dutch, yes. Italians, of course. Some Swedes, maybe. But English? No.'

He put the lager on the table. He'd had a good look at Winter's face by now and Winter knew he was curious.

'You're English?'

'Yes.'

'A tourist?'

'Sort of.'

'You want to live here?'

Winter stared up at him, wondering whether his interest was that obvious.

'Maybe,' he said carefully. 'What do you think?'

'What do *I* think?' The man laughed. His English was good. 'I think people like me would like you to say yes. The winter can be hard.'

'You want my money?'

'Of course.'

'And you're open all the year round?'

'No. We close next week.'

'So what happens then?'

'To me?'

'Yes.'

'I go to England.' Another laugh, softer this time. 'Where the cafés never close.'

After a second beer Winter phoned Maddox, who said she'd had a slow morning. She'd had time to sort out a whole range of properties. Maybe Winter might like to drop by the agency during the afternoon. Then they could go through them.

'And something else. I asked Joe about doing you a tatt.'

'And?'

'He thinks you've got the kiss of death. He fancies something Gothic.'

'Nice.' Winter rang off.

An hour with Maddox leafing through a dozen or so properties plunged him back into gloom. The carefully framed colour shots, with all the come-ons about swirl-pools and solar heating, hid the reality of what probably awaited Winter if he chose to bury himself out here. In Maddox's view the money he was talking would buy him three bedrooms, at least two en-suite, with a bit of land plus a decent view. If he knew where to go, he could pick up a second-hand car for a handful of euros, after which the entire country was his to explore. There was a lovely town down the coast called Rovinj. Venice was only a couple of hours away by high-speed catamaran. She remembered Portsmouth's charms only too well, but life beside the Adriatic definitely had its advantages.

'Why would I want three bedrooms?'

Winter knew she was uncomfortable with questions like these. They led to places she didn't want to go.

'Guests?' she suggested. 'Maybe a girlfriend or two?'

'Dream on.'

'Why do you say that?'

'Because I'll have to be Mr Invisible. Mr Nobody.'

He looked at her, expecting a reaction or at least an ounce or two of sympathy. Instead she glanced at her watch.

'You think I'm being a wuss?' he asked.

'No.'

'What, then?'

'I think you're out of your depth. I think life's got to you.'

'You think I should have stayed in the Job?'

'Only you can answer that.'

'Then the answer's no. It was impossible. In the end those people were totally out of order. Like I said last night, they nearly killed me.'

'Then move on.'

'I did. And look what happened.'

'Then move on again.'

'Sure. And here I am. Some lonely old dosser. Making life hard for you.'

'Not me, Paul. You.'

He was right. He knew it. That night she and Josip were

driving down to Pula for the first night of a friend's new play. She said the guy had a special take on the assassination of Archduke Franz Ferdinand, the incident that had sparked the First World War, and he'd written the piece as a kind of eco-parable. The thrust, she said, was that events had a habit of getting out of control, and only eternal vigilance could save us from oblivion. Winter, who knew a great deal about events getting out of control, was grateful for the invitation but turned it down. The evening would doubtless confirm that Maddox and her boyfriend were inseparable, and that knowledge would probably finish him off. Better, on balance, to get pissed and go to bed.

It didn't work. Maddox left him at the door of his lodgings, gave him a kiss and made him promise to get in touch again in the morning. There was a fridge in the room, and she'd bought some stuff in case he felt peckish. For a while he lay on the bed, watching the early-evening news on the tiny wall-mounted television, trying to make sense of each story as it came and went. The video and graphics helped, but the language was impenetrable, and the longer he watched the better he understood that this pretty much represented where he'd ended up. He'd lost touch. Stuff was happening that he no longer understood. That sureness of touch, that firmness of purpose that had badged his working life, seemed to have vanished entirely.

After the news came a game show. Laughter was laughter in whatever language you happened to speak, but the real appeal lay in the muttered asides and the knowing half-jokes – a territory Winter had made his own – and here, once again, he was totally out of his depth.

He turned the TV off and inspected the fridge. Maddox, bless her, had left him a pile of cold meat brightened with a tomato-and-onion salad. There were a couple of lagers too, and a pot of something that looked like strawberry yoghurt in case he fancied dessert. He cracked one of the lagers, not bothering to hunt down a glass, and raised the tin to his lips. Several streets away he could hear the whine of a motor scooter. Then came footsteps and a brief flurry of movement at the window as someone old and bent shuffled past outside. Then silence again. Winter stood in the gathering darkness, knowing that he had to get out, knowing that this cell-like little room would drive him nuts.

He went back to the sports bar, thinking that Friday nights might be livelier. He was wrong. Apart from a couple of solitary drinkers staring into nowhere the place was empty. Even the bartender seemed to have given up. Winter could make no sense of the scribbled note on the counter but rang the little bell beside it in the hope that someone might appear. A girl came through after a while, poured half a litre of thin lager, ignored Winter's laboured efforts to strike up a conversation and vanished again. One of the drinkers muttered something Winter didn't catch. The other one, a ghost of a man, was perched on a nearby stool. His head was down and he seemed to be barely conscious. Winter studied him for a long moment, wondering whether this was the fate that awaited anyone who swapped real life for self-imposed exile, cutting yourself off, hiding yourself away, looking for comfort in the bottom of a glass. How else could a guy like this get through an evening? And what happened when the money ran out?

Winter shook his head, alarmed by the thought, and reached for his lager. Then he changed his mind and passed the brimming glass along the bar. The guy on the stool lifted his head. It was impossible to guess his age. He had the sunken haunted eyes of someone who always expected the worst. His gaze settled on the glass. He was having trouble working out exactly what was supposed to happen next. Join the club, Winter thought. He picked up his jacket and headed once again for the darkness outside.

The following morning, early, Winter washed and shaved. He locked the room, walked the twenty metres up the street and dropped the key through Maddox's front door. He'd thought about a note to go with it but in the end he didn't bother.

At the bus station he bought himself a ticket for Trieste. From there, with luck, he could get a flight back to London. He was in Trieste by late morning. He took a cab to the airport and found a Lufthansa flight that would take him to Heathrow via Munich. Late afternoon, after the Tube ride in from the airport, he was crossing the concourse at Waterloo. A couple of hours later, back at the Harbour Station in Pompey, he paused to pick up a copy of the *News*.

The day's headline story, yet again, centred on Fratton Park. Portsmouth Football Club had recently been sold to an Emirates-based businessman. After the worst start to a season in recent memory, fans were expecting an injection of cash. Under the old owner the club had sold a clutch of star players. Now, before it was too late, they wanted Sulaiman al-Fahim to put his hand in his pocket. But al-Fahim had other ideas. From a chess tournament in Valencia he'd sent word that money was unavailable for new signings. Even worse, he'd just cancelled an appearance at a fans' forum back in Portsmouth to explain his vision for the club's future.

Winter's interest in Portsmouth FC was limited. What caught his attention was a paragraph at the bottom of the story. According to the *News*, a leading city businessman might be riding to the rescue. Winter, turning to page 3 for more details, found himself looking at a photo of his boss. Bazza Mackenzie was posing in front of the Royal Trafalgar. Winter recognised the suit Marie had bought him only last month. Tight-lipped, serious, he looked – in a word – the business. This was someone who knew a thing or two about football. This was someone you'd be glad to have around in a crisis.

Winter read on. Mackenzie, it seemed, had been monitoring events at Fratton Park and was 'deeply concerned'. On behalf of a huge army of lifelong fans he felt compelled to do whatever he could to bring sanity and order to the current shambles.

To that end he was in conversation with a prominent Russian businessman, a man whose commitment to football was deep and unquestioned, a man who'd made a fortune out of canny foreign investments, a man whom he counted as a close friend. It was still way too early to make any kind of official announcement, but Pompey fans shouldn't give up hope. Why? Because Bazza Mackenzie was on the case. And why was that? Because Pompey, as ever, always came first.

Winter folded the newspaper. He was still without a mobile. There was a public phone on the station. Winter dialled a number from memory. Jimmy Suttle answered on the second ring. Winter turned his back to the queue of travellers waiting for tickets, catching his reflection in the panel of a nearby billboard. He looked wrecked.

'It's me, son,' he said. 'You're on.'

Chapter sixteen

The night before Christmas Eve, for only the second time in his life, Andy Makins was drunk. Apart from a flicker of light from a dying candle, Room 452 was in darkness. He and Gill Reynolds had been in bed since seven o'clock. She'd arrived with two bottles of champagne and a packet of Waitrose mince pies. They'd done the champagne but they'd yet to start on the pies. Gill couldn't remember when she'd last had sex like this.

'You want to do it again?' Her fingers were still busy under the duvet.

Makins frowned. His brain was posting letters to his crotch but nothing seemed to be happening.

'Later?' He swallowed a hiccough. 'Does later sound OK?'

The question made Gill laugh. She laughed a lot when Andy was around. Not because he was especially funny – he wasn't – but because the dwindling trickle of newsroom gossip about the ex-house geek was just so wrong. In real life, unlike most people she knew, this man of hers knew exactly where he was heading. More to the point, he was incredibly good in bed.

The first time they'd done it, back last month, she'd put it down to beginners' luck. Not any more. His stamina was extraordinary, his love of oral sex totally unfeigned. For all his preoccupation – the unyielding sense of mission that seemed to

189

armour him against the silliness of life – he knew exactly how to relax her, how to caress her, how to coax her to orgasm after orgasm.

Sometimes, in her head, she strung these moments on a necklace like beads and tucked them away to think about later. The record so far was four. Andy, who had little patience with numbers, told her she was crazy to even think of doing something like that. Looking back, treasuring memories, had never formed part of his life plan. Better, he always told her, to forge ahead, to look for fresh challenges, new routes up the rockface, summits unconquered by anyone else. If doing it a certain way made her feel that good, then how about trying this? Or this? Or this? A willing accomplice, she did his bidding, only too happy to chalk up the occasional disappointment to her own lack of imagination. The situations Andy invented for them both, and his talent for choreography, never ceased to amaze her. She'd never felt so tactile, so lucky, so *alive* in her entire life. At forty-four, she had nearly a decade and a half on Andy, yet he was the one who was doing the teaching. No wonder Megan had hung on to the relationship way beyond its sell-by date.

She offered him a morsel of mince pie. He peered at it in the darkness as if he'd never seen anything like this in his life. Then he checked his watch.

'Shit,' he said.

'What's the matter?'

'I'm supposed to be downstairs.'

'Why?'

'There's some kind of party. You don't say no around here. Bad move.' He started giggling and disappeared beneath the duvet. Moments later Gill could feel him between her thighs. It was sticky down there but he didn't seem to mind. She lay back, her hands cupping his head through the duvet. After a while he stopped. She saw a thin hand feeling around beside the duvet. Then the hand found one of the empty bottles.

A face re-emerged.

'With or without?'

'What?'

'Foil.'

'Forget it.' She was laughing. 'Go to your party.'

While he got dressed, she asked him whether he minded if she stayed the night again. She'd been careful, never making assumptions, never taking liberties, aware that Andy put a lot of store by life's small print. You always asked first. And normally the answer was yes.

'Afraid not,' he said.

'No?' She turned on the light. She wanted him to see her disappointment. 'Are you sure?'

'I've got a breakfast meet.'

'Where?'

'It doesn't matter.'

'Who with?'

He ignored the question. She could hear the splash of water from the bathroom. He's trying to sober up, she thought. Ready to tempt some other woman into bed.

When he stepped back into the room, she threw back the duvet. Andy was climbing into a pair of cargo pants she'd just given him for Christmas. She was secretly glad the fit was less than perfect.

'You look great.' She held her arms out. 'Kiss me.'

He shook his head.

'Use the back entrance,' he said. 'It's safer.'

'Is that a come-on?'

'No.' He had the grace to smile. 'You've worn me out.'

The pre-Christmas party at the Royal Trafalgar had become the must-have invite on the Pompey social scene, but this time round Marie and Bazza had cast the net wider than ever. The night had been blocked off for months in the reservations book, and the entire ground floor was a swirl of Pompey's movers and shakers.

Between them, Bazza and Leo Kinder had spent the best part of a year taking the *Pompey First* message into every corner of the city's establishment. At first the response had been lukewarm. Bazza Mackenzie came with baggage. He was interesting company to have round to dinner, a laugh a minute when he was pissed but a potential liability if you looked too hard at his past.

Were you dreaming when an ex-football hooligan, one of the 6.57's legendary scrappers, told you he was going to stand for Parliament? Were you tempted to laugh when he told you that money wasn't a problem but he'd value your support in other more important ways? And when he phoned you again, inviting you to the hotel for a drink and maybe a meal, and carefully explained just exactly what he and his team had in mind for this city of yours, did you put the whole thing down to half a lifetime on the white powder?

The answer, in all three cases, was probably yes. But then the vibe about Bazza's little wheeze began to change. People in the know, people with brains in their heads, started to take a harder look at the draft manifesto Leo Kinder was discreetly circulating. One or two elements were wildly inappropriate – how could the city ever afford a tunnel to Gosport under Portsmouth Harbour? – but there was other stuff in there that was surprisingly refreshing. Like the bid to attract Chinese investment capital into the dockyard, thus making it easier for the next government to protect the carrier programme. And like Bazza's determination, against all odds, to sort out the city's wayward youth.

In the latter respect, of course, the guy had form. In his youth he'd been as evil and wanton as the next Pompey toerag, but over the last couple of years he'd turned all that experience to good account, founding a charity called Tide Turn Trust. T3, as he'd started calling it, was dedicated to bringing Pompey wrong 'uns face to face with the real consequences of the stuff they'd been up to, and under the guidance of a gifted Dutch social worker, T3 had begun to make modest headlines in specialist journals across Europe. This did the city no harm at all, a welcome twist on the age-old Pompey reputation as a good place for a ruck, and there were people in this very room who – at the end of Whitehall committee meetings – had taken senior civil servants to one side and whispered about the blessings of grass-roots visionaries like, yes, Bazza Mackenzie. The guy's as rough as a badger's arse, they'd murmur. But by God he gets things moving.

Stories like these always found their way back to Bazza, and as the *Pompey First* roadshow began to gather speed, people who knew him well noticed a change in his behaviour. He was quieter, less aggressive, more reflective. He'd never had a problem with self-belief. He'd always known he was sharper, and braver, and altogether more up for it than any other fucker. But he'd lost that raw punchiness which, in his prime, had been his trademark. Today's Bazza was a businessman who knew his way around a balance sheet, a father who'd defend family values against any left-wing muppet who thought he had better ideas, and – most important of all – the favoured son of a city that, in Bazza's view, had always drawn the shortest of straws. In time of war, as he always liked to point out, Pompey got the best of everything. But the moment the ink dried on the peace treaty, the money went back to London. Pompey, in his view, had always been short-changed. And that had to stop.

The buffet dinner was nearly over. Guests were circulating in the huge dining room, moving from table to table, pausing for an exchange of gossip or a shared confidence, their conversation warmed by a well-thought-out menu and excellent wines. Later, when Bazza judged the moment was right, there'd be entertainment.

Tonight, a little to Leo Kinder's dismay, he was showcasing a tyro local comedian Andy Makins had found at the university.

He was a young sociology lecturer, Pompey born and bred, who did a brand of stand-up that he'd cleverly adapted for this evening's audience. Bazza had thrown him some tasty morsels about the local politicians he'd be fighting in the coming election. He'd also made it possible for the guy to meet these people in person. The resulting routine he'd rehearsed in Bazza's office only this afternoon, a witty mix of impersonation, risqué gossip and other local scuttlebutt. Bazza had loved it. And so, in his judgement, would the audience. It represented *Pompey First*'s coming of age. This lot were clued in. They knew where the bodies were buried. They were *sophisticated*.

A table by the window was currently occupied almost exclusively by lawyers. Bazza slipped into the spare chair. The port was circulating, but Bazza declined. He'd kept a clear head all evening, drinking nothing but San Pellegrino, but now he poured himself a modest glass of wine. He wanted to know what the guys round the table made of the latest rumblings from Fratton Park. The club, it was said, was bust. The busy Christmas fixture list was nearly upon them. More stumbles would push them deeper into relegation trouble. Manager Avram Grant was doing his best, but the money still wasn't there. So where next for Pompey?

Howard Crewdson, as everyone knew, couldn't stand football. Bazza didn't know whether his downturned thumb meant curtains for the club or argued for a change of conversational subject.

A mate of Crewdson's, a younger defence brief with a real flair for scoring impossible results in court, wasn't having it.

'It'll come good,' he said. 'In time.'

'Yeah, but how? Who's in the driving seat? Who's making the decisions? Uncle Avram's going to walk in the end. He won't have any other option.'

'What about Wembley?' This from Michelle Brinton, the only woman at the table. 'Another cup final? Don't we have form here?'

'You have to be joking. You need a decent squad to get to Wembley. A couple more injuries, and Uncle Avram's gonna start raiding the Sunday pub sides.'

A ripple of laughter ran round the table. Then Crewdson topped himself up with more port and lifted his glass in a toast.

'Here's to your Russian, Baz. What the fuck ever happened to him?'

Mackenzie fingered his glass. Mercifully, the report in the *News* back in the autumn had made little impact. In the general madness at Fratton Park what was a rumour about one more Russian oligarch?

'Bit of a disappointment, mate. He seemed keen enough at the time, but you know how these things play out ...' Bazza shrugged, keen to change the subject.

'You talked to him?' Crewdson never gave up easily.

'Of course I fucking talked to him.'

'And what did he say?'

'He said he'd love to help. Best league in the world? Football to die for? Fortress Fratton? Global TV audiences? What's not to like?'

'But nothing happened.'

'You're right, son. Nothing did. You try, though, don't you? And there ain't no law against trying, is there? Not that I can remember ...'

Bazza knew at once the mood had darkened around the table. These guys were lawyers. They were watching him carefully. Crewdson, with his silky courtroom skills, had touched a nerve, and they all knew it. This was a glimpse of the old Bazza, the guy who'd take the bait at the merest hint of an insult. Down to Crewdson, therefore, to reel him in.

'So he's still on the radar, your guy?'

'Definitely.'

'Chequebook ready?'

'Without a doubt.'

'So when do we expect him?'

Bazza wouldn't answer, not for a moment or two. But he was back in control now, knowing exactly how to throw the hook.

'To be honest, guys, I'm not the bloke you should be talking to. Paul's your man. He's riding shotgun on this one. Me? I do the hearts-and-minds stuff. When it comes to the moolah, Paul sorts most of that out.'

There was a collective murmur around the table. Everyone knew Paul Winter.

'So where is he?' Michelle Brinton was looking round the blur of faces.

'Haven't a clue, love. He phoned earlier, said he'd been delayed.' Mackenzie reached for his glass at last and raised it in a toast. 'So here's to Uncle Avram, eh?'

Paul Winter was helping himself to another Stella. He'd never been a fan of safe houses. Last time he'd played a role like this the Special Ops guys had found a crappy ground-floor flat in the backstreets of Bournemouth. The thermostat on the central heating had stuck on forty degrees, the place stank of cat's piss, and there was never anything in the fridge. This, though, was much much better. Jimmy Suttle had done him proud.

They were out in the country, deep in the flatlands above the Meon Valley. Soberton Heath was a scruffy collection of bungalows, red-brick cottages and infill newbuilds that had recently become the address of choice for Portsmouth and Southampton commuters who couldn't afford prettier villages like Wickham or Droxford. One of the newbuilds belonged to a D/I who'd recently retired from Major Crime. He'd spent his last year of service working a wide variety of contacts and was now in Uganda, advising the local cops on interview protocols. Winter had known him well, as had Suttle, and they'd enjoyed the latest postcard from Entebbe. 'Everything's fine,' the ex-D/I had written to Suttle, 'except these guys can't get their heads around the word "interview". They prefer "interrogation" – and you know what? They might have a point ...'

Winter cracked the can and emptied it into a pint glass. Suttle was drinking tea. Thanks to carburettor trouble on the way back from Southampton, Winter hadn't turned up until nearly ten. Now it was almost half past. Lizzie had a mountain of presents to wrap. Already Suttle was dreading the inevitable scene.

'Willard's after a sitrep first thing tomorrow,' he told Winter. 'He's getting nervous again.'

'Why?'

'The Chief came back from an ACPO meet with a flea in his ear. It seems the Home Office have wised up about our friend. The piece in the *Spectator* didn't help.'

Winter smiled. Leo Kinder's latest media coup had arrived in the shape of an urbane young freelance who had a line into some of the higher-profile news magazines. He'd come down to Pompey for the day, and Mackenzie had done him proud. Over lunch at the Royal Trafalgar he'd bent the journo's ear, tabling the tastier bits of what was likely to become the *Pompey First* manifesto. The journo, who'd had the good sense to do his research well in advance, was more interested in his interviewee's background, and Bazza had fed him enough detail to confirm what the guy already suspected.

In this strategy Kinder was a willing accomplice. The whole country loved a decent villain, he reasoned. Most politicians these days had no hinterland, no backstory. They were, at best, prisoners of their own limp ambitions, grey apparatchiks with office complexions and a mania for statistics. Baz, on the other hand, had done stuff, interesting stuff, stuff that had earned him a few bob. So why – without spelling out the details – waste all that?

Kinder had tagged this the Bobby Sands strategy, in memory of a convicted IRA gunman way back who'd got himself elected to Parliament while banged up in the Maze prison, and the gambit, as ever, had worked. The journo had originally been pitching for the *New Statesman*, but on the train to London, reviewing his notes, he realised that provocative copy like this belonged in a right-wing mag, partly because the hot favourite in Portsmouth North was the Conservative candidate and partly because Bazza's life story chimed very nicely with what Kinder called the 'Tory narrative'. Bazza Mackenzie had done very well for himself without taking a penny from the state, and in the shape of *Pompey First* you were looking at the perfect template for the thrust of the coming Central Office campaign. If it was true that no one in the country had the first clue what David Cameron meant by the Big Society, then maybe they ought to start listening to the likes of Bazza Mackenzie.

The article had appeared in the *Spectator* at the end of last week. And every broadsheet paper in the country had quoted it over the weekend.

'So what did the Chief say?' Winter helped himself to more peanuts.

'I've no idea. But Willard's spitting bullets.'

'You've talked to him?'

'I talked to Parsons. Most days it's the same thing. If Mackenzie takes this thing to the wire, people like the Chief are going to be ducking some hard fucking questions.'

'Like what?'

'Like how come we've never laid a finger on this guy? Like how come Pompey's narco-king ends up in *Parliament*?'

'But he'll never make it, son. He'll never get anywhere near it.'

'That's not the point. The point is that he *might*. And that's enough, believe me. At their level, people like the Chief deal in possibilities. That's the language they speak. The trick is to identify the threat and neutralise it.'

'Meaning Mackenzie.'

'Of course. And that means you.'

'Us, Jimmy. Us.'

Suttle shrugged and checked his watch again. 10.43. Nightmare.

'So tell me the latest …' He pulled his pad towards him and produced a pen. 'You know the deal. I need hard-core facts, the truth plus provable lies. Once I've typed this stuff up, you've got to attest it, sign it, the lot.'

Winter nodded. This was the protocol he'd agreed after a series of covert meetings back in September. Behind Suttle, who was his lead handler and prime point of contact, lay an Operational Management Team that numbered upwards of half a dozen officers. Under Parsons' overall command, with the CPS lawyers on her shoulder, each of these guys had a specialist input – intel, comms, surveillance, disclosure – and later, once the operation began to mature, the going would get tougher.

The intention just now, though, was to monitor the development of *Pompey First* while acquiring a detailed analysis of exactly how Mackenzie managed his business interests. In Winter's view, the real opportunities lay in the narrow space between the two. Putting it crudely, soon his boss was going to run out of money. And once that happened, given his ever-rising exposure to electoral expenses, Bazza would have to take a risk or two.

The entrapment of Mackenzie had earned itself a code name: Operation *Gehenna*. It was generally agreed that the next phase of the operation wouldn't begin for a couple of months yet, but in the meantime it was Suttle's job to keep Winter legal. Any u/c operation like this carried enormous risks. In court *Gehenna* would face an army of highly paid lawyers who would pick over every shred of the prosecution case. Any slip at any stage – an unattested detail, provable enticement, unfair harassment – and six months' work could be down the khazi. That was a result that neither Suttle nor Winter was prepared to contemplate. Suttle because the prospect of promotion was beginning to matter. And Winter because he had literally no-where else to go.

For the next half-hour or so Winter talked while Suttle made notes. Mackenzie, he said, was riding the crest of a wave, most of which had been generated by his recent recruit.

'Name?'

'Makins. Andy Makins.'

Suttle recognised the name. This was Megan's ex.

'And he's full time?'

'Yeah. Three grand a month. Mackenzie thinks he's got a bargain.'

Makins had been around for a while, Winter said, and to be honest no one had taken much notice of him. He was young, probably very bright, but a bit of a recluse. From Mackenzie's point of view, he was exactly the guy he needed to sort out the youth vote. Kinder had crunched the numbers and reckoned a registration drive might yield a four-figure windfall for *Pompey First*. These were kids who'd never even thought about voting, largely because they couldn't be arsed, and it was Makins' job to give them a shake and get them in line.

'How?'

'By using the Internet. Kids live and die on the net these days. Baz thinks it's all nonsense but knows he can't ignore it.'

Winter told Suttle what he knew about Makins' input. There'd been lots of talk about Facebook groups and some kind of Tweeting operation, and he knew Makins was banging out a whole load of blogs under various names. Despite his impatience with the Internet generation, Bazza was hugely impressed. Makins was monitoring traffic on the sites and they'd begun to attract a sizeable following. The trick was to generate stuff that would push people towards *Pompey First* without revealing the fact that the whole operation was masterminded from the War Room.

'The what?' Suttle had stopped writing.

'The War Room. Bazza loves all this stuff. He should have been a commando or a para or something. I'm going to buy him a dagger for Christmas and a stick of dynamite.'

'But you're serious? The *War Room*?'

'Yeah. It's down in the basement. That's where Kinder works.'

'And Makins?'

'He's got a hotel room upstairs. Says he needs space to think. He's the golden boy. Whatever young Andy wants, he gets.'

Winter told Suttle about the soap opera he was producing. The first episodes of *Smoutland,* he said, were due to hit the net early in the New Year. He explained the concept, three generations of Pompey inbreds to give YouTube fans a good laugh. Suttle didn't see the point.

'Neither does Marie. And neither, if you're asking, do I.'

'You've seen this stuff?'

'I've seen a couple, yeah. It's Makins again, his idea. He's doing it with a couple of guys at the uni. They're using a bunch of amateur actors from Portsea. You don't need to pay people these days. Fame's enough.'

'So what's it like?'

'It's funny. And cruel as fuck. Makins scripts the things himself. He says it's Voltaire with bells on. The word he's using is *Candide.* Ask me what the fuck he's talking about, I haven't got a clue. But Baz is convinced he's got a real line to the kids, always finds the sweet spot, never fails.'

'But what will it do for *Pompey First?*'

'Spreads the word. Puts it on the map. That's Makins talking, not me.'

'And Kinder? The pro? What does he think?'

'He's hedging his bets. The way I read it, the big ask is to get yourself noticed, get yourself talked about. You remember those horrible Benetton ads? Bleeding bodies? People dying of Aids? Boatloads of Albanian refugees? Apparently they worked.'

'Weird.'

'Yeah. But that's what you have to do these days.' He shrugged. 'You want to take a look at this lot?'

Winter handed over a sheaf of figures. He'd spent most of

the afternoon over in Southampton with Bazza's accountant, checking the health of every arm of the Mackenzie business empire. From Pompey tanning salons to a multi-million-euro retirement complex on the Costa Dorada, he was glad to report that the news was grim.

Suttle flicked through the figures. Lots were in red. On the fourth page his finger paused on the Kubla Khan investment in Montenegro. He'd known for months about Winter's Budva adventure. Indeed, Operation *Gehenna* owed its very existence to Winter's night on the carpet in the Hotel Neptun. After that, he'd told Suttle, there was no way back. He and Mackenzie were through.

Suttle wanted to know if the Russian was still in touch.

'Kokh?' Winter shook his head. 'Not a peep.'

'So the Pompey thing? Mr Moneybags?'

'All bullshit. We've been dicked, son. The guy's taken us for a million and a half. We won't see a penny.'

'And Mackenzie knows that?'

'Mackenzie's in denial. He thinks there's a great big moolah tree out there just waiting for us to give it a shake. I tell him there isn't, and I tell him we're in the shit, and I stack all the bills up on that great big desk of his, and I ask him very nicely who's going to pay them, and you know what he says? He says talk to the bank.'

'And?'

'The bank don't want to know. They used to be into lending. That's all changed. Some days, son –' he tapped his head '– I think Mackenzie's got a problem.'

'So what happens?'

'The shit hits the fan ...' Winter grinned '... just the way I said it would.'

Mackenzie and his family were back at Sandown Road by just gone midnight. At Mackenzie's insistence, Makins had come too. When he'd appeared at the party Bazza had known at once he'd been drinking and now he was determined to help the boy finish the job.

'Scotch? Brandy? Name it, son ...'

They were in the big sitting room at the back of the house. French windows opened onto the south-facing terrace, and during the summer Ezzie's kids practically lived here. Guy, the oldest, had developed a special run-up that took him the length of the living room, out onto the terrace and thence into the swimming pool, and Marie could always judge the day's success by the number of tiny wet footprints on the living-room carpet.

Ezzie was Mackenzie's daughter, a striking blonde with her mother's leggy good looks. She'd qualified as a lawyer but after marriage to Stu, a hedge-fund manager, she'd settled down in a big Victorian house nearby. She and Stu had three kids, and sharing Christmas together had, to Marie's delight, become a family tradition.

Neither Ezzie nor Stu had met Makins before, and Ezzie in particular was underwhelmed. She believed in the importance of first impressions and could only suppose that Makins had got dressed in the dark. She'd been aware of him from the moment he'd slipped into the party at the hotel, his cargo pants at half-mast, and from the start she had him marked down as a loner. For whatever reason he didn't make the effort to mix with the other guests and after the third glass of wine he'd had to find somewhere quiet to sit down. He'd remained there for the rest of the evening, his legs crossed, his head slumped, his eyes closed, untroubled by passing revellers. To be frank, she wasn't surprised. A haircut like that, she thought, would put anyone off.

Makins had asked for a Bacardi topped with Coke. He'd never been to the house before and was very obviously out of his depth. Busy families talk in code, laugh a lot and tend to ignore anyone who doesn't get stuck in. By the time Mackenzie returned with the drinks, Makins was in the far corner of the room, pretending an interest in one of Marie's watercolours. Mackenzie, who could be surprisingly sensitive in situations like these, gave him his drink, took him by the arm and steered him towards the door. His den lay on the other side of the house. He switched on the light, nodded at one of the two chairs and told Makins to make himself at home.

Makins peered around. The den was a shrine to Bazza's passion for Portsmouth Football Club. A pinboard was covered with snaps from the 2008 Wembley FA Cup final, while the truly classic shots qualified for proper frames.

'Who's that?' Makins nodded at a tall figure with an explosion of wild hair flinging himself across a goal. The shot was tightly framed, with a blur of Pompey faces on the terraces behind.

'David James. On a good day he can be brilliant, and that was a good day.'

'Why?'

'He saved the penalty. Other days he can lose it completely. That's why they call him Calamity.'

Makins laughed. He liked it. Calamity James.

'And that one?' He indicated another shot.

'Steve Claridge. Pompey legend. Titchfield boy. Not his fault. Old-style centre forward, brave as you like, couldn't wait to get stuck in, used to run and run all afternoon. He was all elbows and knees, Stevie. Defenders loathed him. No style. No finesse. Just a bagful of goals waiting to happen. Can you imagine someone like him in *Hello!* magazine? Players like him can be a bit of an embarrassment these days.'

'A bit like Pompey?'

'You mean the club?'

'I mean the city.'

'You think it's an embarrassment?'

'No, I think it's everything you say. All elbows and knees. All right angles. This isn't the prettiest place I've ever lived.'

'You're telling me you know somewhere better?'

'Of course I do. Maybe not better but prettier, more re-strained, less in your face all the time.'

'Is that what we are? In your face?'

'Definitely. Maybe it's the island thing, too many people. We're all banged up. Wherever you look there are queues. Traffic lights. Shops. The railway station. Car parks. It has to be sorted.'

'Says who?'

'Says me, for starters. But it's out there on the net. I read this stuff every day. People love living here, don't get me wrong, especially the students, but then students are dossers by nature, animals really, hunting in packs, so it probably doesn't affect them. I'm talking older people. You can feel the vibe. They're pissed off. They want to get things *moving*.'

'So what do you suggest?'

'I suggest we go with it – launch a new transport policy, frame the thing up properly, make an offer the punters can't refuse.'

'Like what?'

'I dunno.' Makins was relaxing now, back on his own terri-tory, '*Pompey Fast* might be a start.'

'*Pompey Fast?*'

'Yeah.'

'Brilliant, son.' Bazza gave him a congratulatory pat on the arm and nodded at his glass. 'Have another one. Happy Christmas, eh?'

Jimmy Suttle had perfected the art of getting into his house without waking the baby. He stood in the street, feeling for his keys. As far as he could see, the lights were off downstairs. With luck, Lizzie would be asleep as well.

He fed the key into the lock and slipped inside. At the far end of the hall a tiny strip of light beneath the door told him he was wrong. Lizzie was perched on a stool in the kitchen. She had a pile of presents on one side and rolls of wrapping paper on the other. Late-night jazz was playing very softly on the radio and steam was still curling from the kettle. As far as Suttle could see, none of the presents had been wrapped.

Lizzie gave him a kiss. She seemed to mean it. She didn't mention how late it was.

Suttle dumped his anorak on the tiny two-seat sofa and hunted in the fridge for something to drink. He rarely checked on the state of their booze supply, far from it, but he swore the bottle of vodka had been half full last night.

'It was.' Lizzie giggled.

'You're telling me you—'

'We. She's in the front room. I let her kip over. Insisted, actually.'

'Who?'

'Gill.'

'Fuck.'

'Exactly.' She started to giggle again, abandoning the scissors and beckoning Suttle closer. Then she kissed him properly, tenderly, running her tongue around his. Suttle responded, trying to mask his surprise. He could feel fingers exploring the zip on his trousers, then the gentlest tug.

'You could fuck me if you want,' she murmured.

Suttle could taste the vodka on her breath. He eased himself back an inch or two and then cupped her face in his hands.

'What's going on?' he said. 'What is this?'

'Nothing. Passion. Sex. I love you. I want you. Fuck me. Just fuck me.'

'Now?'

'Yeah.'

'Here?'

'Wherever you like.' She put her tongue in his ear.

With some difficulty, she discarded her jeans. Then the thong she'd taken to wearing again. Then pulled her T-shirt over her head. Back on the stool, naked except for a pair of ankle socks, she opened her legs.

'Help yourself,' she said.

Suttle sank to his knees. She loved oral sex nearly as much as he did. She came within a minute. World record.

'Fuck.' Suttle was impressed.

'Don't stop.'

He bent to her again. This time it took longer. Towards the end she lifted his head and told him to take his clothes off. Then she nodded at the other stool and settled herself on his lap.

'As quick as you like.' She kissed him. 'I'm Santa.'

Suttle wanted to laugh. He couldn't remember sex like this ever. Not with her. Not with Trude Gallagher, Not with any of the women he'd known. Ten minutes ago he'd been dreaming up clever ways of avoiding a row. Now this.

She began to move, her eyes half-closed, her hands cupping her own breasts. This, too, was new, and a definite turn-on. Maybe she's been on the Internet, Suttle thought. Maybe Gill has a favourite site and they've been getting in the mood. Seconds later Lizzie came, Suttle too. She clung to him for a long moment. Suttle could feel the thump of her heart through her tiny frame.

'Happy Christmas,' she whispered. 'I love you.'

Misty was asleep when Winter made it back to Hayling Island. The sale on his Gunwharf apartment had finally gone through, and his solicitor had organised completion for 2 January. What was left of his belongings occupied a modest stack of cardboard boxes in the otherwise empty sitting room, and he'd called by to pick a couple more up. These last few weeks he'd been living full time with Misty, an arrangement that seemed to be working remarkably well.

He returned to the Lexus and carried the boxes into Misty's hall. She'd cleared a couple of rooms downstairs for the bits of furniture he wanted to keep, pending – in Misty's phrase – whatever the fuck happened next. This subject, to Winter's relief, they were both leaving well alone. Misty was sentimental about Christmas, and the last thing she needed was a row. Over the last couple of months he'd noticed a slight reticence on her part, a hint of detachment he'd never seen before, but he'd been careful to fence off the weekends so they could have a bit of time together, and after a couple of drinks things went pretty much the way they'd always gone. Plenty of laughter. Some excellent sex. And still friends next morning.

He padded up the stairs, soaped his face in the en-suite, returned Misty's discarded gown to the hook behind the door and stepped back into the bedroom. Misty's light was still on and he was bending to find the switch when she stirred.

'Paul? Is that you?'

'Yeah.' He gave her hand a squeeze.

'I thought I heard the phone earlier. I was probably dreaming. You mind checking it, pet?'

Winter went downstairs. He hadn't been in the kitchen so he hadn't seen the message light flashing on the phone console. He lifted the receiver and keyed playback. A woman's voice. Lots going on in the background.

'This is a message for Mrs Gallagher. Please can she call this number and ask for Sister Ballantyne. I'm afraid it's urgent.'

It was a Southampton number. Winter scribbled it down. His first thought was Trudy. As far as he knew, she was in for the night. He went back upstairs and checked the room she was using. The bed was empty, the brightly patterned duvet half on the floor. A litter of shoes led to the wardrobe. The wardrobe door was open. Returning downstairs, he phoned the Southampton number. Another voice answered, male this time.

'ICU.'

Winter was staring at the phone. He knew a great deal about intensive care units. He gave his name and said he was calling on behalf of Mrs Gallagher.

'Who?'

'Mrs Gallagher. Someone left a message earlier.'

'One moment please.'

There was a longish pause. He could hear the clank of a hospital trolley in the background. Next came a low murmur of conversation. Then he was talking to the woman who'd left the message. He listened for what felt a very long time, nodded, said he understood. Then he put the phone down.

Misty was calling him from upstairs. She'd heard the tinkle of the phone connection. She wanted to know what was going on.

Winter took a deep breath and closed his eyes. Then he went up.

Misty knew at once that something was wrong. She was up on one elbow, rubbing the sleep out of her eyes. She reached out for Winter. Her hand was icy.

'What's the matter, pet?'

Winter sank onto the bed, put his arm round the bareness of her shoulders. All he could think of was Karl Sparrow, hanging from his hoist, totally helpless.

'It's Trude, Mist. We need to go to Southampton.'

The Princess Anne Hospital was in the north of the city. Winter left the Lexus in the car park and followed the signs to the main entrance. It was half past one in the morning, and away from A & E the hospital was nearly deserted. The woman at reception directed them to the Intensive Care Unit. The doors to the ICU were locked. Winter, hugging Misty close, rang the bell. After a while a male nurse appeared, inspected them through the glass panel and opened the door. Winter gave their names. The nurse nodded and led them through to a nursing station in the centre of the unit. The sister in charge was on the phone, he explained. She'd be with them as soon as she'd finished.

They took a seat. Misty was hyperventilating, her head back, her eyes half closed. She kept clutching at Winter's hand, the way a child might. She wanted information. She needed reassurance. She prayed that nothing really horrible had happened. She wanted them all back at home in Hayling Island. Intact.

The sister asked them to come into her office. She shut the door. She explained that Trudy had been in a road accident. Mid-evening there'd been a pile-up on the M3 north of Southampton. A lorry had jackknifed, trying to avoid a car joining the motorway. Traffic behind had hit the lorry, and the impacts had rippled back. The police would know more, but as far as the sister understood, Trudy had been a passenger in a car that had hit the lorry. The initial impact had thrown her forward, then multiple impacts from behind had snapped her neck back. She had fractures of the skull, probable broken ribs and damage to her spine. The latter was especially problematic. Just now, she was still unconscious, breathing with the aid of a ventilator. Paramedics had done what they could to stabilise her neck and spine, and soon, God willing, she'd be transferred to the hospital's neurological unit.

'God willing?' Misty looked terrified.

'She's very sick, Mrs Gallagher. I can't pretend otherwise.'

'So will she ...' Misty couldn't complete the sentence.

'We hope so.'

'But you can't be sure?' This from Winter.

'No, I'm afraid not. In these situations there are never any guarantees.'

'Can I see her?' Misty seemed to have recovered. 'Is she close? Can I sit beside her?'

'Of course.'

Misty and Winter followed the sister to a shadowed open-plan ward. Trude was in the bed at the end. Her head, swathed in bandages, was immobilised, and there was clearly damage to her legs as well because the bed was tented with some kind of frame. Tubes ran out of her body to a variety of bottles and drips, and the silence was broken by the steady sigh of the ventilator. Misty crept towards the bed. She wanted to touch her daughter, to stir a flicker of movement, a hint that it was still Trudy in there, but she seemed to have lost her bearings.

'Go ahead, Mrs Gallagher.'

Misty stood at the bedside, bent low, put her cheek to Trudy's. Then she took her hand and stroked it, murmuring something Winter couldn't quite catch.

He asked the sister how long this was likely to go on.

'Unconsciousness, you mean?'

'Yes.'

'We never really know. Guessing would be unkind. She might come round in a minute or two. It might take days. It might ...' She offered Winter a tired smile. 'We just can't say.'

'What about the rest of the people in the car?'

'I understand the driver died. That's all I know.'

There was a waiting room, she explained, if they wanted to stay. Trudy's condition would be reviewed by a couple of consultants in the morning. They'd probably be able to tell them a great deal more than she could.

Winter thanked her. He found a chair for Misty, another for himself, and settled down to wait. Misty couldn't take her eyes off her daughter's face. A screen above the bed displayed a series of lines that monitored various vital signs, and when a peak or a trough caught her attention, she'd glance up and frown as if the machine was somehow to blame for this terrifying event, but her real focus was Trude. She had to know her mum was with her. She had to know she wasn't alone. They were going to see this thing through together. Come what may.

After a while Winter fetched a couple of coffees from a vending machine in the corridor. He selected double sugar for Misty's, thinking she might need it, but when he carried the coffees back through she barely registered his presence. Mother and daughter occupied a bubble cut off from the rest of the world. Nothing else mattered.

By six o'clock in the morning there were stirrings in the ward. Nurses came and went. Cleaners. Someone important-looking with a clipboard and a pen. No one spared Misty and Winter a second glance. Trudy was still deeply unconscious, her chest rising and falling at the bidding of the ventilator.

'Do you think she feels any pain, pet?' Misty's hand found Winter's.

'No.'

'And when she comes round? What then?'

'She'll be confused, Mist. You need to be here. She needs to see a face she knows.'

'And you, pet?'

'I'm here too.'

'Bless you.' Her hand tightened in his. 'You're a good man.'

The ICU consultant was Indian. Misty refused to leave Trudy's bedside, so he took Winter to the room reserved for friends and family. The rows of stuffed animals reminded Winter of Misty's bedroom. He was glad she wasn't here.

'So what's going to happen?'

The consultant wouldn't go much further than the sister. Except to warn Winter that the neurological consequences could be lifelong.

'I'm not with you, Doc.'

'We did X-rays last night. She has fractures here and here.' He touched the nape of his own neck. 'We call them C5 and C6. Until she's fully conscious again we'll have no idea of the extent of the damage. The spinal cord runs down through these vertebrae. Spinal nerve tissue is very sensitive and it doesn't heal. If it's damaged the effects could be permanent.'

'Like how?'

'Like having no sensation below here –' he touched his shoulder blades '– and no control, either.'

Winter nodded and said nothing. Karl Sparrow again, banged up in his Tipner bedroom with a lifetime of DVDs to look forward to. Helpless. Incontinent. Fuck.

The consultant wanted to know whether there was anything else he could help Winter with. He knew it was tough, but there was still a chance Trudy could pull through without permanent damage.

'How much of a chance?'

'A chance. That's all I can say. Good luck, my friend. We're all doing our best.'

He gave Winter's arm a tiny pat and left. Winter settled heavily into the nearest armchair and let his head fall back. Then he closed his eyes and squeezed them very hard. He felt totally knackered. In his own way he loved Trude as much as her mum did, a different kind of love maybe but no less real. The kid had always been alive, always on the move, always ready with a quip or a little dig. If anyone could bounce back from something like this then she could. But then he knew only too well that the body wrote its own script, did its own bidding, and that from certain kinds of injury you never came back. How was he going to break this to Mist? What on earth would he say?

By the time he got back to her, he'd decided to say nothing. Trudy was still away in her private world, somewhere beyond reach. Misty asked what the consultant had said but Winter shook his head. 'No news is good news,' he muttered. 'These guys won't commit themselves.' Misty nodded, happy enough not to know. She looked exhausted, but when Winter suggested she might go back to the car and have a kip she wouldn't hear of it. Trude might come round any moment. And when that happened she had to be there.

Winter put his hands on her shoulders and started to give her a massage. He loved the way she'd said 'when' and not 'if' but he could feel the tension in her neck. After a while an orderly asked whether they'd like something to eat. He could offer scrambled eggs and toast. Misty barely heard him. Winter said yes.

He ate breakfast alone, back in the room with the stuffed toys, wondering where he could find some pepper and salt. Then he heard a flurry of movement in the corridor outside, a couple of nurses hurrying past, and he put the paper plate to one side, getting to his feet, sensing that something might have happened. He could remember three or four patients in the surrounding beds. Please, he thought. Please let it be Trude.

It was. She couldn't move her head, but her eyes were open. She was looking at Misty. And she was trying to smile.

It was midday before they headed back to Hayling Island. Trude was still in the ICU, still on a ventilator, drifting in and out of consciousness, but her vital signs were improving and the medics seemed to have no doubt she'd make it through. What kind of damage her spinal cord had suffered was still unclear. She reported no sensation below her neck, but these were early days and according to the neurological consultant she could yet make a full recovery. Limb by limb, sensation and control might return as the swelling around the injury began to subside. Either way, staff would be monitoring her very closely over the coming hours and days. Better, therefore, that Misty and Winter took the chance to get their heads down.

Misty slept most of the way back. When they turned into the drive, she jerked awake and Winter knew that for a split second she was telling herself nothing had happened, it had all been some vile dream, Trude was upstairs, tucked up in bed, nothing had changed. Then she looked across at Winter's face and knew none of that was true. They were in deep, deep trouble. All three of them.

In the kitchen Winter made a pot of tea. Misty sat on her favourite bar stool, staring out at the rain. She'd put up decorations only a couple of days ago, cheerful little loops of tinsel that ran around the kitchen and moved in the draught when she opened the window. Christmas Eve, Winter could sense her thinking. What a fucking joke.

He poured the tea and asked whether she wanted anything to eat. When she shook her head he told her she ought to get something down her. They needed to stay strong for whatever lay down the road. No one could live on fresh air alone. Misty didn't seem to be listening. After a while she turned her head towards him.

'I need to ask you a question,' she said. 'I'm sorry, but it's something I have to do.'

'Go on then.'

'A while back Trude and I came across something on your answerphone at the flat. We weren't snooping, I promise. It just happened.'

'And?'

'Who do you know in Croatia?'

Winter gazed at her for a long moment, finally understanding where the last few months had come from. The reticence. The faint un-Misty hint of withdrawal.

'You mean a woman? A woman's voice?'

'Yes.'

'Her name's Maddox.'

'And did you go and see her?'

'Yes.'

'In Croatia?'

'Yes.'

'Why?'

'Because I had to sort out some stuff.'

'And did you?'

'Yes, I did.'

'And does she matter?'

'No, Mist, she doesn't.'

Winter took her in his arms and hugged her. She was sobbing now. He let her cry for a while and then found a box of tissues. She dabbed at her face, smudged blue with eyeliner. Then she swallowed hard and looked him in the eye again.

'Promise?'

'Promise.'

'Thank fuck for that.' She started to cry again. 'Toast, please.'

*

Later that day, in the Polish city of Lublin, a fight broke out in a bar. Three men who'd been drinking for most of the afternoon disputed the bill, and the owner, a newcomer to the city, had to step in when one of the drinkers attacked the barman. In the resulting chaos the owner headbutted the guy he judged to be the ringleader and broke his nose. Unfortunately, the drinker turned out to be an off-duty cop. Police were summoned and the bar owner was arrested. He spent Christmas Day in a cell and was subsequently charged with assault. A week later an alert administrative assistant at Lublin police station keyed the bar owner's name into an Interpol database and scored an interesting hit. The news arrived at Hantspol HQ early the following day.

III

Chapter seventeen

Gordon Brown called the general election on Tuesday 6 April.
He drove to Buckingham Palace, asked the Queen to dissolve
Parliament, and returned to Downing Street to launch the
Labour Party campaign. That same morning, oddly enough,
Bazza Mackenzie got some very bad news.

He was in the War Room with Kinder, Makins and Winter
when his mobile rang. All eyes were glued to the live BBC
news feed on the big plasma TV Kinder had installed. Gordon
Brown was emerging from Downing Street to address a mob
of reporters.

Mackenzie bent to his phone. Already visibly irritated, his
frown deepened. He brought the conversation to an end and
sat back to watch Gordon Brown at the microphone. The election was to take place on 6 May. The future, Brown said, is
ours to grasp, a future fair for all. So let's get to it.

'Too right, mush.' Mackenzie got to his feet. He caught
Winter's eye and jerked his head towards the door. They
needed to talk. Now.

Upstairs in his office, Mackenzie seized the phone and
punched in a number. When he was especially tense he had a
habit of sitting on the very edge of his seat. Just now he hadn't
even sat down.

'Julie? I need to talk to Conrad.'

Winter knew at once what this was about. Conrad Whittiker was Mackenzie's point man at the bank, the guy who oversaw his various accounts, the senior manager who made all the key credit and loan decisions. Whittiker was a very bad man to cross. Especially now.

Mackenzie was at full throttle. The moment Whittiker came on the phone he let fly. Some muppet had been on about a couple of mortgage payments. She seemed to think there were insufficient funds available. The payment had therefore been blanked. What the fuck was going on?

Whittiker spoke at some length. Winter watched Mackenzie's face darken.

'That's bollocks, Conrad, and you fucking know it. I've put hundreds of thousands your way, squillions of fucking quid, and now you tell me there's a *problem*? What fucking planet are you people on? First you trash the economy, get it so totally fucking wrong we're all back in the Stone Age, monkeys up fucking trees, then you take it out on people like me. Some of us have a living to make, believe it or not, and you tossers don't make it fucking easy. So do us a favour, eh? Sort this nonsense out.'

He put the phone down and stared at it, daring it to ring again. It was Winter who broke the silence.

'Well?'

'You don't want to know, mush.'

'I do, Baz. I do.'

'They're threatening to withdraw the overdraft.'

'Threatening?'

'They've done it. Bang!' His fist hit the desk and made the phone jump. 'Just like fucking that. No consultation. No warning. These guys think they *own* us all.'

'They do, Baz.'

'Bollocks. You believe that? You really believe all that bullshit? Jesus ...' He turned away from the desk and stormed towards the window. Out on Southsea Common Winter could see a couple of girls flying a kite. One was very pretty. He thought of saying something but knew there was no point. Bazza in a mood like this was beyond reach.

'Great fucking timing,' he muttered. 'This has to be a spoiler, doesn't it? There has to be some evil fucker behind all this, some Tory cunt. The Labour lot haven't got the brains and the Lib Dems are away with the fairies. So who wants to hurt us, mush? Who is it?'

He was talking to himself, a man cornered by months of spending money he didn't have, a man desperate to put a name and a face to this monstrous twist of fate. In Bazza's world, as Winter knew only too well, the blame never settled at his own door.

'Which account is it, Baz?'

'All of them, the lot. He's telling me there's nothing left in the pot.'

'We knew that.'

'He means his pot. We're halfway up the fucking mountain, mush, and he's just cut the rope. Mortgage payments, direct debits, cheques, credit card payments, the lot, finito. Not another fucking penny, he says. Not one.'

'So what do we do?'

'We look elsewhere. We work the phones. We call in favours. Stu's got a quid or two if it really comes to it. Marie too.'

Winter said nothing. If Bazza was relying on his wife and son-in-law, things had to be really bad.

At length there came a knock at the door. It was Leo Kinder. For days, in anticipation of this morning's news, he'd been planning a big press conference to launch the *Pompey First* campaign. The London papers would be sending stringers. TV and radio were standing by. The *News* was talking about a big splash on the front page plus a feature inside. This was the raw meat of politics. Even Kinder, Mr Cool, couldn't mask his excitement.

'You want me to make the calls, Baz?' Winter asked.

Mackenzie was still at the window. He didn't turn round. 'Of course I fucking do,' he said.

Misty Gallagher was on the road again. Three or four mornings a week she drove the fifty miles to Salisbury District Hospital. Trude had been in the Duke of Cornwall Spinal Treatment Centre for nearly three months now. It felt like for ever.

Misty found a space in the car park and walked to the unit. It was a long modern-looking red-brick building on the edge of the main hospital site with views across the surrounding downland. In the early days she'd had a long conversation with another relative who visited her son daily, and the woman had been keen to stress how lucky they were to have a place like this on their doorstep. Misty had a very different take on 'lucky' and 'doorstep' but had kept her opinions to herself.

This morning was Trude's first visit to the unit's swimming pool. Misty knew she'd been looking forward to this landmark for weeks. Trude had always loved the water and had swum like a fish since early childhood. Misty signed the visitors' book and followed the signs to the pool. There was a viewing area on one side, and Misty slipped in through the glass doors, strangely comforted by the familiar smell of chlorine. This, she thought, might be a step back towards a life her daughter could recognise as her own.

Trude was in the shallow end, attended by a physio called Awaale, an absurdly handsome Somali with a smile that would make anyone feel better. Trudy adored him but Misty knew at once that something was wrong. Her daughter was struggling. She was clinging to Awaale. Every time he tried to make her swim free, she wouldn't have it.

After nearly two months of what the medics called spinal shock, Trude had begun to recover some sensation in her arms and lower body. She could feel the difference between hot and cold. She could register pain and pleasure. The bedside physios had done a brilliant job maintaining her muscle tone, and she had a full range of movement in every limb. Week by week, she was even getting back in charge of her bowels and bladder. All of this was brilliant news – she wouldn't, after all, be paralysed for life – but coordination remained a real challenge. Hence the pool.

Misty, aware that Trude seemed embarrassed by her presence, retreated from the pool and bought herself a coffee from a nearby machine. There'd been many moments since the nightmare that had been Christmas when she'd doubted her own ability to carry on. The sight of the hideous metal clamp they screwed into her daughter's skull. The existence of the 'specialist swallowing team', gathered around a neighbouring bed. The endless talk of skin integrity, and renal function, and bladder management. Stuff like this was gross, nothing to do with her beautiful Trude, yet here she was, as helpless as a baby and nearly as frightened as Misty herself.

She finished the coffee and walked through to the day room to wait for Trude's return, shoulders back, head erect, telling herself to get a grip. They weren't out of the woods yet, far from it, but compared to the early days – as Winter kept pointing out – Trude was definitely on the mend.

She was there within minutes, wheeling herself in through the door with Awaale providing the lightest of course corrections from behind. Misty was as smitten as Trude. Awaale beamed down at them both.

'She did great, Mrs G.'

Misty knew at once that Trude had been crying. She turned her head away.

'I was crap,' she muttered. 'This is never going to work.'

Operation *Gehenna* had a new safe house. The ex-D/I who'd gone to Uganda was now back in Soberton Heath, and Winter had been summoned to an address in St Cross, a wealthy enclave on the southern approaches to Winchester. This was handy for Willard, whose office at headquarters was five minutes up the road. The Head of CID was waiting for Winter in the kitchen of what resembled a Victorian rectory. The place was fully furnished, though Winter's taste didn't run to flock wallpaper and heavy drapes. He'd been in upmarket Indian restaurants that felt a bit like this and he wasn't impressed.

Willard had the kettle on. He assumed Winter wanted coffee. Winter, who hadn't seen Willard since the day of Faraday's funeral, was surprised by the change in his appearance. He seemed to have lost a bit of weight and there was something new – almost wolfish – in his face. According to Suttle, Willard had completed the ACPO course and was heavily tipped for an Assistant Chief Constable post in the West Midlands. The Brummies, Winter thought, were in for a bit of a shake-up.

Parsons and Suttle turned up minutes later. Willard had already cleared a space in the dining room. The big window looked out onto a blaze of daffodils, but Willard had pulled the curtains against the world outside. They sat around the table beneath an elaborate chandelier. It might have been the middle of the night.

Willard kicked off. To Winter's surprise, he already appeared to know about Mackenzie's exchange with the bank.

'You're telling me you set that up?'

Willard ignored the question. Far more important was Mackenzie's reaction.

'He kicked off big time,' Winter said. 'Just the way I told you he would.'

'But what's he going to do for money?'

'He's phoning around, calling in favours, leaning on old mates. He's trying to set up a fighting fund. Baz thinks he's back in the 6.57. The one thing he won't do is give up.'

'Excellent. And his chances of success?'

'Nil. Add up all the liabilities, all the outgoings, all the unpaid bills, and we're talking six figures. And that's *before* the campaign kicked off.'

'So he's still going ahead?'

'Of course he is.'

'How?'

'Skelley.'

'But how?'

'That's down to me.'

Willard nodded, then shot a look at Suttle.

'You told Mackenzie about this guy Beginski?' Suttle began. 'Like I asked?'

'Yeah.'

'And did he bite?'

'Of course he did. I put it the way yŏu suggested. I said Beginski was a Polack driver, used to work for Freezee. I told him he was very likely the guy Skelley had asked to drive Johnny's body up to the Lake District. That's why he got a big fucking pay-off and did a runner back to Poland. Johnny was what did it for Baz. He accepts he's probably dead and now he's thinking all that's down to Skelley, which is where it becomes personal. That's why I'm off up to London.'

Suttle nodded. Johnny Holman had been an old mate from Mackenzie's 6.57 days, a washed-up drunk baby-sitting two and a half million quid's worth of Bazza's precious rainy-day toot.

Winter wanted to know where Operation *Gehenna* was heading next. At Suttle's direction he'd explained to Bazza that Beginski had boasted about the size of the pay-out from Skelley and that his mates had naturally been pissed-off. What did Suttle want him to do now?

'There's a woman you need to meet,' said Suttle. 'Her name's Irenka. She's half-Polish. She runs an agency in Isleworth, Home From Home. She sorts out accommodation for Polish workers. It turns out she's Pavel Beginski's sister.'

'And?'

'We think she might know where he is.'

'Fuck.' Winter was impressed.

'Exactly.'

'So what's she saying?'

'Nothing. Not to us, anyway.'

Winter stared at Suttle, trying to juggle the implications.

'So I'm a cop now. Is that it?'

Even Willard laughed. Winter hadn't finished. He'd been aware of Beginski for some time, ever since Suttle slipped him the intel file on Martin Skelley. But the fact that he had a sister was something new.

'So how come you lot know about this Irenka?'

'We ran various checks.' Suttle said. 'Cross-matched Beginski to other databases.'

'Like?'

'HMRC. DWP.' Her Majesty's Revenue and Customs. Department of Work and Pensions.

'And you're telling me they've got the same surname? Brother and sister?'

'Yeah. It seems she's never married.'

'Lucky, eh?'

'For her?'

'For you lot. Bit of a break, I'd say.'

Suttle nodded and shot an amused glance at Parsons. Winter had never been an easy sell, and nothing had changed.

Winter wanted to know where to find the woman.

Suttle passed across an address in Isleworth. 'I think it's pretty basic,' he said. 'Maybe just a couple of rented rooms.'

'You haven't checked it out?'

'No. We thought you might do that. The lead only came in a couple of days ago.'

Winter was still looking at the address. His plan for the afternoon wrote itself. Find Irenka. Get some kind of lead on Beginski's whereabouts. And sort whether he might be up for a conversation. If he'd burned through his pay-off and could do Skelley real damage, then he might want more. And if that was the case then Winter would be only too happy to act as his agent.

Winter sat back, took his time. Everyone round the table was waiting.

'This is kosher, right?' Winter was looking at Willard.

'What's kosher?'

'The woman. Irenka.'

'What do you think?'

'I don't know. That's why I'm asking you.'

Willard smiled, then glanced at Suttle.

'She's kosher, sir.' Suttle nodded. 'One hundred per cent.'

Willard nodded and reached for his briefcase. He was looking at Winter again. He didn't bother to hide his amusement.

'Happy now?' he said.

It was early afternoon by the time Mackenzie finished his first round of phone calls. One by one he'd drawn a line through the long list of names on his pad. These were people who only hours ago he'd have relied on for a grand or two or maybe even more, but most of them had already kicked in modest sums for a couple of *Pompey First* fund-raisers during the spring, and given the current squeeze none of them were up for more. As he got towards the bottom of the list, his pen strokes became angrier, and by the time Kinder and Makins joined him for a pre-launch meet in his office at the Royal Trafalgar, his mood was grim.

Kinder told him they were looking at 90 per cent acceptance for the five o'clock launch. They were using the big function room downstairs. Staff were already bannering the stage Mackenzie would be using, and Kinder had just taken receipt of the specially commissioned colour blow-ups from the framers. These shots featured Bazza in a number of Pompey settings from the Fratton End at the Chelsea game to the top of the Round Tower overlooking the harbour mouth. In every case Baz was locked in conversation with a bunch of punters. These were Pompey faces, Bazza's people, the men and women he'd be only too happy to serve, and on most of the shots the strap line was the same: *Pompey First ... because we all deserve better.*

Kinder had brought what he judged to be the best of the photos with him and now he propped it against the door. BazzaMac, as some of the bloggers were beginning to call him, was standing in the empty bowl of Hilsea Lido, a 1930s open-air swimming pool at the top of the city. This had always been a must-visit attraction on hot summer days, especially popular with young families, and for thousands of older voters it represented a Pompey that was close to disappearing. In recent years the council had abandoned plans for a major refurb, and only a vigorous local campaign had saved the place from demolition.

Mackenzie leaned forward over his desk, staring at the shot. Kinder's photographer had got him to spread his arms wide and asked for a gesture of despair. Mackenzie, who had no time for despair, had found the photo shoot a pain in the arse, but now he saw what the photographer had been getting at. Across the bottom of the shot ran a different strapline: *Pompey First ... before it's too late.*

'Perfect,' he said. 'Fucking great.'

His mood began to lift. Kinder ran quickly through the plan for the late-afternoon media launch. When he got to the drinks, Mackenzie told him to cancel the champagne. Kinder raised an enquiring eyebrow.

'Too flash,' Mackenzie grunted. 'Make it tea and coffee. This is the austerity election. We don't need Moët.'

He reached for the speech Kinder had prepared him. Kinder pointed out an extra paragraph he'd added after monitoring the lunchtime news round-ups. *Pompey First,* he wanted Bazza to announce, was the Big Society in action. Not some puppet show controlled by the faceless honchos up in London but the real thing. Local votes, local voices, plus a big fat local vibe. Your Pompey, not theirs.

No problem. Mackenzie put the speech to one side. He wanted an update on the Future-Proofing Conference. This

228

had been on standby for nearly a month. Kinder had lined up a panel of speakers from across Europe to descend on the city for a two-day brainstorm: an Italian architect who specialised in the use of public space, an academic from Frankfurt who knew all about tram systems, a Swedish engineer with some radical thoughts on green energy, plus a handful of English experts with international reputations in the field of urban planning. The conference, said Kinder, would attract national media attention and add a coat or two of gloss to the *Pompey First* campaign. These guys on the south coast, went the implicit message, aren't the country bumpkins you might think they are. They care about their city's future. And they're doing something about it.

'I need costings, Leo.'

'You've got them. We've budgeted twenty grand with a 2K buffer.'

'Which takes care of what?'

'Transport, fees, accommodation, hire of the venue, entertainment, plus various sundries.'

'Halve it. We can hold the conference here. Fly them economy. And forget the accommodation costs.'

'How does that work?'

'I'll shift it to another budget, pretend they're just regular guests.'

'We can't do that, Baz. You know we can't.'

'I can do whatever I fucking like, Leo. OK?'

Kinder locked eyes for a moment, then shrugged. After the election was over he would have to submit full accounts to the Electoral Commission. Exceeding the allowance for expenses was a criminal offence. Already, given what they'd spent since the turn of the year, they were dangerously close to the limit. The New Year's Eve firework display had cost seven thousand. An earlier conference on juvenile delinquency, a showcase for Tide Turn Trust, another eighteen. Given these constraints, he could hardly object to reductions in the budget, but hiding expenditure away was madness. He'd dealt with the Electoral Commission before. They weren't stupid.

Mackenzie wanted a schedule for the first week of campaigning. Kinder opened a file and studied it for a moment. They were kicking off tomorrow with a visit to the QA site. Two hundred and fifty-six million pounds had bought a new superhospital, the jewel in Pompey's crown, but *Pompey First* was calling for better coordination between patients' groups, hospitals and GPs.

'You got a brief on that?'

'It's joined-up care, Baz. No point buying a Bentley and putting the wrong fuel in.'

'What else?' Mackenzie jotted himself a note.

'Friday we're hitting the Cosham Shopping Centre. Loads of balloons plus some local kids. They call themselves the Silver Majorettes. Business rates are going up from 2K to 10K. Footfall's down 40 per cent. Most of the shopkeepers are suicidal, and there are lots of regulars who see it their way. Hundreds of votes, Baz.'

'And the weekend?' He made another note.

'There's a huge gig at the Student Union on Saturday night. We've bunged some money in.'

'How much?'

'Five hundred.'

'Halve it.'

'Too late, Baz.'

'Get a rebate then. Any fucking thing.'

'Are you kidding?' Kinder was close to losing it. 'We pledge five hundred? They spend the money? Then we want half *back*? How does that play in the *News*? Students are key, Baz. You know that.'

'Students are dossers.'

'Whatever. But we need them. Andy?'

Makins agreed. On the back of the video work, he'd persuaded a bunch of guys from the uni to organise a registration drive. A lot of the students lived in the north of the city and the reg rate was beginning to pick up.

'How many? Tops?'

'Could be more than a thousand. Easily.'

Mackenzie nodded, knowing that he'd lost this one. He looked at his watch. Andy Makins hadn't finished.

'Just to say we're starting the *Pompey Passion* slots. The first lot are going up on YouTube this afternoon. Sixty seconds each. Just thought you ought to know.'

The *Pompey Passion* videos had been Bazza's idea. He had told Makins to find a whole load of punters who did odd things with their spare time. He knew the city was full of characters like these – anything from stuffing crows to meticulously constructed models of Nelson's fleet for Trafalgar re-enactments on Southsea Boating Lake – and if each of the slots ended with a full-on *Pompey First* endorsement, he thought it might have some impact. Makins had agreed but had come up with his own twist.

'We're kicking off with the actors from *Smoutland*.' He offered Mackenzie a rare grin. 'Only this time they're playing themselves.'

'Doing what?'

'That was the problem. In real life they're all a bit boring so we had to invent stuff. The old guy on the allotment turns out to collect fire extinguishers. Young Shel's got a thing about fur-trimmed knickers.'

'Brilliant. Top stuff.' Baz was grinning at last. 'Go for it.'

He brought the meeting to a close and agreed to hook up later. The guy doing the PA for the media launch wanted a sound check at 16.45. Mackenzie said he'd be there.

Kinder and Makins left the office. Mackenzie crossed to the door, locked it, then returned to his desk. He'd already made a note of the number he needed. He looked at the phone for a moment then picked it up. This was the last call he'd ever wanted to make but he knew he had no choice.

The number rang and rang then a voice he recognised only too well came on the line.

'It's me ...' he muttered, 'Bazza Mackenzie.'

Chapter eighteen

Winter was in Isleworth by mid-afternoon. Studland Close was a scruffy parade of shops off the Twickenham Road. The agency was perched on top of a second-hand white-goods store and had a flight of steps to an upstairs entrance at the back.

Irenka Beginski was having a late lunch. She answered Winter's knock with a plate of salad in one hand and a TV remote in the other. She was a big woman – tall, with startling make-up and a slightly intimidating smile.

'And you are?' Flat London accent. Definitely home-grown.

'My name's Paul Winter.'

'Do I know you?'

'I doubt it.'

'You're after somewhere to live?'

'No.'

She gave him a long appraising look then stepped aside.

'First room on the left,' she said. 'People normally phone first.'

The office was spartan but larger than Winter had expected: a desk, three chairs, two filing cabinets, a whiteboard listing current tenants, a TV balanced on a stack of phone directories, a chipped mirror, plus a huge badly framed poster. Winter paused to look at it. Crowds of what looked like tourists stood in a square gazing up at a clock tower. A frieze of picturesque buildings brightened the background.

233

'You know Cracow at all?'

'No.'

'You haven't missed much. It used to be lovely.' She eased herself behind the desk and began to pick at the salad. 'How can I help you, young man?'

'I understand you've got a brother.' Winter was still on his feet.

'I have. You're right.'

'Name?'

'I beg your pardon?'

'His name? Your brother?'

'I'm sorry, I'm not quite up to speed with this. Are you police? Immigration? VAT? None of the above? Only I'm a busy girl.'

'I can see.' Winter was looking at the empty desk.

Irenka put her plate down with some care. Then she reached for the phone. When the number answered, she said something rapid in what Winter assumed was Polish and rang off.

'Friend of mine.' There wasn't a trace of warmth in the smile this time. 'Big guy. Lives round the corner. You'll like him.'

Winter took this as a warning. He sat down. To his relief Irenka turned the TV off. He'd never much liked *Copycats*.

'I'll start again,' he said.

He explained he'd come up from Pompey. He worked for a businessman in the city. The businessman had issues with a guy called Martin Skelley and was keen to talk to an ex-employee of his who happened to be Polish.

'His name's Pavel Beginski,' Winter said. 'Am I getting warm?'

'Go on.'

'My boss wants to get in touch.'

'Why?'

'Because Skelley owes him money.'

'Lots of money?'

'Lots of money.'

'And Beginski? Where does he come into all this?'

'We think Pavel knows a thing or two about Skelley. And we think Skelley might pay a great deal of money for what Pavel knows.'

'So why doesn't this Pavel talk to Skelley direct?'

'Good question. We think he might have done. And knowing Skelley the way we do, we think he'd have told Pavel to fuck off.'

'I see.' Irenka had reached for a pad. 'And you can make a difference, can you? Supposing you're right about Pavel?'

'Most definitely.'

'How could Pavel be sure about that?'

'He couldn't. He'd have to trust us.'

'Sure. But supposing you're right, what's in it for Pavel?'

'Ten per cent of what we're owed.'

'Which is?'

'One million.'

'Pounds or euros?'

'Euros.'

Irenka made a note, then frowned.

'Poles like to drive a bargain,' she said. 'I can imagine someone like Pavel wanting 25 per cent.'

'Imagine?'

'Imagine.'

'Fifteen, then.'

'Twenty-three.'

'Seventeen five.'

'Twenty-one, young man. You're starting to bore me.'

'OK.' Winter shrugged. 'Twenty-one per cent it is, but this is strictly payment on results. Pavel does the business, gives us a sworn statement on paper, properly witnessed, plus we need a recorded message on video with date evidence in frame. Date evidence has to be that day's paper, preferably in English. The moment we get paid, Pavel gets his slice transferred to whatever account he nominates. You think he might be up for all that?'

Irenka wanted to know what this statement of Beginski's would be about, but Winter refused to go into details. Instead he repeated his question.

'You think he'll do it?'

'He might. I can only ask.'

'You're in touch?'

'Yeah.' She nodded, her eyes returning to the salad. 'What's the time frame?'

'Tight. Tighter than tight.'

'Fine.' The smile this time was unforced. 'So let's go back to 25 per cent, eh?'

Winter broke the news to Bazza Mackenzie back at the hotel. The last of the journalists had just left after filing their copy, and Bazza had at last broken out the champagne.

As far as Winter could judge, the press launch had been a stonker. Bazza had nailed the speech, departing from Kinder's set text and going on a wild riff about the little guys who always get dumped on. Making your own way in life, he'd said, was everyone's birthright, and he was sick of politicians telling everyone how to live and captains of industry feathering their own nests. The time had come for people to sort things out for themselves. That's what *Pompey First* was all about, and it was his privilege to carry the flag for the little guy.

Kinder, not the least upset by Bazza going off-piste, was delighted with the press reception. Media people rarely stooped to applause, and when it came it had felt sincere. Now, at the bar, he was using words like unprecedented and historic. Some of this euphoria was probably down to the Moët, but Bazza seemed equally fired-up. He pressed another glass on Winter and told him to pack his bags.

'Where are we going?'

'Westminster, mush.' Bazza clinked glasses. 'Enjoy.'

He towed Winter out of the bar and along the corridor to his office. Calls were stacking up on his answerphone, but he dismissed them with a flourish. A good day, he said. One of the fucking best.

Winter was nonplussed. When he'd left this morning, Bazza had been at rock bottom. It was never something he'd share with the likes of Kinder, but there might come a time, he confided to Winter, when he'd have to chuck it in. What 'it' was remained a mystery, and Bazza wouldn't explain, but driving over to Winchester Winter could only conclude that he meant the campaign. This would very definitely be a pity, holing *Gehenna* beneath the waterline, but he needn't have worried. *Pompey First*, for reasons Winter could only guess at, was in the rudest of health.

'So what's happened?' he asked.

'I got a loan. Raised some cash.'

'Who from?'

'None of your fucking business.'

'How much?'

'Enough to tide us over.' He leaned forward. 'Until chummy pays up.'

'You mean Skelley?'

'Yeah. This has to be down to you, Paul. We're going to owe you. Big time. All of us.'

Winter nodded. No problem. Glad to be of assistance. Then he took Bazza through the day's events. He'd found Beginski's sister. She knew where to find Pavel. Pavel could take Martin Skelley to a very bad place. Unless he came up with the money.

'How much is he costing us?'

'Two hundred and fifty grand.'

'*What?*'

'Think of it as a bargain, Baz. Skelley plays hardball. Assuming this Pavel comes through, he's going to be putting his neck on the line. He's pricing the risk at 25 per cent. That still leaves us with seven hundred and fifty grand.'

Mackenzie nodded. He needed to know that Winter had bargained him down.

'Her, Baz. And yes, I did, or at least I tried. No money changes hands until we get repaid by Skelley. And I've drawn the deadline for Pavel as tight as I can.'

'Like when?'

'The 16th. That's the end of next week. I've told her we need everything from Pavel by then.'

He explained the details. Bazza held his gaze.

'And we're sure this guy's in the know? We're absolutely sure he's got something on Skelley?'

'Yeah. For my money, like I told you last week, he was the driver that took Holman's body up to the Lake District. It turns out Skelley's got a big pad up there, bang on the water.'

'Who told you that?'

'She did. And the only way she can possibly know is from Pavel.'

'So Johnny's at the bottom of some fucking lake? Is that what you're saying?'

'Yeah. Think it through, Baz. We knew the state of Johnny before he disappeared. We knew he probably nicked off with your toot. That made him an obvious target. One way or another, that toot ended up with Skelley.'

'Then how come we got a settlement from Lou Sadler?'

'Fuck knows. The way I see it, she was the broker. She flogged it on to Skelley, gave us 350K from the proceeds, and he did the business. That kind of weight, you're looking at a couple of mil, give or take.'

'Which we want back.'

'Exactly.'

Mackenzie nodded. He seemed appeased. Any minute now, thought Winter, he's going to start talking about Johnny Holman. To date, in the absence of a body, the poor guy was in limbo, denied both a funeral and a memorial service. The

Bazza of old would have thought that outrageous. Not any longer.

'Johnny dicked us,' he said. 'I find that hard to forgive.'

'Forgive or believe?'

'Forgive. The state of the guy at the end. Pathetic.'

He brooded for a while, twirling the champagne glass between his fingers. Then he shook his head, the way a dog might shake the rain off, and asked about Pavel. Who was going to sort this guy out? What was supposed to happen next?

'His sister's going to bell me tonight. My guess is she lifted the phone the moment I left, sounded him out, checked whether he's up for the deal.'

'And if he's not?'

'Fuck knows. I could try some police contacts. They might have nailed him by now. The file's still open.'

'How come you know that, mush?'

There was an edge to the question Winter didn't much like. He took his time replying.

'Because I was a copper once, Baz. And because coppers never change their ways. A multiple homicide? Four bodies in a burned-out farmhouse? Johnny Holman wiped off the face of the earth? Those guys don't stop looking. Ever.'

'So who would you talk to?'

'I haven't a clue. It's just a possibility, a way forward, that's all. Hopefully the sister comes back tonight, Pavel's said yes, and it's all sweet.'

'But say it's not. Who do you talk to?'

'Dunno.' Winter shrugged. 'Jimmy Suttle might be a good place to start.'

'The lad who tried it on with Trude?'

'Yeah.'

'The one who married the bird from the *News*?'

'Yeah.'

'The one who asked you to be godfather to their nipper?'

'That's right.'

239

Mackenzie was smiling now, the mirthless smirk he reserved for moments in his life when he wanted to pass a message. Don't fuck around with me, he was saying.

'You thought I didn't know, didn't you?'

'About what, Baz?'

'About young Grace. About you and Suttle tucked up together. He's Filth, mush. And you work for me. And from where I'm sitting that spells big fucking trouble.'

'He's like a son, Baz. I taught him everything I know.'

'That's what worries me. You were a decent cop in your time. Better than the other dickheads.'

'So what are you saying? I resign as godfather? Would that make you feel better?'

'Don't be a twat.'

'What then?'

'Nothing. Except you said it yourself, didn't you? Once a copper always a copper.' He leaned forward across the desk, his voice a whisper. Then he reached for Winter's tie and pulled him even closer. 'I'm gonna say this once, just once, OK? Don't even think of dicking me around. Because if you do I'll tear you into fucking pieces. You got that, mush? You understand my drift?'

Winter nodded. There was a long silence. Mackenzie's grip slackened and he sat back, a tiny figure behind the big, big desk.

'You know something, Baz?' Winter was on his feet now. 'This fucking city really deserves someone like you.'

'I'll take that as a compliment, mush.' The smile again. 'Lucky I've got a sense of humour, eh?'

On his way out of the city, stuck in traffic, Winter brooded. Sometimes, like now, he felt it might be cheaper, quicker and altogether more merciful to simply shoot Mackenzie. For the price of a bullet or two he could bring this whole pantomime, with its alarming plot twists, to an end. Baz would be dead, the nation would be spared the possibility of a *Pompey First* MP, and – with the crime mysteriously undetected – Winter could ghost away into something resembling a peaceful life. But then, as the queue of commuter cars began to inch forward again, he thought of the downside. The tabloids would declare his dead boss a martyr to the democratic cause. And Willard would put a homicide charge together to bang him up for fuck knows how long.

So where would that leave Misty? Over the last few months, since Trude's accident, Winter knew they'd grown closer than they'd ever been. He'd always admired Misty's gutsiness, her absolute refusal to buckle under any of life's pressures, but what had happened to Trude had tested her to the limit, and some nights, as the weight fell off her, Winter could see the gauntness and the despair in her face.

As proud and independent as ever, she'd insisted that this on-going trauma was hers to handle. On the night of the accident Trude had been with virtual strangers. The boy at the wheel, the one who'd died, was out of his head on a cocktail of Class A drugs and Trude herself had been drinking heavily. None of that was Winter's doing, and the last thing Misty wanted was to lumber him with a family that had no one to blame but themselves. That, though, wasn't the issue. In Winter's book Misty deserved all the support she could get.

As a result, he'd spent most weekends with her at the Spinal Unit over in Salisbury. The drive was a pain in the arse and he'd always loathed hospitals, but as Jimmy Suttle had pointed out, this was no more of a cross than Faraday had volunteered to bear. At the time, Winter had wondered about the comparison, but the more he thought about it the more he knew that Suttle was right. Before his breakdown Faraday had been going to a different part of the hospital, the Burns Unit, but both men were supporting someone they loved. In Faraday's case it had been his partner Gabrielle, who was desperate to adopt a little Palestinian girl badly burned in Gaza. For Winter it was Misty

Gallagher, fighting every inch of the way to bring her errant daughter back to life.

He eased the Lexus off the motorway at the Hayling Island exit, still thinking about Faraday, surprised that he missed him so much.

Misty had been at home since mid-afternoon. The news from the hospital wasn't great.

'They think she's got something called posterior cord syndrome, pet. Here, I got them to write it down.'

She fumbled in her bag and gave Winter a scrap of paper. These days, without her glasses, Misty couldn't read a thing.

Winter peered at the handwriting. Capital letters. Easy. 'You're right, Mist. So what's posterior cord syndrome?'

Misty was at the fridge, sorting out a Stella for Winter. She was drinking white wine this evening. The bottle was already two thirds done.

'I think it's got to do with the back of the neck ... here.' Winter felt her fingers pressing against the collar of his shirt. 'That's where the cord got damaged, on the back bit.'

'But what does it *mean*, Mist?'

'It means she's going to have problems getting it together. She can feel OK. She's got sensation. But getting her legs to work properly won't be easy.'

The consultant, she said, had been pretty upbeat. In the end, over time, he thought there'd be no reason why Trude shouldn't be able to lead a normal life. But afterwards Misty had talked to the occupational therapist, who'd warned her to take nothing for granted. The coming months, once she was back at home, were going to be tough. With sensation restored, PSC patients always expect to be walking within days. Sadly, posterior cord syndrome doesn't work that way.

'And Trude? She knows all this?'

'Yeah. That's the problem. She's just like the OT woman described. She thought an hour in the pool would do it.'

'And?'

'It didn't. She said she felt helpless as a baby. She was really upset.'

Winter nodded, said nothing. For months now he'd been wondering whether Trude's accident had been karmic payback for borrowing Karl Sparrow's name for his new passport. Mercifully Trude would never be as kippered as Sparrow, but for the first time in his life he'd started to feel the sheer weight of circumstances crowding him into a corner. Last year, once he'd taken the decision to grass Bazza up, the way forward had seemed simple. Now it was anything but.

Misty wanted to know how the media launch had gone. Winter sensed she was fed up talking about spinal injuries. There had to be more to life than catheter hygiene and the ceaseless battle to prevent pressure sores.

'It went fine, as far as I know.'

'So where were you?'

'In London.'

'Really? You never mentioned London this morning ...'

'That's because I didn't know about it this morning. It was Baz's idea. He sent me up.'

'Yeah? And how is Mr Pompey?'

'Like a dog with two dicks. You're right, Mist, he can't get enough of all this politics shit.'

'That's because he's bored.'

'Maybe.'

'What else?'

'I think he believes it. It started as a game, as a bit of a piss-take. You know how he loves winding up the suits.'

'And now he is one? Is that what you're saying?'

'Yeah. Exactly. He'll never fit the mould because that isn't his way, but Kinder and the other guy, the young guy, have built him the train set of his dreams.'

'That's cruel. Baz never had a train set in his life. The only train that ever got his interest was the 6.57. And look where that took him. He's done all right, though, eh? We all have.'

Winter could only agree. In the immediate aftermath of Trudy's accident Mackenzie had played a blinder. Trudy had always been family to Baz, and in situations like these he'd spend whatever it took to make things happen.

Impatient to get Trude back on her feet, he'd told Winter to find the top American neurosurgeon in the field and see whether something couldn't be sorted. Winter had done his bidding, chasing down a high-profile specialist in southern Florida. With some reluctance the consultant at the Salisbury Spinal Unit had emailed Trudy's X-rays to Fort Lauderdale, and after a lengthy transatlantic phone call Winter found himself looking at a prospective bill for £63,500 to fly Trude over for an operation which might, just possibly, work. This was money that Bazza simply didn't have, as Winter was the first to point out, but the gesture had touched Misty deeply. More importantly, it made Winter realise just how much his boss still meant to her, yet another complication as Operation *Gehenna* hit top gear.

Mist was talking about Trudy again. However hard she tried to change the subject, everything still revolved around her daughter.

'They're talking about sending her home, pet.' She'd reached for the bottle again.

'When?'

'First week in May. That gives us a month.'

'To do what?'

'Get her room adapted. Get a bed at the right height. Get the taps changed in the bathroom. Put grab handles in the shower. I've got a list somewhere ...'

'So you think she'll be walking properly by then?'

'I doubt it. You're supposed to get loads of backup after they've left hospital, but reading between the lines it's going to be down to you and me, pet.' She leaned across and cupped his face. Her eyes were moist. 'We just have to keep at her, make sure she keeps trying, make sure she doesn't give up. I know it doesn't sound like Trude, but loads of these PCS people just throw the towel in. You know what I mean?'

'Yeah.'

'But we won't let that happen, will we pet?'

'Of course not.'

'What's the matter?'

'Nothing. It's just ...' He shook his head.

'What?'

'That first week in May.'

'What about it?'

'Are they talking a specific date?'

'Of course.' She frowned, trying to remember. 'The 6th? Would that be right? A Thursday?'

'Spot on, Mist.' Winter could only shake his head. 'Election day.'

'Does that matter?'

'Only if Bazza wins.'

'Why?'

'Because then we'll *all* be legless.'

She stared at him for a long moment. Then she got it. Legless. Very funny.

Winter was starting to apologise for the lapse in taste when he was interrupted by his mobile. It was a London number he didn't recognise and he was about to ignore the call when he remembered Irenka.

He slipped off the stool and nodded when Misty reached for his empty glass. Only when he was at the far end of the hall, safely out of earshot, did he answer the call. He was right. It was Irenka. She kept it brief. Winter nodded and checked his watch. He'd have some conversations and get back to her.

'Fine,' she said. 'Your call.'

Chapter nineteen

Portsmouth's Marriot Hotel lies to the north of the city, surrounded by a cat's cradle of new roads. Bazza Mackenzie was in the new ground-floor restaurant, as arranged, by eight in the morning. The hotel was handy for his first political engagement of the day, an appearance at the newly refurbed Queen Alexandra Hospital, just up the road. To his surprise, Cesar Dobroslaw had already arrived.

Dobroslaw was a big man in his late fifties, powerfully built. Over the years, at a handful of meetings, Bazza had never seen him in anything but a suit. Today's was a subtle grey with the lightest stripe. The white shirt looked box-fresh, and Mackenzie was betting the chunky cufflinks were solid gold. Dobroslaw spent a lot of money on his appearance and it showed.

Mackenzie stepped across to the table, extending a hand, expecting Dobroslaw to get up. When the Pole didn't move, he slipped into the chair opposite and tried to catch the attention of a nearby waitress. Dobroslaw was already drinking coffee. His big flat face was mapped with tiny broken veins, and Mackenzie caught the faintest hint of a tremor as he lifted the cup to his mouth.

'Fancy a bit of breakfast?' Mackenzie was eyeing the spread at the buffet. 'It's the least I owe you.'

Dobroslaw shook his head. He'd eaten already. He had to

be back in Southampton by nine. The traffic at this time of the morning was a joke.

Mackenzie wanted to know whether he'd got the money.

'With me?'

'Yeah.'

'Of course not. We have solicitors. Solicitors draw up agreements. That's the way we do business, no?'

Mackenzie tried to mask his impatience. Only yesterday afternoon he thought they'd struck a deal. He should have known better.

'You're backing out?'

'Not at all. We just need to be clear about the details. A hundred thousand is a lot of money, Mr Mackenzie. Or at least it is to me.'

Mackenzie knew he'd come to gloat. Over the years they'd had a number of run-ins, often violent, and on the phone Bazza had sensed the Pole's intense pleasure at finding his Pompey rival up shit creek. Dobroslaw was one of the richest men on the south coast. A small army of Belorussian toms, imported from Minsk, had laid the foundations for a thriving business empire, and unlike Bazza he'd invested the profits wisely.

'My solicitor tells me we'll need the deeds to your house,' he said.

'The bank's got them. I told you yesterday. Eighty per cent of the place is on a mortgage.'

'A copy, then.'

'That's gonna take time. Listen, this is a handshake, right? Your guy draws up an agreement, I sign over my share of the remaining equity, and you give me a cheque. It's that simple, or am I missing something here?'

'We need the deeds.'

'OK. No problem. I'll get the bank to fax them over. It's in their interests too.' He paused, aware that he was beginning to sweat. 'Are we on the same page here? Or shall I go through it all again?'

Dobroslaw was smiling now. He had Mackenzie exactly where he wanted him.

'There's the question of interest,' he said slowly.

'We agreed that too. Three per cent for the first month. If it goes any longer we're talking a one per cent compound escalator per quarter.'

'Per month.'

'You have to be joking.'

'And one per cent is too low. We need at least two.'

'No way.' Mackenzie shook his head. 'I don't have enough equity left to cover that.'

'Fine.' Dobroslaw reached for the cashmere coat folded over his briefcase. 'Then I'll be back in Southampton earlier than I expected.'

'Wait.' Mackenzie shut his eyes a moment, trying to do the maths. 'We're talking ball park around 30 per cent annual interest. Have I got that right?'

'Yes.'

'You don't think that's a rip-off?'

'Not at all. Thirty per cent is high. Of course it's high. But you're telling me this is a short-term loan. I'm doing you a favour, Mr Mackenzie. I'm giving you every incentive to repay the capital and the interest by this time next month. What kind of rip-off is that?'

'Say it goes tits up? Say there's a glitch? Say I need the money for longer than a month?'

'Then I do you another favour and call the loan in.'

'Sure. And that way I lose my house.'

'Exactly.' The smile again. 'Which is why you'll pay the money back next month.'

Mackenzie turned the deal over in his head. Whichever way he looked at it, he knew he had no choice. Without the Pole's money, he was dead in the water.

Dobroslaw, with an extravagant apology for his nosiness, was curious to know why Mackenzie needed the money. He'd caught the odd mention of *Pompey First* on the local TV news. He'd even read a profile of Mackenzie in his wife's copy of the *Daily Mail*. Were these two things perhaps connected? The firework blaze of *Pompey First* and yesterday's phone call pleading for a bail-out?

'Politics can be an expensive business—' Mackenzie began.

'Business?'

'Commitment. Calling. Vocation. Whatever.'

'Then why do it?'

'Because I think it matters.'

'Really? You believe that? Someone with your background?'

'What's wrong with my background?'

'Absolutely nothing, my friend. You come from where I come from. You come from absolutely nowhere, and you make a great deal of money, and you make life sweet for your family, and you have nice holidays, and you drive a nice car, and then along comes this politics thing, and maybe it's more complicated than you think, and suddenly you're on the phone to someone you don't like at all asking for rather a lot of money. I'm just curious, that's all. Because maybe politics is more complicated than you think it is.'

'That's crap.'

'You think so?' Dobroslaw glanced at his watch, then slipped a card from his pocket and placed it carefully on the table. 'My solicitor. He'll be glad to get the deeds. Sooner rather than later, eh? From your point of view?'

He began to get to his feet then sat down again at the approach of the waitress. She'd finally noticed Mackenzie and had a very big smile on her face.

'It's you.' She was fumbling for her pad. 'BazzaMac.'

Mackenzie acknowledged her with a terse nod. This kind of thing was happening more and more often in Pompey, a tribute to Leo Kinder's promotional skills, and normally Bazza loved the attention. Not now, though. Not in this kind of company.

'I've changed my mind.' He was looking at the order pad. 'I'm not staying.'

'That's fine. I just want your autograph.'

'Yeah?' Mackenzie took her pad and scrawled a signature across the top page.

'Do I get a kiss? Only my mum's not going to believe this.'

Mackenzie glanced up at her, then put a cross under his name.

'Thanks, Baz. And good luck, eh?'

Dobroslaw watched the waitress pick her way between the tables. A chef was ladling out scrambled eggs behind the buffet bar. When the waitress showed him the pad he looked across, grinned and gave Baz the thumbs up.

'The price of fame, eh?' Mackenzie tried to hide his embarrassment.

'Not at all.'

'You don't think so?'

'No.' Dobroslaw pushed the solicitor's card gently across the table. 'This is the price of fame, my friend. Let's just hope you can pay it back.'

Winter and Suttle were at the safe house in Winchester. In the absence of anything drinkable in the kitchen, Suttle had acquired a couple of take-out coffees from a café in nearby St Cross.

Winter explained about last night's phone call from Irenka. She'd talked to Pavel and got the nod for the proposed arrangement. He'd been sticky at first, but the moment she'd mentioned the money on offer his reservations had vanished.

Suttle wanted to know how much he was after.

'It's not him, son. It's her. She's screwing us for 25 per cent.'

'Of a mil?'

'Yeah.'

'That's 250K.'

'Exactly.'

'And you've told Mackenzie?'

'Of course I have.'

'And what did he say?'

'He hates it. Pennies matter to Bazza, always have. He thinks a quarter of a million is a little bit on the high side.'

'But he agreed?'

'He had to. He has no choice. Worse still, he knows it. Bazza's the kind of guy who invented the word options. Just now, my son, he hasn't got any.'

'You sound pleased.'

'I am. Most of the time you roll with the punches. Bazza gives you lots of shit, but he pays you well and on a good day you have a laugh or two. But when times get really hard there's another guy in there, a total fucking animal, and when he's like that believe me you don't want to be around.'

'So what's happened?'

'Don't ask.'

'But I am asking. And we need to know.'

'We?'

'Me, Paul. Me.'

With some reluctance Winter told him about the confrontation in his office last night. The warning had been explicit. One step out of line and Winter was a dead man.

'You believe him?'

'Too right. I'm not playing the health and safety card, son, but under this kind of pressure the guy's a ticking bomb. I've seen it before. He's unpredictable. He can kick off at the slightest thing. And when that happens, you seriously don't want to be in the firing line.'

'You think he's sniffed something?'

'Yeah.'

'What?'

'You.'

He explained about the godfather thing. Baz believed in

251

families, always had, but the Filth were the Filth and you never crossed the line.

'So how did he know?'

'That's a very good question. There's a guy called Andy Makins who works for us now.'

'I know. You mentioned him before.'

'He used to be with the *News*, and Baz seems to think he's shacked up with another reporter called Gill Reynolds who Baz just happens to fancy.'

'That's right. He is.'

'You *know* about this?'

'Sure. Gill's big mates with Lizzie.'

'Great. Thanks a fucking million. So you're telling me that Gill Reynolds or Makins or both of them know all about little me and little Grace?'

'Bound to.' Suttle reached for his coffee. 'And I imagine that's how it got back to Mackenzie.'

'Right ...' Winter did his best to fight the rising tide of anger. 'Do any of you muppets understand the first thing about Mackenzie? That he hates you lot? That he wouldn't cross the road if you were lying on the pavement fucking *dying*? That stitching you lot up is a point of fucking *honour*? Is any of that stuff on your fucking radar? Because if the answer's no, then I'm out of here.'

'Calm down, mate. I'm sure you handled it.'

'I did, son, I did. And you know how? By playing the only card I have left. By telling him that you and me were close, really close, father-and-son close, and that you mattered to me. Not just because I made you the cop you are but because you helped save my fucking *life*.'

'A pleasure, mate.'

'Yeah, well bear that in mind because you might just have to do it again.'

'It's not that critical. It can't be.'

'*Critical?*' Winter exploded. 'That's a management word,

son. What's this job doing to you? Have you lost it completely? Have you forgotten what people are like out there? In the real world? Bazza Mackenzie, in case you hadn't noticed, has people *killed* when it suits his fucking business plan.'

'Does he?'

The question brought Winter skidding to a halt. He looked away. He frowned. He shook his head. He mumbled something about losing it, about going over the top. Of course Bazza didn't kill people. That was just a figure of speech, a spur-of-the-moment thing, whatever.

Suttle didn't believe him for a moment.

'Tell me more,' he said quietly.

'There is no more.'

'Of course there's more. Just tell me.'

'No.'

'What does that mean?'

'It means no, son. It means we're changing the subject. It means I lost it for a moment there. I apologise.'

'I don't want an apology.'

'I bet you fucking don't.'

'Just tell me what happened.'

'No.' Winter tried the coffee and pulled a face. 'This stuff's cold.'

There was a long silence. Winter heard a lorry rumble past on the main road.

'It happened abroad, didn't it?' Suttle wouldn't let go.

'I've no idea what you're talking about.'

'France? Spain?'

'Pass.'

'Recently? The last couple of years?'

'This is a waste of breath, son. Let's talk about Mr Beginski.'

'Sure.' Suttle extracted a sheet of paper from his file and gave it to Winter. 'Why not?'

Winter found himself looking at a sheet of timings. There

was a BMI flight from Heathrow to Warsaw tomorrow morning at half past six.

'You want me to go to Poland?'

'We do.' Suttle nodded. 'There are twelve trains a day from Warsaw to Lublin. The journey takes about two and a half hours. You could be with our friend by mid-afternoon.'

'Fine. Then what?'

'You get what you need for Skelley.'

'The statement, you mean?'

'Yeah. You'll have to find a lawyer to witness it. Shouldn't be a problem.'

'And the photos? The video? All that bollocks?'

'Here ...' Suttle bent to his briefcase and gave Winter a smallish box with the cellophane wrapping still intact. 'Canon Ixus. State of the art. Does both stills and video. Gives you everything you need. The instruction manual will be inside.' He looked in the briefcase again and produced a tiny slip of paper. 'Have a practice tonight, eh? This is the receipt.'

'Receipt?'

'Yeah. I assume Mackenzie's paying.'

'And you want the money back?'

'Of course we do. No rush.' Suttle nodded at the airline timings. 'Listen. If we're right about Beginski, then you've got Skelley up against the wall.'

'Yeah, son. And so have you.'

Suttle said nothing, just smiled. Then he went through the sequence of events they wanted Beginski to attest. Major Crime believed that Johnny Holman's body had left the Isle of Wight on 9 February aboard a Freezee van driven by Beginski. The next day, according to worksheets seized from Freezee, Beginski had made a run north. The destination was logged as Carlisle, but Suttle suspected he'd driven deep into the Lake District and offloaded Holman's body at Martin Skelley's house on Derwent Water. What happened after that was anyone's guess, but it was a matter of record that Pavel Beginski, after returning to London, had binned the job and left the country.

'With a whack of money? Like I told Bazza?'

'That's the rumour.'

'You've talked to Beginski's mates?'

'Of course we have.'

'And they stand it up?'

'Yeah. It turns out Pavel was a bit of a drinker. Threw a party before he left. Lots of vodka. Lots of sausage. That's something he might regret.'

'So why haven't you scooped him up?'

'He's disappeared. Or that's what the Polacks tell us.'

'You issued a European Arrest Warrant?'

'Yeah.'

'Nothing?'

'Zilch.'

'Lucky then.'

'How?'

'Finding that sister of his.'

'Too right.'

Suttle, unblinking, held Winter's gaze. Then he asked whether Winter was prepared to make the journey to Warsaw.

'Of course I am. Does that surprise you?'

'Yeah, it does.'

'Why?'

'Because you told me you were bricking it over your own Euro-warrant. You said you expected a knock on the door from our lot. Van to Heathrow. Extradition without a court hearing. The rest of your life in some foreign jail.'

'Never.' Winter shook his head. 'You've got that wrong, son.'

'I don't think so.'

'Then I must have been pissed. If I was that worried about a Euro-warrant –' he reached for the BMI timings '– there's no way I'd risk leaving the fucking country.'

Bazza Mackenzie did his best to make sure that the bank faxed his house deeds to Dobroslaw's solicitor by noon. His appearance at the Queen Alexandra Hospital attracted a modest media posse. He was photographed in one of the paediatric wards, perched on the bed of a convalescing six-year-old, and another snapper caught the moment he presented an Aruna Dindane Pompey shirt to the sister in charge of the Renal Unit. According to Kinder, she was a regular at Fratton Park and would be thrilled by the gesture. As it turned out there'd been a shift change, and the shirt ended up with another sister, who couldn't stand football. This logistical glitch didn't affect Mackenzie in the slightest. He gave the woman a kiss and told her he'd bung her a couple of comp tickets for the Fratton End so she'd know what she'd been missing.

Later, on the pavement outside the hospital's main entrance, Mackenzie held an impromptu press conference and told the assembled reporters that the National Health Service would be safe in his hands. In the background, thanks to Kinder, eight students dressed as nurses were jumping up and down with *Pompey First* placards.

Back at the hotel, preparing for an afternoon descent on a senior citizen bingo session in North End, Bazza took a phone call from Conrad Whittiker, his account controller at the bank. Whittiker was apologetic. There seemed to have been a hiccough with the dispatch of the house deeds to Mr Dobroslaw's solicitor.

'How come?' Mackenzie was checking his watch.

'We had to get in touch with your wife, Mr Mackenzie, and confirm her approval. She's co-owner of the property of course.'

'So what did she say?'

'I gather she's not happy. Maybe you ought to have a word.'

Mackenzie phoned her at once. She was, as Whittiker had suspected, extremely disturbed.

'This is crazy, Baz,' she said. 'Please tell me what's going on.'

Late that afternoon Andy Makins ducked out of the Royal Trafalgar and walked the quarter-mile to the Sunlight Café, a squalid Southsea backstreet eatery he favoured when he needed time to think. Gill Reynolds had phoned him earlier, insisting they were due a conversation, and she was already tucked into a corner when he arrived. Texting on her phone, she was doing her best to avoid the lowlife around her.

Makins made his way through the litter of greasy unwiped tables. The regulars knew his face by now, and he sensed a kind of tacit approval of the way he dressed and the fact that he kept himself to himself. His favourite was a hollow-faced junkie with nose piercings and a dragon tatt down the side of her scrawny neck. She lived in a bedsit round the corner and called in for soup and toast between the men she shagged to fund her habit.

Gill was under-impressed.

'This place is horrible.'

'Real, Gill. It's real.'

'Is that right?' She offered her face for a kiss but Makins wasn't interested. Gill, uncomfortably aware that they hadn't had sex for more than a month, wanted to know how the campaign had kicked off. By now she knew that this was the surest way to talk him into bed. Andy's conversation had always been limited, but just now his entire life seemed to have shrunk to a single subject. Nothing mattered except *Pompey First.*

'It's going OK,' he told her. 'You want another coffee?'

'No, thank you. Tell me more.'

Makins explained about the websites. These were his children. He'd dreamed them up, nurtured them and then set them free at an early age to wander the streets of the Internet. Some had prospered, others were back home within days, friendless, ignored, the Billy No-Mates of the blogosphere.

The phrase made Gill laugh. She loved Makins in a mood like this.

'Actually it's Leo's phrase, not mine.'

'But you're out there, my love. You're doing the heavy lifting.' Her hand closed over his. 'You're the daddy in all this, am I right?'

'Yeah.'

'So which one's your favourite?'

'You mean site?'

'Yes.'

Makins frowned. The question called for a little thought. He never took himself less than seriously.

'*Frontline Pompey*,' he said at last. 'It's a bid for the far right. BNP. Hard-core Pompey fans. All those nutters in the English Defence League. You pitch your tent and see who turns up. It's been amazing these last few days. I never understood how many punters have got a bit of squaddie in them.'

'And they'll vote for *Pompey First*?'

'They'll vote for whoever gives them their country back.'

'We're talking immigration?'

'Too right. It's huge. None of the mainstream lot'll touch it, but Bazza just gets stuck in.'

'He contributes to these sites?'

'No. He hasn't got the time, so I do it for him. I'm fluent in Bazza-speak, believe it or not.'

'But he checks this stuff?'

'Rarely. To tell you the truth he's shit on the small print. I think it bores him.'

'But he trusts you?'

'He must do. And that's nice.'

'So what do you say? On the immigration thing? When you're pretending to be Bazza?'

'I say some of my best friends are Pakis. I say I love 'em all to bits. I say they've got the best food in the world. And I say they're great when it comes to the family thing.'

'And how many squaddie votes does that win you?'

'I also say I love my country the way it used to be. Just like the Pakis must love theirs. Everyone deserves a little bit of their own England. In case you're wondering, that's code for fuck off home.'

'Clever.'

'Obvious. And bloody effective. People love this stuff. The Internet's like a pub. You can say what you like, spout any kind of nonsense, but it's being there that matters. Bazza's right. We're all pack animals. We move in herds. We like company. We like mixing it. We like a bit of a ruck.'

'Is this you speaking?'

'Bazza. He might be crap on detail but he's very sharp, he learns very quickly. People would be nuts to write this thing off as some kind of stunt. It's not a stunt. Believe it or not, he means it.'

'So how is he?'

'Stressed out of his head. Up one minute, down the next. I like him, don't get me wrong. Leo Kinder says he's authentic, and that seems to matter. It's a brand thing, apparently. It's what they teach in business school. Whatever you're selling, it has to be *real*.'

'Like this place?'

'Yeah. It might not be your taste but –' he shrugged '– who gives a shit?'

'Maybe I do.' She gave his hand a squeeze.

'Yeah?'

'Yeah … but hey, what's not to like?' She was looking at an elderly dosser by the window. A heavy cold had coated the sleeve of his jacket with drying mucus, and he badly needed a shave.

Makins was oblivious. He was also on a tight schedule. His video crew at the uni were prepping for a night shoot with a bunch of feral kids in Portsea and they needed a proper brief.

'Can't tempt you to the gym then? It's half-price on Wednesdays.'

Makins ignored the invitation. Exercise was a planet he'd

yet to explore. He wanted to know why Gill had phoned him. What was so pressing it couldn't wait?

'I've got a proposition.'

'I'm stuffed, Gill. Really busy.'

'It's not that. Mark's asked me to have a word.'

Mark Boulton was editor of the *News*. Gill had at last caught Makins' attention.

'What does he want?'

'He's looking down the road, post-election. He hasn't got a clue how your lot are going to perform on the night because no one has, but he likes what he's seen so far.'

'He does?'

'Big time.' She nodded. 'He thinks you've put Pompey on the map and that's no bad thing.'

'Already he thinks that?'

'Yeah.'

'Excellent.' Makins shook the hair out of his eyes. 'Because there's lots more to come.'

'I bet. And that's the point really. He wonders whether you're keeping any kind of diary.'

'Why?'

'Because he'd like to publish a special supplement after the election – the inside story, what made your lot tick. He's serious, believe me. We're talking a 25K print run. He'd even pay you for it.'

Makins laughed. One of the many reasons he'd left the *News* was their obsession with cutting costs.

'The answer's no,' he said.

'Really?' She didn't hide her disappointment. 'Am I allowed to ask why?'

'No.'

'Why not?'

'Because it's none of your business. Or Mark's.'

She nodded, then reached for her phone and slipped it into

her bag. There were moments when he couldn't hide the truth from her, and this was one of them

'You've had a better offer, haven't you?' She kissed him and then stood up to leave. 'Good luck, my love. Don't forget me, eh?'

The message from Marie was waiting for Mackenzie when he got back to the hotel. His wife needed to talk to him urgently. Please ring.

Bazza sank behind his desk and briefly reviewed the pile of other stuff that had come in. He made a couple of calls on issues that couldn't wait, checked in with Leo Kinder and then turned his attention once again to Marie.

She'd been trying to contact him all afternoon. His phone had been on divert throughout the bingo session but she'd sent two texts, both of them terse. The second one left little room for negotiation. *Just pick up the phone 4 Gd's sake.*

Bazza kept a photo of Marie on his desk. In her late forties she was still a handsome woman, blonde, leggy, gym-fit, and when friends and business associates told him he was the luckiest guy in the world he knew they were right. Not because Marie had kept her looks but because she was the real strength in the marriage, the family's centre of gravity around whom everyone else revolved. Bazza's orbit had been the giddiest, wild excursions into deepest space, but he'd always come back to her. Not just because she was sexy and popular and all the other stuff, but because she made him feel good. She was class. She cared about him. Without Marie there was nothing.

With some reluctance, he lifted the phone. He knew she wouldn't rant at him. That wasn't her style. But he braced himself for a bollocking all the more effective for being so reasonable and low-key.

'Ma? It's me.'

He made his excuses, said he was sorry for not getting back, explained how busy he was. He was about to tell her about this evening's campaigning schedule when she cut in.

'We need to talk,' she said. 'All of us.'

'Have you signed the bank thing?'

'No.'

'Why not?'

'I've just told you. We need to talk. Stu's coming over this evening with Ezzie. We have to straighten things out, Baz. We can't go on like this.'

'Tonight's impossible. I'm up at Mountbatten for a meeting at seven. Then there's—'

'Cancel it. The kids are coming over at half seven. OK?'

She put the phone down.

The Mountbatten Centre, in Kinder's phrase, was the key to Pompey's heart. The complex of sports facilities lay on the city's western shore beside Tipner Lake. The recent addition of a multi-million-pound Olympic-size swimming pool offered a world-class launch pad for young local swimmers, and in a city as sports mad as this one, Mackenzie knew it deserved lots of electoral attention.

He and Leo Kinder drove up together. The Secretary of the Boxing Club was waiting in reception. Upstairs, in the café, he introduced Bazza to a couple of star prospects who were keen to shake his hand, and the candidate happily posed for a couple of phone shots to squirt off to their mates. Afterwards, with the Secretary, they got down to business. The Boxing Club was planning a big tournament for the autumn. Mackenzie confirmed that he'd be happy to chuck in a bit of sponsorship, though he wasn't yet able to go firm on a definite figure. When the Secretary enquired whether he'd be prepared to present the trophies on the night, Mackenzie beamed. My pleasure, he said.

A glance at Kinder prompted an idea for a poster. Kinder had roughed it out earlier in the War Room. He wanted to come with a photographer to the club's Friday night training session. They'd choose one of the younger lads and take some action shots to feature on a poster for the closing week of the campaign. Kinder showed the Secretary the strapline: *Pompey First ... striking a blow for city pride*. The Secretary was impressed. Like Mackenzie, he was Copnor born and bred.

'On the fucking nose,' he said. 'Brilliant.'

With Kinder en route back to the hotel, Mackenzie hijacked a girl from the Mountbatten management team and did an impromptu walkabout, visiting the cycle track, the squash courts and the weights room, dispensing cheerful waves and Pompey wisecracks. In the sports hall his entrance brought a netball game to a halt. This was a face from the local TV news. When the ball came Mackenzie's way he made four attempts on the basket and missed every time. Being a short-arse, he said, was sometimes a pain in the bum. The women loved him, and even his escort – an ultra-cool nineteen-year-old from Baffins Pond – was impressed.

'You're like that Prince Charles,' she said, 'but tastier.'

Mackenzie's last call was the fitness suite. At this time in the evening, once the after-work crowd had left, it was nearly deserted. A couple of guys in the corner were going head to head on the rowing machines, and an older woman in a scarlet leotard was on the running machine, her eyes closed, her lips moving to whatever was playing on her MP3. Mackenzie spared her no more than a glance, then took a second look. Gill Reynolds.

He walked over. For someone her age, maybe early forties, she was in excellent nick: sleek legs, neat arse, flat stomach. Mackenzie reached for the controls and wound the speed down. Gill frowned and slowed her pace. Then the machine came to a complete halt and she opened her eyes.

'Awesome.' Mackenzie threw her a towel. 'Drink?'

The bar was upstairs. Mackenzie drank a bottle of Becks

while Gill showered. When she finally turned up, she settled for a spritzer.

'You look knackered,' she said.

'I am. Totally wrecked.'

'You should try some of this.'

'That's a woman's drink.'

'I meant exercise.'

'Really? You think I'm sat on my arse all day? Jesus …' He called for another Becks, no glass.

They talked about the campaign. Gill, who'd already penned a long feature piece for the *News* some months ago, was fascinated by the way all the schemes and dreams were now playing out. The election, at long last, was upon them. The public could be unforgiving. Mistakes would begin to matter.

'Too right.' Mackenzie took a suck at the Becks. 'So are you still shagging Andy?'

Gill laughed. After what she'd heard about Mackenzie, nothing came as a surprise.

'I thought we were talking about *Pompey First*?'

'Well? Are you?'

'No. Not right now.'

'Heartbroken?'

'I miss him, yes.'

'Why?'

'Is that a serious question?'

'Of course it fucking is.'

'Then I'll give you a serious answer. That guy was the fuck of my life.'

'Was?'

'I dunno –' she reached for her glass '– but probably yes.'

Mackenzie took his time digesting the news. He could think of lots of nice things to say about Andy Makins but this wasn't one of them.

'Surprised?' Gill was watching him carefully.

'Yeah. Tell you the truth, I'd never have thought he had it in him.'

'But he does, Baz. In spades.'

'Great.' Mackenzie lifted his bottle in salute. 'Here's to Andy.'

Gill ignored the toast. She wanted to know whether Bazza was keeping a diary.

'Why?'

'Because we might be interested.'

She explained about her editor on the *News*. The special supplement, in her view, would offer a post-election chance to draw breath, part the curtains and show the public how the campaign had *really* worked.

'You really think I've got time to keep a fucking diary?' Mackenzie liked the bit about parting the curtains.

'Probably not.'

'Then who does the grafting?'

'Me.' She smiled at him. 'We'd have to touch base pretty regularly, probably every day. You give me five minutes of your precious time and I can sort the rest.'

'I bet you can.' Mackenzie loved her fingernails. The way she shaped and varnished them reminded him of Misty. 'So do I get time to have a think? Make a decision?'

'No.' She shook her head. 'You don't.'

'Then the answer's yes.' He tipped the bottle again. 'Game on?'

It was nearly ten by the time Mackenzie finally got home. He'd made a detour to the hotel, collecting his schedule for tomorrow's appearances, which seemed to include a brief speech at a dog-walking class in the depths of Buckland. Buckland was inner-city Pompey, the real thing, and when he asked Kinder what he was supposed to say, Kinder rolled his eyes. The kids were worse than the dogs, he said, so watch your back. Mackenzie laughed, heading out of the hotel's front entrance.

Makins happened to be leaving as well, and Mackenzie paused for a moment beside the Bentley, wondering whether he ought to offer the boy a lift, but then decided against it. The kid had enough going for him. He could fucking walk.

A two-minute drive took him to Sandown Road. Mackenzie let himself in and headed for the kitchen. The moment he opened the door, he knew he'd made a big mistake. He should, after all, have binned all the nonsense up at the Mountbatten.

Stu Norcliffe, his son-in-law, was asleep, his bulk filling the tiny two-seat sofa. Ezzie was perched on a stool, watching something inane on the big plasma. Of Marie, ominously, there was no sign.

'She's gone to bed, Dad. You ought to wake her.'

Mackenzie went upstairs. There were a couple of clean sheets neatly folded on the landing outside one of the spare bedrooms. He stared at them for a moment, then walked into the master bedroom. He could hear the splash of water from the en-suite. Marie was washing her hair, oblivious to his presence. He watched her for a moment or two. Beautiful.

'It's me, Ma. Got held up.'

Marie turned the shower off and began to dry her hair. She told him to go downstairs and get Ezzie to put the kettle on. She'd join them in a minute.

'I don't want tea.'

She shot him a look, stepped very close, lifted her head, wrinkled her nose.

'You've been drinking. Great.'

'Big deal.' He asked her about the sheets in the hall.

'They're for you. There's a duvet on the bed already and spare blankets in the wardrobe. Help yourself.'

'Thanks. I will.'

Downstairs, Mackenzie roused Stu. He had a bottle of decent malt in one hand and a couple of glasses in the other. Stu, still groggy, said yes to the malt. Ezzie was still watching the telly.

Marie appeared in her dressing gown. She wasted no time

on small talk. She'd spent most of the day on the phone to the accountant. This was a call, she said, that she should have made months ago. Probably years ago. Even now, even after God knows how long on the phone, she'd no idea where the money had gone.

'Hard times, love. There was a banking crisis. You probably heard.'

'But there's nothing left, Baz. Spain? France? Montenegro? Dubai? It's all gone, it's all mortgaged. And for why? Because you couldn't stop buying, because you had to get bigger and bigger, because you're like a kid, because you're so bloody *greedy* and so fucking *stupid* you had to have more all the time.'

'More is good.'

'More is the kiss of death, Baz. More is what's got us into this mess. You can't just keep building and building and you know why? Because in the end the thing will just fall over. Are you with me, Baz? Do you understand that?'

Mackenzie shrugged. The first malt had gone down rather nicely. He helped himself to another and offered the bottle to Stu. Stu shook his head.

'She's right, Baz,' he said. 'I've gone over the figures. I'd no idea it was so bad.'

'This is short-term, mush. Things change all the time. A couple of months and we're in the clear.'

'You think so?'

'Definitely.'

'So how does that work?'

'It's a question of bottle, Stu. Some people have it and some don't.'

Mackenzie seemed to think this settled the argument. Ezzie had other ideas.

'Mum says our houses are on the line.'

'Mum's wrong. I've got that sorted.'

'Yeah?'

267

Mackenzie nodded. He'd negotiated a bridging loan only this morning. Thanks to Marie it would take longer than he'd like to lay hands on the cash, but the deal was done and there wouldn't be a problem.

'So who's this guy Cesar?' Marie again.

'A business associate. A friend of mine.'

'What kind of business?'

'Home entertainment. He also rents vans.'

'And you think a hundred thousand will be enough?'

'Ample. Like I say, it's short-term, a month tops.'

'And after that?'

'After that –' Mackenzie smothered a yawn '– you can all come up to Westminster and I'll show you around.'

Marie closed her eyes and squeezed them very hard. Lately she'd begun to suspect that her husband was off his head. This was the clincher.

'You're mad, Baz,' she said quietly. 'I could get you sectioned.'

'Thanks.'

'I mean it. This whole political thing, you know what it is?'

'Tell me.'

'It's a wank, Dad.' This from Ezzie. 'The whole thing's a wank. Even Stu thinks so.'

'Stu?' A hint of something dangerous had crept into Mackenzie's voice. The question was a challenge, a test.

'I think you're overstretched, Baz. Maybe *Pompey First* wasn't such a clever move.'

'You're a London cunt, mush. You wouldn't know the first thing about Pompey.'

'Yeah, but even so—'

'Even so, bollocks. You listen to me, son. There are some people in this town who know a thing or two about loyalty, about sticking with something through thick and thin, about getting a fair deal for the little guys that get screwed by the likes of you, and you know what? I'm one of them. That's

268

where *Pompey First* comes from. That's why I get up in the morning. That's why I've just spent most of my fucking evening playing Mr Nicey-Nicey to a bunch of netball witches over in the Mountbatten who might, just might, give me their precious fucking vote. That's commitment, son. That's the kind of graft that built this city. Not that anyone ever fucking listens.'

He tipped his glass to his throat and swallowed the contents in one. Then he was gone.

Marie told Ezzie to turn the telly off. No one wanted to break the silence. Finally it was Stu who asked about Cesar.

'Just who is this guy?'

'I haven't a clue, my love.' Marie glanced at her watch. 'I was hoping we might find out.'

Paul Winter finally made contact with Marie past midnight. He was in a hotel near Heathrow. He was sorry he hadn't returned her calls.

'What's going on?'

Marie explained what she'd learned from the accountant. None of this was news to Winter.

'We're fucked, my love,' he said. 'Excuse my French.'

'As bad as that?'

'Probably worse. I've been trying to explain the facts of life for the best part of a year. In the end you just give up. It's like talking to a child.'

Marie mentioned the bridging loan Bazza appeared to have negotiated. She didn't know the details, but her husband seemed to have pledged the last few bricks of the house not already held by the bank.

Winter wanted to know more about the loan. Where was it coming from? Who had Bazza tapped up?

'His name's Cesar. He's a Polish guy. As far as I know, he's local.'

'Cesar Dobroslaw?'

'Why are you laughing?'

'He's a gangster, my love. Worse than that, he's a Scummer, lives in a huge pad over in Rownhams. Baz must be desperate.' Scummer was Pompey-speak for anyone who lived in Southampton. Not a compliment.

'Does he have the money, this Cesar?' Marie asked.

Winter said yes. Dobroslaw was a wealthy man. The last time Winter had tried to take a proper look, one of his goons had kicked the shit out of him in a Portakabin beside Southampton Docks.

'Kicked the shit out of you?'

'Me. Dobroslaw's no gentleman. He settles arguments the way Baz does. Birds of a feather, my love.'

Winter asked about the terms of the loan, knowing Dobroslaw would love to warm his hands at a bonfire of Mackenzie's assets. Marie said again that she had no details.

'He'll screw us –' Winter yawned '– and he'll enjoy every last second.'

Marie fell silent. It had been a very long day, deeply depressing, and every conversation she had seemed to make things worse. At length she roused herself and asked Winter what he was doing in London.

'You don't want to know, my love.' He was laughing again. 'Tell Baz I'm on the case.'

Chapter twenty

Winter was at the big central railway station in Warsaw by mid-morning. The place was awash with scarlet-faced drunks and there wasn't a single signboard that made the slightest sense. Finally he located the ticket office and bought himself a single to Lublin.

The train left within twenty minutes, clattering out through the suburbs of Warsaw on a day of filmy sunshine sharpened by a biting easterly wind. To his relief, he had a compartment to himself. He'd been up since four in the morning and by the time they hit the open country he was asleep.

The ticket collector woke him up a couple of hours later. It turned out he'd spent some time in the UK visiting relatives in Norfolk and spoke decent English. He also lived in Lublin, and when Winter showed him the address Irenka had emailed him for Pavel Beginski, he drew a pencilled map. The bar, he confirmed, was called Krzywa Wieza. He'd never been there himself, but a friend of his knew it well. Apparently it had changed hands recently and gone downhill, since when his friend, along with the other regulars, had taken their money elsewhere.

Winter thanked him and pocketed the map. He took a cab from Lublin station and sat back as the driver eased his way through heavy traffic, heading for the city's industrial quarter. The road was flanked by high-rise flats. Smokestacks loomed beyond. On the plane coming over, flicking through the Polish airline magazine, he'd read about the unforgettable hive of cobbled streets that made up the Old Town. Lublin, it seemed, was bidding to become the next must-visit Euro-destination. Fat chance.

The cab dropped Winter in a side street off a major road that funnelled traffic out of the city. It was raining by now, and Winter ducked into the shelter of a shop across the road. The Krzywa Wieza, as far as he could see, was off the plot. The windows had been boarded up and a new-looking chain and padlock secured the front door. It was a two-storey building, flaking grey render, and the curtains in the two upstairs windows were pulled tight. If this was the key to Operation *Gehenna,* thought Winter, the prospects were deeply unpromising.

He lingered for a moment, wondering what to do. The shop had the look of a neighbourhood convenience store. If he was after local knowledge, this might be the place to start.

The woman behind the counter spoke no English. Winter had bought a copy of this morning's *Telegraph* at Heathrow as a prop for the video session with Beginski. He got it out of his holdall and carefully wrote Pavel Beginski's name across the top of the paper, big capital letters, and pointed at the property across the road. The woman fetched her glasses and squinted at the name. Then she nodded.

'*Tak.*'

'He lives there?' Winter had no idea how to mime a question like this. 'Is he there? Now?'

The woman didn't understand. She came round from behind the counter and took Winter out to the street. Then she pointed at one of the upstairs windows.

'He does live there?'

The woman looked confused again, then closed her eyes and laid her head against her flattened hands.

'He's asleep?'

'*Tak.*' She looked pleased. 'Sleep.'

She stepped back inside the shop, leaving Winter on the street. He put the paper back in the holdall and crossed the road. Whorls of fading graffiti decorated the render at street level. There was no bell beside the door. He rapped hard on the wooden panel and stepped back, looking up at the curtained windows. Nothing. He did it again, louder. Still no response. He was about to head down the road and try and find some way of circling the property when he became aware of two men crossing the street. They wore plain clothes and were young, crop-haired, tidy. Cops, Winter thought.

One of them spoke a little English. His leather jacket was zipped up against the chill of the wind. He asked what Winter was doing.

'I've got a friend.' Winter nodded at the bar. 'I'm paying a visit.'

The rain was harder now. The guy with the leather jacket indicated a black Skoda parked across the street. 'Come,' he said.

When Winter resisted the pressure on his arm he found himself looking at a laminated ID card. He was right. *Policja.*

The car smelled of cheap tobacco. Winter sat in the back.

'You're English?'

'Yes.'

'Passport?'

Winter handed it over, then stared out at the rain while the guy in the leather jacket checked the airline tickets Winter had slipped inside and then flicked to the back page of the passport and carefully wrote down the details. When he'd finished, he bent to the radio. The conversation went on for longer than Winter might have expected. He didn't understand a word but assumed they were checking him out against various databases. Thank God for Karl Sparrow, he thought.

The woman who'd helped him had appeared in the doorway of the shop. She was looking at the car and seemed to know what was going on. When she realised Winter was watching her she disappeared again.

The cop in the leather jacket had finished with the radio. He returned Winter's passport and then pointed at his bag. Winter handed it over. The cop unzipped it, peered inside. The sight of the camera didn't seem to trouble him. He zipped up the bag again and passed it back. Then Winter heard a metallic click as he released the locking mechanism on the rear door.

'Goodbye,' the cop said. 'Have a nice day.'

Out in the street again, Winter was aware of the cops watching him as he walked away. He turned up the collar of his suede car coat, spotting a café at the next corner. He ducked inside, glad of the warmth, and pointed at the coffee machine.

'Big.' He made an expansive gesture with his hands. 'With sugar.'

Marie authorised transmission of the house deeds to Dobroslaw's solicitor shortly after lunch. In a brief early-morning encounter with her husband she'd flatly refused to do anything until he told her a great deal more about this sudden addition to their social circle.

'He's not a mate, Ma. It's not like that.'

'That's what Paul said.'

'You've talked to him?'

'Of course I have. At least he gives me answers.'

'And what did he say?'

'He said the guy was a gangster. And he said he'd once had Paul beaten up.'

'Gangster's harsh, Ma. The guy runs a decent business.'

'And the beating-up thing?'

'That was unfortunate.'

'But true?'

'Yeah.' Mackenzie laughed. 'Paulie's fault. He should have seen it coming.'

With this Mackenzie had brought the conversation to an

end. He'd phone her later to tell her more, and when he did so – from the lobby of the Buckland Community Centre – he tried to convince her that there was another side to Cesar Dobroslaw.

'This guy's a Pole, Ma. That's where he begins and ends. Southampton's full of Poles, has been for ever – hundreds of them, thousands of them – and he's bang at the top of the pile. Does loads of community stuff, knows them all, digs them out of the shit when times get hard, sprays money around when he has to. Pillar of the fucking community, our Cesar.'

Marie wasn't sure whether her husband was making this stuff up but gave him the benefit of the doubt. A sleepless night had also convinced her that the last thing they needed was an ongoing ruck. The coming weeks and months, she suspected, were going to be tough. Better to hang in there together.

'I'm amazed he's not standing for Parliament,' she said drily.

'Very funny, Ma. You talk to the bank yet?'

'No. But I will.'

Winter, after a second coffee, was still reviewing his options. The brief encounter with the police had shaken him. Thank Christ he'd invested £3,000 in a new passport. Otherwise he might be looking at the inside of a Polish prison cell while his new friends dialled a number in Malaga.

That was bad enough, but there was something else bothering him. As a working detective Winter had never had much time for coincidence. In his experience it was rare that policemen, who were an expensive resource, just happened to be at the right place at the right time. So how come the two guys had been parked up across the street from Beginski's bar? Had they been expecting a visitor? And if so, who?

Winter knew he couldn't expect an answer to these questions. Not, at any rate, until things were a good deal clearer. In the meantime he knew he had to find some way of getting into the derelict bar down the road. Going back empty-handed was unthinkable.

He paid for the coffees and returned to the street. The cops had gone, no sign of the Skoda. A final try at the bar's locked front door raised no response, so he set off down the street again, counting the properties one by one until he found an alley on the left. There were puddles in the alley, and he had to manoeuvre himself around a couple of dumped supermarket trolleys before he got to the end. From here a second alley, wider, led past the rear of the houses in the street. He walked back, retracing his steps, tallying the addresses until he was back outside what he judged to be Beginski's bar. The rear of the property was bare brick. Over a high wall topped with broken glass Winter could see a rusting fire escape that led to a door on the upper floor. The adjacent windows, once again, were curtained.

A wooden door in the wall barred entrance to whatever lay inside. Winter gave it a push. It was locked, but the wood was beginning to rot and the door was loose on its hinges. Winter checked left and right and dumped the holdall. He kicked the door twice, aiming for the lock. On his third attempt he felt something give and a final kick did the trick. The door swung in, shedding bits of rotting timber, and Winter bent to retrieve his holdall before limping quickly inside.

A small courtyard was piled high with junk and rubbish from what must have been a kitchen. The carcase of an oven lay abandoned beside a fridge. Rotting food spilled from sodden cardboard boxes. A mountain of yellow crates was partly shrouded by a dripping tarpaulin. Winter picked his way between the debris. The flagstones were greasy underfoot. A door beside the foot of the fire escape was locked. He thought about kicking it in but abandoned the idea. Doing the back gate had knackered his ankle.

He struggled up the fire escape. To his relief, the door at the top was unlocked. He pushed it open. First he could smell weed, then came a heavy sour gust of old chip fat. He closed the door behind him and paused to get his breath back. The place was in semi-darkness. When his eyes accustomed to the gloom, he could make out a primitive kitchen: a two-ring electric burner, a tiny fridge, dripping taps in a cracked sink. A table was littered with food. A slice of bread felt soft to the touch. Winter smiled. The woman across the street had been right: someone was living here.

He stepped into a tiny upstairs landing, trying to map the flat in his head. There were three doors. The first was probably a bathroom, the other two maybe bedrooms. Winter chose the middle door, pushing it open, telling himself that this was probably where you'd sleep, away from the noise of the street. He was wrong. The room was bare except for an abandoned pair of muddy boots.

He returned to the landing. A slow *drip-drip* from somewhere ahead told him that the roof was dodgy. He paused in front of the remaining door, then knocked. When nothing happened, he knocked again. Then came a voice, a grunt, something in Polish he didn't understand. He opened the door and went in. The curtains had seen better days and a thin grey light washed into the room. A big double bed was set against the back wall. Something was stirring under the duvet and Winter waited until a face appeared. Male. White. Unshaven. And very confused.

'Pavel Beginski?'

The name prompted a nod. Beginski's English, to Winter's relief, was excellent.

'Who the fuck are you?' he said.

Mackenzie's afternoon campaigning took him to a Sure Start Centre at the top of the island. Fat Pompey mums sharing packets of custard creams. Kids learning graffiti skills with finger paints and sky-blue chalk. Harassed staff fretting about the imminent spending cuts. Kinder had briefed Mackenzie on the latter issue, and Bazza, in keeping with his normal MO, had revved up the statistics to make a decent impact.

'Whatever the Tories say, you're looking at 40 per cent cuts across the board,' he told the centre's Secretary. 'Because they lie all the time, I'd make that 50 per cent. The Labour lot, credit to them, have given us sixteen Pompey centres. Let the Tories in and you can kiss goodbye to half of them. Do the sums, love. Odds like that, and I'd be looking to put my vote somewhere else.'

The gambit was effective. Towards the end of his visit, trying to explain the offside rule to a stroppy three-year-old, Mackenzie found himself suddenly in conversation with another parent. Her name was Kelly. She looked about twelve. What she'd heard from the Secretary had upset her deeply. Mackenzie could see the alarm in her eyes.

'There's no way they can do that, is there? Just close a place like this down?'

'Of course they can. They'll dress it up. They'll tell you it's in the national interest. They'll say we can't afford luxuries like this any more.'

'But that's so wrong. I work for a living. Without this place, me and little Rosa would be back on the dole.'

'That's another thing.'

'What?'

'The dole. Benefits. Vote Tory and you'll lose the lot, Kell.'

'Shit.'

'Exactly.'

'So what will you do?'

'Me? I'll make sure none of that happens. Why? Because people like you matter. How? Because I'm a businessman, because I've got loads of experience, because I understand all this stuff.'

'What stuff?'

'Money, Kell.'

Mackenzie broke off to take a call on his mobile. It was

Whittiker again, phoning from the bank. He had some good news. Mr Dobroslaw's solicitor had been in touch. The loan would be in Mackenzie's account by close of play.

Mackenzie grunted his thanks. He looked up to finish his conversation but Kelly had drifted away.

It was late afternoon before Beginski was in any kind of state to address the recent past. To begin with, Winter simply assumed the man was a piss head. The place was littered with the evidence – empty bottles of vodka as well as half-crushed cans of Tyskie strong lager – but once he'd taken a proper look, watching the guy fumble his way round the kitchen, squeezing another cup of coffee from yesterday's dregs, hunting for something to go on his two remaining slices of bread, he began to wonder whether there wasn't something more to it than alcohol.

He was older than Winter had anticipated, probably older than Winter himself. He was tall and slightly cadaverous. His lank grey hair was beginning to thin, and a rare smile revealed a row of blackened teeth. There wasn't much in this man's face to tempt drinkers in from the street. No wonder the bar had failed.

Winter did his best to find out more, but Beginski wasn't in the mood for conversation. He'd taken the bar over from a friend of a friend. It had cost him far too much money and he should never have done it. It was closed now because he'd run out of credit with the brewers, and that was that. He owed the bank. Next he'd probably find himself out on the street.

He seemed to accept this prospect as inevitable. When Winter asked him whether he'd expected this visit – a total stranger knocking at his bedroom door – he said yes. His sister had been on a couple of days ago from London. He'd never much liked her, but for once in his life she seemed to have done him a favour.

'She told you what we want?'

'Sure. You'll have to tell me again, though.' He tapped his head. 'No good.'

Winter explained the deal. Already he'd decided to skip the visit to a solicitor to witness a written statement. In this man's state, given the possible involvement of the local cops, that was a risk he wasn't prepared to take.

'I've got a camera with me,' Winter said. 'I'm going to ask you some questions.'

'About what?'

'Martin Skelley ...' Winter gazed at him. 'Skelley? The guy who used to employ you?'

'Sure.' He nodded. 'Freezee.'

'You drove a van for him?'

'That's right.'

'And before you chucked the job in we think you took something up to the Lake District ... is that right?'

'Yeah ...' he was concentrating hard now '... I did.'

'What was that something?'

'Who wants to know?'

'We do.'

'Why?'

'Because we think Mr Skelley owes you some money. Quite a lot of money. And we think we're the people who can make that happen.'

They were sitting in the kitchen. The single bare bulb threw harsh shadows. After coffee and a slice or two of bread Beginski looked even more wrecked. He got to his feet and looked around until he found an inch or two of vodka at the bottom of a bottle under the sink. He drained the bottle and sat down again. The alcohol did him a power of good. Finally he seemed to remember what he'd signed up to.

'OK,' he said. 'We do it.'

Winter unpacked the camera. He'd practised last night in the hotel room, interviewing himself in the bathroom mirror. The screen on the back of the camera was a handy size. All he had to do was select video mode, keep Beginski's face in shot and hit the play button.

'Right.' Winter had the camera ready. 'So let's go through it ...'

He asked Beginski to hold up this morning's copy of the *Telegraph*. Then, step by step, exactly the way he might have handled it in the interview room, Winter took Beginski through the series of events that had led to his decision to bin his job with Freezee. How he'd joined Skelley's firm in the first place, after a heads-up from a mate. How he'd spent the best part of a year delivering cut-price burgers to various outlets, chiefly in the south. How one morning Skelley had intercepted him in the yard, called him into the office and asked whether or not he was up for a special job.

'What did he mean by that?'

'I didn't know.'

'What did he tell you?'

'I had to go to a place on the Isle of Wight. A farm, it was. Someone would meet with me and give me a parcel.'

'Did you ask what was in the parcel?'

'No.'

'So what did you say?'

'I said yes. Of course I said yes. I worked for Skelley. I was on the Isle of Wight, making deliveries. And he said he'd give me extra money.'

Winter knew from the file he'd read that the pick-up must have happened on a Monday.

'Sure. I can't remember.'

'Describe the parcel.'

'Big. Heavy. Like a log. Except ... you know ... bendy.'

'What colour?'

'Black. You know those bin liners? On the roll? All over, lots of tape. Grey tape.'

'You put the parcel in the back of the van?'

'Sure. There was another guy there – a big guy, foreign, young, not Polish. He helped me.'

Beginski drove the van back to the Freezee depot off the M4 in Brentford. Skelley told him to keep the refrigeration on and come back next morning. During the night the parcel began to leak.

'How do you know?'

'There was stuff all over the floor. Blood. Other stuff. There was a smell too. Not good.'

'So what did you do?'

'I asked Skelley what was in the parcel. He said it didn't matter. He wanted me to drive up north to a house of his. He gave me a map. Showed me where it was. I had to get there when it was dark. Someone would be there to meet me.'

'So what did you say?'

'I said no.'

'Why?'

'Because I knew it was a body, someone dead. You want the truth? I was scared.'

'And what did Skelley say?'

'He said I had to do it. He'd give me much more money, a lot of money. And he said I could leave afterwards, get away, go home.'

'How much money?'

'Ten thousand pounds.'

'Was that enough?'

'That was plenty. Skelley scared me. He scared everyone. A scary person. You know what I mean?'

Beginski drove north the following day. He slept in a lay-by near Carlisle, waiting for darkness to fall, then delivered the body. The person waiting for him was wearing a face mask. He was a small guy, very strong. He never said a word. Back at the Brentford depot Beginski spent half the afternoon steam-cleaning the back of the van, every corner, every crevice. By the weekend he was back in Poland, wondering about a new career as a bar owner.

'But you had a party, didn't you? Before you left?'

'Some guys came round, yes. Friends from the depot.'

'And they knew about the money you were getting? You told them?'

'I can't remember. I was drunk. Maybe I did. I don't know.'

'And anything else? Did you tell them about anything else?'

'The body? What I saw? What I smelled? Never. This is the first time.'

'What about Irenka?'

'Who?'

'Your sister. You must have told her.'

'Sure. But later. Much later. From here. On the phone. When I need more money.'

Winter nodded. Two decades in the Job told him that this was enough, at the very least, to put Skelley in front of an interviewing team. Corroboration would come from the worksheets. Other guys at the depot might have seen Beginski steam-cleaning the arse off his van. And afterwards, of course, he'd boasted about his five-figure windfall. On a good day the CPS would have the bottle to take this to court. As Skelley would know.

'Do you want to send him a message at all?'

'Who?'

'Skelley.'

Beginski thought about the offer. Then he nodded. 'Sure,' he said.

Winter hit the play button again. Beginski put his head back, staring up at the ceiling, Then he eyeballed the camera and said something in Polish, something terse. To Winter it sounded like a mouthful of broken glass.

'What the fuck does that mean?'

'It means thanks for the drugs.'

'Drugs?' Winter was frowning. 'He gave you cocaine as well as money?'

'Yes.'

'Enough to sell? Enough to make more money?'

'Enough to fuck my head up.'

Beginski reached for the bottle again, forgetting it was empty, then asked Winter for money. Twenty euros would buy him a litre of vodka from the shop across the road. Winter opened his wallet and gave him a fifty.

'Get yourself a couple, mate. And maybe something to eat, eh?'

Beginski carefully folded the note and slipped it into his jeans pocket. Then his head came up again.

'You're a cop, aren't you?' he said.

'What makes you say that?'

'Because I know about cops. I know everything about cops.' He was staring at the empty bottle. 'And I'm right, aren't I?'

Chapter twenty-one

Winter didn't make it back to the UK until the following day. He took an early flight from Warsaw, landing at Heathrow mid-morning. He bought a pay-as-you-go phone at the airport and called Suttle on the dedicated number. Suttle told him to pick up the Lexus from the hotel where he'd left it on Wednesday night and take the A3 south. Beyond the M25 junction he was to look for signs for West Clandon. Half a mile down the road was a pub, the Barley Mow. The first left turn beyond the pub would take Winter a couple of minutes down a narrow country lane. At the end of the lane was a converted farmhouse called Bissett's. The entrance Winter needed was at the back of the property. Suttle would be inside to meet him.

'You and who else?'

'No one.'

'Just us?'

'Yep.'

Winter found the rendezvous without difficulty. He parked the Lexus and got out of the car. The farmhouse door opened before he reached it. Suttle stayed in the shadows, closing the door as Winter stepped into the kitchen.

'Go on through,' Suttle said. 'First on the left.'

It was a smallish room without windows, obviously used as a study. Winter knew better than to ask about the owners. He shed his jacket, folding it carefully over the back of a chair.

'Warm, isn't it? I'm off for a piss.'

'Upstairs.' Suttle told him. 'End of the landing.'

Winter went upstairs. If he had this right, a couple of minutes would be ample. Afterwards he washed his hands, inspected his face in the mirror and then looked unsuccessfully for a towel.

Back in the study, moments later, he found Suttle waiting for him. The passport was on the desk beside the PC monitor, Winter's cheerful note unfolded beside it. *Help yourself, son,* went the invitation. *And then we might have a little chat.*

'Couldn't resist it, eh?' Winter had left the passport inside his jacket pocket, the note slipped into the ID page at the back.

'Where did you get it?'

'That's not a question you should be asking.'

'No? Then maybe you could tell me why you need it.'

'You know why I fucking need it. I told you.'

'The Euro-warrant?'

'Yeah.'

'So it's true?'

'Yeah.'

'Care to tell me any more?'

'No. No way. But here's a question for you, son. How come you bothered looking in the first place?'

Suttle didn't answer. Winter waited and waited. Finally he retrieved the passport.

'The police were waiting for me out there, right? They were waiting because they knew I was on my way.'

'We thought it was a wise precaution.'

'Keeping an eye on me? For my sake?'

'Absolutely. The guy might be unstable. He might be anything. Think of it as health and safety, mate. You're back on the team now.'

'Am I?'

'Of course.' Suttle gestured at their surroundings. 'That's why we're here, isn't it?'

Winter ignored the question. He wanted to know more about the Polish police.

'So you're telling me you contacted the locals? Briefed them up? Just in case there might be trouble?'

'Exactly.'

'And when did you do this?'

'The day before yesterday.'

'Helpful, were they?'

'Very.'

'Surprised?'

'Of course.'

'So when you asked them to look after me, did you expect them to haul me off? Check out my passport? Airline tickets? Bag?'

'No way.'

'So when they got in touch yesterday and told you about Mr Sparrow standing there in the rain, what did you say?'

'We said there must have been some mistake.'

'And what did they say?'

'They wouldn't have it. They described you.'

'Fat old bastard? Suede car coat? No hair?'

'Spot on.'

'And that's why you had to check for yourself?' Winter nodded down at the passport. 'Just now?'

'Of course.'

'OK.' Winter frowned. 'So let's go back to Beginski. So far you know fuck all about him except he worked for Skelley and did a runner to Poland back in February, yeah?'

'That's right.'

'Since when he's been off the radar?'

'Exactly.'

'But you tried to flag him up, right? And that means Interplod, yes?'

'Correct.'

'And failed?'

'Yeah.'

'Which means the guy's got no previous. Right?'

'None that we know of.'

'Else you'd have got a call from the locals?'

'Of course.'

Winter nodded, taking his time. He'd never seen Suttle so uncertain, so shamefaced. He'd been lured into the simplest of traps and now, thought Winter, he hadn't a clue what to do.

'With respect, son, you're talking bollocks,' he said at last. 'Beginski's shot. He's all over the fucking place. But you know something about guys like that? They let you closer than they think. And you know something else? He's been in the shit with the locals recently. That's partly why they were there. You may well have put a call in. I expect you wanted to be sure I'd really turned up. But they did their own checks too because he's already on their radar, and the fact that I turned out to be Karl Sparrow confused the fuck out of them.' He smiled at last. 'Am I getting warm here, Jimmy? Do you want to spare me the next bit? Just get it off your chest?'

Suttle was angry, Winter could see it in his face. Operation *Gehenna* could do him a very big favour and the last thing he needed, just now, was a masterclass in interviewing techniques.

'We do it the way we do it,' he mumbled. 'You know that better than anyone.'

'Of course I do, son. But I expect it to be done *well*. That was what pissed me off last time round. It's not you getting hurt here, Jimmy. It's little old me.'

'So what are you saying?'

'I'm saying you've fucked up. I'm guessing that Beginski's been on your radar for some time. I don't know when the Poles flagged him up, and I don't know why, but that's not the point, is it? The point, Jimmy, is you *knew*. It was never a question of getting to him through his sister. You knew already. Am I right?'

Suttle didn't know what to say. The anger had gone. He looked weary.

'We were giving you a cover story,' he said at last. 'We were trying to help. There was no way you could have access to our intel. Mackenzie wouldn't buy that for a moment.'

'Right. So you gave him a sister. Insisted she wouldn't grass her brother up to the likes of you lot. Sent me along to do the biz. Very clever. Very plausible. And I'm assuming, at the same time, you've done some kind of immunity deal with Beginski in return for the stuff he gave me yesterday. No European Arrest Warrant as long as he grasses Skelley up. Yeah?'

'Yeah. He'll have to give evidence of course, but … yeah.'

'Right. Top class. Brilliant little wheeze. Yours?'

'Ours.'

'Excellent. Except there's one hole, isn't there? Who the fuck is Irenka?'

There was a long silence. Suttle was studying his hands.

'She's u/c,' he admitted at last.

'One of your lot.'

'One of us. She's part of *Gehenna*.' His head came up. 'Just like you.'

'Wrong, Jimmy. Because she's on the inside, isn't she? And you know why that makes her different? Because you or Parsons or Willard or whoever it fucking is has left me out of the loop. Again. For the second fucking time. You've assumed all along I'm too old or too stupid or too fucking *blind* to suss the way you set it up. And that, son, was a very big mistake.'

Suttle nodded. He'd had enough of this humiliation.

'So where's the camera?' he said.

'Is that a serious question? After what we've just been through?'

'Of course it is.'

'Then I'll tell you. I put it in a Jiffy bag about an hour ago. First class. Touch wood, he'll have it by tomorrow morning.'

'Who?' Suttle was lost.

'Bazza, son. My boss.'

Chapter twenty-two

The first weekend of the election campaign found Mackenzie in conference with Leo Kinder. Bazza had descended to the War Room with a bacon sandwich. There were traces of brown sauce around his mouth and he badly needed a shave.

Kinder had news from the front line.

'You know the UKIP candidate we're up against? The guy who works in computers?'

'Yeah.'

'Guess what he's using as his battle bus.'

Bazza was deep in the sports pages of the *News*. Tomorrow Pompey were playing Spurs in the FA Cup, a fixture all the sweeter for the involvement of Harry Redknapp, the ex-Pompey manager who'd ratted on the club by walking out for the same job at Tottenham.

'No idea,' he muttered. 'Tell me.'

'A Volkswagen camper van.'

'You're kidding.' Bazza at last looked up.

'With German number plates.'

'Fuck.' Bazza barked with laughter. 'We'll kill him. We'll eat him alive. The guy's banging the drum for Blighty? Giving it plenty? And he's doing it in a Kraut-reg *Volkswagen*? Jesus ...'

He told Kinder to work up a line or two for the morning press conference. Today's *Pompey First* election theme was law and order, and Bazza was relishing the prospect of an impromptu rally outside the city's Central police station. Months of media exposure was beginning to draw decent crowds whenever Bazza made an appearance, and with luck today's gathering might be spiced with a hooligan or two chucked out of the Custody Centre after a night banged up in the cells. In Bazza's view a couple of scrotes would be the perfect garnish for the hard-hitting speech Kinder had cooked up only yesterday. How Friday-night drinkers, pissed out of their tiny skulls, were giving the city a headache it couldn't afford. How foreign visitors pouring off the ferries hit the motorway to London rather than risk a night in Pompey. How the time had come to bring this lunatic pantomime to a halt.

'And the BIBs?'

'Andy's got the roughs. They look great.'

'When do we go to print?'

'Monday or Tuesday. We're putting them round the libraries and the primary schools. Fingers crossed, eh?'

The *Boys in Blue* campaign had been Makins' idea, a jokey take on the law and order issue. He'd commissioned a gifted first-year art student at the uni to come up with a cartoon featuring the BIBs, a heroic bunch of overweight coppers forever battling the forces of darkness. Most of the time they ended up flat on their fat arses, only to be rescued by the thinly disguised Bazza Mackenzie, a caped crusader toting the colours of *Pompey First*. Bazza loved the idea, mainly because he knew the political message would drive the Filth nuts: only BazzaMac, the city's richest criminal, could return Pompey to peace and quiet.

Kinder was watching the news feed from BBC24. The Tories had just announced a £150 per annum tax break for married couples, and the Lib Dems, in the shape of Nick Clegg, had been quickest on the draw. He'd married his wife, he was saying, for love not an extra three quid a week. It was a good line and drew a cackle of laughter from Mackenzie.

Kinder was also amused. 'We need to get across this,' he

said. 'Gordon Brown will bang on about the tax implications and bore everyone shitless, but Clegg's got it right. The Tories hate people laughing at them.'

'Too right ...' Mackenzie was watching news footage of Clegg's Spanish wife. Miriam Gonzales-Durantes, in his view, was a looker. 'So how do we handle it?'

'You dream up something about Marie. Something original. Something witty. Something *sincere*. We need it by the time you do the stand-up outside the nick. Yeah?'

'No problem.' Mackenzie checked his watch. 'I've got a meet with Gill Reynolds in ten. I need to get a shave. Did I mention this diary thing of hers?'

'You did, Baz.'

'And?'

'Be careful.'

'Always, my friend.' He got to his feet and gave Kinder a pat on the arm. 'Later, eh?'

The door opened and Winter walked in. Neither Mackenzie nor Kinder had seen him since midweek. Not a phone call. Not a text. Not an email. Nothing.

'Thanks for the postcard, mush.' Mackenzie was looking at the Jiffy bag in Winter's hand. The bag had Bazza's name on it. 'What's that?'

'Little prezzie from Poland. I found it in Reception. You got a moment?'

'How much of a moment?'

'Half an hour, tops. Your office would be favourite.'

Winter was already heading for the door. Mackenzie called him back.

'No can do, mate. I've got a meet in five then we're off up to Central. This afternoon's block-booked already. Walkabout in Commercial Road, then a Q and A thing with local traders. These guys are spitting bullets about what's not happening in the Northern Quarter. Zillions down the khazi and nothing to show for it. What a way to run a fucking city, eh?'

He gave Winter a playful tap on his ample belly and told him this evening might be a possibility. A couple of cold ones, maybe, and a chance to catch up.

Winter was about to say something else but it was too late. Bazza had gone.

'What's that about?' Winter turned to Kinder. 'Is he back on the toot or what?'

'It's worse.' Kinder was shaking his head. 'Have you met this woman Gill?'

Suttle had requested a meet with Willard and was summoned to Parsons' office in the Major Crime Suite at Kingston Crescent police station at noon. Willard had driven across from Winchester, collecting Parsons from her house in Fareham en route. To Suttle's relief, Willard seemed surprisingly upbeat.

'He's in the last three for the West Mids job,' Parsons confided. 'And he tells me the competition's crap.'

Willard had disappeared up the corridor for a leak. When he returned he wanted to know about Winter.

'We may have lost him,' Suttle said at once. 'That's why I asked for the meet.'

'*Lost* him? Last time we talked you told me he was practically back in uniform.'

'I never said that, sir. With respect.'

'No, you didn't. And it won't happen either. Not as long as I'm in charge.'

'So what's changed, Jimmy?' This from Parsons.

'He's sussed Irenka, boss. He knows she's u/c.' He explained about Winter's visit to Lublin to see Pavel Beginski. 'He's saying the guy's wrecked. Totally out of it.'

'We didn't know that already?'

'No, sir. When I saw him after Christmas he was still running the bar. He wasn't the sharpest tool in the box but he wasn't a *total* piss head.'

'And now? According to Winter?'

'He's shot. Winter thinks booze is part of it, but maybe he's using other stuff as well. The bar's semi-derelict. The guy's camping upstairs. Winter said the place was evil.'

'So what did Beginski tell him?'

'I'm not sure, sir, but in that kind of state he'd have no chance, not with someone like Winter. Whatever happened, Winter now knows we set Irenka up. And he thinks that's a bit of an insult.'

'That we conned him?'

'That we thought he was stupid enough not to see through it.'

Willard nodded. He knew Winter. He could see the logic.

'So what has he got? What did he bring back?'

'I've no idea, sir. He said he'd posted it on down to Mackenzie. He may have been lying, but I doubt it. He knew I could have arrested him, done the searches, seized whatever I fancied.'

'So why didn't you? You know the terms of the agreement. Winter is working for us. He's under our control. We task him. We send him out there. We have first sight of whatever he brings back. It's called management. Mackenzie only gets to see it when we feel the time is right.'

'Sure. Of course, sir. You're right.' Suttle shot a despairing look at Parsons.

'I think Jimmy's trying to tell us Winter's beyond managing,' she murmured. 'And he might have a point.'

'No one's beyond managing. Not if you ...' He frowned.

'Manage them properly?' Parsons suggested.

'Exactly. We have protocols here. Rules. One way or another, this thing has to get to court.' He was still looking at Suttle. 'Doesn't Winter understand that?'

'I'm sure he does, sir.'

'Then why is he dicking us about?'

'That was exactly his question. He doesn't think we're serious.'

'*Serious?*' All thought of an imminent move to the West Midlands had gone. Willard was close to losing it.

'I think he means competent, sir. Maybe he's right. Maybe it was a mistake to give Beginski a sister.'

'So how else was he going to sell it to Mackenzie?'

'I've no idea, sir. Except that he'd have found a way. Winter might be bent as fuck, sir, but he's extremely resourceful.'

'I don't doubt it. I never doubted it. But he has to make a choice here. Whose bloody side is he on?'

'His own, sir. Winter's in there pitching for Winter.'

'Like always.'

'I'm afraid so.'

'Then fuck him.' Willard glanced at his watch. 'This is more trouble than it's worth.'

'You're telling me it's over, sir?' Parsons looked startled. '*Gehenna*'s finished?'

'I'm telling you we're on the wrong track. Do we still need to scoop Mackenzie up? Expose him for what he really is? Of course we do. Do we try and achieve that by playing Mr Nice to the likes of Paul Winter? I think not. Winter is a rat. Winter is lowlife. The man doesn't understand the word trust. I'm amazed we didn't suss that from the start.'

'With respect, sir—' Suttle began.

'Respect, bollocks. You're too close, son. Rule one of covert ops is perspective and *control*, and just now something tells me you've lost both. It's the same old story. You thought you could take the man at his word and it turns out – surprise, surprise – that you're wrong.'

Suttle looked away. So far he'd managed to fence off Wednesday's call from the Lublin police. Willard didn't know about Winter's dodgy passport and neither did Parsons. Once they did, both Winter and *Gehenna* would probably be history, an outcome Suttle was increasingly desperate to avoid.

'There's something we haven't discussed, boss.' Suttle had

turned to Parsons. 'In my judgement Winter has probably come back with exactly the evidence we need.'

'Meaning?'

'He got Beginski to cough. When I talked to him after Christmas in Lublin he wouldn't go into details. He picked up a package for Skelley and drove it north. That's as far as he was prepared to go.'

'But we got a deal from him, did we not? Immunity in return for evidence against Skelley?'

'Sure, boss, of course we did. But we still didn't have that evidence, not the nitty-gritty, only the guy's word that he'd come through in court if it ever got that far. That was always the logic of using Winter. Winter could do the biz on him because Winter could do the biz on anyone. That's what he's done all his life. That's what he's best at. And from our point of view, of course, it's the sweetest deal. Number one, we can take a pop at Skelley. And two, we can point Mackenzie in his direction at exactly the moment he's desperate for money. That's two Level 3 villains for the price of one. We thought that might be a decent result …' Suttle's gaze strayed towards Willard '… didn't we?'

'We did. Except that Winter's blown it.'

'That's because he's pissed off with us.'

'So what do you suggest we do?'

Suttle said nothing for a long moment. This, he knew, was a bend in the road Operation *Gehenna* simply had to negotiate.

'I suggest, sir, that we apologise.'

'We?'

'You. It would have to come from you.'

'*Me?*' Willard's face was the colour of death. 'Apologise to *Winter?*'

'Yes, sir.'

'What for?'

'For getting it wrong. For allowing *us* to get it wrong. We should have told him about Irenka. We should have known he'd suss her in the end.'

To Suttle's surprise Willard didn't explode. Instead he shot a look at Parsons. Parsons was about to express her own opinion when the phone rang. She glanced at the caller ID and frowned.

'Take it,' Willard told her.

Parsons bent to the phone. Suttle could hear a male voice at the other end. The conversation was brief. Parsons scarcely said a word. Then she put the phone down.

'That was the duty Inspector down at Central,' she said. 'He knows I've got an interest in Mackenzie's campaign.'

'And?'

'It seems Mackenzie's holding a rally outside the nick there. They've got some actors and dressed them up as coppers. He's calling them Bibs but the duty hasn't a clue why.'

'So why the heads-up?' Willard nodded at the phone.

'He says every scrote in the area's piled in. We're talking Somerstown, Portsea, Buckland, the lot. He thinks something might kick off. He's talking to the Chief Superintendent as we speak.' Parsons risked a grim smile. 'And you know Mackenzie's line in all of this? He's posing as Mr Law and Order. The cameras are there, and he's playing the copper. He's saying the scrotes are a disgrace. He's telling them they're losers. He's saying guys like them ought to be put down.'

'He's taking the piss.'

'Of course he is, sir. And unless *Gehenna* works out, it's going to get a whole lot worse.'

Winter got to Sandown Road by late afternoon. He'd taken a call from Marie on his mobile. He couldn't remember when she'd last been in tears.

She was by herself in the kitchen. The final edition of the *News* lay open on the breakfast bar. Marie surrendered to a kiss and hug, and nodded at the paper. The half-page report had been filed in the 'Election Latest' section. The headline read MR TWINKLE TELLS ALL. Winter recognised the accompanying thumbnail photo of the reporter responsible. Gill Reynolds.

'Just read it, Paul. And tell me I'm wrong.'

Winter skimmed through the article. In response to the Tory announcement on a tax break for married couples, *Pompey First*'s Bazza Mackenzie had talked exclusively to the *News*. Like Nick Clegg, he thought the Tory offer was pathetic. If that's the best they could do for something as important as marriage and family life, then they and the other lot should move over and make room for the kind of politician who understood a thing or two about the real world. As a married man, he knew how much he owed to his missus. They'd been together for a while now. They had grandkids. They'd never take a penny from the state because they didn't need to, but that wasn't the point. The point was the man-and-wife thing. You had to have someone you could rely on, someone who saw the world the way you did, someone who'd always be there for you. The article finished with a gushy pay-off: *'I know I've led her a right old dance,' Bazza told me with a twinkle in his eye, 'but she always knows where she belongs.'*

'Can you believe that?' Marie's eyes were glassy again. 'Can you believe he actually *said* something like that? Knowing God knows how many people were going to be reading it? Friends of mine? People who might have some respect for me? People like you? Ezzie? Stu? The kids, for Christ's sake? How can he *do* something like that? What's the *matter* with the man?'

Winter could only agree. He'd seen the madness in Mackenzie's eyes as he left the War Room only that morning and he knew exactly the way the interview with Ms Reynolds would have gone. Bazza lacked finesse in situations like these. He knew how to make a woman laugh and he knew how to exact the price for that laughter. Now, newly minted by all the media coverage, he'd be at maximum revs. An empty bedroom somewhere at the top of the hotel, Winter thought. Fifteen minutes, tops.

'He's lost it, my love.'

'Lost what?'

'Pretty much everything. The business. Any sense of reality. Maybe you as well.' He tossed the paper aside. 'You're right. It's beyond belief, something like that. Must hurt like hell.'

'It does, Paul, and what's worse is there's nothing I can do about it.'

'You could leave. Bail out. Bin it.'

'I could. You're right. You think that would bring him to his senses?'

'I doubt it, not with all this kicking off.' He nodded at the paper. 'Leo tells me he's off up to Wembley tomorrow, FA Cup semi-final. He's angling to be presented to the crowd ahead of the game because it's on TV, but Leo thinks it's a big ask. The people at Fratton Park know the kind of baggage he carries.' He paused and extended a hand. 'I'm not helping, am I?'

'You are, Paul. And you know what? I sometimes think you're the only sane one left.' She offered him a weary smile. 'Apart from me.'

She reached for a tissue and dabbed at her eyes. Winter felt intensely sorry for her, not least because Bazza was right. She *was* someone he could rely on. And by and large she *did* see the world the way he did. Now this.

'There's a chance he's about to blow it,' he said carefully.

'I know. I've seen the sums. Nothing works. Nothing adds up. He's still spending like there's no tomorrow, just pouring the stuff away, and now we're in the hands of some gangster from Southampton.'

'That's not what I meant.'

'It's not?'

'No. It might get worse. A whole lot worse.'

'How do you know?'

It was a good question, and Winter knew he'd already said far too much.

'I just do, my love. It's my job to know. It's what he's always paid me for. I'm the knowledge. I'm there to make sure he never gets surprised, never gets jumped.'

'And?'

'He's stopped listening.'

'Meaning?'

'He's about to get jumped.'

Marie nodded. She was very pale. Winter could see the uncertainty and fear in her eyes. Bazza Mackenzie, in the end, was her man. And in ways that made her increasingly angry she still loved him.

'So what do I do?'

'Seriously?'

'Seriously.'

'You take the Pole's money, buy a bunch of tickets to South America and you all fuck off.'

She nodded, giving the proposition serious thought. Then she looked round at the kitchen, at the gallery of summer poolside snaps on the pinboard, at the Waitrose shopping list for first thing tomorrow morning, at the sheaf of dinner-party invites as yet unanswered, and her eyes returned to Winter.

'But nothing would change, would it? Even if we went to South America?'

Winter took his time coming up with a reply. He knew he owed her this last lifeline before the waters closed over the family's head.

'No, it wouldn't.' He felt for her hand. 'Because Baz would still be Baz.'

Suttle spent the afternoon at home, looking after Grace and keeping up with the football scores while Lizzie went shopping. Uninterrupted family interludes like this were becoming increasingly precious as *Gehenna* zigzagged wildly towards some kind of conclusion. By now Lizzie had come to accept that the Major Crime Team had first claim on her husband's time, but Suttle could often placate her by sharing the odd detail about this job or that. As a journalist, albeit on maternity leave, Lizzie loved the sense of exclusive access, but *Gehenna* left no room for quietly shared confidences. The rules of engagement on all covert ops were tightly drawn, and Suttle knew better than to break them.

Now, with his daughter on his knee, he heard the turn of Lizzie's key in the front door. She struggled in with bags full of shopping. Suttle strapped Grace back in her bouncer in front of the telly and joined his wife in the kitchen. Grace loved *Final Score*.

'OK?' Suttle watched Lizzie storing packets of rusks in a cupboard. 'Survived the excitement?'

Lizzie said she'd run into Gill in Waitrose. They'd gone for a coffee afterwards.

'Andy's dumped her,' she said. 'That guy's got serious form.'

Suttle was trying to remember who Andy was. Finally he got it. Mackenzie's little helper. The guy with the demon dick.

'Heartbroken, is she? Again?'

'Not at all. It's all worked out rather well.'

'How come?'

'There's a new man in her life. She says she's through with the monkey. From now on she's shagging the organ grinder.'

'I'm not with you.'

'Mackenzie. Bad Bazza.'

'You're kidding.'

'Far from it. She says he needs to relax a bit, but she's grateful for small mercies. This morning. Around half past ten. Some tatty disused room at the back of the hotel.' She laughed. 'Amazing, isn't it? I told her she should be keeping notes, and it turns out she's doing that too.'

'Why?'

'She wouldn't say.'

Suttle nodded, trying to hide his sudden interest. Lizzie wasn't fooled for a moment.

'You want me to pass a message? Only I'd prefer if you and Gill were never alone together. That woman is sex on legs.'

'And this is the first time? Her and Mackenzie?'

'Yeah. As far as I can tell.'

'But not the last time?'

'Not if Gill has any say. She thinks he's smitten, but that's what she always thinks. I told her to cool it, not to put out so quickly, but she never listens. It's all or nothing, flat out into the first corner, foot to the floor. She always says that fortune favours the brave and, who knows, maybe she's right?'

Suttle was laughing. This was a perfect description of Mackenzie himself.

'No wonder they got it on,' he said. 'Ferrets in a sack.'

'Yeah? You know him that well?'

'Rumour, love.' He turned away. 'We call it intel in the trade.'

Winter finally cornered Bazza Mackenzie in his office at the Royal Trafalgar around eight. The afternoon's campaigning in Commercial Road had apparently gone well, the shopping precinct awash with Pompey blue and white ahead of tomorrow's outing to Wembley. One old guy in a wheelchair had turned out to be a season ticket holder at Fratton Park. He'd donated his Pompey rosette to Bazza and insisted he wear it to the game. He'd watched the malarkey outside the nick on the lunchtime *Meridian News* and wished Bazza all the best. Kids these days needed a good fucking war, he'd announced before wheeling himself away for a burger and chips.

'He's right too, mush. We don't need an army. You just take Somerstown and empty it all over fucking Afghanistan. Sort the ragheads out in no time. We'd save zillions of quid, and with luck all the scrotes would get blown up as well. Brilliant result.' He spotted the DVD in Winter's hand. 'So what have you got for me?'

Winter didn't bother to set the scene. He said he'd been to Lublin, found Beginski, and this is what happened next.

'Beginski's our guy, right?' Mackenzie said.

'Right.'

'Gun to Skelley's fucking head, right?'

'Right again.'

Mackenzie nodded at the spare chair and slipped the DVD into the player. On the big plasma screen Pavel Beginski looked like a refugee from some natural catastrophe. Winter walked him through the events of February, prompting him when necessary, leaving long silences at other moments while Beginski was digging up tiny details from what was left of his memory.

Early on Mackenzie twigged that the log-like object taped up in black dustbin liners was – in all probability – Johnny Holman.

'So who killed him?' Mackenzie paused the DVD.

Winter said he didn't know. He thought Lou Sadler was involved but couldn't be sure exactly how. Sadler, an old mate of Misty's, ran Two's Company, an escort agency on the Isle of Wight. Winter knew she'd been picked up during the Major Crime investigation but released without charge.

'But this guy didn't do it?' Mackenzie nodded at the gaunt grey face on the screen.

'Definitely not. Helping dispose of the body puts him on the line for a conspiracy charge but nothing more.'

'And Skelley? Remind me?'

'Same charge. I'm pretty certain he also took the toot off Lou Sadler. Which is where we come in.'

Mackenzie watched the rest of the interview without comment. At the end he hit the stop button. He thought it was good. In fact he thought it was brilliant. He could picture exactly how a guy like Skelley would react, thinking he'd got it all weighed off but realising now that he had a big fucking problem on his hands. In Bazza's view, it was a problem that a great deal of money could easily solve, but for the time being he wanted to know exactly how Winter had got to Beginski.

'Through his sister. I thought I told you.'

'Tell me again, mush. Spell it out. Pretend I'm thick.'

303

Winter described tracing Beginski's mates at Freezee a couple of months ago.

'How did you do that?'

'I hung around outside the depot, clocked their private cars, checked out where they drank, had a few conversations.'

'Just like that?'

'Just like that.'

'And these guys were Poles?'

'Some of them.'

'And what did they say?'

'They said that Beginski was an odd guy, sociable sometimes, a bit of a recluse others. Liked a drink. Bit of a loner. They also said he had a sister who ran an agency, a place in Isleworth just down the road. She sorts out accommodation for blokes in from Poland. Some of them had used her.'

'So you got the address?'

'Yeah.'

'Paid her a visit?'

'Yeah. It turned out she knew where her brother had ended up. Not only that but he'd run out of money. As we now know.'

'So you made the offer?'

'I did, Baz.'

'Twenty-five per cent.'

'Afraid so.'

'Two hundred and fifty K.'

'Yeah.'

'For that.' He nodded at the screen.

'That's the deal, yes.'

Mackenzie stretched, then sat back in his chair and put his feet on the desk.

'Get her down, mush,' he said at last.

'Why?'

'A quarter of a mil is way over the top. We've got what we want. We need to renegotiate.'

Winter started to protest but knew it was hopeless. In these moods Mackenzie was immune to reason. To his way of thinking, they now had Skelley exactly where they wanted him. How much they paid some derelict in Lublin was neither here nor there.

'Then just forget him, Baz. Pay nothing.'

'Why's that, mush?' Mackenzie was watching him closely. 'Don't you want her down here?'

'Personally, Baz, I couldn't care whether you paid him or not. It just makes life simpler, that's all. Plus we need every penny we can get.'

'Sure. But give her a bell, eh? No great rush.'

He turned away, a gesture of dismissal, and reached for the phone. A mate was standing the two grand for a chopper to Wembley tomorrow, and Bazza was asking about his favourite champagne. By the time Winter got to the door, he'd managed to blag an extra seat for a friend.

'Woman called Gill,' he said. 'You'll fucking love her.'

Half an hour later, parked up on the seafront, Winter gazed into the gathering darkness. If he needed any confirmation that his days with Bazza Mackenzie were numbered, then here it was. Forget the moment he watched Bazza's hit man execute a lieutenant who'd stepped out of line. Put aside the guy's girlfriend, totally innocent, blown away seconds later. Resist the memory, all too recent, of a bunch of psychos who'd nearly burned him alive in a hotel room in Montenegro. All that stuff, deeply alarming though it was, came with the territory. Mackenzie was a criminal, a gangster, a man of violence. That's what happened. That's the language these guys spoke when everything else turned to rat shit. That's what the likes of Paul Winter had to expect for a decent wage and a nice car and – on a good day – a laugh or two.

But this? Marie in pieces? Abandoned? Fucked over? Betrayed? Today in the pages of the city's daily paper? And tomorrow, quite possibly, on trillions of TV sets? A camera lingering briefly on one of the stadium's executive boxes? Mr Pompey and his new girlie enjoying their moment in the Wembley sun?

Winter shook his head. He knew the time for excuses was over. There was no longer any point blaming Mackenzie's excesses on the pressure of work, or the state of his finances, or the insane demands of a political campaign that was, at bottom, no more than a stunt. No, the guy was in control of his own fate. He knew exactly what he was doing. He was in sole charge of the journey every step of the way. Winter was certain that journey would shortly end in disaster and his responsibility now was to limit the fallout. There were individuals here who deserved a little advance warning, just a shred of protection, and under the circumstances that task was down to him.

A couple of months ago, at the birth of Operation *Gehenna*, it had all seemed so simple. A clever scam would snare Mackenzie in a trap of his own making. The likes of Parsons and Jimmy Suttle would march him to court, a jury would deliver the inevitable verdict, the Proceeds of Crime Act would strip him of everything the bailiffs could seize, and Mackenzie would be contemplating the onset of old age in a prison cell. But life rarely worked out that way – so neat, so perfectly managed – and *Gehenna* had suddenly found itself fogged in. Nothing was clear any more. Trust had broken down. And only one guy, it seemed to Winter, was left with any clear sense of direction.

He smiled to himself, recognising only too well that he was back where he'd always been, teasing advantage out of the surrounding chaos, staying one move ahead, trying to broker a result that would spare him either humiliation or penury, or – if events got totally out of control – an ugly death. The coming days wouldn't be easy, but then he'd be crazy to expect anything different. At moments like this, he told himself, he knew exactly what he was best at.

Surviving.

Bazza Mackenzie didn't eat until nearly ten. The hotel restaurant was beginning to empty. His favourite table by the window had been reserved all evening in expectation of his arrival. He summoned Leo Kinder and Makins, and ordered a couple of bottles of Krug to kick things off. Makins did a double take when he saw Gill Reynolds at his boss's side but did his best to ignore Bazza's extravagant displays of affection. His months with Mackenzie had taught him a great deal about the importance of territory. You could look, and you could remember, but you very definitely didn't stray onto your boss's turf.

Mackenzie wanted to review the week's campaigning. The way he saw it, *Pompey First* had roared off the starting grid and left the opposition for dead. They'd torn up the electoral rule book and pulled stroke after stroke. They were getting oodles of media attention and putting themselves bang in the face of the whole fucking city. Everyone knew about the Smouts, and the brain-dead piss heads at the weekend, and how Bazza cherished the National Health Service and the Sure Start Centres, and what a hefty injection of Chinese capital could do for the city's defence industries, and why the Hilsea Lido deserved a bit of TLC, and how the Tide Turn Trust was turning the wilder kids back into human beings.

All this stuff, Bazza pointed out, had happened in less than a week. The north of the city was plastered with *Pompey First* posters, and YouTube had become the destination of choice for punters looking for something different in the way of political broadcasting. Only this morning Bazza had fielded a couple of emails from *Smoutland* fans in Scotland. When the mini-vids had first aired, everyone had said they were pointless and mad. Now they'd become cult viewing. And that, said Bazza, was exactly what *Pompey First* was about. We're here to give the other lot a kicking. We're here to give the system a shake. Take a long hard look at the Big Society, and what you got – if you were lucky – was *Pompey First*.

Mackenzie raised his glass, first to Andy Makins, then to Leo Kinder.

'You've done brilliant, guys. And you know what? It can only get better.'

Kinder agreed. He'd mapped out the campaign schedule for the coming week. Tomorrow's semi-final at Wembley would bring the club – and hence the city – a great deal of publicity, so they needed to hit the ground running. Right, Baz?

Mackenzie offered a vigorous nod. He wanted lots of good strong positive stuff about Fratton Park's long-term future. Just now the club's finances were a car crash and there were all kinds of issues about ownership, but he knew Pompey would pull through the way it always had, and once all the aggro and madness had settled down he could see nothing but success. A brand-new stadium out at Horsea Island. Big-name signings on the back of the club's huge core support. Regular top-five finishes in the Prem. Plus unforgettable nights of Euro-football, with Pompey caning the arse off the likes of Barcelona and AC Milan. Mackenzie reached for his glass, enjoying the prospect of this glorious fantasy. His club. His city.

Kinder took up the running again, outlining the week's other themes. The way investment always seemed to drain to the south of the island. The way Southsea and Gunwharf hogged the lion's share of National Lottery money. The way *Pompey First* planned to restore a bit of city-wide fairness in the scramble for funds. Bazza signalled his approval as Kinder planted a tick in each of these boxes, utterly certain that the electoral tide was running in his favour, and when conversation turned to the imminent Future-Proofing Conference, he let his mind wander, gazing out of the window.

This was one of his favourite views. Beyond the sweep of Southsea Common and the frieze of coloured lights on the seafront lay the busy darkness of the Solent. At this time of night there was still plenty of traffic out on the water – a FastCat heading for Ryde, huge container ships inbound for

Southampton – and Mackenzie reached for Gill's hand, giving it a little squeeze, proud of the niche he was carving for himself in Pompey's rich history.

Informally, among people in the know, he'd been prince of the city for years now, the Copnor boy with the bollocks and the brain to turn oodles of toot into serious moolah, and with luck the next three weeks would become a kind of coronation. Bazza had never been to an election night count in his life, but now he was relishing the prospect: getting in the faces of all the Establishment suits, scoring some kind of result and acknowledging the cheers in the Guildhall Square afterwards. This was the Copnor boy made good. This was how far you could get as long as you never lost your bottle. He was having a think about the speech he'd be making on election night when Gill touched him on the arm.

'Those two were outside the nick at lunchtime.' She was looking at a couple of youths standing in the hotel forecourt, staring up at the restaurant. She'd seen the same faces on the midday news.

Mackenzie followed her pointing finger. She was right. One was a skinny little scrote, baseball cap, dead eyes, hoodie, brand new Nikes. The other one was bigger, taller, broader. He was wearing a Pompey shirt over Lacoste trackie bottoms. He had something in his right hand. He drew his arm back and took careful aim at the faces in the window.

Moments later the half-brick shattered the glass beside the table. Gill screamed, covering her face as the next missile showered them with more glass. Mackenzie was already on his feet, already heading for the door, towing Makins behind him.

Kinder pulled Gill to safety as a third object, a rock this time, sailed in through the open window and scattered a party of late diners on the other side of the restaurant.

On the steps of the hotel Mackenzie paused. The kids were crossing the road, heading for the Common, cool as you like. The skinny one turned to give him the finger, and Mackenzie caught a derisive yelp as they launched into one of the chants from the Fratton End.

Mackenzie shot Makins a look and set off in pursuit. Makins, with some reluctance, followed. The kids had broken into a trot now, still in no hurry. As far as Mackenzie could judge, they were heading for the seafront. Mackenzie ran a little faster, closing the gap, thankful he'd only had the single glass of Krug. Fuck sweet reason, he thought to himself. Fuck the army of sociologists who'd rocked up for the Tide Turn Trust conference. Fuck all the speeches about social deprivation and the miracles of restorative justice. These inbreds needed a slap or two. And he was only too happy to oblige.

By the time they got to the seafront, Mackenzie was knackered. He paused on the promenade, catching his breath, waiting for Makins. The kids had slowed and were walking backwards towards the pier, still screaming abuse.

Makins wanted to know what was supposed to happen next.

'We fucking do them.'

'How?'

'*How?*' Mackenzie had set off again. What a question.

Southsea Pier was a quarter of a mile away, a long dark finger silhouetted against the lights of the seafront. The tide was out and the kids jumped onto the beach, heading for the gleaming stretch of wet sand down by the water. Mackenzie could hear the tramp of their feet on the pebbles. They'd started on the songs again. 'I'm Pompey Till I Die.' Too fucking right, he thought.

By now, still on the promenade, Mackenzie and Makins were abreast of the kids. A final effort would do it. Mackenzie led Makins onto the pebbles. The kids began to run again. The blackness beneath the pier loomed before them. Then they were gone.

Mackenzie plunged after them. Under the pier it was suddenly cold. He could feel the clammy breath of the pebbles. He stopped, wiping the sweat from his face, letting his eyes get used to the darkness. The curl of the breaking waves echoed around the rusting iron pillars. From somewhere overhead came a slow *drip-drip* from a leaking pipe.

'Sweet or what?'

He spun round. A line of bodies barred the way back to the beach. There were more faces to his left, maybe a dozen of the little bastards, maybe more. He'd been set up. He'd been ambushed. These tossers had taken his rant outside the nick a little too literally and now they wanted payback. Sweet indeed.

'Fuck you,' he said softly. 'Fuck the lot of you.'

He'd been in situations like this before, often with the 6.57. You were chasing some rival firm or other. You thought your mates were behind you. You went steaming round the corner only to find yourself in a cul-de-sac, surrounded by hostile faces just itching to kick you to pieces. The odds against were enormous. The immediate future held nothing but pain. You were probably crapping yourself. But you never let the bastards see it.

'Who's first then?' Mackenzie had adopted the punchy crouch he remembered only too well.

There was a stir of movement in the darkness. No one knew quite what to do next. Then the kid in the Pompey top, the one who'd done the damage back at the hotel, told Mackenzie he'd been out of order.

'When, son?'

'Lunchtime. Outside the nick. What you said.'

'I said you were all losers. Am I wrong?'

'Yeah. Cos we ain't. We might be loads of things but we ain't losers.'

There was a general murmur of agreement. Another kid wanted to know what Mackenzie was doing in politics.

'You was a right laugh once. Don't understand that.'

'Maybe I mean it. Maybe I want to make things better. Have a bit of a sort-out. Put tossers like you lot back in your fucking kennels.' He peered round, trying to make eye contact, trying to shorten the odds against a serious beating. 'So who's going to offer me out then? Any volunteers? Anyone up for it?'

There were no takers. Then Makins tried to bolt. He got as far as the gleam of light on the pebbles beyond the pier before three of the kids hauled him back. He was still struggling when a couple of them punched him to the ground and began to kick him around the head and shoulders.

Mackenzie didn't hesitate. He pushed past the stone thrower and dragged the kids off. The one doing the real damage was way bigger than Mackenzie. Bazza spun him round and drove his forehead into his face. He felt bone splintering under the force of the blow and the kid fell back, his broken nose pumping blood.

His mates turned on Mackenzie. Bazza lashed out, catching the nearest one on the side of his head, sending him sprawling, but he was too slow and too old to get them all. Curled up beneath the blur of flailing limbs, he tried to protect his head and groin. He felt a sharp pain under his eye. A blow to his ribs drove the breath from his lungs. Another caught him on the side of the knee. Then, as suddenly as it had kicked off, the kids had gone – tramping away over the pebbles – and all he could hear was the steady rasp of the incoming tide and that same *drip-drip* from the leak overhead.

He felt for Makins in the darkness, asked him if he was OK. Makins was trembling with shock, his eyes wide in the whiteness of his face, blood around his broken mouth. Mackenzie helped him to his feet. There were taxis back on the seafront. The hotel was down the road. Everything would be fine.

'Yeah?' Makins didn't believe him.

'Yeah.' Mackenzie helped him up the drift of pebbles towards the promenade. 'Welcome to Pompey, son.'

Chapter twenty-three

Jimmy Suttle was alone when the front door bell rang. It was five past four in the afternoon. Lizzie and Grace were round at Lizzie's mum's in North End and the game had just started. Yesterday's Premiership results had confirmed certain relegation for Pompey, but today's semi-final in the Wembley sunshine gave them a chance to salvage a little pride from the wreckage of a disastrous season.

It was Winter at the door. Suttle stared at him. This broke every rule in the book.

'You're out of your head coming round here.' He hustled Winter inside. 'I thought we had an agreement?'

'We did, son. You lot broke it.'

He followed Suttle through to the living room and made himself at home on the sofa.

'You're staying?'

'I've come for the match.' Winter beamed. 'And the company.'

'You want tea?'

'No, thanks.' He nodded at the bottle of Stella beside Suttle's chair. 'One of those might be nice.'

Suttle left, returning in moments with another Stella. At Wembley the crowd were roaring on a Spurs attack. Defoe was making for the Pompey goal, but Rocha held him off with a forearm nose-smash.

'I thought you hated football?' Suttle tore himself away.

'I do. But so does Lizzie. Am I right?'

'Yeah.'

'So ...' he shrugged '... I thought we might have the place to ourselves.'

'And the footie?'

'Help yourself, son. Enjoy. We've got all afternoon.'

After a frantic start the game settled down. From time to time Winter asked about this player or that, but his real interest seemed to be the state of the club. Like most people in the city, he'd lost track of who owed or owned what. Was it true the club had run out of money? Was there nothing left for oranges at half-time?

'Not a bean,' Suttle confirmed. 'They've been in administration since February. You're looking at monthly wages of over a million quid and nothing left to pay them with. Fuck knows how they got into a state like this. No one's holding their hands up.'

'That's robbery, isn't it?'

'Probably. Shit!' Yebda had just curled a pass into Piquionne. With all the time in the world, the Pompey striker had smashed it into the arms of the Spurs keeper. 'One–nil that should have been.'

Suttle stole a look at Winter, trying to gauge whether his interest in the game was genuine. Winter was looking at his empty bottle. Suttle fetched another.

'Mackenzie given you the day off?'

'He's up there.' Winter nodded at the screen. 'Spot the candidate with the black eye.'

'You *what*?'

'A couple of scrotes attacked the hotel last night, ruined Bazza's day. Needless to say, he chased them down.'

He told Suttle about Makins. X-rays had revealed a couple of broken ribs and a hairline fracture to the skull.

'You're serious?'

'Absolutely.'

'And Mackenzie's pressing charges?'

'Bazza doesn't do charges. I gather he's called a little meet for tomorrow night – 6.57 reunion. Leo Kinder knows a thing or two about the Third Reich. He thinks it's the Brownshirts all over again.'

'Brownshirts?' For the time being Suttle had given up on the game.

'Hitler's private army. Bunch of Bavarian thugs who did the biz for the young Adolf. Bazza thinks you can always learn from history, and maybe he's right.'

Suttle's gaze returned to the screen. It was nearly half-time.

'So where are you in all this?'

'With Bazza you mean?'

'Yeah.'

'I'm where I always was. I'm the guy with the whistle, trying to keep some kind of order. At this rate, son, you won't need Skelley. Just wait for Bazza to self-destruct.'

'You're telling me he's going after these kids?'

'Yeah. And let's hope he means it. Number one, he might kill a couple, which would make a promising start. And number two, you lot might notice, which means we could all get on with our lives.'

'But seriously ...'

'Seriously, I doubt it. He might put the word around. A couple of the kids might end up at A & E. But Kinder's no fool, and he's telling Bazza to behave.'

'And Mackenzie listens?'

'Kinder's the key to Pompey's door. That's the way Bazza figures it. So of course he listens.'

The players were trooping off the pitch. One end of the stadium was a sea of blue. Not to have conceded by half-time was definitely a result.

Winter found the remote and killed the sound. Then he told Suttle they had to sort a deal.

'For who?'

'Me.'

'We're talking *Gehenna*?'

'Of course we are. How long is half-time?'

'Fifteen minutes.'

'Perfect.' He produced an envelope from his pocket. Inside was a DVD. Suttle stared it.

'Beginski?'

'Yeah.' Winter nodded. 'Help yourself.'

The game had restarted by the time Suttle was through with the interview. The last time he and Winter had met, at the safe house up in Surrey, he'd sensed that the expedition to Lublin had been successful. Now he knew that *Gehenna* was looking at a giant step forward.

'I can keep this?' Suttle had retrieved the DVD.

'Of course. I've got copies.' Winter smothered a yawn. 'So what next?'

'I show it to Parsons. And Willard. We frame up a strategy. Then we call you in.'

'Wrong, son. That's what you did before. This time you leave it to me. I do the legwork. I choose the moment to make the approach to Skelley. I decide when and where this whole thing kicks off.'

'And us? Do we get to play as well?'

'Of course you do. I keep you informed. I tell you what I need and when I need it. But the pecking order won't ever be the way it was.'

Suttle smiled. He'd half-imagined a conversation like this but knew it was a non-starter.

'Willard's prepared to apologise,' he said softly. 'And believe me, that's a first.'

'Apologise for what?'

'For keeping you out of the loop. About Irenka.'

'Big deal. I don't want an apology, son. I want control.'

'They'll never agree.'

'Fine.' Winter drained the second bottle. 'Mine's a Stella.'

Suttle didn't move. On screen Piquionne had just missed another sitter. Pompey supporters had their heads in their hands. At this rate they'd be looking at extra time.

'Bazza wants to meet this Irenka,' Winter said. 'You think she's up for that?'

'I'm sure she is. Why the interest?'

'Because he thinks the way I do. It's too neat, too convenient. He wants to check her out for himself.'

'Fine.' Suttle shrugged. 'I'm sure she'll be delighted.'

'But can she pull it off? Can she *do* it?'

'Of course she can.'

'What makes you say that?'

'Because Covert Ops are choosy when it comes to u/c.'

'Is she Hantspol? Met? Somewhere else?'

'I haven't a clue. And that's the truth.'

'You want to find out?'

'I can try.'

'Yes please, son.' Winter waved his empty bottle again.

Suttle fetched another. They watched the remainder of the second half in companionable silence. With the score still 0–0 at full time, the players gathered around their respective managers. Harry Redknapp was taking it easy, the occasional word in a Spurs ear, a pat on the shoulder, a shared joke with a couple of the big defenders. Avram Grant, on the other hand, had gathered his players around him, serious, intense, making point after point with little trademark jabs of his right hand.

'What's he saying?' Winter was intrigued.

'He's telling them they don't get paid for extra time. The administrator's been on to him. Nothing left in the kitty.'

Winter laughed. Then he told Suttle exactly what he wanted out of *Gehenna*. The fact that Suttle knew Misty and Trude made it a whole lot easier.

'I want them both taken care of,' he said.

'I'm not with you.'

'You give me a whack of money. Resettlement's no problem. Neither is ID. I can sort both. But I need the pair of them with me, and that's going to cost. If there's any equity left in Misty's place it'll end up seized. When that happens she'll have nowhere to live. And neither will Trude. So ...' he raised an eyebrow '... you think that might be a runner?'

'It's possible. I can at least try. You got anywhere nice in mind?'

'Of course I have.'

'Like to share it?'

'No.' Winter shook his head.

Extra time was under way. Twelve minutes later Piquionne at last came good. A beautifully flighted ball from the right wing beat the Spurs central defender. Flat on his arse, he watched Piquionne score with a simple tap-in.

Suttle was on his feet, punching the air. From next door, through the thin walls, came the thunder of feet on bare floorboards and wild cheering. Across the road a woman in a dressing gown had appeared at her front door, waving a Pompey scarf. Even Winter looked impressed. *Gehenna,* for the next fifteen minutes, was history.

Spurs brought on a replacement striker. Gareth Bale was slicing through the Pompey defence, putting in quality cross after quality cross. At the other end Utaka led a break, two against one, with Dindane in support. But his pass was useless, and Dindane's botched return went straight to a Spurs defender. Finally, minutes later, Dindane atoned by tempting Palacios into conceding a penalty. Prince Boateng stepped up to the plate and slotted it. Two–nil. Game over.

Suttle grabbed his phone and got through to Lizzie. Her mum had insisted on watching the game and had just broken out the sherry. Suttle could hear his daughter in the background. He got Lizzie to put the phone to her mouth. Over the roar of the crowd on the telly Grace was gurgling with contentment.

Suttle made kissy-kissy noises and pocketed his mobile.

Winter was still watching the celebrations. The Pompey players had run to the blue end to salute their travelling support, and the crowd had gone wild. After a while Winter reached for the remote again and lowered the sound. A line in the match commentary had amused him.

'This guy Prince Boateng. The one who took the penalty. He's ex-Spurs, right?'

'Right.'

'Scored against his own club, yes?'

'Yes.'

'Put the game beyond reach?'

'Absolutely.'

'Excellent.' Winter emptied the bottle and got to his feet. 'Bit of a lesson there, eh?'

Suttle studied him a moment, working it out.

'That sounds like a threat,' he said at last.

'Threat?' Winter was looking pained. 'Why don't you talk to your bosses? He's there for the taking, son, if we play this my way.'

Chapter twenty-four

Weeks two and three of the campaign weren't kind to Bazza Mackenzie.

On the Monday after the triumph at Wembley his suggestion of a *Pompey First* photo call with the all-conquering FA Cup team was ignored by the management at Fratton Park.

On the Tuesday a bid to upstage the launch of the Tory manifesto spectacularly misfired when *Pompey First*'s hired launch sprang a leak in Portsmouth Harbour and nearly sank. Bazza, rescued by a tender from HMS *Iron Duke*, kept hammering away at his script but to no avail. When he accused the Tories of preparing to torpedo the aircraft carrier programme – thus shafting hundreds of Pompey dockyard workers – the Portsmouth North candidate, who happened to be a Royal Navy reservist, simply queried his entitlement to voice any kind of view on maritime affairs. This is a guy, she said, who has difficulty staying afloat on a sunny day with no one trying to kill him. Would you seriously entrust the nation's defence to *Pompey First*?

On the Thursday, after a merciful lull, things went from bad to worse. Secretary of State for Industry Lord Mandelson was extensively photographed waltzing with a woman in pink in the Blackpool Tower ballroom. The news coverage caused a flurry of excitement across the nation, and it was Gill Reynolds' idea to stage *Pompey First*'s very own photo shoot at Hilsea Lido's

Blue Lagoon. That afternoon they were staging a Festival of Jive. Reynolds, who happened to be a talented jiver, offered to partner Bazza and guaranteed coverage in the *News*. The candidate himself was less than keen, but a couple of TV crews also turned up and he did his best. The black eye had gone by now but even Reynolds' twirls couldn't mask Bazza's clumsiness. The results, beamed into thousands of homes across the city, proved beyond doubt that Bazza Mackenzie had two left feet, and although he won a sizeable sympathy vote for his gameness, it did nothing for either his self-esteem or his marriage.

That evening, after watching *Meridian Tonight,* Marie threw him out and had the locks changed. She'd never much liked politics and she'd certainly had enough of this kind of public humiliation. Bazza, who viewed this development in his private life as a temporary blip, moved into one of the nicer bedrooms on the Trafalgar's second floor, often with Gill Reynolds in attendance. That night, pissed, he tried – and failed – to shag her. This was a situation he'd never encountered before. She was as dexterous and inventive as ever, but nothing she did for him seemed to work. Early next morning, to his growing alarm, he drew another blank. She gave him a massage. She ran a bath. She tried to cup him between her breasts and told him he was the best fuck she'd ever had. He didn't believe her. And nothing happened.

By now Bazza suspected she was getting a better offer from Andy Makins. *Pompey First*'s IT wizard was out of hospital now, and it was no secret that Gill Reynolds was popping round to his flat most afternoons to make sure he was OK. Makins, to Bazza's disgust, wasn't keen on hurrying back to front-line electoral duties, a situation Leo Kinder put down to post-traumatic stress disorder. PTSD, according to Kinder, could incapacitate someone as sensitive as Makins for months.

Bazza, who had no time for fancy excuses like these, issued Makins with an ultimatum. Either he resume work for *Pompey*

First or he was off the payroll. Makins, to his credit, did his best, but by midway through week three it was obvious that his heart wasn't in it. The ceaseless flow of ideas had dried up. He stopped monitoring the various Internet forums he'd fathered. Messages from Bazza demanding a response went unanswered. From the room he was using as an office, Makins seemed to spend half the day checking the street outside for possible threats. And when the time came to go home, he either blagged a lift from Gill Reynolds or insisted on a taxi.

From Bazza's point of view this was a sinister development. He'd never trusted anyone else with a woman he happened to be shagging. Gill Reynolds managed to coax a performance or two, but Bazza was increasingly haunted by what she'd once told him about Andy Makins. The guy had the knack. The guy knew what a woman really needed. The guy took her places she'd never been before. Again and again and again. Bazza was honest enough to know that he simply wasn't in this league. He could make a woman laugh. He could spend money on her. He could make her feel like the princess of her dreams. But when it came to bed, he rarely wasted the kind of time and attentiveness she seemed to crave. The sex was OK. It did the business. But he was uncomfortably aware that it didn't hold a candle to what she'd come to expect from Mr Makins.

And so, as the campaign gathered pace, Bazza began to flag. The Future-Proofing Conference, so carefully prepared, was a huge disappointment. Half the speakers didn't turn up and neither did the media. In the days that followed, Mackenzie seemed to lose it. His speeches lacked that buccaneering spark that had lit a bonfire under the Pompey hustings. Crowds once numbered in hundreds began to thin. He started muddling important statistics, handing his opponents a series of open goals. Postings on various group sites registered disappointment, then hostility, then derision. Even Leo Kinder, who Bazza had always regarded as rock-solid, began to show signs of losing his nerve.

Then, with election day barely a week away, *Pompey First* hit the buffers. Since the incident under the pier there'd been no sign of the kids Bazza had insulted in his haste to grab the law-and-order vote. Glaziers had restored the hotel restaurant to its former glory. Bazza had waived the bill run up by the party of diners who'd been on the receiving end of the third rock. And when the *News* phoned the following day, enquiring about an incident at the Royal Trafalgar, he'd told them they were imagining things. Life was sweet. Business was good. Find yourself a headline somewhere else. This smokescreen of denials seemed to work, and within days the only real casualty of the incident was Andy Makins.

But the kids hadn't gone away. Towards the end of the month Bazza arrived in the Guildhall Square to make a speech about political funding. How the Tories were simply frontmen for big business. How the Labour lot were putty in the hands of the trade unions. How the only candidates worth voting for were the guys with clean hands and a clear conscience. Like Bazza Mackenzie. He'd touched on elements of this issue before, but Leo Kinder had worked deep into the night and produced something really punchy he thought might reboot the *Pompey First* campaign. He'd also been on his knees to various media contacts and managed to secure a decent turnout. TV was there, and radio, and a couple of print journalists.

Their very presence attracted the beginnings of a respectable crowd, and Bazza was deep into his speech, giving it plenty of welly, before he noticed the kids at the back. He'd last glimpsed these faces in the half-darkness under the pier. A lot of them were carrying posters. The posters were crude – hand-scrawled black capital letters – but they all spelled the same message: *Pompey Last.*

Bazza did his best to ignore them. He talked about the fat cats in the city. He had a rant about dinosaur trade union leaders. He even made a half-decent joke about political cross-dressing, accusing Lord Mandelson of cosying up to Russian oligarchs. All this was good political knockabout, exactly as Kinder had intended, and Bazza knew the crowd was on his side, but the moment the kids arrived he felt the momentum slipping away. They were chanting – they'd obviously been rehearsing – 'Loser ... loser ... loser ...'

Bazza started to shout. Then he lost his thread. The chanting got louder. Finally he'd had enough. Appealing directly to the nearest camera, he pointed out the faces at the back of the crowd. 'That's the scrote vote,' he yelled. 'Take a good look, because that's the future of this fucking country.'

The quote, discreetly bleeped, made the national news. Within hours it was on the front page of the London *Evening Standard*. The Pompey *News* devoted two inside pages to the story: instant rebuttal from the kids themselves, from angry parents, from shocked teachers, from despairing social workers. Who was Bazza Mackenzie to condemn an entire generation? Who, indeed?

And it got worse. Over the next two days, no matter how carefully Bazza and Kinder tried to outfox them, the scrote vote was always waiting at the next campaign stop. More posters. More chants. Increasingly desperate, Kinder began to reschedule, insisting on indoor venues and putting 6.57 security on the door. The tactic was a disaster. Intimidated by a bunch of middle-aged thugs, the audiences got smaller and smaller while the scrote vote picketed the road outside, drawing the kind of crowds *Pompey First* could only dream of. But these people had come for a ruck. They were the kind of gawkers who slow down on motorways when they see a tangle of wreckage and a couple of winking blue lights. *Pompey First*, it was widely agreed, had become a car crash.

Winter consented to attend a *Gehenna* meet at the end of that last full week of campaigning. He drove to the safe house in Winchester and found himself confronted by the entire management team: half a dozen faces around the table, all of them eager to find out what was really happening at the heart of the *Pompey First* electoral machine.

'It's all turned to rat shit,' Winter was smiling. 'As I told you it would.'

Willard, who'd been fed the media coverage by Parsons, wanted to know about the kids with the placards, the *Pompey Last* lot. How come they'd turned out to be so politically savvy? And how come they were always one step ahead?

Winter was happy to explain. He described the night the kids had turned up outside the hotel and what happened afterwards. Makins, he said, had been hospitalised for a couple of days. Returning to his Southsea flat, he'd found a note pushed under his door. Liam and Billy were the kids who'd put the boot in under the pier. And now they wanted a little chat.

'How did they know where to find him?' This from Parsons.

'I told them.'

'You traced these kids?'

'Of course I did. We had the news footage from the law-and-order thing. I printed out some faces. Showed them around.' He smiled. 'The way you do.'

Willard wanted to know what happened next.

'Liam and Billy went round to see Makins. Makins was bricking himself, but all they wanted was advice.'

'What kind of advice?'

'Political advice. It turned out they were really pissed off by what Mackenzie had said. They thought it was unfair for starters. Makins explained Bazza had never really meant it – it was just stuff for the cameras – but that just made it worse. These kids hate people taking advantage. And that's exactly what Mackenzie had done. Big time.'

Makins, he explained, had promised to help them.

'Why?' Willard again.

'Partly because he didn't want to end up in hospital again and partly because he's had it with Mackenzie. He thinks the bloke's off his head, and from where I'm sitting he's dead right.'

'So what happened?'

'He told the kids to wait, to hang on. He knew Mackenzie would never last the course. Then he came up with the *Pompey Last* line and the "Loser" chant. That's what really did it for the kids in the first place, being labelled losers. They really hate that. Loser's the worst. So turning it on Mackenzie when his campaign's going tits up was really sweet. You know what they think of Makins now? They love him to death. And you know why? Because Bazza reacted just the way Makins knew he would. He can't handle stuff like that. He needs to be in control. Otherwise he starts foaming at the mouth.'

Heads nodded round the table. Winter had always promised that the campaign would take Mackenzie to a very bad place, and that's exactly what had happened.

'But how come the kids always know where he's off to next?' Suttle asked.

'Big mystery. Mackenzie's starting to think it might be a woman called Gill Reynolds. She's a reporter on the *News*. He's briefing her every night for some kind of special she's doing afterwards. This is a woman who can't wait to be famous. Bazza is her best shot. Another possibility is Andy Makins. He's got access to the intranet we use, chiefly because he set the thing up. He knows these kids. He knows where to find them. Plus he's happy to shaft Mackenzie.'

'Is that wise?'

'Probably not. But he was shagging Reynolds before Bazza helped himself.'

Winter looked briefly troubled. Mackenzie had tasked him to stop the leaks and bring him a name. Suttle wanted to know if that was a problem.

'Of course it is.'

'Why?'

'Because the leaks are down to me. I bung the kids a schedule every night. They've no idea where it comes from but it's always kosher stuff. They turn up next day and Bazza goes ape, blames everyone, Reynolds, Makins, even Kinder. No wonder the fucking thing is falling apart.'

A ripple of laughter ran round the table. This was textbook Winter, a masterclass in manipulation. Even Willard looked impressed.

'So what happens next?' he said. 'What's your recommendation?'

Winter held his gaze. He didn't much like the word recommendation, but he decided for the time being to live with it. Willard had a great deal of face to save, but in truth *Gehenna* was now in Winter's hands. He was the spider in the middle of the web. His strategy. His call.

'Jimmy?' Winter had turned to Suttle. 'You've talked to Mr Willard?'

'About?'

'Me? Misty? Trude?'

'I have, yes.'

'And?'

'It's OK. In principle.' Suttle glanced at Willard for confirmation. Willard simply nodded.

Winter wanted to know what 'in principle' meant. He was looking at Willard now.

'It means we'll meet your demands. Given a satisfactory outcome.'

'Which is?'

'Mackenzie in front of a jury. And you in the witness box.'

'Fair enough. You want to talk about timings? When Misty and her daughter can be ghosted? Exactly when that happens?'

'No.' Willard shook his head. 'We'll sort that later.'

'When?'

'Later. Once we know where this thing is headed.'

Winter studied his hands for a moment. Unlike everyone else around the table he'd brought no paperwork. Everything, every last detail, was where it should be. In his head.

'Like I say,' he began, 'Mackenzie's in a very bad place. His missus has washed her hands of him. The money's running out again. He's getting calls from the bank. The business could fold any day now. *Pompey First* is a joke. Any one of those factors could push him towards the edge. Put them all together, and he's looking at oblivion.'

'Except Bazza doesn't do oblivion.' This was Willard.

'Exactly. You're right. What Bazza does is tight corners. And what he does best, what he *loves*, is getting out of them. This is the tightest of tight corners. This is a corner so tight that even he thinks it might be a stretch getting out.'

'So what's the trick?'

'Skelley. We had a meet about him this morning, Baz and I.'

'And?'

'I'm off up to London after this.' He was still looking at Willard. 'You've seen the Beginski material?'

'Of course I have.'

'And?'

'It's OK.'

'Just OK?'

'It's good.' The admission pained Willard. 'With the right corroboration, it should do the job.'

Winter nodded, then tallied his demands. He wanted twenty-four-hour surveillance on the hotel. He wanted another team permanently targeting Mackenzie. He had a list of Mackenzie's various mobile numbers and of the direct line he used in his office. He was no longer up to speed on comms intercepts, but he imagined the science had moved on.

The D/I from Covert Ops said his guys would need access to the hotel. Half an hour in Mackenzie's office, undisturbed, should be enough to put a decent rig in.

'Impossible.' Winter shook his head. 'He's got CCTV every-where. There's no way you wouldn't be clocked.'

'Then maybe we can give you a radio mike. You'd have to put it in his office. We can monitor the feed.'

Winter gave it some thought. The microphone and

transmitter would be hidden – maybe in a book or an ornament of some kind – but to get a result it had to be reasonably close to Mackenzie's desk. Winter, knowing how territorial Bazza could be, shook his head again.

'He'd probably spot it,' he said. 'That's a risk we shouldn't be taking.'

'You mean *you* shouldn't be taking.' This from Willard.

'Exactly.'

'How about a fallback?' Willard again. 'Would you be prepared to wear a wire?'

'No way.' Winter shook his head.

Willard raised an eyebrow. No one else said a word. Finally it was Winter who broke the silence.

'This woman Irenka,' he began. 'The u/c. Bazza wants her down to the hotel.'

Willard wanted to know why.

'He needs to check her out.' Winter said. 'I already mentioned it to Jimmy.'

'I know. We've discussed it.'

'So where does she come from?'

'The Met.'

'And she's good?'

'The best.' The Covert Ops D/I again. 'Trust her with my life.'

'Thanks.' Winter wasn't smiling. 'Except it's mine, old son, not yours.'

Chapter twenty-five

Freezee's southern distribution depot lay on the edges of a west London trading estate beside the M4. Winter found a lay-by up the road from the main entrance and pulled in. Through the chain-link fence he could see rows of refrigerated lorries. Beyond them a couple of guys in overalls were steam-cleaning a white Transit van. Overhead, on the elevated motorway, traffic roared towards central London. It was mid-afternoon.

Mackenzie answered on the second ring. Winter bent to the phone.

'I'm here, Baz. I'm about to go in. If I'm not out by six, call the rozzers.'

'Have you seen the woman yet? That Irenka?' Mackenzie ignored the joke.

'Later, Baz. Providing I'm still in one piece.'

Winter ended the call without waiting for a reply. He drove back to the main entrance, where a security guard checked his name against a list on his clipboard. Winter had called Skelley's secretary earlier. Mr Skelley would see him at half past three.

In reception Winter accepted a mug of lukewarm tea and browsed a copy of the *Sun*. The Lib Dems were promising shock gains in Thursday's poll while Gordon Brown had likened Nick Clegg to a game-show host. Winter was wondering whether to risk a peek at his horoscope when Skelley's secretary appeared. He followed her down a long corridor to an office at the end.

The office, to Winter's surprise, was modest: a desk, a small conference table, no windows. On the plain white wall behind the empty chair hung a framed photograph. Pale grey light gleamed on a huge stretch of water, and there was a bare odd-shaped mountain in the background. Winter had never been to the Lake District but suspected that this was the view from Skelley's house. He stared at the water. Johnny Holman must be down there somewhere, he thought.

The secretary had gone. Winter waited. At length the door opened again and he turned to find himself looking at a proffered handshake.

'Martin Skelley.' The voice was soft, Scouse accent.

'Paul Winter.'

'You want another tea?'

'No, thanks.'

Skelley settled behind the desk. He was a big man, well built, and one look at his face told Winter that there must be West Indian blood in his family: the skin colour, the tiny button ears, the tight whorls of greying hair, the blackness in his eyes. He studied Winter for a long moment.

'I understand you've got something for me?'

'I have.'

'So why should I be interested?'

'Because it ties you to a murder.'

He nodded and said nothing. A new-looking PC occupied one end of Skelley's desk. Winter gave him the DVD. Skelley slipped it into the slot and reached for his mouse. Moments later Winter heard Beginski's trademark cough.

The interview lasted twenty-two minutes. At the end of it Skelley returned his attention to Winter.

'You've got copies of this?'

'Of course I have.'

'Are you Filth?'

'No.'

'So what do you want?'

'A million quid.'

For the first time Winter sparked a reaction, but there was no warmth in the smile.

'This is a joke, isn't it?' Skelley said. 'Some chiselling fucker on the take?'

'His name's Mackenzie,' Winter said. 'And he's my boss.'

'Tell me more.'

'He had a stash of toot buried on the Isle of Wight. A guy called Johnny Holman was the babysitter. We think Holman ended up in the back of Beginski's van. And we think you took care of him after that.'

'You can prove any of this shit?'

'No, but I know people who can.'

'That's a threat, I take it?'

'Of course it is.'

'So why the million quid?'

'Because it wasn't just Johnny who disappeared. My boss lost his bugle too, all of it. He thinks you had it off Lou Sadler. And he thinks a million quid is a reasonable settlement.'

'Then he's crazy.'

'Fine. You're telling me you never had the toot?'

'Of course I am.'

'Sure.' Winter nodded at the PC. 'In which case we're talking straight extortion.'

The smile again. This time Skelley seemed genuinely amused.

'You *are* a cop,' he said. 'It's fucking obvious.'

'Was once.'

'Yeah?' He was frowning now. 'Does Lou know you?'

'She does.'

'Business or pleasure?'

'There's no difference. Not with Lou.'

'You're right.' The laughter died on his lips. He wanted to know where he could find Mackenzie.

'Down in Southsea. The Royal Trafalgar Hotel. He's

expecting a call.' Winter flipped a card onto the desk and stood up. 'Cheers for the tea, eh?'

Isleworth was a ten-minute drive from the Freezee depot. Winter climbed the stairs at the back of the agency, knocked twice and stepped inside. Next door he could hear voices raised in anger. One of them was Irenka's. They weren't speaking English. Another satisfied customer, Winter thought.

He waited in the outer office until the door opened. A small thickset guy in his early thirties pushed past Winter without a backward glance and wrenched the door open. Winter heard the clatter of his feet on the concrete steps. He shut the door and went into the office. Irenka was looking at some kind of bill. She shook her head.

'The man's in there a week, gets trashed on vodka every night, winds up the stereo, upsets the neighbours, buys himself an electric fire, then expects me to pick up the tab. Fucking Poles, who needs them?'

'Mackenzie wants you down at the hotel.' Winter hadn't got time to waste.

'Does he? When?'

'As soon as.'

Irenka abandoned the bill and consulted her diary.

'I can't do tonight. Tomorrow I'm in Scotland. It'll have to be Wednesday.' She looked up. 'What does he want?'

'Number one, he wants to check you out. Number two, he thinks 250K is a joke.'

'For Pavel, you mean?'

'Yeah.'

'He's right. What was he like, this Pavel?'

'Shot. Wasted. I never realised why so many Poles came over here until I met him. I think Lublin must have got to him. There are nicer places in the world, believe me.'

Winter told her everything he could remember about

333

Beginski: the way he'd looked, the conditions he was living in, how life seemed to have shrunk him to nothing.

'I gather you're the sister.'

'That's the legend, yes.'

'So how well are you supposed to know our Pavel?'

'We didn't meet until he came over here. I helped him find a place, waived the commission, did the family thing. We don't get on, not really.'

'I'm not surprised. You should see the state of him.' Winter paused. 'Mackenzie's a bloke you shouldn't underestimate. He can come across as a bit of a hooligan sometimes, but it's a game he plays. Don't be fooled. He's sharp as a tack, doesn't miss a trick. What you see isn't always what you get.'

'Yeah?' She frowned. 'Tell me something ...'

'Go on.'

'Why is he standing for Parliament?'

'Good question. Some days I think he means it. Others he seems to be taking the piss. Just now the wheels have come off. Getting elected is harder than he'd ever thought.'

'You know him well?'

'Probably as well as anyone.'

'You like him?'

'I used to.'

'So what's changed?' She nodded at the paperwork that littered her desk. 'What's led to all this?'

'It's complicated. Some bits you don't want to know. Other bits I'm not going to tell you.'

'Why not?'

'Because ...' Winter tried to find the words. 'I dunno ...'

'Try.'

'I can't. I don't want to.'

'Why not?'

Winter gazed at her for a long moment. It was rare to find someone this blunt yet this persuasive.

'Honestly?'

334

'Honestly.'

'Because it doesn't make me feel so great about myself.'

Irenka nodded. 'You mean you feel ashamed? You regret binning the Job?'

'No, it's not that. The Job had become impossible.'

'So what is it?'

'It's hard. I don't know. Disgust? Fuck knows. Mackenzie can be an animal, a total arsehole, but then we all can.'

'So there's more?'

'Of course there's more.'

'And?'

'The man's starting to frighten me.'

'It's fear. You're talking about fear.'

'Yes.'

It was the truth. Winter gazed at her, admiring the way she'd managed to dig it out of him. It would have been nice to get some response, but her gaze had returned to her diary.

'I've got an aunt in Southampton.' She reached for the bill for the electric fire and threw it in the bin. 'She's due a visit. How about Wednesday evening?'

'I'll ask him.'

'And Skelley? He's seen the interview?'

'He has. There's another scary man.' Winter flashed her a smile that wasn't quite convincing. 'Fingers crossed, eh?'

Winter was back in the Trafalgar by early evening. On the first Monday of every month the hotel always hosted a supper for the local Rotary Club, a gathering of local worthies. They booked one of the function rooms and normally gathered in the bar before wandering through with their drinks. This evening attendance was thin. Winter asked the receptionist why.

'Dunno.' She shrugged. 'Loads of them have phoned up and cancelled. I'm not sure they like all this political stuff. Mr M isn't best pleased.'

'I bet.'

Winter stepped into the bar. Over the last week or so, as word spread that Bazza was in trouble, familiar faces had begun to appear. These were names Winter had known since way back, old mates of Mackenzie, rallying to the flag. Many of them were ex-6.57, fellow infantrymen from Pompey's army of travelling away fans. In the 1980s and 90s they'd exported recreational violence to the furthest corners of the kingdom, returning late on Saturday nights to feast on the day's mayhem and get even more pissed. A decade or so later, still tattooed, still shaven-haired, many of them had made decent careers in the motor trade or the property game. The T-shirts were tighter over the belly and the jeans a little baggier round the arse, but the light in their eyes told Winter they still had it. In a city as tribal and closely knit as Pompey, this was muscle Bazza could rely on.

Gill Reynolds was sitting at a table in the corner. She was by herself. Winter knew this was the hour Bazza normally reserved for their tête-à-têtes, a diary catch-up on the day's campaigning and a preview of what tomorrow might hold.

'Buy you a drink?'

She asked for a spritzer. Winter went to the bar. A couple of the guys on stools gave him the nod. One of them had gone into the music business and supplied bands city-wide. The other drove a taxi. In another life Winter had nicked them both on a variety of minor drugs offences.

He carried the drinks back to the table. Gill looked up at him.

'How's the man?' Winter asked.

'Knackered. Knackered and depressed. Apparently he did three venues today. He got single-figure audiences in two of them, and when he made it to the third no one could get in.'

'Where was it?'

'Wymering. The caretaker had been taken to hospital. No one else had a key.'

'Shit.'

'Exactly.' She stared at her drink. 'This is turning into a nightmare, isn't it?'

'The campaign, you mean?'

'Of course.' Her head came up. 'What else is there?'

Winter held her gaze. It was a direct question. She was a journalist. She'd sniffed the wind. She kept her eyes open. She had a gift for putting bits of the jigsaw together. She might even have arrived at a conclusion or two.

'There's nothing, love,' Winter said. 'Only the campaign.'

'I don't believe you. He's in deep shit, isn't he?'

'Of course he is. A couple of hundred votes come Thursday? Lost deposit? All those suits in his face? That's not what our man had in mind.'

'I'm not talking about the campaign.'

'Oh? You think there's something else?'

'I know there's something else.'

'Like what? His marriage?'

'That's not down to me.'

'Did I say it was?'

'No, but you didn't have to.' She reached for her drink. 'You don't like me much, do you?'

'I've never really thought about it, to tell you the truth.'

'Thanks.'

'Pleasure.'

'Is it because of Marie? Is that why? Only I know you two are close.'

'Who told you that?'

'Bazza. Sometimes I think he's jealous.'

'You have to be kidding. If we're talking fuck-ups, Bazza needs no help from me. He's been a twat and he knows it.'

'Great. I'll take that as a compliment.'

'You should. You've been clever.'

'You think I'm doing this for me?'

'I doubt whether you're doing it for any other reason.'

'Love?'

'Very funny. I can think of lots of reasons for screwing the boss but love isn't one of them.'

Winter tipped his glass in salute and Gill returned his smile. She enjoyed this kind of banter. Winter could sense it.

'He's broke, isn't he? It's a money thing.'

'What makes you say that?'

'I heard him on the phone last night. We were in the office. He was talking to someone about Cyprus.'

'Yeah?' Winter pretended not to be interested.

'Yeah. He must have a place out there. Is Famagusta in the north?'

'Pass.'

'It is. I checked it out this morning. It's where all the gangsters end up. Guys like Asil Nadir. Am I getting warm?'

Winter smiled. This was a big story, and she knew it.

'You're telling me Bazza's bailing out?' he said.

'I'm telling you he might have to.'

'That's supposition.'

'I know. It's what people like me do for a living.' She fingered the rim of her glass. 'Well?'

'No comment.'

'No comment meaning you don't know or no comment?'

'No comment.'

Minutes later Mackenzie appeared. Gill got to her feet and reached for her bag, but Bazza ignored her. He wanted a word with Winter. They left the bar and went into his office. The Venetian blinds were down and a recording of the FA Cup semi-final was playing on the TV in the corner.

'Well?' Mackenzie closed the door and locked it.

'Well what?'

'Skelley, mush. I need to know what happened.'

'He hasn't called you?'

'Not a fucking peep.'

Winter described the afternoon's meet. Skelley, he suspected, would play it long.

'What does that mean?' Mackenzie was watching the game.

'It means he'll deny all knowledge.'

'He can't. It's all there on the disc.'

'I meant the toot.'

'Then he's lying. He must have had it. We know he had it. You fucking told me he had it. You told me he gave some to the Polish bloke. That was ours, mush, and he's bang up for it.'

'You're right, but that's nothing we can prove.'

'Who cares a fuck. Give the man a ring. Tell him he's out of order. Tell him we'll fucking be up there sharpish unless he sorts something out. Otherwise that DVD goes to the Old Bill. You got that?' Winter nodded, said nothing. 'And what about the woman? The sister? You saw her too?'

'Yeah. She can make Wednesday evening.'

'That's too late, mush. She needs to know that brother of hers isn't getting a quarter of a million quid off me.'

'Then phone her up and tell her.'

'That's not the way it works. I want her down here.'

'She can't do it, Baz. She's away. Wednesday she's got some aunt she needs to see in Southampton. She can come across afterwards.'

'Yeah?' Mackenzie abandoned the TV and turned his attention to the big campaign grid on his office wall. Wednesday evening was a blank. A couple of weeks ago they'd all been hatching plans for a storming finish to the campaign, but Bazza's appetite for yet more humiliation had gone. 'Tell her eight o'clock. I'll stand her dinner.'

'No problem.' Winter got to his feet but Mackenzie waved him down again. He was still staring at the campaign grid. His mood had changed. Some of the air had left his balloon. He looked, in a word, deflated. 'Where did we go wrong, mush? Who's fucking leaking all this stuff?'

Today's efforts, he muttered, had been a total waste of time, half a dozen retards at the first event, a bunch of deaf pension-ers at the second. And both times, just to salt the wound, the audience had been outnumbered by the usual flying picket of scrotes outside.

'They won't leave us alone, mush. They're evil little inbreds, but they're way ahead of the game and they fucking know it. So who's giving them the wink? Where's this stuff coming from?'

Winter said he didn't know.

'Leo thinks it's Gill Reynolds.'

'Why?'

'Because the *News* is often there as well. Stands to reason, doesn't it?'

'Maybe the kids tip them off.'

'Sure.' He nodded. 'And maybe they don't.'

'Why don't you ask her?'

'I have.'

'And?'

'She says I'm off my head.' At last the hint of a smile from Mackenzie. 'And fuck knows, the woman's probably right.'

His eyes returned to the wallboard. Tomorrow, in the run-up to election day, *Pompey First* had announced an event at Fort Nelson, a showpiece military museum up on Portsdown Hill. Bazza would be addressing the arts and culture issue head on, pledging support for more resources, more exhibitions, more celebration of the city's glorious heritage. The management at Widley had been really helpful, but in his battle against the scrotes Bazza had decided on yet another last-minute change of venue.

'The Tipner scrapyard, mush. Gill's idea. Fucking perfect. Leo's fixed for a BBC South crew to be there. We don't need the punters, just the background. I'm going for a piece to camera. Flagship Pompey. Trafalgar. Jutland. D-Day. Where we've come from. Who we are. None of the other lot would dream of anything like this, but that's because they've never looked hard enough. It's there, mush. Under our fucking noses.'

'What is, Baz?'

'Blood, mush. And treasure.'

For a moment the old spark, the old mischief, was back. He was animated, alive, pumped-up, surfing that same wave that had carried *Pompey First* through the opening week of the campaign. This was the city he loved. And it might still be his for the taking.

'Tipner, then?' Winter didn't know what to say.

'Spot on, mush. Half eleven.' His eyes were back on the semi-final. 'Do yourself a favour. Join us.'

Winter left the hotel soon afterwards. Of Gill Reynolds there was no sign. Neither was he able to clock the surveillance from *Gehenna* that was undoubtedly in place. He drove along the seafront and then pulled a left into Craneswater. Darkness was falling and the dog walkers were out in force. Winter parked along the road from Mackenzie's house and fetched out his mobile.

Skelley wasn't picking up so he left a message. His boss, he said, was anxious for a meet. If he didn't hear back by close of play tomorrow, he'd draw his own conclusions. A second call went to Irenka. She was in the bath.

'Mackenzie wants to buy you dinner,' he said. 'Lucky girl.'

They agreed half seven at the Trafalgar Wednesday evening. Irenka said she'd be driving over from Southampton. Winter gave her directions.

At the end of Sandown Road there was a public call box. Winter had used it a number of times over the last few days. He strolled down and dialled a number from memory.

'You know the scrapyard at Tipner? Out beyond the dog track?'

'Yeah.'

'Half eleven.'

He put the phone down and backed into the gathering dusk. The Tipner scrapyard was visible from the motorway, acres of assorted debris, a very Pompey welcome to the city. Winter had never understood why the site hadn't been snapped up by the developers and turned into yet another retail experience, but in a way he was glad it had been spared. The place was much emptier now, but over the years, driving into the nick at Kingston Crescent, he'd been strangely gladdened by the sight of a rusting submarine awaiting the scrapyard blowtorch or a line of derelict battle tanks parked among the puddles. It spoke of a Pompey he knew only too well, martial, gruff, matter of fact, a city that rolled up its sleeves and threw its weight about, resisting the picturesque curtsey that would put it on the front of everyone's Christmas calendar. Bazza felt this way too, and unlike Winter he could probably put it into words.

Winter walked on past the car and stepped into Bazza's drive. This, he knew, would probably be the last time he'd ever set foot in the property, but for his own peace of mind he was determined to say a kind of goodbye.

Marie was in the kitchen. She watched him cross the patio beside the pool and beckoned him in. She knew he loved a good malt. 'There's a bottle in the den,' she said. 'Help yourself.'

Winter fetched a bottle of Glenmorangie, pausing to look round. This single room – cluttered, intimate, slightly claustro-phobic – told you everything you'd ever need to know about Bazza Mackenzie. The trophy football shots on the wall. The framed snap of a younger Marie beside the PC. More photos of Stu and Ezzie and the grandkids. A big framed poster advert-ising the beachside retirement apartments south of Barcelona, Bazza's first serious venture into the foreign property market, a success he'd parcelled up and given to Marie as a surprise Christmas present. This space charted the journey Bazza had made, and Winter could only imagine how he must be feeling without it. Pompey's favourite son, like everyone else in the world, needed a comfort zone. And this was it.

'So how is he?' Marie couldn't hide her anxiety.

'Lost.'

'I know.'

'You've talked to him?'

'Every night. He phones up every night.'

'And what does he say? You mind me asking?'

'Not at all. It's sad, Paul. He's got terrible problems. Lost is a good word. You've nailed it completely. Lost.'

Her husband, she said, had run out of steam. It had never happened before in his life and there was no instruction book to tell him what to do. She thought it began and ended with money – money ran everyone's life these days – but that wasn't all of it.

'He can't get it up any more, Paul. It's worrying him sick.'

'Get it up?'

'Do it. Screw. Shag. Fuck. He says it doesn't work.'

'And he *tells* you all this?'

'He does.' She nodded. 'And in a way I'm glad.'

'Why?'

'Because it probably means there's no one else to talk to.'

'And that matters?'

'Of course it does.'

'Because you miss him?'

'Yes, oddly enough I do.' She turned away and sorted out a couple of glasses. Winter had never seen her drink malt whisky.

'Cheers,' he said. 'Here's to Baz, eh?'

She nodded but said nothing. Her glass was still on the breakfast bar. At length she took a tiny sip, the way a child might. In this light she looked much younger. Winter hadn't been around when they'd first met but could imagine the chemistry. The posh young thing with the high school education and the Old Portsmouth address. The apprentice estate agent from over the tracks with his Lambretta 200 and endless supply of quality weed. The way Bazza sometimes told it, Marie had made the running. Not that he'd ever complained.

'So what happens next?'

'I don't know, Paul. We were talking last night. I hope you don't mind.'

'About what?'

'I mentioned what you'd said.'

'About what?'

'Buying a ticket to South America. Packing our bags. Doing a bunk.'

'And what did he say?'

'He laughed. He said he wouldn't blame me. Then he said something else. He said he'd like to come too. Maybe not South America. Maybe somewhere else.'

Winter was thinking about Famagusta. Gill Reynolds was right. If you made it to Northern Cyprus you were probably safe.

'And you?'

'I don't know. Some of the stuff he's been up to lately is hard to forgive.'

'She's a journalist, my love. They'll shag anyone for a story.'

'You really think so?' She forced a smile. 'But it's not like they're even shagging, is it?'

Whether this knowledge was a comfort or not Winter could only guess. The message he'd come to deliver seemed suddenly irrelevant. She missed him. She wanted him back. The only questions that mattered were when and how.

They had another drink. They talked about some of the good times – excursions abroad to view this property or that, wild nights in London when Bazza had scored a particularly sweet deal, a July week in a big rented house in Cornwall, three generations under one roof, the kids underfoot, days on the beach, nights around the barbecue, the feeling – new to Winter – that he was part of the warm rough and tumble of a real family, with all its chaos and laughter.

'You liked that? Sennen Cove?'

'I loved it.'

'We did too. It was good having you along. The kids thought

you were great, Guy especially. He still talks about it.'

Guy was the oldest of Bazza's grandchildren. Winter had taught him how to pick up crabs and jellyfish in the rockpools beneath the cliffs. He remembered the icy kiss of the water and Guy's upturned face. Dad stuff. Family stuff.

'Yeah ...' he said. 'Good times.'

Marie poured them a nightcap. She was drunk by now, moist-eyed at the memories. She reached for his hand and told him about a miscarriage she'd had only a couple of years back. Women her age had no business getting pregnant, but somehow it had happened and what made it all the sweeter was the knowledge that Bazza wanted it too.

'We were going to call him Paul,' she said, giving Winter's hand a little squeeze. 'And guess who was going to be the godfather?'

Winter stared at her. Then astonishment gave way to something else and he pulled her towards him and gave her a long hug. He could feel how thin she was under the T-shirt and sweater. Stress, he thought. Small wonder.

'Would you have liked that?' She was peering up at him. Her eyes were shiny with tears.

'Like what?'

'Being a godfather?'

Winter nodded. Now wasn't the time to talk about Jimmy Suttle, and Lizzie and Grace. Now was the time to try and make her feel just a little bit better.

'You've been brilliant. A brilliant wife. A brilliant mum. And brilliant to me too.'

'Been?'

'Are.' He tried to smile. 'I was always crap at grammar.'

She turned away and said she had to go to bed. This whole thing would sort itself out, she knew it would. Winter nodded, saying nothing, wondering why Bazza hadn't put in his nightly phone call. Maybe he rings late, he thought. Maybe he waits until he knows she's tucked up.

Then came a ring at the front door. Marie glanced up at the clock and frowned. Nearly eleven.

'I'll get it,' Winter said.

He walked through to the hall. The porch light wasn't on, but he could see the foggy shape of someone waiting through the frosted glass. Marie had bolted the door top and bottom. Winter drew the bolts and opened the door.

Bazza.

He looked Winter up and down. He too had been drinking.

'This used to be my place ...' he said. 'Mind if I come in?'

Winter didn't get back to Hayling Island until gone midnight. He'd stayed long enough for a coffee and a bit of a chat before leaving Bazza and Marie to it. In his heart he knew Bazza was back for good, and he was glad for Marie's sake, but that didn't make the parting any easier. Next time they met he knew the circumstances would be very different. He just hoped, way down the line, that she'd forgive him.

Misty was asleep when he crept into the bedroom, but the moment he rolled into bed she woke up.

'Where have you been, pet?'

'With Baz and Marie.'

'They're back together?'

'Yes.'

'Thank fuck for that. She should chop it off. Bloody man.'

She switched the light on. She was parched. Too much Stolly. Drinking alone would be the end of her.

Winter padded downstairs and made a pot of tea. Returning to the bedroom, he settled beside her. He'd tried to rehearse what was coming next but had never quite managed to find a way of softening bad news. Better, perhaps, to just say it.

'The shit's about to hit the fan, Mist.'

'What shit?' She was brushing sugar off the duvet. 'What fan?'

'Bazza. There's no way I'm going into details, but he's fucked.'

346

'Broke, you mean?'

'Big time. And other stuff as well.'

The gravity of what Winter was trying to say was evident in his face. It dawned on Misty that this was serious.

'So what's going to happen?'

'They'll have the house off you.'

'Who's they?'

'It doesn't matter, Mist. We're in queue territory here. We could start with the bailiff but it doesn't end there.'

'So what do we do?'

'We move.'

'But what about Trude? She'll be home in a couple of days.'

'She comes too.'

'Where? Where would we go?'

Winter hesitated. He could try and flannel her. He could try and pretend he'd just dreamed up the idea. But neither option would work because Misty Gallagher had been around for a while and very little got past her.

'Abroad, Mist. We'll have to go abroad.'

'*Abroad?* Why, for fuck's sake?'

'Because we have no choice.'

'We?'

'Me.'

'Why?' She peered at him. 'Are you in trouble?'

'Yes.'

'Big trouble?'

'Yes.'

'Have you killed someone?'

'Sort of ...' He nodded. 'Yes.'

She gazed at him for a long time. At first Winter misread her reaction as disbelief. Then he realised she was, in some unfathomable way, proud of him.

'Pet ...' She abandoned the cup and gave him a hug. 'You should have told me. What's a girl for, for fuck's sake?'

Winter tried to fight her off. She wanted to know where they were going.

'Croatia,' he said, 'for starters.'

'Really?' She was in his face again. 'And is that why you went out there? To get things ready?'

'Yeah.' Winter was happy to lie. 'So now you know.'

'And this friend of yours? This woman? She's all part of the plan?'

'She is.'

'Thank fuck for that. Trude'll be pleased too.' She paused, struck by another thought. 'And Baz? Marie? They're coming too?'

Winter looked at her, holding her at arm's length, knowing he couldn't ride his luck any further. Enough was enough.

'No, Mist.' He leaned forward and kissed her. 'I'm not sure that would ever work.'

Chapter twenty-six

Winter phoned Maddox from Hayling Island. Upstairs he could hear Misty padding round the bedroom. She'd been up since dawn, going through her wardrobes, pulling out stuff she wanted to hang on to, making another pile for the charity shop. After a fitful night's sleep she'd decided that relocating abroad would be an adventure.

Maddox finally answered from Porec. She said she was at the agency. She'd had one customer all morning and he'd only come in to make a pass at her.

Winter, relieved that she hadn't put to sea with Josip, said he was about to change all that. He had money. And he wanted her to find a six-month rental.

'How much have you got?'

'Enough.'

'One bedroom? Two?'

'Three, minimum.'

'*Three?* What haven't you told me?'

'Long story. Think me and a lady called Misty and a twenty-five-year-old with a walking problem.'

'Croats are useless around disability.'

'Then find us a carpenter. Or someone who can sort out the aids we'll need.' Winter grinned. The prospect of money made things so simple. 'Deal?'

He hung up in time to catch Misty doing a twirl in a low-cut cocktail dress he'd last seen her wearing in the days when she was still pulling Bazza. She struck a pose, pushed her chest out.

'What do you think? Yes or no?'

'I think yes, Mist.' Winter's grin widened. 'Come here.'

Mid-morning, contrary to what he'd told Winter, Bazza turned up at Fort Nelson. Leo Kinder, who was beginning to despair about the campaign, was struck by the change in his candidate. The gloom seemed to have lifted. He was his old self again, Pompey's bantam cock, strutting his stuff.

'Alright, are we?'

'Never better, mush.' Bazza shot him a wink. 'Thank fuck for marriage.'

Kinder looked at him a moment, wanting to know more, but time was moving on.

'The piece to camera? You're happy to go for it?'

'No problem. I've got it nailed.'

Kinder had struck a deal to bus in a couple of classes of kids from a local primary school, and the Royal Armouries, who ran the museum, had been as good as their word in offering help. Bazza was best mates with the young cameraman who turned up from BBC South and even the weather was on *Pompey First*'s side. Best of all, for the first time in nearly a week there was no sign of the scrote vote.

The cameraman set up for the master shot. Leo wanted a gaggle of kids around Bazza as he walked along a line of artillery pieces. Some of these monsters had been installed to defend Pompey against the marauding French, and the plan was to track slowly backwards until Bazza and his eager young posse got to the last cannon. This one had been primed with a blank charge, and it was Bazza's job to order the attending gunner to let fly.

Kinder knew enough about media set-ups like these to understand how much he was asking of Mackenzie. The walk was timed at around three minutes. From start to finish Bazza had to cover more than five hundred years of history, from the sinking of the *Mary Rose* to the dispatch of the Falklands task force. This was a challenge that would stretch a seasoned professional. Bazza had never done anything like it in his life.

Kinder needn't have worried. From the moment he set foot in the fort and saw the guns, Bazza was in top form. He rallied the kids, led them yelping and screaming down the ramparts, and then bullied them into a wide circle around him. He let the sound recordist fit a radio mike, jogged along the line of artillery for a word with the gunner, then returned. The cameraman, who was shooting this first take hand-held, had organised someone to guide him backwards as he held Bazza in shot. All that remained, in Bazza's phrase, was nailing it.

On Kinder's cue taping began. Bazza, who'd established a rapport with the kids, kicked off with Henry VIII. Big fat guy, he said, nodding down towards the city below. The Frenchies arrived off Southsea Castle, the battle started, the *Mary Rose* heeled over and hundreds of men died. These were local blokes, he said. Blokes like your dad and your grandad. All dead. For why? Because Pompey, your Pompey, our Pompey, *mattered.* We were in the right place at the right time fighting the right enemy. After Henry's precious flagship came Admiral Byng – total wimp, executed by firing squad in Spithead. And then HMS *Victory* smashing through the French line of battle. And then the world's first ironclad, HMS *Warrior*. And then the Dreadnoughts chasing the Germans at the Battle of Jutland. And then the D-Day armada thundering south towards France. And finally HMS *Hermes* sailing halfway round the world to put the Argies back in their box. These, said Bazza, were Pompey blokes. Something we ought to remember. Something we ought to be proud of. Something we ought to celebrate. Why? Because Pompey had always been the guardian of the nation's flame.

This last line was Kinder's but the rest was pure Bazza. And as he came to a halt beside the last gun, he turned to the kids with a question: 'You want to send the French a message? You do? Then here it is ...'

A nod to the gunner cued the blank charge. The girls screamed. The boys covered their ears. Even the cameraman was impressed.

'Brilliant,' he muttered to Kinder. 'How the fuck did he manage that?'

Winter was in Winchester by half past two. Suttle and Parsons met him at the safe house. Parsons wanted to know about Skelley.

'He's coming down tonight. Mackenzie talked to him first thing this morning.'

'And what do you think he's going to say?'

'I think he'll tell us to fuck off. As far as I can see, he's not having it.'

Parsons, like Suttle, was worried about the strength of the evidence. The DVD interview was a taster, no more. Lublin police were on standby with a European Arrest Warrant, and Beginski could be back in London by the weekend if Willard chose to trigger proceedings.

Suttle needed to be sure that Winter would be present when Skelley met Mackenzie.

'I'm assuming yes.'

'Then you'll need to wear a wire unless there's some other way we can put a rig in. I know you don't want to, but there's no alternative.'

Winter knew he was right. Whatever transpired at this evening's meet would be priceless ammunition when it came to arrest and interview, and the transcripts would probably end up in a court of law. But there was a downside, too. Winter had never been much interested in risk assessments but on this occasion he was prepared to make an exception.

'Skelley's a quality criminal,' he said. 'I'm assuming he'll bring protection. He might insist on a pat-down. The rest writes itself, doesn't it?'

Parsons and Suttle exchanged glances. They'd been anticipating exactly this conversation for days. It was Suttle who voiced the obvious.

'Without hard evidence, Paul, it could get sticky. If we're relying on your testimony, Skelley's briefs will be dancing in the aisle.'

'A bit harsh, son, isn't it?' Winter looked aggrieved.

'Not at all. They'll turn the entire trial into a test of character. How much reliance can we place on a police officer who ratted on his mates? Who joined forces with a known criminal?'

'But he's not a known criminal, not a *proven* criminal, that's the whole point.'

'Sure, but here's the catch-22. Mackenzie is a Level 3. He's built an entire empire on Class A narcotics. We need to take him down. We need to put him away. But if the evidence boils down to you, we've got a problem.'

'Beginski?'

'He'll certainly help.'

'And Baz himself?'

'I'm not with you.'

'He's bang up against it, son. Everything I promised has come true. He's skint. He's totally potless. And *Pompey First* has become a joke. All Skelley has to do now is tell him to fuck off and you're looking at blood on the walls.'

'Is that a guarantee?'

'Of course it's not. But it'll happen.'

'Says you.'

'Says me.'

'When?'

'By the end of the week. Bazza's burned through the loan he got. The bank's back on the phone.'

Parsons nodded, scribbled herself a note, said nothing. Suttle wasn't convinced that *Pompey First* was finished.

'I was talking to one of the surveillance guys just now. He was up at Fort Nelson this morning, doing the punter thing. Apparently Mackenzie played a blinder, not a scrote in sight. The guy was so impressed he's thinking of voting for him.'

'That's because he got a decent screw last night. God bless Marie.'

'He's back home?'

'Yeah.' Winter paused. '*Where* did you say he was this morning?'

'Fort Nelson. The Royal Armouries place.' Suttle frowned. 'What's the matter?'

A phone call took Winter to the offices of the *News*. Gill Reynolds collected him from reception and led him upstairs. The editor, Mark Boulton, was waiting in his office overlooking the production floor. Winter settled for a milky coffee, two sugars.

Boulton looked far too young to be bossing a paper as big as the *News*. His body language suggested that Reynolds was heading for stardom.

'She's been keeping a diary for Mackenzie,' he said, 'as you probably know.'

Winter nodded. The coffee was vile.

'We're building all this into a post-election special,' Boulton went on. 'She might have told you that as well.'

'Mackenzie mentioned it.' Winter checked his watch. 'Where's all this going?'

'Good question. Like most of the rest of the city, we think we know about Mackenzie. About where his money came from. All that.'

'Really?'

'Yes.'

'Have you got a good lawyer?'

'You think we'd need one?'

'Yeah, I do, if you put any of this shit into print.'

Boulton smiled. Reynolds, it seemed, had her suspicions about Mackenzie's immediate short-term plans.

'She thinks he's going to leg it. She think's he's a flight risk.'

Flight risk was a CID term, and for one crazy moment it occurred to Winter that Reynolds too might be u/c, a particle of *Gehenna* that Jimmy Suttle and the rest of them had swept under the carpet Then he told himself it was impossible. He'd have sussed it earlier. Maybe.

'She mentioned something about it last night,' he said. 'Famagusta?'

'That's right. But now she's got a number.'

'How come?'

Boulton glanced at Reynolds. She couldn't wait to share her little secret.

'I was in the Man's office this morning. He was sweetness and light. He had to pop out for a wee-wee.'

'And?'

'He left his mobile on the desk. The Northern Cyprus code is 09032. The calls go through Turkey.' She smiled. 'The number was sitting there in his directory. I just helped myself.'

Winter said nothing. Boulton was watching him closely.

'You don't seem surprised.'

'I'm not. I told you just now. I knew already.'

'That's not what I meant. As I understand it, you're Mackenzie's right-hand man. You work for him. Here's Gill telling you about Northern Cyprus. About raiding the man's mobile. And you haven't turned a hair.'

'What do you expect?'

'I expect you to be defending your boss's best interests. I expect a little ...' he frowned '... reaction.'

Winter shrugged. His day was getting worse. He knew exactly what was coming next.

'Gill tells me you used to be a copper.'

'That's right.' He glanced at Reynolds. 'How did you know?'

'Bazza told me. It was one of the first things he said when we

355

did that first interview. He boasts about it. You're his trophy catch. The way it comes across, it was Bazza who saved you from a fate worse than death.'

'Staying in the Job?'

'Exactly.'

'He's probably right.'

'He said that too. And he thinks you owe him.'

'So *do* you?' Boulton again. 'Or are we on a different page in the script?'

Winter shuddered. This was less than artful. Reynolds, for whatever reason, had come to the conclusion that Winter was back where he belonged. Talking to the Boys In Blue.

'I work for Mackenzie,' he said stonily. 'That's where it begins and ends. Nice coffee.' He stood up.

Boulton didn't move. He glanced across at Reynolds and raised an eyebrow.

'I was with Joe Faraday for a while.' She was smiling. 'And he told me he never really understood how you could live with working for Mackenzie.'

'Really?'

'Yes. And he said something else too. He said once a copper always a copper. And he said you were one of the best.'

'Thanks.'

'Pleasure.'

Boulton got to his feet.

'We think you might one day have a story to tell.' He extended his hand. 'And when that day comes we'd be delighted to help in whatever way we can. In the meantime, under the circumstances, you might want sight of that number.'

Winter gazed at him for a long moment, then shook his head and left.

Under the circumstances?

Winter knew he was in deep, deep trouble. If Gill Reynolds had put the story together then Bazza couldn't be far behind.

That's why he'd set last night's trap, telling Winter about the change in location for the heritage piece and then sitting back and seeing what happened. This morning, in all probability, the scrote vote had turned up at the Tipner scrapyard, and Bazza doubtless had someone in attendance to report back.

Their next conversation would be fraught, and he knew he had to make a decision. Aborting *Gehenna* at this stage would solve nothing. With Bazza home free or settling into a new life in Northern Cyprus, there was no way Winter could avoid the shadow of the Malaga executions. One day would come the knock on the door. And that he had to avoid at all costs.

And so *Gehenna* had to run its course, earning him the deal he needed. A fresh start. A new ID. Somewhere sunny. With Misty and Trude.

The thought of Misty took him out of the city. By now she would have acquired a mountain of cardboard boxes from the Londis down the road. For an hour or so he'd be only too happy to lend her a hand, a down payment on this new life of theirs. By the time he was back at the hotel, with luck, he'd have worked out a line for Mackenzie.

It was a glorious day, and traffic was heavy onto Hayling Island. Winter drove past thicket after thicket of blue Tory posters, musing about where the election had taken them all. The master plan for *Gehenna* had been his, and in theory it was a beautiful piece of entrapment.

To no one's surprise, Bazza had generated a perfect storm for himself. His trademark mix of recklessness, mischief, ambition and raw nerve had led him to take a tilt at Parliament. At the start of the campaign, to everyone's surprise, he'd done extremely well. There'd even been rumours that the mainstream candidates were beginning to worry. But then, as Winter had predicted, it had all unravelled until Pompey's favourite drug baron found himself in a trap of his own making. According to the *Gehenna* script, at this point it would only take a tiny push to topple Bazza over the edge. That push, fingers crossed,

357

would come from Skelley. After which Bazza would lose it completely.

Did Winter still believe it? Was he still signed up to *Gehenna*? He knew the answer was yes. Because, God help him, there was no alternative.

He was already turning in through Misty's gate when he saw the Bentley. It was parked beneath the tree at the edge of the drive. The kitchen was at the back of the house, and Winter could see Mackenzie swivelling at the breakfast bar, alerted by the crunch of gravel outside. Shit.

He knew Bazza was at his most dangerous when nothing in the world seemed capable of upsetting him. He met Winter at the door, big smile, pumping handshake, the smell of fresh coffee on the go, even the tang of grilling bacon.

Misty was in the kitchen, reaching for an extra plate. As Winter had predicted, the kitchen was littered with cardboard boxes. Whatever else awaited them in Porec, they wouldn't be short of glasses.

'Mist tells me you're off?' Bazza couldn't have been more affable.

'Yeah.' Winter shed his jacket. 'It's Trude, really.'

'Likes the sunshine, does she?'

'Always.'

'Bit of a surprise, though, eh? Mist assumed you'd told me.'

'Didn't want to get in the way, Baz. No distractions. Not this week.'

'Well done, son. Good darts. Everything for the cause, eh?'

Winter nodded. He was wondering about the surveillance guys. Were they parked up outside? Somewhere down the road? Had Bazza clocked them? He felt physically ill. Mackenzie was playing with him, goading him, setting him up. This was beyond dangerous. He had to do something. He had to somehow seize the initiative, restore – at the very least – a little self-respect.

'If you want the truth, Baz, I've had enough. I said I'd see you through, and that's what I've done.'

'See me through to what, mush?'

'Thursday. Election day. Whatever happens after that, you're on your own.'

'Is that right?'

Misty, still attending to the bacon, caught the change in tone. She glanced over her shoulder towards the breakfast bar. Winter could see the anxiety in her eyes. He turned back to Mackenzie.

'Look on the bright side, Baz. You can flog this place now. Fuck knows, you need the money.'

Mackenzie ignored him. He was standing by the window now, gazing out.

'We've been a good team,' he said softly. 'What do you think, Mist?'

'Me and you, Baz?'

'Me and Paulie here.'

'The best, Baz. Totally the best.'

'That's what I think.' He stepped back from the window. 'So what do *you* think ...' there was no warmth in the smile '... Paulie?'

'I think it's been fun. But like I say, I think the time's come to call it a day.'

'Shame.'

'Definitely.'

'No regrets?'

'Plenty.'

'Like what?'

'Like ...' Winter frowned, then shook his head. 'No way. I'm not going there.'

'Where, Paulie?' He'd come close now. The smell of mint on his breath was something new. All that campaigning, Winter thought vaguely. All those strangers you suddenly had to talk to.

'Ketchup or brown sauce?' Misty was trying to head Bazza off. It didn't work.

'It's Westie, isn't it? It's fucking Westie that's done it for you. Him and that girl of his? Couldn't hack it, could you? Couldn't just accept it was something that happened? People get hurt, mush. That's life. People fuck up. They get in my face. And then they get hurt.'

'You had them killed, Baz. You had them blown away. That's not hurt.'

'Whatever. It doesn't matter, mush. It's gone. It's over, unless ...'

'Unless what?'

'Unless I think different.'

'I'm not with you.'

'No, you're not, mush, are you? And I tell you something else. You're fucking bricking yourself. I can smell it, mush. Any minute now you're going to do what old men do. You're going to dump in your kacks. And you know why? Because I frighten you shitless. Good. I'm glad. Because you fucking deserve it.'

He stared up at Winter for a long moment, then headed for the door. En route was an empty cardboard box. He gave it a kick, then turned round and strode back. His finger was in Winter's face.

'I don't know what's going on in that evil little brain of yours, mush, but you listen to me. I'm saying this once and once only. If you even think of dobbing me in with the Filth, you'll end up like Westie. Except worse. Much worse. Westie was lucky. *Bam!* End of. For you, mush, I can dream up something really tasty. We understand each other? No? Then talk to Misty here. She knows exactly what I'm about.'

He turned on his heel again and left. Moments later came the slam of the front door. Winter watched the Bentley execute a savage turn, gravel kicking from the rear tyres. Then Mackenzie was gone.

Winter turned round to find Misty behind him. She was offering him a sandwich.

'Can you manage a couple, pet?' She did her best to smile. 'Be a shame to waste them.'

Winter activated the emergency procedure in mid-afternoon. By now he was taking no chances. The scene with Bazza was a declaration of war. Surveillance worked both ways. He had to assume Mackenzie would detail someone to keep tabs on him.

'Son?' Winter was parked on the hard shoulder on the motorway. 'There's no way I can wear a wire tonight.'

'You OK?'

'No.'

'Wanna talk about it?'

'No.'

'You're telling me we're blown?'

'No. He's still in play. But only just.'

'Take care, eh? Nothing silly ...' Suttle rang off.

Skelley was due down from London between six and seven. On the phone Mackenzie had skipped the usual dinner invite. This was to be strictly business, no frills, no fraternising. Mackenzie sat in his office watching the early-evening news. Gordon Brown, it seemed, had at last thrown caution to the winds and come out with a barnstorming speech. Within hours, poor man, one of his own candidates had described him as the worst prime minister ever. Winter sank into the proffered seat, wondering aloud why anyone ever went into politics. The higher you got the more shit you had to take.

Bazza agreed. The venom and the anger had gone. He was quiet, almost reflective. For once his desk was empty of paperwork, and he'd abandoned the campaign suit for jeans and a loose cotton shirt. Famagusta, Winter thought.

'How's Trude?' Bazza said at last.

'Fine, Baz. On the mend.'

'And up here?' He tapped his head.

'Frustrated as fuck. She wants everything back the way it was, but that's going to take a while.'

'But it's going to happen, yeah?'

'Probably.'

'Probably's not good enough.'

'That's what she says.'

'I'm serious. If it takes some fancy operation, like I said before, I'm up for it. The offer's still there.'

'Thanks. I'm grateful.'

'It's not for you, mush. It's for her. She's my girl, always was.'

It was true. After years of shagging Misty Gallagher, Bazza had assumed that young Trude was his daughter. Years later a blood test had proved otherwise, assigning paternity to a motor trader called Mike Valentine, but Bazza still regarded himself as Trude's honorary dad.

'I'll make sure we bring her round before we go, Baz.'

'Do that, yeah?' His eyes finally left the screen. 'Old times' sake?'

'Of course.'

The waiting went on. A lengthy trailer detailed the treats in store for election junkies on Thursday night. Programming would start the moment the polls closed. By midnight it should be pretty clear who'd won.

'Enjoyed it, Baz?'

'Yeah, most of it. Until the fucking scrote vote turned up.'

'I'm sure.' Winter managed a grin. 'I'm glad Tipner worked out, though.'

Mackenzie shot him a look, said nothing. Then he smiled.

'Put them off the scent, did you?'

'Of course. I knew the effort you'd put into the other place. Fort Nelson. Everyone deserves a break, even you, Baz.'

'Fort Nelson was good.' He nodded at the screen. 'They're running it tonight.'

The phone rang. Skelley was in reception. He seemed to have brought a colleague.

'Show them in, love.'

Winter arranged the chairs in a semicircle around the desk. Moments later there was a knock at the door. Skelley was wearing a beautifully cut business suit that flattered his bulk. His companion, equally well dressed, was younger, fitter, black.

'Sit down, gents. You're welcome.'

The receptionist backed out of the office and closed the door. The TV was still on but Bazza muted the sound. Then he leaned forward and looked Skelley in the eye.

'So what have we got?'

Skelley reached inside his jacket pocket and for a split second Winter wondered exactly what he had in mind. Then he produced a white envelope and put it carefully on the desk.

'What's that?'

'It's yours.'

'But what is it?'

'Open it.' Skelley looked briefly amused. 'Then you'll find out, won't you?'

Mackenzie opened the envelope. Inside was a folded sheet of paper. He looked at it, uncomprehending, then passed it to Winter. It was a printout of some kind, presumably off the Internet. It was in Polish.

'What's the *Lubelski Kurier*?'

'The Lublin local paper. The bit you need is at the bottom on the left.' Skelley leaned across and pointed out a paragraph ringed in blue biro.

Winter was no wiser. Then he recognised the name. Pavel Beginski.

'So what does it say?'

'It says a friend found his body yesterday morning.'

'He's dead?'

'I'm afraid so.'

'How? Why?'

'Pass.' He shrugged, a gesture of infinite regret. 'Apparently the bloke wasn't too well. Drink? Drugs? Fuck knows. You have to take care of yourself these days. Otherwise anything can happen. George?'

Skelley's minder had another envelope. He gave it to Mackenzie. Bazza ignored him. His hand had found the remote.

'That's me, guys.' He nodded at the screen and turned up the volume.

Skelley seemed genuinely interested. The report lasted four minutes, ending with the boom of the cannon. Afterwards came reactions from other candidates. Their message was broadly the same. A vote for *Pompey First* was a vote wasted. Only the major parties could make any real difference.

Bazza turned the sound down again. He wanted to make it clear that this wasn't the end of the story. He still had the interview. Skelley could save himself a lot of aggravation by squaring up for the toot.

'Maybe not a million,' he conceded. 'Let's call it 750K.'

Winter did his best to hide a smile. Pavel Beginski was in no state to be claiming his commission.

'Well?' Mackenzie was still looking at Skelley.

Skelley, as impassive as ever, got to his feet. He had to be back in town by half nine. He had a business to run, contracts to tie up ahead of the election result. By the weekend a new government might change everything. He'd enjoyed his trip to the seaside, but in the real world there were more serious conversations to be had than this.

By the door he paused, then nodded at the TV.

'You were good,' he said. 'Maybe it's time for a change of career.'

Skelley and his minder left. Mackenzie gazed at the door for a moment, then reached for the envelope. Inside, as Winter had already guessed, was the DVD. Mackenzie picked it up and flipped it into the bin.

'What now then? You want me to go to war? Ambush the guy up the road? Rip his throat out?'

'No, Baz.'

'Good. Then maybe you can tell me what else I can do.'

'I dunno, Baz.'

'You dunno, Baz. Great. You know what Marie said to me last night? She said you were the best thing that had happened to us for years.'

'I'm flattered.'

'You fucking ought to be. And I tell you something else. It's just as well she said "us".' He narrowed his eyes. 'Are you with me?'

Chapter twenty-seven

Suttle called on the pay-as-you-go early in the morning. It was barely light. Winter eased himself out of bed and took the call in the bathroom. With the door closed and a tap on there was no way Misty could eavesdrop on the conversation.

Suttle wanted to know what was going on.

'Beginski's dead.'

'*What?*'

'The Poles haven't told you?'

'The Poles tell us fuck all.'

'Give them a bell. It's in the Lublin local paper. Those guys ought to get out more.'

There was a long silence. Then Suttle was back on the line.

'You're telling me we have to pull the operation? Bin it?'

'No way.'

'What the fuck do we do then?'

'You do what you always did, son. You leave it to me.' Winter was studying himself in the mirror. He looked terrible. 'Mackenzie's a flight risk, by the way. So keep the surveillance on.'

'Flight risk?'

'Northern Cyprus.' He started laughing. 'How come fucking journalists always get there first?'

*

Suttle had the full story by mid-morning. Parsons called him into her office in Major Crime. She had Willard on a secure link from headquarters in Winchester. As far as Suttle could judge, he was developing a heavy cold.

'Winter's right, sir,' Suttle said. 'I talked to the Poles this morning. A neighbour discovered Beginski's body on Monday morning. The police found a forced entry at the back of the property.'

'What sort of state was he in?'

'Nothing obvious, sir. No signs of violence. They did the PM on Monday afternoon. At the moment they seem to be thinking suffocation.'

'Definitely homicide?'

'Yes.'

Willard wanted to know about Winter. What was his take on this latest development?

'He's saying it makes no difference. He still thinks it's do-able.'

'What is?'

'*Gehenna*, sir. He wants us to keep the obs on. He says it's just a matter of time.'

'So Skelley's still in play? Is that what he's saying?'

'That's not clear, sir.'

'Why not?'

'He won't tell me.'

There was a long silence. Suttle exchanged looks with Parsons. Twenty-four-hour surveillance was costing Willard a fortune. With Beginski dead and the DVD interview potentially tainted by Winter's role in proceedings, *Gehenna*'s prospects were suddenly far from rosy.

'So Mackenzie might not be going after Skelley? Is that what we're saying?'

'It's possible, sir. And he thinks Mackenzie's a flight risk.'

'Because?'

'Because he might have sussed what we're up to. At the

moment we've got nothing on him. He's a free agent. We can't do him for *Pompey First*. He can go wherever he likes, whenever he likes.'

'Then it's over, isn't it? We're blown? We're fucked?'

'That's not what Winter's saying.'

'But why? On what grounds?' Willard was fast losing patience.

'I think Jimmy's saying we haven't got an option, sir.' This from Parsons. 'If we want any kind of result we have to hang in there. The only guy at the coalface is Winter. Either we trust him or we don't.'

'Quite. Extremely well put. So what do you think?'

Parsons nodded at Suttle. He was grateful for her intervention.

'I think we give it forty-eight hours, sir. To be fair, Winter's always talked about election day. That's tomorrow.'

'Wonderful.' Willard sneezed. 'So what will he be giving us?'

'Mackenzie, sir.'

'And you believe that?'

'Yes.' Suttle nodded. 'I do.'

Pompey First, after overnight raves for Bazza's performance at Fort Nelson, was cranking up for a final day of flat-out campaigning. To Kinder's delight his candidate appeared to have shaken his feathers and decided to fight to the last. Victory might be beyond them, but the voice of the real Pompey wasn't going to let the city down. They'd end the way they began. On a high.

At Mackenzie's suggestion, Kinder organised a series of impromptu rallies. The first, hastily announced on the Internet, took place at the entrance to Fratton Park. Bemused players returning from the morning's session at the training ground found themselves picking their way past a sizeable crowd of *Pompey First* supporters while Bazza name-checked the first-team squad one after the other.

These, he said, were the guys who'd be returning to Wembley in a couple of weeks' time to set about Chelsea. Against all odds, in the teeth of financial meltdown, they'd kept their bottle and played their football and done the city proud. The price of a single Chelsea player, said Bazza, could buy the entire club. That was the Pompey spirit. That was the city's story down through the ages. Make and mend. Get stuck in. Take the battle to the enemy. The last player to appear was David James. He acknowledged the cheers and paused for a word or two. Good luck tomorrow, guys. Break a leg, eh?

Bazza was delighted. The crowd was swelling by the minute. He wanted to tow them across the city to Southsea Castle, turning an impromptu rally into an impromptu march. Many of these people appeared to have time on their hands, and when Bazza put the proposition to the vote there was a roar of approval. Better to be out in the spring sunshine with a bunch of like-minded mates than stuck at home in front of crap TV.

Bazza had found a beer crate to stand on. Of the scrote vote there was no sign.

'Pompey, Pompey, Pompey ...?' He cupped his ear.

'First, first, first,' came the bellowed reply.

Winter spent the morning at home in Hayling Island. He'd never been much good at DIY but he raided Misty's modest supply of tools and began to install the handholds and other aids that Trude would need on her return from the Spinal Unit. Misty had been to B&Q only yesterday, taking a list drawn up by the occupational therapist, and by lunchtime Winter had nearly finished.

Misty was still packing boxes, trying to sieve a lifetime's possessions ahead of the move abroad. Winter, pleased with his morning's work, showed her what he'd done in the bathroom and then took her into Trude's bedroom.

Misty stood beside the bed. Winter had raised it on wooden blocks and swapped the old mattress for something thicker and more resilient. He'd screwed handholds at key locations around the room and installed a bedside bell push Trude could use if she needed to summon help.

Misty looked round. He could certainly have used a spirit level for the handholds and one of the wooden blocks seemed to have given the bed a tilt to the left, but she knew Winter was under pressure and was warmed by the fact that he cared enough to make this kind of effort.

'I'm still a bit fuzzy about the timetable, pet,' she said. 'Trude comes back tomorrow, right?'

'Yeah.'

'And then we're here for a while?'

'Yeah.'

'How long?'

'Dunno, Mist.' Winter bent to retrieve a Rawlplug. 'Depends.'

'On what?'

'Stuff,' he said vaguely. 'A couple of weeks? Maybe a bit longer?' He checked his watch and reached for his jacket. 'Gotta run, Mist. Gotta get back to the ranch.'

Winter drove the half-mile to the beach. He parked the Lexus and stepped onto the drift of sand and pebbles that fringed the road. The tide was out, and he made his way across the dunes. It was a glorious day, not a cloud in the sky, and he watched a lone jogger down by the waterline, a black silhouette against the dazzling brightness of the morning sun. Away to the right, beyond the entrance to Langstone Harbour, he could see the distant curl of the Pompey shoreline, and he paused, thinking suddenly of Joe Faraday. Life, unless you were careful, could spring all kinds of surprises. Faraday had been one such victim, kippered by events that had spiralled out of control. How would he feel now, in Winter's shoes? What would he do? What *could* he do?

He walked west, towards Langstone, reviewing the decisions he'd taken, the risks he'd run, the consequences he'd ignored.

Winter had never been one for introspection. Unlike Faraday, whom he'd once accused of thinking too hard about more or less everything, Winter had always been happy to surf whatever waves turned up. In general this MO had served him well. It kept him on his toes. He'd seldom if ever been bored. But his carefree buccaneer passage between life's dodgier reefs had, in the end, landed him in deep, deep shit. He had no illusions about Bazza Mackenzie. He'd always recognised how dangerous and unpredictable the man could be. And just now he knew that one mistake on his part, one tiny miscalculation, could spell disaster.

He paused to watch a bunch of kitesurfers out among the breakers curling over the sandbar, brilliant brushstrokes on a canvas of the deepest blue. A guy with a scarlet kite launched himself from one of the bigger waves, judging the somersault perfectly, touching down in time to catch the face of the wave behind. His whoop, carried by the wind, brought a smile to Winter's face.

He checked his watch and fumbled for his pay-as-you-go. Jimmy Suttle was at his desk in Major Crime. He told Winter to hang on while he shut the door.

'Paul? You still there?'

'Yeah.'

'How's it going?'

'Beautiful day.'

'*What?*'

'I said beautiful day.'

'I'm sure, mate. Are we on the same page here?'

'Always, son.'

'Thank fuck for that. So what do I tell my bosses? Only they're just a tad anxious.'

'Tell them I'm grateful.'

'I'm not sure it's you they're worrying about.'

'Oh?' The kitesurfer had just performed another miracle. 'So what's the problem?'

Suttle told him to stop fucking about. *Gehenna* was eating money by the hour and no one seemed to have a clue where it might head next.

'And does that include you, son?'

'To be frank, yes. So just tell me where we are.'

'We are where we always were.'

'Stop talking in fucking riddles.'

'I mean it. Mackenzie's on the point of doing something very silly.'

'To Skelley?'

'No, son. To me. Just keep the obs on, yeah?'

He ended the call. The kitesurfer, on his third jump, had blown it.

The *Pompey First* campaign came to an end on the quayside opposite HMS *Victory*. The crowd had thinned a little, some of the older men peeling off to share a late-afternoon pint or two in one of the pubs en route. Bazza, on the promise of good behaviour plus a hefty whack of public money for heritage projects after a *Pompey First* triumph in tomorrow's polls, negotiated half an hour's access to the Historic Dockyard and led his swelling army towards the towering masts and yardarms of Nelson's flagship.

This, as every child in the city knew, was the spirit that badged Pompey. This was the flagship that had broken the French and Spanish lines one stormy October day off the coast near Cadiz. These were the guns that had sent broadside after crashing broadside into Pierre de Villeneuve's fleet, splintering enemy decks, spilling enemy blood, breaking enemy spirits. The price, of course, had been high. Bazza found a bollard to stand on, gathering the crowd around him. He talked of generations of sacrifice – not just Nelson, but the thousands of other men and women who'd fallen in foreign wars, unknown, barely mentioned – and at the end he suggested a minute's silence before calling for three rousing cheers. One for Nelson.

One for the Wembley final. And the last for *Pompey First*.

Kinder, watching the crowd flooding back towards the Victory Gate, shook his head in admiration.

'We might not win –' he offered Mackenzie his hand '– but what the fuck, eh?'

Winter was under instructions to be at the Trafalgar by six o'clock. Irenka was due at seven but Mackenzie was expecting another guest around half six. Given the fact that Pavel Beginski was now dead, Winter had offered to cancel his sister, but Mackenzie wouldn't hear of it. He wanted to meet this Irenka. He needed to have a chat. She might, he told Winter, have something unexpected to stick in the pot.

Winter, pondering this latest development, made his way downstairs to the War Room. Mackenzie and Kinder were watching the BBC twenty-four-hour news channel. Kinder had his feet up on the conference table and was wearing what looked like a new T-shirt. Winter glanced at it. Over the left breast, surprisingly discreet, was the Spinnaker Tower *Pompey First* logo. Kinder leaned forward in his chair, showing Winter the back. *Leo Kinder,* it read, *Vote Meister, 6th April–6th May 2010.*

'Yours is on the table, mush.' Mackenzie nodded at a plastic bag. 'A little something to remember us by.'

There was another T-shirt in the bag, same logo. On the back it read, *Paul Winter. Scheisse Meister.* Same dates.

'Shit-stirrer?' Winter queried.

'Something like that.' Mackenzie nodded at the screen. 'Look at Cleggie. What a muppet.'

Winter helped himself to a chair and watched the coverage. The party leaders were winding up their separate campaigns and heading back to their constituencies for tomorrow's vote. After a month on the road, thought Winter, they looked knackered.

Minutes later Mackenzie took a call from reception. His

visitors had arrived. With Winter in tow, Mackenzie mounted the stairs to the lobby. His guests had already moved on in search of a drink. Even back view, Winter recognised the tall bulky figure at the bar: the mane of jet-black combed-back hair, the sheer breadth of the man's shoulders, the beautifully cut suit. Cesar Dobroslaw.

Mackenzie was intercepting the proffered fifty-pound note. Drinks were on the house.

'Cesar, meet a colleague of mine.'

The sight of Winter drew the faintest smile from Dobroslaw. The last time the two men had met, Winter had paid the price for a piece of Bazza mischief that had badly misfired. The beating he'd taken that night belonged in the same mental drawer he reserved for Westie's execution and the aborted Budva barbecue. Memories like that, thought Winter, probably lasted for ever.

'This is Alan Chudleigh, my solicitor.' Dobroslaw introduced a thin ill-looking man who'd settled for an orange juice. His rimless glasses gave him a slightly bookish air, and something about Mackenzie had already unnerved him.

Mackenzie led the way through to the restaurant. At this time in the evening, still early, it was virtually deserted. The four of them sat down at the reserved table by the window. Chudleigh opened his briefcase and took out a slim Manila file. Winter stared at it. He hadn't a clue what was going on.

Mackenzie reached across and helped himself to the file. Inside was a sheaf of papers. He flicked quickly through them, then nodded.

'Fine,' he said. 'Paul here can be witness.'

'Witness to what?'

Mackenzie didn't answer. Instead, he reached inside his jacket pocket, unfolded a document and passed it to Chudleigh. Winter recognised Marie's signature.

'It's an assignment, mush.' Mackenzie was talking to Dobroslaw. 'It gives me power to OK the deal on her behalf.'

'Deal?' Winter again.

'Cesar here is helping me out.'

'How?'

'By taking over bits of the business. It needs someone else in the driving seat, mush. Someone with half a brain in their head.'

He pushed the open Manila file towards Winter. Mackenzie's signature would transfer the hotel, the house and Misty's place on Hayling Island to Przyjemnosc Ltd, the company through which Dobroslaw did most of his business.

'For how much?' Winter looked up.

'A quid. Most of it's debt. Don't tell me you hadn't noticed.'

'You're mad.'

'No, mush, I'm skint. There's a difference, eh, Cesar?'

Dobroslaw was staring out of the window. His drink was untouched and he didn't seem much interested in the conversation. Winter turned to his solicitor.

'What about the rest of it? The stuff abroad? Businesses around the city?'

'We've had a good look.' Chudleigh had his pen ready for Mackenzie to sign. 'But regrettably most of it's rubbish, hopelessly over-leveraged. The properties we've bought will offer a good return in time, but I'm afraid the rest is a can of worms.'

Winter nodded. He knew he was right but it was chilling to hear it spelled out with such frankness.

'That's a shame,' he said.

'No, it's not.' Mackenzie had been watching him carefully. 'You've been telling me this for months.'

'I have, Baz. But ...' he shrugged '... it needn't end like this.'

'No? You got any other ideas? Apart from kicking Skelley in the bollocks and nicking a million quid off him?'

Winter said nothing. Mackenzie reached for Chudleigh's pen and scribbled a signature at the foot of each page of the document. When he'd finished, Winter did the same. Dobroslaw was still inspecting the view. Four years of graft, of deal-making, of helter-skelter madness, Winter thought. Gone.

Mackenzie wanted to propose a toast. Winter assumed it would be to *Pompey First* but he was wrong.

'Here's to sunshine,' Bazza said, 'and all that lovely Efes.'

Winter caught his eye. Efes was a premium Turkish beer available in – among other places – Northern Cyprus. The deal made sense now. Bazza was on his way out.

Irenka arrived. Winter saw her first as she walked into the restaurant, unknotting her scarf as she made for the table by the window. Dobroslaw clocked her too, and for the first time a smile warmed his face. He got to his feet, his huge hands outstretched, then opened his arms for a hug.

'Stephania.' He was beaming now. 'How long has it been?'

Mackenzie's eyes never left Winter's face. Dobroslaw and Stephania were still on their feet. Dobroslaw's delight was unfeigned. Stephania, despite her acting skills, couldn't mask the panic in her eyes.

Mackenzie beckoned Winter closer.

'Irenka?' he queried softly.

Chapter twenty-eight

Willard called a full *Gehenna* meet for half past midnight. The Covert Ops D/I had belled him on the secure line hours earlier. Irenka, his u/c, had been blown.

'She grew up in Southampton,' he told the faces round the table. 'Belonged to a prominent Polish family. She was in the navy before she joined the Job and hasn't been back to Southampton since, but these people have long memories. Dobroslaw's the godfather. He knows everyone. Stephania did well for herself. Dobroslaw keeps up with stuff like that.'

Willard wanted to know about the link with Mackenzie. The Covert Ops D/I said Bazza had recently tapped Dobroslaw up for a loan.

'We should have known about that.' Willard was looking at Suttle.

'We did, sir. But no one expected the two to meet.'

'Except Mackenzie. We've done this before, haven't we?'

'What, sir?'

'Underestimated the man. A couple of hours down the line it all looks so simple, doesn't it? He has to have a meet with Dobroslaw. He still thinks Irenka might be dodgy. He's sussed there's a Southampton connection. Game, set and fucking match. Jesus ...' He turned away in disgust.

Parsons wanted to know about Winter. She put the question to Suttle. Had he been in touch?

377

'He has, boss. He belled me about an hour ago.'

'And?'

'He was at home at Misty's place. He was just going to bed.'

'Lucky man.' Willard had gone beyond anger. He couldn't wait to bring this pantomime to a halt. 'We've blown it completely,' he said. 'That man's running rings round us.'

'Winter?'

'Mackenzie.'

Suttle shook his head. 'Winter doesn't see it that way at all, sir.'

'He doesn't?'

'No. He admits the Skelley thing's gone tits up but says everything else is on track.'

'Then he's crazy.'

'You might be right, sir. But from where I'm sitting we can't afford to assume that.'

This was brave talk. Heads turned around the table. Suttle was putting a great deal on the line.

'Go on ...' Willard had stopped looking at his watch.

'Number one, he's certain Mackenzie is about to bail out. He'll stick around for tonight's count but after that he's away.'

'How do you know?'

'He's thrown in his hand. Most of the business is worthless. He sold the rest to Dobroslaw last night. For a quid. That's his house, his hotel, Misty's place. Winter says it was inevitable, had to happen, but it must have hurt like fuck. The man's up to his eyes.'

'Skint?' Willard visibly brightened.

'Totally boracic. Except there'll be some kind of side deal because that's the way Mackenzie works. This is Winter speaking, sir, not me.'

'So where's he going?'

'Winter thinks Northern Cyprus, like I said this morning. Probably on Friday and probably with his wife.'

'So how do we stop him?'

378

'We can't, sir. There's nothing to charge him with. And once he's gone, we can't get him back.'

There was a collective nod around the table. No extradition treaty existed with Northern Cyprus. Hence the endless beach-side estates of wanted British criminals.

'So what are you suggesting?' Willard was still looking at Suttle.

'It's not me, sir. It's Winter.'

'Same difference, isn't it?'

'With respect, sir, no. Winter says he can spark Mackenzie up, make him do something very silly.'

'When?'

'Tonight. All he asks is that we keep obs in place.'

'On?'

'Mackenzie. He'll be out and about all day. I assume he'll end up at the Guildhall election count.'

Willard nodded. Another day's surveillance, given the sums already expended, wouldn't break the bank.

'So what's the downside? What's our exposure?'

'You want an honest opinion?'

'Don't fuck around, son. Just tell me.'

'Worst case, Winter ends up dead.'

There was a brief silence. Then Willard wanted to know how.

'Bazza kills him.'

Willard sat back, digesting the news. Then came the first hint of a smile.

'That's worst case?' he said.

The meeting went on deep into the night. Willard, at last glimpsing the logic behind Winter's confidence, wanted a Command Post established here in Parsons' office. Gold commander would be Willard himself. Silver went to Det Supt Parsons. Bronze would fall to D/S Suttle. The surveillance teams, appropriately reinforced, would report to the Covert Ops D/I, who'd have a desk of his own in Parsons' office. Comms, he said, would be the key to success. He needed a set-up flexible and responsive enough to give real-time overall command to the *Gehenna* management team.

'What time does Winter anticipate kicking off this morning?'

'Half past eight, sir. There's a champagne breakfast at the hotel.'

'And they're still on speaking terms? Mackenzie and Winter?'

'Yes. That's what we never allowed for. Mackenzie's being very grown-up. We thought he'd lose it. He hasn't.'

'Wrong. *Winter* thought he'd lose it. In fact he practically guaranteed it.'

'You're right, sir. And if it's worth anything, he's offered an apology. He admits he fucked up.'

'And tonight? We get more of the same?'

'He says tonight will be different.'

'And you believe him?'

'I do, sir, yes.'

'Why?'

'Because he can't afford to have it any other way.'

'But that's Mackenzie's line, isn't it? That's why he's behaving himself?'

'Exactly, sir. Which is why we should wait and see.'

'You mean take Winter at his word?'

'I mean wait and see.'

This first hint of caution wasn't lost on Parsons. She was looking at Willard.

'With respect, sir, I think we need the TFU on standby.'

The Tactical Firearms Unit was based at Netley, a pocket army of tooled-up ninjas, guys who patrolled the fragile front line between operational prudence and something a great deal more direct.

'You think that's appropriate?' Willard wasn't convinced.

'I do, sir. Winter knows Mackenzie better than most. Personally I'm amazed he's still in there pitching for us.'

'So am I, Gail.' Willard was looking at Suttle. 'And you have to ask yourself why.'

Misty Gallagher slept badly. For long periods of the night she lay awake, aware of Winter tossing and turning beside her. Sometimes she thought of Trude spending her last night in the Spinal Unit, and she wondered what kind of life awaited them all once she got home. At other times she tried to imagine this new future of theirs out in Croatia, what kind of arrangements Winter had really made, whether or not this awkward three-some, complicated by Trude's injury, could easily adapt to a couple of years on the Adriatic coast. Once or twice she reached across to Winter, alarmed at how clammy and unsettled he was, and when his eyes finally opened, shortly after dawn, she hung over him, whispering in the half-darkness.

'What's the matter, pet? You're dripping wet.'

'Nothing, Mist.' He sniffed, reached for his watch. 'I'm fine.'

'You're not. Something's wrong. What is it?'

'Nothing. Zilch. You want tea?' He pulled back the duvet, reached for his dressing gown and made for the door. Then he seemed to have second thoughts. Back in bed, he took Misty in his arms and gave her a long hug.

'I love you, Mist, I really do. I just wanted to say it.'

She returned his kiss and then held him at arm's length.

'Christ ...' she couldn't hide her alarm '... it must be serious.'

The champagne breakfast at the Trafalgar was a subdued affair. At Kinder's insistence, Mackenzie agreed to hold it in the War Room. Makins turned up in a taxi Mackenzie had dispatched, and to no one's surprise Gill Reynolds was with him. Bazza himself served scrambled eggs and bacon from the kitchen while Marie circled with the Moët. Kinder had shipped in a couple of extra TV screens, offering a choice of live election coverage, but there was a strange sense of anticlimax as they watched a long succession of Establishment worthies placing their votes.

For four long weeks *Pompey First* had fought tooth and nail to upset the political order, and the unvoiced suspicion around the table was that nothing would probably change. More meaningless promises about non-essential budget cuts. More stern warnings about holes in the national coffers. The usual bollocks about Whitehall and Westminster stepping aside to give the locals a fighting chance.

In the end it was Gill Reynolds who put this feeling into words. She'd spent the last week or so working on the special post-election supplement for the *News*, and this exercise had made her realise how much sheer graft had gone into the BazzaMac campaign. If democracy didn't deliver the right result in Pompey North, she said, then it was no fault of *Pompey First*.

'At least you guys tried.' She raised her glass. 'Respect.'

Bazza spent the rest of the day touring various outposts of the *Pompey First* machine in the company of three 6.57 heavies and a plentiful supply of Moët for the front-line troops. A stop at the uni got rid of half a dozen bottles, chiefly to the tyro video kings who'd serviced Andy Makins' YouTube operation. They insisted on cracking the bottles on the spot, toasting Bazza's electoral fortunes, and Mackenzie returned the compliment by inviting them down to the Trafalgar War Room to watch the results come in. Free bar all night, he promised. And somewhere to be sick once the Tories hit the lead.

Mid-afternoon, back in the hotel, he bumped into Winter.

'Five'o clock,' he grunted. 'Spinnaker Tower.'

Misty was still waiting for Trude to be discharged from the Spinal Unit. She'd spent most of the day being checked over by an endless queue of specialists, and Misty was getting tired of re-reading all the information that had been pressed upon her.

Most of this stuff she'd known already, and in the long hours waiting beside Trude's empty bed she began to fret about Winter.

Finally she made her way out of the unit and back into the car park. It was still glorious, the sun warm on her face. She rummaged in her bag for her mobile and dialled a number from memory. It took an age to answer but finally there was a voice in her ear.

'Baz? It's me.'

The Command Post nesting in Gail Parsons' office was operational from mid-morning. Techies fine-tuned the comms, and by early afternoon the Covert Ops D/I was happy with the results. He was keeping the surveillance logs, with updates forwarded hourly to Parsons and Suttle. Mackenzie, he said, had been touring the city all day to say his electoral thank yous. His last bottle of Moët had gone to the Custody Sergeant at Central police station in recognition, according to Bazza, of 'services rendered'. At first the custody skipper had refused to accept it, but then Bazza asked for it to be registered as lost property. This, it seemed, had done the trick.

When Parsons arrived at her office, thirty minutes ahead of Willard, she wanted to know where Mackenzie was headed next. The Covert Ops D/I sent a message to the surveillance shift leader and got a reply within seconds.

'Spinnaker Tower, boss. He's just arrived.'

Mackenzie and Winter rode the express lift to the upper viewing platform. Mackenzie had abandoned his escort of 6.57 in the café on the ground floor, leaving them with a twenty-pound note and instructions not to drink it all. As the lift slowed at the top of the shaft, Mackenzie moved towards the exit door. So far he hadn't said a word.

Except for a gaggle of Asian tourists, the viewing platform was empty. Late afternoon, at this time of year, the sun hung over the distant swell of the Isle of Wight, throwing a long golden stripe across the Solent. From this height Pompey was a child's plaything, a busy maze of tiny streets and houses stretching inland as far as the eye could see. Winter walked to a window to peer down at the narrow alleyways of Old Portsmouth, then watched one of the Fishbourne car ferries churning past the end of Spice Island. The benches outside the Still and West were beginning to fill, and Winter could just make out a solitary figure at the rail gazing out at the harbour mouth. Faraday, he thought. His favourite pub. His favourite view.

'Amazing, eh?' Mackenzie was at his elbow. Winter followed his pointing finger. The sturdy facade of the Royal Trafalgar was clearly visible, headbutting the huge green spread of Southsea Common.

Mackenzie drew Winter to another window, the northerly aspect this time. Beyond the clutter of the dockyard lay the continental ferry port. Then came street after street of houses, receding into a blur of rooftops, before the island nudged the lower slopes of Portsdown Hill. From here, thought Winter, it was easy to see what had been the making of Portsmouth. It was defensible. It had two huge harbours. It was bang on the English Channel. And thousands of acres of marshland, once drained, sucked in the men and women who'd finally made it what it was.

'There, mush, there.' Mackenzie was pointing again. Winter guessed he meant Copnor. He was right.

'Well done, Baz. Some journey, eh?'

'Yeah.' He nodded. 'Yeah.'

'You should be proud.'

'I am.'

Mackenzie grinned. It had been fun, he said, the whole trip.

'Are we talking *Pompey First*?'

'No, mush. The whole deal. Start to finish. If my old man was alive he'd die to think of me tucked up in Craneswater. Silly, isn't it? How that generation couldn't get their heads around money? What it can buy you? Where it takes you? What sort of bloke you become at the end of it?'

Winter spared him a look. He'd rarely seen his boss so reflective, so philosophical. In this mood, he thought, he could give Joe Faraday a run for his money.

'No regrets, then?'

'Hundreds, mush. Thousands. You get let down, all the time, but that's life, isn't it? You think people are going to measure up and they don't. You have a rant, or even a ruck maybe, and you think you've sorted it, but you're always wrong. And you know why? Because some people are born to be cunts.'

'And I'm one of them?'

'You are, mush. You are. I never thought I'd hear myself saying it, but it's true. Down where it matters you're an evil little grass, just like the rest of them.'

'The rest of who, Baz?'

'The Filth, mush. People said I was off my head when I took you on, people I respect, and I always told them they were wrong. That Paul Winter, I says, that Paul Winter's a one-off. He's got a brain. He's funny. Get to know the geezer and you realise you can trust him. Worth every penny, mush. Worth every fucking cent. And you know what they said? They said just wait. What you see ain't necessarily what you get. One day the fucker will turn you over. And when that day happens, you know where to come for help.'

Winter was thinking of the 6.57 tucked up in the café below with their pints of Foster's, sharing the back pages of the *News*. Was this the moment Mackenzie had chosen for a settling of accounts? Something told Winter the answer was no. This was a subtler Bazza Mackenzie. But he still had to get it off his chest.

'What were you thinking last night, mush?'

'When?'

'When you realised I'd sussed it. The Polish woman. Pavel

385

fucking Beginski. That evil little trap you all dreamed up. Bazza desperate for moolah. Bazza chasing Martin fucking Skelley with a meat cleaver. Bazza making it easy for you cunts at long last.'

'What was I thinking?'

'Yeah. Be honest. I'm not going to hurt you.'

'OK.' Winter nodded. 'I thought I'd like to get home. I thought I'd like to see the back of all this shit. And I thought I'd like to give Mist a cuddle.'

'I know. She phoned.'

'She did?'

'Yeah. This afternoon. And you know what she said? She said she wanted us all to be friends. Fuck me ... *friends*? With a fat old grass like you?' He shook his head, staring out at the view again. 'I dunno what you've done to her, mush. That woman used to be proper Pompey, she used to have a bit of pride.'

Winter smiled. He'd no idea where this conversation was heading next but he knew the time had come to take the initiative.

'You're right, Baz. We all make decisions, and mine was the wrong one. I thought you were a decent bloke once, but that's all gone. You hurt people. You make people's lives a misery. One of them happens to be your wife, which is a very great shame, but she seems to love you so that must be OK.' He glanced at his watch. 'Nice view, Baz. Thanks for the ride.'

He shot Mackenzie a final glance, recognising the sudden flare of madness in his eyes, then turned on his heel and made for the exit signs. The lift was full of chattering Japanese. Back at ground level, in the shadow of the Gunwharf promenade, Winter paused to look up. A tiny figure was still framed in one of the observation windows, his arms rigid on the handrail, staring out at the city of his birth.

*

386

The polls closed nationwide at ten o'clock. Gail Parsons, who'd had the wit to order a small portable TV for the *Gehenna* Command Post, was glued to the set when the titles rolled for the start of the BBC's live coverage. David Dimbleby kicked off with the night's big headline: the shock results of an exit poll conducted by all three major broadcasters. After bossing the political scene for the last couple of years, the Tories were forecast to fall just short of a working majority. Another bombshell suggested the Lib Dems would win no more than sixty-one seats, one short of their total in 2005. Nick Clegg may have turned heads throughout the campaign, but celebrity didn't, in the end, win votes.

Willard was helping himself to a second biscuit, another of Gail Parsons' thoughtful little additions to the evening. She knew he had a weakness for Waitrose Classic Gingers and had laid in ample stocks. Willard, who lived and voted in Winchester, made no secret of his disappointment at the exit poll. A Tory government with a decent majority would, in his view, be excellent news for the forces of law and order. Now, with a hung Parliament a distinct possibility, anything could happen.

'This could get ugly,' he growled, reaching for another biscuit.

In the War Room at the Trafalgar Hotel the exit poll brought whoops of approval. As Leo Kinder had predicted, the electorate were much more volatile than any of the pundits believed. If the results mirrored the forecasts, the election could offer rich pickings for the likes of *Pompey First*.

Winter had found himself a perch in a corner of the room near the door. Unlike the hordes of students who'd descended on the hotel, he'd so far limited himself to a single bottle of Stella. Like Bazza himself, he anticipated a long night and knew that getting pissed was the last thing he needed to do.

Half an hour ago, once it was dark, he'd gone upstairs and

made his way out onto the street. Twenty years in the Job had given him a keen eye for spotting surveillance, and he'd been comforted by what he'd found. A couple of unmarked cars were parked up with line of sight to the hotel, and when he ducked back inside he recognised the guy on obs in a corner of the bar. *Gehenna*, for once, had done him proud.

Houghton and Sunderland South was the first seat to declare at 22.52. Labour clung on with a decent majority, but the swing to the Tories was 8.4 per cent, which appeared to confirm the findings of the exit poll. At midnight, with most of the students out of their heads, Bazza decided it was time to go to the Guildhall for the count. The 6.57 were still in attendance, remarkably sober, and Winter joined Leo Kinder and Gill Reynolds in a second car.

They followed the Bentley north through Southsea and walked the final hundred metres across the Guildhall Square. The square boasted a huge TV screen, and Winter was amused to watch their progress live as they were filmed by a local BBC crew. This had to be Kinder's work, he thought, as Mackenzie stopped for a word with the young reporter. Asked how he fancied his chances after the exit poll, Bazza reckoned there was everything to play for. 'People have come to their senses,' he said. 'People have realised that this is about them, not a bunch of has-beens up in London, and that can only be good for us.'

Alas, the hard evidence suggested otherwise. In Pompey the count was complicated by local elections in all fourteen of the city's wards, and progress was going to be slow, but already the whisper on the floor of the huge auditorium was that *Pompey First* would be lucky to hang onto its deposit.

All the parties, including *Pompey First,* had stationed tellers outside polling stations throughout the day. Bazza, in what he regarded as a masterstroke, had insisted that potential *Pompey First* voters be greeted by 6.57 volunteers, beefy men from Bazza's past. At the time this had seemed a good idea, but now it seemed that voters, sensing intimidation, had put their cross elsewhere.

Winter stepped onto the floor of the auditorium. The last time he'd been here was for a Tom Jones concert years back. Now the theatre seating had been cleared away, making space for big open oblongs of tables. Inside sat the counters, most of them women. Opposite stood little knots of party supporters, making sure their votes ended up on the right pile. Once again Bazza had briefed 6.57 to defend his interests, and Winter circled the room, following in Bazza's footsteps, checking on *Pompey First*'s progress.

The news wasn't good. Votes were tallied in bundles of twenty-five. In ward after ward the *Pompey First* pile was dwarfed by those of the major parties. Despite four weeks of wall-to-wall publicity, hundreds of posters, a major media profile, trillions of postings on the Internet and some truly inventive stunts, Bazza Mackenzie was heading for electoral oblivion.

Winter, hidden in the swirl of bodies on the floor, was watching Mackenzie, who was doing his best to ignore his opponents. For four hectic weeks he'd done his level best to destroy these people. He'd mocked them, belittled them and badged them as spineless puppets bossed by their masters in London. As an electoral strategy this had appeared to work. Digs about dancing to their masters' tunes always raised a laugh. People nodded in approval when he wondered whether any of the other candidates had a single original thought in their empty heads. Now, though, reassured by towering piles of votes, it was their turn to gloat. When they managed to catch Mackenzie's eye, a nod and the faintest smile was all it took. *Pompey First*, the express train of Bazza's dreams, had finally hit the buffers.

By half past two in the morning Mackenzie had seen enough. He slipped through the press of media by the door, no longer interested in anyone's microphone. Winter found him sitting on the flank of the Guildhall steps, his elbows on his knees, gazing sightlessly up at the BBC live feed on the huge outdoor screen.

The news arrived at the *Gehenna* Command Post via the Covert Ops D/I. He signalled to Willard, who was sitting at the end of the long conference table.

'Winter's with Mackenzie, sir. They seem to be talking.'

'Where?'

'Outside. In the square.'

Willard nodded. Like everyone else in the room, with the single exception of Suttle, he'd written off *Gehenna*'s chances of any kind of result. It was good news that Pompey North was going to be spared a *Pompey First* MP, but it was equally obvious that Mackenzie had no interest in making life easy for the men in blue.

'Winter's got it wrong again,' he grunted. 'Surprise, surprise.'

It was chilly on the steps. Mackenzie had donned a suit for the count, a sober two-piece that Marie had found in a Debenhams sale, and Winter was amazed he didn't feel the cold. Live election coverage had switched to Luton South on the big screen, and they were both watching Esther Rantzen trailing in a poor fourth.

'I know how she feels, mush. What's wrong with this fucking country?'

Winter said nothing. He'd never much liked Esther Rantzen. Coverage switched to Jacqui Smith, another loser. Winter asked what Bazza was up to next.

'I stick around, mush. They're estimating six or seven in the morning for the declaration. Joy, eh?'

'That's not what I meant, Baz.'

'No?'

'No.'

Mackenzie shrugged and turned away. It was times like

390

these, he said, when he regretted giving up smoking. One of those little cigarillos would be nice. And maybe something serious to drink.

'Northern Cyprus, is it? La-la land?'

Mackenzie shot him a look. Winter was taking the piss. Had to be.

'Yeah,' he said. 'Since you're asking.'

'So what do you do for money? Only a quid doesn't go far these days. Not even in Northern Cyprus.'

'Fuck off.'

'I mean it.'

'You really think I'm that skint? Down to rock bottom?'

'I know you are.'

'Then you're fucking wrong, mush. Since when did I leave myself *that* wide open?'

'So where's it coming from?'

'Cesar's standing the flight. Southampton. Charter jet. Just like the old days.'

'And?'

'Nikki does the rest.'

'Nikki?'

'Kokh, your old mate.'

'You took the offer?'

'I did, mush. A hundred grand in euros, sitting in a bank in Famagusta, just waiting for me and Ma. Plus another two hundred down the line if he ponies up. Sweet, eh?'

'Yeah. Shame it couldn't have been the three of you.'

'Three of us?'

'The baby, Baz. The one who never made it.' He smiled. 'The one you were going to call Paulie.'

Mackenzie was staring at him. His eyes were the deepest black.

'You know about that?'

'Of course I know about that.' Winter's smile widened. 'So what makes you think the baby was yours?'

391

For a moment Mackenzie didn't move. Then he was on his feet, taking the steps two at a time, racing back towards the entrance to the Guildhall. Winter watched him disappear into the swirl of bodies beside the door. Then he settled down to wait.

'Something's up, sir.' The Covert Ops D/I was on his feet.

Willard was asleep. Gail Parsons bustled past Jimmy Suttle and gave him a nudge. Suttle glanced at his watch. 02.47.

The Covert Ops D/I had crossed the room to the big street map of Pompey. Mackenzie's Bentley, he said, had appeared from nowhere and was parked on the corner of Guildhall Walk.

'And Winter?' Willard was rubbing his eyes.

The Covert Ops D/I bent to his radio. He nodded a couple of times, then looked up.

'Still sitting on the steps, sir. But something's definitely kicking off.'

Winter knew it too. Mackenzie had reappeared at the top of the Guildhall steps flanked by three 6.57. Silhouetted against the blaze of light from the open Guildhall door, they made Winter deeply uncomfortable. He had no idea what might happen next but knew he'd finally put a match to the firework that was Bazza Mackenzie.

He came down the steps towards Winter.

'On your feet, mush.'

Winter began to struggle upright. One of the 6.57, a scrapper of some talent, lent a hand. Winter shook him off.

'What's the problem, Baz?'

Mackenzie didn't answer. The 6.57 marched Winter across the square towards the waiting Bentley. The rear door was already open. At the kerbside Winter hesitated a moment before a push sent him sprawling onto the back seat. Fear, he thought, smells of new leather.

The car rocked under the weight of bodies piling in. Two of

them were sitting on Winter. The car began to move. It seemed to be Mackenzie at the wheel. Winter could hear him on the phone. He hoped to God he wasn't talking to Marie.

They were going faster now, picking up speed, then came the sudden lurch of a roundabout and Winter gasped with pain as an elbow caught him in the face.

'Sorry, mush.' The 6.57 was laughing.

Winter could smell roll-ups. He thought of trying to negotiate, of trying to calm Mackenzie down, but he knew there was no point. This was what he'd been promising *Gehenna* since the operation began. The fact that it was him in the firing line rather than Skelley was immaterial. The next half-hour, he knew, would decide his fate. In these moods Bazza never hung around.

The Covert Ops D/I was still at the street map.

'Fratton Road, sir. Signalling right by St Mary's church.'

Suttle was trying to picture the journey, Winter banged up with a bunch of hooligans, Mackenzie for some reason deciding it was time to take a drive. Where were they off to? And what could possibly have sparked this sudden development? According to the D/I, they were now passing the big cemetery beside Kingston Prison. Beyond that lay a short cut to the Eastern Road, which funnelled traffic north onto the motorway.

'They're bailing out,' he muttered. 'Mackenzie's had enough.'

He glanced down the table. Willard occupied the seat at the end. He was still watching the election coverage, one ear cocked. Nick Clegg had just acknowledged a disappointing night for the Lib Dems. Life, he said, sometimes takes you by surprise.

Too fucking right, thought Suttle.

The Bentley was slowing down, and Winter could hear the gentle *tick-tick* of the indicator. They turned sharp left, accelerated, braked, then pulled a hard right. Moments later the big car glided to a halt. For a moment no one moved. Then Winter caught the faint tinkle of keys.

'Out.' It was Mackenzie.

The weight of bodies on Winter suddenly eased. Doors opened. Then he felt hands tugging at his legs and he found himself dumped on the pavement. He'd caught his hip on the sill of the door on the way out of the car and he reached down, trying to ease the pain. Mackenzie watched him for a moment and then drove his foot in at exactly the same spot. Winter yelped with pain. Mackenzie did it again, telling him not to fucking squinny, then he was across the pavement, keys in his hand, hunting for the lock in the darkness.

Winter tried to focus. Everything hurt. It looked like a shop of some kind. The pattern on the door looked faintly familiar. Above the display window he could just make out a name. His blood froze. Pompey Reptiles.

Bazza had the door open. Winter felt himself being dragged inside. Then came that smell again, the smell of the urban swamp, the stench of caged flesh, a hot smell, a smell that promised nothing but pain.

Mackenzie was screaming for Sanouk. Winter could hear the patter of footsteps overhead. Then the little man was among them, rubbing the sleep from his eyes. Mackenzie had lost it completely. He wanted to know why Sanouk hadn't changed the name of the shop, like he'd told him to. He wanted to know why no one in this fucking world ever did what they were told. And he promised retribution.

'Rope, son. We need a rope. Rope? Fucking rope? *Comprende?*'

Sanouk, plainly terrified, disappeared. Seconds later he was back with a length of cord. It looked like the belt from a dressing gown. Mackenzie tossed it to one of the 6.57. Then he found a chair in the corner of the shop and kicked it across the floor.

394

'Knife? You've got a knife?'

Sanouk disappeared again. When he came back he was carrying a knife. Winter stared at it. It was huge.

Mackenzie told the 6.57 to cut the cord in two. He wanted Winter tied hand and foot, then secured to the chair. The 6.57 did what he was told. One of his mates helped. Looking into their faces, Winter could sense their uncertainty. They knew about Bazza. They knew what he could do. And they knew, above all, that there was no stopping him.

It was Suttle who voiced the obvious question.

'How long do we let this run?' he asked.

Willard wouldn't answer. The surveillance team had Pompey Reptiles plotted up. One of the guys had reported the violence on the pavement. They knew Winter was inside, and it was a reasonable assumption that something horrible was about to kick off. Pompey Reptiles was the only clue you'd ever need. Suttle knew how much Winter hated snakes.

Willard wanted to know whether the Tactical Firearms Unit was at full readiness yet. The TFU liaison D/S had been in the Command Post since mid-afternoon. The last couple of minutes he'd been busy on the emergency frequency, calling in his guys from their holding point at Kingston Crescent.

'Give me five, sir?'

'And then?'

'We can go in.'

Bound to the chair, Winter could see nothing but Mackenzie. By now he'd lost it completely. He bent low, stabbing his finger into Winter's face. Every accusation, every insult, was flecked with spittle. Winter could do nothing but shut his eyes and wait. When Mackenzie wanted to know more about Marie, more about this fucking fairy-tale affair they were supposed to have had, he simply turned his head away, but every denial, every refusal to reply, simply sparked a deeper anger.

Finally he seemed to accept there'd be no more from Winter. Not, at least, until he'd learned the error of his ways.

He turned on Sanouk again. He wanted the biggest snake he'd got. He wanted Sanouk to wrap it around Winter's throat and talk to it nicely and get it to do something evil. Then he wanted another snake, smaller this time, something venomous, something with loads of attitude. He wanted this snake in a really bad mood. And he wanted it to end up in Winter's boxers.

While Sanouk disappeared to find the cage keys, Mackenzie turned on Winter again.

'You hear what I said, mush?'

Winter nodded.

'And you know why I'm going to stuff it down your kacks?'

Winter shook his head.

'Because that's all your todger's good for, mush. Snake fucking fodder.'

Winter had given up thinking. What was about to happen was beyond his imagination. He was sure about the surveillance. He knew these guys were good. So what the fuck was happening? How much proof did these people need?

In Parsons' office the TFU liaison D/S was bent to his radio. The guys had left Kingston Crescent eight minutes ago. This time of night there shouldn't be a problem with traffic. Then came a muttered voice on the radio. Something had gone wrong. Suttle knew it.

'Give us a couple more minutes, sir?' The TFU liaison was looking worried.

Sanouk had produced a baby boa constrictor. The snake was beautiful, green and yellow markings, sleek, perfectly balanced, and the head swayed from side to side, the tiny forked tongue flicking in and out. The 6.57 had backed away but then one of them took a step forward. He'd always wanted to touch a snake and he'd never had the chance.

'Very valuable.' Sanouk angled it towards him. 'Cost much money.'

The 6.57 reached out a hand. The snake reared away. Winter was trying not to look. Of Mackenzie there was no sign.

Then, like an eruption, he was back. He grabbed Sanouk. He'd been looking for something and he couldn't find it. Sanouk nodded and muttered something Winter didn't catch. Then Mackenzie was gone again.

The 6.57 was stroking the snake.

'You want it?' Sanouk asked. 'You want hold it?'

The 6.57 shook his head. Then he nodded at Winter and told Sanouk to put it round his neck, just like the man had said.

Sanouk obliged. Winter squeezed his eyes shut. The snake felt surprisingly warm against his flesh. He could feel it moving under his chin. Think scarf, he told himself. Think windy day. Think any fucking thing except being here, in this shop, waiting for a boa constrictor to throttle the life out of you.

Sanouk had reappeared with another snake, much smaller. It was the colour of liquorice. He held it very carefully, his thumb and forefinger under its gullet. The body of the snake lashed around. One of the 6.57 thought it was well pissed off.

Then Mackenzie was back. He had something in his hand Winter couldn't see. He wanted to know about Marie again. He wanted to know when this thing of theirs had started. He wanted to know when they'd done it, how many times, how long this fucking piece of shit he'd called a mate had been sniffing around his wife.

'That's you, mush. You. The guy I fucking trusted. The guy we took down to fucking Cornwall with the kids, for fuck's sake, the *kids*. Did you have them too, you paedo? Is there anyone in my family you haven't fucked?'

The violence in his face was terrifying. He told Sanouk to get rid of the boa constrictor. Winter felt the pressure on his throat ease. Relieved, he tried to turn his face away, but Mackenzie hit him. Then did it again. And again. Winter felt the bite of knuckles in his face. He could do nothing, absolutely fuck all. His mouth was pouring blood. He blew hard through his nose. More blood. He tried to suck in air, knowing he had to keep his head up, knowing he had to stay conscious for long enough to somehow survive.

'Baz ...' he managed.

'Don't Baz me, you cunt. You know what this is? You know what happens next?'

Winter tried to focus. Instead of a snake, he found himself looking at a tube. He squeezed his eyes hard, shook his head, took another look. It was a tube of expanding foam, the kind you use for insulation. The last time he'd seen it was here in this very shop.

'You know what this stuff does, cunt? It expands like fuck then it sets rock hard. And once that's happened, there's fuck all you can do. You know about this stuff? Just nod.'

Winter nodded. He could remember the stickiness on his palm when he'd shaken Sanouk's tiny hand the first time they'd met. And he remembered how hard it had been to scrape the stuff off afterwards.

'So listen, cunt ...' Mackenzie was back in his face. 'What happens is this. We forget the snake. We open your mouth. And then I fill it full of this stuff. *Comprende?* It's something really special we use for grasses in this city. It gets bigger and bigger inside. It tastes fucking horrible, and after not very long you can't breathe. Not through your mouth. So by now you're choking to death, so if we're kind, and that's a big if, we squirt a little more up each nostril. And after that, mush, you're well dead. Yeah? All that make sense? You fucking grass?'

He stepped back. Sanouk had found the injector that went with the tube of foam. Mackenzie slipped the tube into the barrel, withdrew the nail that capped the nozzle and applied a little pressure. A tiny dribble of foam appeared, getting bigger and bigger on contact with the air. Mackenzie waved it under

Winter's nose. It smelled chemical. It smelled of death.

'One more chance, you fucking grass. Just get it off that fucking chest of yours.'

'What, Baz?'

'Marie, you cunt.'

In the Command Post the TFU liaison D/S signalled to Willard. The guys had finally arrived. They were ready.

'Where are they exactly?'

'Parked up round the corner, sir. Thirty seconds, max.'

Willard nodded, taking his time. Suttle checked his watch again. Winter had been inside for more than fifteen minutes. How much time did *Gehenna* need?

'For fuck's sake, sir ...' he began.

Willard ignored him. He told the TFU liaison to go ahead. The D/S was already on the radio.

'Pompey Reptiles,' he said softly. 'Number 49.'

There was a long silence. Suttle tried to imagine the guys piling out of the van and spilling round the corner of the street. On an operation like this there'd be half a dozen of them. One would be carrying the ram to put the door in. They called it the Big Key. On most occasions that would draw a smile from Suttle but not tonight. Winter, he thought. Poor bloody Winter.

'They're outside the property, sir.' The TFU liaison again.

Another pause. Another silence. On the TV the face of David Cameron appeared in close-up – sleek, pink, almost cherubic. Parsons had turned the sound down. Suttle hadn't a clue what he was saying.

'They've done the door, sir. There's a guy tied to a chair.' The TFU liaison was looking at Willard. 'Mackenzie's got something pointing at his mouth.'

Willard wanted to know what the something was.

'Hard to say, sir.'

'Who's the guy in the chair?'

'We think Winter.'

'Is he under threat?'

'Yes, sir, definitely.'

'And is Mackenzie backing off?'

'No, sir. We've warned him twice. He's not having it.'

Willard was leaning forward in his chair, his body tense. In these situations, operational responsibility lay with the TFU commander on the spot. Only he could take the decision to open fire. Willard told the liaison D/S to wind up the volume on the comms. Then he sat back and closed his eyes. He was smiling.

A single shot. Then silence.

Afterwards

The Portsmouth North election was won by Penny Mordaunt, the Conservative Party candidate, with a 44 per cent share of the vote. She beat the incumbent MP, Labour's Sarah McCarthy-Fry, by 7,289 votes. Bazza Mackenzie, had he been alive, would have lost his deposit.

Bazza Mackenzie's death at the hands of the Tactical Firearms Unit was lead story in the Portsmouth *News* for a couple of days. The killing sparked remarkably few protests within the city, but the Chief Constable, after consultations with Det Chief Supt Geoff Willard, felt obliged to call in a team of officers from a neighbouring force to conduct an independent inquiry. The results of that inquiry are still pending, but inside sources report no cause for concern on the part of Hampshire Police.

Marie Mackenzie had nothing to say about her husband's death in response to enquiries from the *News* and a variety of other media outlets. She also declined to speak to reporter Gill Reynolds in connection with a special post-election *News* supplement. Neither would she take calls from Andy Makins, who appeared to be writing a book about her husband's rise and fall.

Marie and her immediate family headed the sizeable crowd of mourners who filled the city's Anglican cathedral for her husband's funeral. She resisted suggestions that Bazza's coffin should be paraded through the city in a horse-drawn hearse but consented to decorate it with a single Pompey scarf when half a dozen 6.57 shouldered the coffin on its arrival at the cathedral. More 6.57 formed an honour guard to line Bazza's path to the south door, and there was an impressive turnout of accountants, solicitors, city councillors and sundry other officials waiting inside. Bazza's grandson Guy read a poem he'd composed specially for the occasion, and Marie voiced a simple, elegant tribute to the man she said she'd always loved. In good times and bad Bazza had always been her rock. No one could ever replace him.

Off the record, in response to an enquiry from the 6.57, Marie emphatically denied that she'd ever had a relationship with Paul Winter. Neither did she know where he was. Nor did she ever want to see him again. When Cesar Dobroslaw seized her house, she moved in with her daughter and son-in-law.

Paul Winter left the country the day after Mackenzie's death. Thanks to a generous, if discreet, settlement from Hampshire Police, Misty and Trude joined him shortly afterwards. To date, they still occupy a roomy rented house in pinewoods across the bay from Porec. Winter is mulling over whether to make an offer for the freehold but is still struggling with Serbo-Croat. To Misty's astonishment, he's also developed an interest in fishing. Trude's mobility is slowly improving. On good days she accompanies Winter to his favourite cove and helps sort out his lures. Misty, though she won't admit it, is beginning to miss home.

Det Chief Supt Geoff Willard is now an Assistant Chief Constable with West Midlands Police. He recently acquired the firearms portfolio on behalf of the Association of Chief Police Officers (ACPO).

Pompey went to Wembley on Saturday, 15 May and gave a spirited account of themselves. Had they not missed a penalty early in the second half they might even have got a result. As it was, they lost to Chelsea 1–0. No shame.

Two months after the conclusion of Operation *Gehenna*, with the new coalition government in place, Jimmy Suttle got a phone call from Ulyana, J-J's partner. She said that J-J still had his father's ashes and wanted to scatter them from the top of Tennyson Down, Faraday's favourite walk. Would Suttle and Lizzie be prepared to be part of this last farewell? Suttle said yes.

They met on a blustery day in mid-July. Tennyson Down is on the Isle of Wight. They took the FastCat to Ryde and caught a bus across the island to Freshwater Bay. From there a stiff walk took them a couple of miles to the very top of the down, marked by a huge granite cross. J-J was carrying his father's ashes in a plastic container. The wind was blowing in from the sea. They all stood at the top of the cliff, peering down at the churn of the waves below.

Suttle had brought the eagle poem, but J-J didn't want him to read it. Instead, he knelt briefly on the springy turf and bowed his head. Then he got to his feet, unscrewed the lid of the container and scattered his father's ashes. The wind, billowing up from the cliff face, carried most of the thin grey cloud away, but J-J was still finding tiny particles of grainy ash in his pullover on the bus ride back to Ryde.

Six weeks later Jimmy Suttle got a letter from the Personnel Department at Devon and Cornwall Constabulary. They were happy to inform him that his application for a post with one of the force's Major Crime Investigation Teams had been successful. Suttle carried the letter back upstairs with a cup of tea for Lizzie and a warmed-up bottle for Grace. Lizzie read the letter and returned it to the envelope.

'Happy days,' she said.

Acknowledgements

This is the twelfth and last book in the Faraday series and is, in so many ways, a personal farewell to Pompey. Over the last decade, I've name-checked the army of cops, pathologists, nurses, social workers, immigration officials, priests, naval officers, accountants, coroners, yachtspeople, train drivers, local government officers, journalists and politicians plus assorted adventurers, friends and family who have given me priceless help – and in this respect *Happy Days* owes yet another debt to these folk, too numerous to list here. You know who you are, and you have my deepest gratitude.

Hugh Davis has copy-edited most of the series and has disentangled my punctuation with forensic skill and enormous patience. Diana F ranklin has been through the proofs with a magnifying glass and nailed a thousand typos. My editor, Simon Spanton, has remained on board to the last and has played an absolutely key role since Joe Faraday made his debut in 2000.

My agent at Blake Friedmann, Oli Munson, has been a tower of strength, especially with respect to D/S Jimmy Suttle's imminent transfer to the Devon and Cornwall force.

But my biggest thank you must go to Lin, my wife. She's weathered the Faraday years with immense good humour, an acute feel for character, and a huge appetite for shedding light on some of life's nastier secrets. She's also been the best possible friend and travelling companion when the ever-widening plots took us into some of the darker corners of Europe and the Middle East. I treasure those journeys that Joe Faraday made possible.